About the Au

Two-time Golden Heart® Award f been reading romance since she was a teen and writing for even longer. Now she can be found drinking gallons of iced tea at her local coffee shop while doing one of her favorite things – convincing two characters they deserve their happy-ever-after. When she's not writing, she spends time at the lake, hangs out with her family, and reads. Ami lives in Michigan with her four kids, three cats, and very supportive husband.

USA Today bestselling author **Janice Maynard** loved books and writing even as a child. Now, creating sexy, character-driven romances is her day job! She has written more than seventy-five books and novellas which have sold, collectively, almost three million copies. Janice lives in the shadow of the Great Smoky Mountains with her husband, Charles. They love hiking, travelling, and spending time with family. Connect with Janice at JaniceMaynard.com and on all socials.

A typical Piscean, award-winning *USA Today* bestselling author **Yvonne Lindsay** has always preferred the stories in her head to the real world. Married to her blind-date sweetheart and with two adult children, she spends her days crafting the stories of her heart and loves to read or travel when she's not working. Yvonne loves to hear from readers, contact her via yvonnelindsay.com or Facebook.com/YvonneLindsayAuthor

Christmas Nights with the Ex

AMI WEAVER
JANICE MAYNARD
YVONNE LINDSAY

MILLS & BOON

First Published in Great Britain 2023
By Mills & Boon, an imprint of HarperCollins*Publishers* Ltd,
1 London Bridge Street, London, SE1 9GF

www.harpercollins.co.uk

HarperCollins*Publishers*
Macken House, 39/40 Mayor Street Upper,
Dublin 1, D01 C9W8, Ireland

Special thanks and acknowledgement are given to Janice Maynard for her contribution to the *Dynasties: Seven Sins* series.

ISBN: 978-0-263-32108-1

This book is produced from independently certified FSC™ paper to ensure responsible forest management.

For more information visit: www.harpercollins.co.uk/green

Printed and Bound in the UK using 100% Renewable Electricity at CPI Group (UK) Ltd, Croydon, CR0 4YY

A HUSBAND FOR THE HOLIDAYS

AMI WEAVER

To the baristas at my local Biggby,
who keep me supplied with gallons of iced tea
and a place where I can write without feeling I
have to clean my house. You guys are awesome!

Chapter One

"She's back."

The grim tone of his brother's voice told Mack Lawless all he needed to know, and his heart gave an unwelcome thump. Still, since he hadn't heard from the *she* in question in almost a decade, he deliberately uncoiled more of the pine garland he was hanging on the front of his veterinary practice and kept his voice level. "Who's back?"

Chase moved so he was at the periphery of Mack's vision. Even out of the corner of his eye, Mack could see the tight set of his brother's mouth. Damn. He willed his hands not to shake. He refused to let on that the mention of *her*—even indirectly—could still affect him. He came down the ladder, leaving the boughs hanging and ignoring the sting of the snow that pelted his face. "Chase?"

Chase met his gaze. "Darcy."

Darcy. Her name was a hard punch to his gut. Still. After seven freaking years. He'd gotten over her, and yet…

And yet hearing her name tore the lid off the memories he'd worked so hard to bury.

He forced himself to hold Chase's gaze and not show anything but indifference. "Are you sure?"

Chase nodded. "Saw her at the gas station a bit ago. Thought I'd—thought I should be the one to tell you."

The wind kicked up and the tail of the abandoned garland lashed Mack in the face. He winced, caught it and turned back to the ladder. Mack and Chase were planning to buy her family's tree farm after Christmas. He hadn't thought it would matter to Darcy. She hadn't been back since their divorce, even to visit her aunt and uncle.

His brother angled so the wind was at his back. "You okay, man?"

Irritation flared, but Mack tamped it down. Chase meant well. They all would mean well. As if he was still the heartbroken mess Darcy'd left in her dust all those years ago. "Yeah. It was a long time ago." He fitted the garland over the next hook and pretended the acid in his stomach was because he'd had a burrito for lunch and not because the only woman he'd ever really loved had returned to Holden's Crossing. The woman who'd broken him into shards when she left.

But his damn heart had never fully let her go.

"All right, then. Let me know if you need anything."

In spite of the tension coiling through him, Mack laughed. "Like what?"

Chase shrugged. "Whatever you need. We can talk to her…"

"Oh, no. No talking." He could just imagine how that particular conversation would go. He could almost pity Darcy. *Almost.* "Leave her alone, Chase. I'll deal with her when I have to."

"If you say so." Chase jingled his keys, then walked away. Mack heard his brother's truck start up and forced himself to focus on his task. Now he felt exposed. Anyone who'd seen Darcy, anyone who knew the story—or thought they did—could be driving by right now, staring at him, whispering.

He hated the whispers.

He looped the last of the decoration over the final hook and secured it so the winter winds wouldn't rip it free. Since the weather was steadily getting worse, he opted to leave the Christmas lights for another day. He hoped the wind wouldn't rip them down—the way Darcy had ripped his heart.

He closed the ladder and tried damn hard to ignore the mental picture of his ex-wife, with her long coppery locks and golden brown eyes. Damn it. Now he'd have Darcy on the brain after he'd been so successful at getting her out of it. He forced himself to turn away and haul the ladder back inside, banging it hard on the door. He swallowed a curse as pain radiated up his arm.

"All done?" Sherry's voice was cheery and he relaxed for a moment. His office manager didn't know anything too personal about him, thank God. At least not yet.

"Weather's getting worse," he said as he lugged the ladder down to the hall closet. "Wind is picking up, so I'll finish tomorrow."

She gave a quick nod. "You've had a bunch of calls in the past half hour," she said. "Your family, mostly."

She held the messages out, her attention back on the computer screen.

"Ah. Thanks." He took them and beat it back to his office. He skimmed through them quickly, then dumped them in the trash. Mom. Chase. His sister, Katie. How sad was it to be a thirty-two-year-old man and have your entire family band together over an ex-wife? Had the whole thing really been that bad?

He closed his eyes, then opened them.

Well, yeah, actually it had. Worse, probably.

He stared out his office window at the snow, which had changed from pellets to flakes. The radio station playing in the waiting area announced, between Christmas tunes, that three to six inches of the white stuff was expected by morning. It'd be a white Thanksgiving. Not uncommon in northern Michigan.

Darcy's uncle would be thrilled. And so should Mack.

Mack rubbed his hand over his face. Had Joe and Marla told their niece how he'd been helping out at the farm? Would she have come back if she'd known? He liked them. He enjoyed the labor of trimming the trees, mowing, whatever Joe needed done on the farm. They'd become friends, even with their shared history, but it was funny how the older man hadn't mentioned Darcy's imminent return. Mack was supposed to go out there tonight and help with some of the prep for the tree farm's official opening the day after Thanksgiving. He wanted to make sure this last year went off flawlessly.

Canceling wasn't an option. He knew Joe needed the extra hands more than ever.

Would Joe inform Darcy of the evening's plans?

A small part of him acknowledged the appeal of

showing up and seeing her shocked reaction. Letting her see he was fine and completely over her. He'd moved on with his life. Seven years was a long time and he wasn't that man anymore.

Maybe she isn't that woman anymore, either.

It didn't matter. He didn't want to go there. He'd managed to compartmentalize his relationship with Darcy's uncle away from what he'd had with her. That part of his life was over. At least until now, when it looked as though the past had come back to haunt him.

Sherry appeared in his door. "Jim Miller and Kiko are here. Jennifer's not back from lunch yet," she said, then really looked at him and frowned. "You okay, Mack? You look as if you've seen a ghost."

She wasn't too far off the mark. In a way, he had.

"I'm fine," he assured her. "I'll be with them in a few minutes."

As she exited his office, he sighed and pulled up Kiko's chart on the computer. Kiko was one of many pets he'd see today. Jim and his wife were getting a divorce, and the older man had gotten Kiko, a Siamese cat, as company. Some marriages weren't meant to be, no matter how promising they started out.

Like his and Darcy's.

He filed the unhelpful thoughts away and went to get his patient, whom he could hear yowling from the waiting room. Still, in the back of his head, all he could think was *She's back.*

His ex-wife was back.

Darcy Kramer drove through downtown Holden's Crossing, her hometown until she'd fled after the bust-up of her marriage at the young age of twenty-three.

She'd always loved the town at Christmas. The cheery decorations, the snow, the old-fashioned charm of the buildings added up to magic for a young girl. Somehow there was comfort in knowing it hadn't really changed.

Had it really been almost eight years since she was here? She truly hadn't intended to stay away so long. Shame tugged at her conscience. She knew Mack's older brother, Chase, had seen her back at the gas station. The look he'd given her was far colder than the wind that whipped outside. Had he gone straight to Mack? Probably.

Pain bloomed in her chest. The Lawless family pulled together tight when one of their own was hurt. Except, apparently, those related only by marriage. Those weeks after the accident and the loss of their baby, as her marriage crumbled under the weight of shared grief and her guilt, they'd set themselves firmly in Mack's camp. And he'd turned to them for comfort, rather than her.

She inhaled deeply and forced the memories down. To get through these next two weeks, she had to keep Mack out of her mind as much as possible. Her focus was helping her aunt and uncle, who'd raised her after she lost her parents, with their last Christmas season with the farm.

She gripped the wheel a little tighter. One last Christmas before the tree farm went up for sale. Before he'd died, her father had asked his brother to include Darcy in the final season if they ever sold the farm. So she'd agreed to take two weeks' vacation from her PR job in Chicago and come home.

Home.

Even though she hadn't been here in many years, it was still her childhood home, entwined in her heart and her memories, both the good and not so good. She'd missed being here. But coming back—and possibly facing Mack—hadn't been an option. Until now.

She accelerated as she exited the town limits. The steadily falling snow wasn't yet sticking to the roads, though it was starting to coat the grass. Figured, she'd get up here just in time for the first real snow of the season. Good timing, really. The snow added to the festive holiday atmosphere Kramer Tree Farm prided itself on.

She flexed her fingers on the steering wheel. Two weeks. She could do it. Then she could go back to Chicago and her carefully ordered life. She'd worked so hard for some measure of peace.

She turned on the road leading to the farm. Right away she saw the fences lining the property by the road were faded, even broken in some places. She pulled over in one such spot and got out, zipping the down vest she wore over a fleece jacket to her chin as she walked over to examine the broken board.

The chill that ran through her had nothing to do with the cold. The farm's financial situation must be much worse than her aunt and uncle had let on. Why hadn't he or Marla said anything to her? She'd offered help over the years as her career took off, but they'd always turned her down. She touched the jagged end of the wood, and tears stung her eyes. Her uncle and father had always been so adamant about the appearance of the farm. She swallowed hard as she looked out over the field beyond, with its neat rows of trees. Those, at least, looked well cared for. The wind bit through her fleece jacket and she folded her arms tight over her chest as she walked back to the car.

The farm entrance came into sight up the road and

she turned into the drive with a sense of trepidation. She drove past the low-slung barn that housed handmade wreaths and other decorations, relieved to note at least here the fencing here was in good shape and the area was trimmed festively. There were a half dozen cars parked in the lot and she knew inside the barn would be four or five people making wreaths, grave blankets and other decorations. No doubt her uncle was out in one of the fields somewhere, when he should be taking it easy. The road forked just past the barn, and since her aunt had requested she come to the house first, she continued up the driveway.

The house, a white-painted bungalow with green shutters, already sported lights and garlands and little wreaths hung from wide red ribbons in every window. Smoke curled from the chimney and a sense of relief, of rightness settled in Darcy's bones. When she pictured home, this was exactly how she thought of it. She grabbed her purse and reached for the door handle.

But she couldn't open the door. She'd been gone for so long, for reasons that seemed to pale in light of the farm's plight. Even though she knew she'd done the right thing for both her and Mack, she couldn't stop the wave of guilt that washed over her.

Marshaling her courage, she got out of the car, pulled her bags out of the trunk and trudged across the drive, the snow falling on her face and stinging her cheeks. The weight of her luggage was nothing compared to the weight of the baggage she carried within her. She knocked on the back door and waited. She could see the lights in the kitchen through the curtains, see the shadow of someone hurrying toward the door. Her aunt, of course.

Her breath caught as Marla opened the door, a smile wreathing her ageless face. “Darcy Jane! So nice to see you, honey.”

Darcy stepped through the door into her aunt’s embrace, letting her bags slide down to the floor. “Hi, Aunt Marla,” she said, breathing in her aunt’s familiar scent of Jean Nate. She squeezed her eyes shut against tears. Thank God some things didn’t change.

Her aunt gave her a squeeze and stepped back. “Let me look at you. My goodness, you don’t look any older! You’ve got your mama’s good genes. Come on in, let me shut the door.”

Darcy stepped all the way into the kitchen and rejoiced in the smell of pot roast. She never cooked like that for herself. “Mmm. Smells wonderful in here.”

Marla opened the oven and took a peek. “I try to have a hot meal for us after these long, cold days of getting ready for the opening. This roast is a bit of a splurge, since you’re here. Normally, we don’t eat red meat anymore. Trying to keep Joe on a better diet to help his heart.”

Darcy toed off her boots. “How is Uncle Joe?”

“He’s doing good. He needs to take it easy, which is very hard for him this time of year, but he restricts his working hours and we’ve got some wonderful employees who pick up any slack. Selling is going to be hard, but it’s the right thing to do. It’s time.”

Darcy hesitated. “I see it needs a little work,” she said softly.

Marla nodded. “We’ve focused on the trees, not that fence out by the road. We couldn’t do it all, although—” She stopped, and Darcy could have sworn guilt crossed her aunt’s face.

"Although what?"

Her aunt gave her head a quick shake. "Nothing. We've done what we can. Now it's time to turn it over to someone else." She nodded at Darcy's bags. "Why not take those up to your room, honey? It's all fresh for you. We'll eat shortly. I hope you're hungry."

Her stomach chose that moment to unleash a rolling growl. Her aunt cocked an eyebrow. Darcy gave a little laugh. "Guess that's your answer." She'd been too much of a wreck about coming back to Holden's Crossing to do much more than nibble on a protein bar in the car.

"Good thing, too. We've got a lot of food and I don't want your uncle to eat it all. Here, let me help you." Marla picked up one of her bags and Darcy grabbed the last two.

As she followed her aunt to the stairs, she noted the decor hadn't changed much, either. Clean, same plaid couch from when she'd left, same curtains. A large blue spruce stood in front of the big window, lit with hundreds of lights and covered in ornaments. A fire crackled on the hearth, which made the whole place seem homey and cozy.

Sadness gave a little twist under her heart. She'd miss this house when they sold it.

Marla set the small duffel on the bed. "I know it was hard for you to come. I just want you to know how much we appreciate it. And I wish—I wish you hadn't thought you couldn't come home."

Caught, Darcy sank down on the bed. "You know why I couldn't."

Marla held her gaze and Darcy saw understanding and compassion there. "I know why you thought you couldn't. There's a difference."

Darcy dropped her gaze to the quilt and ran her hand over it, the slightly puckered fabric cool under her hand. Leaving gave both of them a chance to start over after the divorce. "Not to me."

"I know that, too. Your dad would be proud of you for coming back. So." She headed for the door. "Come down when you're done. Dinner'll be ready soon. Then we've got work to do."

Darcy stayed on the bed, hearing the stairs creak as her aunt went downstairs. She took a deep, shaky breath.

The memories weren't going to go away. In fact, being here pretty much ensured she'd be assaulted by them at every turn. So she'd deal.

Determined, she stood up and unzipped the nearest bag. She wasn't that naive young woman anymore. She'd been to hell and back. She'd lost her baby and her marriage. There was nothing the Lawless family could dish out she couldn't take.

But she did need to make things right. So she'd apologize to Mack, make him see her intention had never been to cause him any more pain. Maybe then she could forgive herself.

Maybe.

Two hours later, at the kitchen table, her stomach full of Marla's excellent roast, she smiled at her aunt and uncle. "Thank you. That was the best meal I've had in a long time." And tomorrow was Thanksgiving. Two excellent home-cooked meals in a row. Amazing.

They exchanged glances, and then her uncle spoke, his face serious. "Darcy, there's something we need to tell you."

Worry rose so fast she thought she'd choke. "Are you okay, Uncle Joe?"

He patted her arm. "Yes. Oh, yes, Darce, it's not me. It's—well, it's just that Mack has been working here."

That couldn't be right. She clearly had her ex on the brain, because she thought she'd heard her uncle say he was working here. At the farm. Which wasn't possible. Why would Mack be out here? He was a vet. "I'm sorry. What was that?"

He met her gaze. "Mack's been helping me."

The air whooshed out of her lungs. She hadn't misheard. *No. Way.* "*My* Mack?" She winced at her mistake. He hadn't been hers for seven years. "Why?"

Marla laid her hand on Darcy's arm. "He's young and strong. He's been out here for years helping. I know this must be upsetting for you."

She looked away, betrayal humming in her veins. *Upsetting* put it mildly. But they were all adults. What right did she have to expect her family, who lived in this community, to not interact with the Lawless family? "Ah. Well, that's nice of him. I know his vet practice must keep him very busy." She gave a little shrug, trying for casual and fairly sure she'd failed. "Why would it be upsetting? It's been a long time."

Her aunt made a distressed little noise. "Oh, Darcy."

Joe cleared his throat. "One more thing. He's on his way here."

Her gaze snapped to his, panic coiling in her belly. "What?"

Marla looked at her with concern. "He's been out here every night for the past couple of weeks. I know this is a shock—"

"You couldn't have given me a little more warning?" Oh dear, was that a squeak of hysteria in her voice?

"We didn't want to upset you," Marla said simply. "We thought it would be best not to tell you. We talked about it at length, trying to decide how to handle it. Things were so hard for you after the divorce."

She shut her eyes and inhaled deeply, trying to calm her quickly frazzling nerves. Or course they meant well; she didn't doubt that. They were only trying to protect her. Mack, at least, wouldn't be blindsided. Chase would have taken care of that before Darcy got back in her car at the gas station.

"When will he be here?" Amazing, her voice sounded almost calm. Thank God.

Joe glanced at the wall clock. "He's usually here by six thirty. Please understand, Darcy. I know we should have said something before now, but…" He trailed off and looked helplessly at his wife.

She jumped in seamlessly. "But we weren't sure how you'd react. It was hard enough for you to come back as it is. I'm sorry."

Darcy managed a laugh. "I've been over Mack Lawless for years now. If he helps you out, that's great. I've got no problem with it at all."

That wasn't entirely true. But she chose to believe it was because they hadn't told her.

It had nothing to do with maybe not being over him.

Chapter Two

"Well," Marla said as she stood up and began to stack dishes. "I'm going to take care of these and then I'll join you in the barn. Darcy, if you'd rather not go out there tonight, we'd understand."

"No. I'll be fine." She hoped like crazy it was true. She couldn't let her aunt and uncle know how rattled she was.

Marla wouldn't hear of Darcy helping her clean up, which was probably a good thing, as her hands hadn't stopped shaking since they'd told her about Mack, so she got into her down jacket and boots and followed her uncle down the snowy path to the barn. Any other time, she would have found the quiet and the falling snow peaceful. Right now, she found herself too keyed up to enjoy it.

"Finances are a little tight around here, as I'm sure you noticed when you drove up," her uncle said finally.

"Mack offered to help out. He won't accept any pay. Likes the work, he says."

Her heart tugged. That sounded like the Mack she'd known and loved.

"It's okay, Uncle Joe."

He took her hand for the rest of the brief walk and she was grateful for the simple touch. In the workshop, he introduced her to his employees, then said, "We'll be in and out. You remember how to make a wreath?"

In spite of her nerves, she smiled. "I can do it in my sleep, Uncle Joe."

He gave her a quick hug. "Stay strong, honey." He headed outside with his crew and left her alone.

She took a moment to inhale the sharp scent of pine. Some things never changed, and this room was one of them, thankfully. Long scarred tables, open shelves with wire, twine, cutters, pinecones and different colors and styles of ribbon along with boxes of assorted decorations. She admired a finished wreath. It was beautiful—spruce and juniper, with berries, pinecones and a big gold ribbon.

Forcing herself not to watch the clock and failing—just how much longer till six thirty anyway?—she kept busy by gathering supplies for and starting a wreath. Her aunt walked in five minutes before Mack was due to arrive.

"I thought maybe it'd be best if I were here," she said, and Darcy gave her a tremulous smile. "I see you haven't lost your bow-tying skills."

Her aunt kept up a steady chatter, not seeming to expect Darcy to reply, which was good because she had one ear tuned for an approaching engine. When she finally heard it, she took a deep breath.

Marla gave her a sympathetic look. "Relax, honey. It'll be okay."

But Darcy barely heard her as the barn door rolled open and Mack's familiar, long-legged form stepped through. Her breath caught.

He hadn't changed. If anything, he'd gotten even better looking, even in old jeans, boots and a down vest, with a Michigan State ball cap. His brown hair was a little longer, curling slightly at the nape of his neck. He'd always hated the curl, worn it short. Somehow the new style was a sign of how much she'd missed.

His gaze landed on her and he gave her a cool nod. "Darcy. Nice to see you."

It'd been seven years since she heard her name on his lips in that delicious deep voice of his. Longer still since he'd said it with affection, love or passion. Pain and regret hit her like a tidal wave. She'd botched things so badly. She swallowed hard. "Mack." Her voice wasn't much more than a whisper.

Before she could say more he shifted his attention to her aunt. What they talked about, Darcy couldn't say. She turned back to the table to busy herself by tying bows. Her hands shook so hard she kept fumbling the ribbon.

Watching Mack now—because her gaze kept pinging over there on its own—it was clear to her that he wasn't having the same issues she was. He'd gotten over her.

That was good, right? That was why she'd left. Mission accomplished.

Too bad she didn't feel accomplished. She felt torn up inside. Raw.

She started to reach for the scissors when her neck tingled. When she looked up, her gaze locked on Mack's.

Even across the barn and over her aunt's head, she felt the heat of it to her toes.

Oh, no.

She looked down at the bow she'd botched and untied it with trembling fingers. Oh, this was bad.

True, in the years since the divorce she'd barely dated. The few times she'd gone out? Her friends had talked her into it and there'd never been a second date.

She'd never reacted to anyone the way she did to Mack.

"We need to talk."

Darcy jumped at the sound of his voice right behind her. She turned and looked up at him, at the hard set of his jaw, the iciness of his blue eyes. Oh, how she'd hurt this man she'd loved with all her heart. If only she could go back and undo the past.

But she couldn't.

"About what?" Panic fluttered in her throat. He couldn't want to get into their failed marriage already, could he?

"Why we're here."

Darcy put down the scissors she could barely hold anyway and crossed her arms over her chest, needing the barrier it signaled to both of them. "I know why I'm here. My aunt and uncle asked me to be."

His eyes flashed. "You could have come home at any time."

She inhaled sharply. "No. I couldn't. You of all people know why."

"I don't even know why you left in the first place." The words were simple but stark and sliced through her as cleanly as a sharp blade.

She lifted her chin, fought the threat of tears back.

"Of course you do. But it doesn't matter now. I'm going to help my aunt and uncle out, then I'll be out of your life."

He looked at her, his intense blue gaze unreadable. "You'll never be out of my life," he said, his voice low.

Darcy stared after him as he strode out of the barn, his words vibrating in her soul.

Marla hurried over to her. "You okay, dear?"

Darcy forced her lips into what she hoped passed for a smile. "Of course." At her aunt's skeptical look she added, "A little shaken, but I'll be fine, Aunt Marla. It's been a while."

The phone rang and her aunt glared at it, then went to answer, clearly reluctant to leave Darcy alone.

She picked her scissors back up and decided right then not to show how much the encounter had affected her. As she started a new bow, determination set in. It might be too much to hope she could get Mack to understand now what he'd been unable to back then. But she absolutely had to try so she could finally move on.

Wasn't Christmas a season for miracles?

She'd need one.

Mack strode out into the cold, thoughts whirling. He thought he'd been prepared for the shock, but he'd been wrong. Way wrong. Seeing her wasn't easier after all these years.

Especially when she looked so damn appealing.

But it'd been the look in her big brown eyes that killed him—wary, hopeful, sad all mixed together. Regretful.

Regrets. He had a few of those himself.

The still falling snow swirled around him as he approached Joe, who was readying to bale and load cut trees into a truck for delivery at a local store. Joe looked distinctly guilty as he approached.

"You saw Darcy?"

Mack gave a curt nod. "Yeah."

Joe's look was assessing and it made Mack uncomfortable. He didn't want the older man to see how rattled he was. "I'm sorry we didn't talk to you about Darcy. We were afraid you'd quit or that she wouldn't come. We didn't want either to happen."

Mack shook his head. He wouldn't have quit. And he wouldn't have discussed Darcy with her uncle anyway—it would be disloyal and he'd never ask Joe to do that. "It's all right. So where are these going?" He pulled a fresh-cut spruce off the trailer.

"Tom's. Said delivery would be first thing tomorrow." With that, Joe turned the equipment on.

It suited him.

It didn't take nearly long enough to load the truck with the trees and wreaths the grocery store owner had ordered. By the time he'd completed several other tasks and he ducked back into the barn, he didn't see Darcy.

The stab he felt wasn't disappointment. It couldn't be. He'd been there, done that.

He wasn't able to fool himself.

With a sigh, he trudged toward his truck through a good four inches of snow. Joe's voice stopped him.

"Are you going to talk to Darcy?"

Mack turned around. "About what?"

"About what happened."

Anger surged through him, but he forced it down. "There's nothing left to say. It's been a long time, Joe. A long time," he repeated, even though seeing her made it all feel like yesterday. He wanted to forget, to keep it buried. She hadn't wanted them, their family. What good was it to rehash the whole thing now?

"Maybe so. But you two have unfinished business. Talk to her." When Mack opened his mouth, Joe held up a hand. "I'm not going to say any more on this. You're adults. Thanks for the help tonight. We'll be back at it after dinner tomorrow."

Mack said good-night and swiped the fluffy snow off his windshield. He stood there for a second and watched Joe walk up the lane that led to the house. With a sigh he climbed in and started the engine. As he drove back out to the road, exhaustion washed over him. No doubt there'd be no sleep for him tonight. Or he'd dream of Darcy all night. Frankly, he'd prefer no sleep.

He turned in the driveway of his little house, the one he'd bought and restored after Darcy left. He'd needed an outlet for his grief, and this house had provided it. He came in through the front door, and was greeted by enthusiastic barking. Sadie and Lilly came barreling out of the living room and threw themselves at him, barking as if they'd thought he wouldn't be back. He rubbed ears as he waded through them and headed for the kitchen.

"You guys want out?" They zipped to the door and he let them out in the snow in the fenced-in backyard. His phone rang before he even got his coat off. A glance at the caller ID had him bracing himself.

"Hi, Mom."

"Mack. How are you?" There was concern in his mother's voice.

"Fine." And because he was feeling a little contrary with how his family assumed he wasn't, he added, "Why wouldn't I be?"

His mother sighed. "I don't know. Because Darcy is home. And you help out at the tree farm. Did you see her?"

Mack shrugged out of his jacket. "I did." There wasn't anything else to say—at least not to his mom.

"How did it go?" Her voice was gentle.

"I don't know. Fine." He raked a hand though his hair, remembering Darcy's huge, stricken eyes. "Mom. What do you think I'm going to do?"

She sighed. "I don't know. I know how torn up you were when she left. How we thought we'd lose you, too. I know you're an adult, but you're still my boy. And I don't want to see you go through that again."

Mack turned as he heard a noise at the back door. The dogs were ready to come in. He opened it and they tumbled through in a flurry of wet paws and snow and cold air. "It's all in the past, Mom."

She made a little noise that could have been disbelief. "Okay, then. I won't keep you. We'll see you tomorrow."

Tomorrow. Thanksgiving. He'd spent one of those with a pregnant Darcy as his wife. Just before—well, before. It was how he divided everything. Before. And After. He shut the images down. "Sounds good."

She talked a few more minutes and Mack made all the appropriate noises before hanging up with a promise to be on time.

He tossed the phone on the counter and sank down at one of the bar stools lining it. He covered his face with his hands and braced his elbows on the counter. Darcy. All those things he'd worked so hard to avoid were staring him in the face.

He slammed his palms on the surface, and both dogs looked up from their bowls.

"Sorry, guys," he said, and they looked at him as if they saw more than he wanted them to. Wanted anyone to, for that matter.

After a shower, he lay on his bed and turned the TV on, more for distraction than anything else. He flipped through the channels until he found a hockey game he wasn't going to watch anyway.

She'd looked shocked when he said he didn't know why she'd left. How could that be? She'd never told him, she'd just said she wanted a divorce. She'd left in a hurry after that, without so much as a glance back.

He'd been looking for her ever since.

Thanksgiving passed in a blur of fantastic food and frantic preparations for the season opening of Kramer Tree Farm the next morning. Darcy knew Mack was around, but there were so many other people and so much to be done she had no time to dwell on it.

But she was always aware he was in the vicinity. Somehow she was very tuned in to him. That wasn't a good thing.

She hadn't slept so well the previous night, dreaming of Mack. Now, fired up on caffeine and nerves, she figured tonight would be a repeat of the last.

She thought of her quiet condo in Chicago, her refuge from all this emotion and pain. She missed it and the safety it offered—even if it was apparently safety from herself and her memories.

The chatter of the employees, the Christmas music, all combined to make a festive atmosphere. The fresh six inches of snow added to it. Her aunt and uncle were thrilled. She tied the last sprig of bittersweet to the wreath she'd made as Marla came over.

"Looks lovely," she said with a smile. "You haven't lost your touch."

Darcy laughed. "I think I can make these in my sleep. Everything going okay?"

"Yes, thankfully. We're pretty much set. Can I get you to take the ATV out to the warming stations and make sure they are ready to go in the morning? Hot chocolate and coffee out there, and both that and mulled cider up here."

"Sure." Darcy left the completed wreath where it was and stripped off her pitch-sticky work gloves. It only took a couple minutes to gather the supplies she needed and put them in a bag. Outside, she fired up the ATV and drove down the plowed paths to the first—and largest—warming shed. Someone had left the lights on. She parked outside and went in.

Mack turned around, surprise on his face. Darcy squeaked.

"What are you doing here?" she blurted, and realized as his expression closed up how rude she sounded. "I mean—I didn't mean—"

"I know what you meant." He nodded toward the heating unit. "Wasn't running right, so I told your uncle I'd take a look at it."

"Oh. Well. I'll be just a minute." She held up the bag as she edged inside. "I've got cocoa mix for tomorrow. Got to stock up."

She had every right to be here. She couldn't let him intimidate her, not that he was trying. She had nothing to hide or defend to this man. Their marriage was over.

So why were her hands shaking?

When she stood back up, she bumped a can of coffee, which fell off the table and crashed on the floor, leaving a fragrant trail of grounds as it rolled around. Her face burning, she practically dived for it the same moment Mack reached for it.

"I got it," she muttered, then inhaled sharply as Mack's hand closed over hers. His palm was warm, and while she knew she should yank hers back, her gaze flew to his and locked on.

He was only inches from her. His blue eyes were serious and heat sparked in them—and an answering heat spread through her. She wanted to lean forward, just a little and close the gap, see if he tasted like she remembered—

She couldn't afford to remember. She'd spent far too long trying to forget.

"Darcy." His voice was low, a little rough. She swallowed hard and pulled away, gathering the errant coffee can in her arms like a shield. His gaze was shuttered as he sat back on his heels. "Need a broom?"

She blinked at the coffee mess on the floor. "Looks like it." Hopefully, there was a backup coffee can somewhere, or else everyone would have to make do with cocoa. "There's one in the closet. I'll just clean this up and get out of your hair."

She couldn't even tell the heater wasn't working. It was awfully hot in here right now.

She suspected it had everything to do with how Mack managed to kick up her internal temperature.

"You're not in my way," he murmured and retreated to the heater when she came back with the broom. It was as if they were performing some kind of awkward dance. She managed to clean up her mess and stock up the packets with no further incidents, even though she kept sneaking looks at his broad back as he worked on the heater.

She put the broom away and turned toward the door, wanting only to escape the oppressiveness of the room.

"Okay, well, bye," she said in an overly bright tone. "Sorry for the interruption." She made a beeline for the door, unable to resist a last look at him.

He looked up and caught her. "No apologies necessary," he replied quietly.

Darcy escaped outside and took a deep lungful of the cold, crisp air in hope it'd settle the crazy butterflies in her belly.

She didn't care so much about making a mess in front of Mack—though she really hoped Aunt Marla had an extra can of coffee on hand—but her response to him scared her. She'd worked long and hard to move on past the guilt and grief, to build a new and successful life in Chicago. It'd been a long road, and hard won. But seeing Mack threatened all those carefully constructed walls. She couldn't afford that. If she hadn't promised her dad all those years ago she'd be here for this, she'd pack up and leave on Monday.

It wasn't running away when your sanity was on the line. Right?

Chapter Three

Opening day flew by in a merry haze of families and Christmas trees. Darcy was thrilled with the number of people who came out to the farm. The weather co-operated, too, with a very light snow and no wind. She worked the register, greeting old friends and new faces alike. She saw Mack often from her post, as he was helping with tree processing and loading for anyone who needed it. She actually began to suspect there were a few women who didn't need it, but took advantage of the fact they'd get his attention for a few minutes.

She wasn't sure how she felt about that.

She tried very hard not to stare at how perfectly the faded jeans he wore hugged his butt and strong thighs. She also tried to avoid eye contact with him, but it seemed they glanced off each other every time he came into her line of sight. She did note how much the people loved him. Which made sense. As a Lawless, he'd be well-known.

And sometimes she caught him looking at her. Those small moments thrilled her in a way she knew they shouldn't. There was nowhere it could go that would end well.

Only a handful of people alluded to their past and none of them made hurtful comments, even though Darcy had been braced for the worst.

So she was relaxed and happy when they closed at eight that night. Enough that when Marla invited Mack to the house for a hot supper and a drink, she smiled at him.

He accepted without even looking at Marla.

Talk at dinner was minimal, as Marla and Joe were clearly exhausted and they were all starving. But the stew was hot and good and just spooned from the slow cooker. After dinner, Darcy sent them to relax. "I'll get the dishes."

"We both will," Mack said and stood up from the table.

Marla and Joe exchanged a look and Darcy wished he hadn't said anything. Now it was clear what her aunt and uncle were thinking. She didn't want to give them the chance to do any misguided matchmaking.

"Okay," Marla relented. "Thank you."

In silence, Darcy and Mack cleared the table. She was thankful there were only a handful—Mack was doing the suck-all-the-air-out-of-the-room routine that made it hard to concentrate. And he smelled so *good*, like fresh air and snow and pine. She wanted to burrow into his plaid flannel shirt and just breathe him in.

Wait. No, she didn't. She was over him, remember?

She turned the water on and added soap while he quietly got out a clean towel. From the living room, the TV added a nice undertone and helped fill the silence, but didn't do anything to cut the tension.

"So," she said as she slid plates into the sink, "a good day, huh?"

"Very," he agreed. He took the plate from her instead of waiting for her to put it in the drainer. She pulled away quickly. She'd have to be very careful not to touch him accidentally.

"Tell me about your job," he said.

She relaxed. This was a safe topic, not likely to venture into territory she wasn't comfortable with. She filled him in on her PR career, stressing how much she enjoyed it and the city.

Or used to. No point in mentioning the dissatisfaction she'd had over the past few years.

"You love Chicago."

It wasn't a question, almost an accusation. Surprised, she forgot she wasn't going to make eye contact and looked at him. His jaw was tense.

"I do," she said because it was true. She loved the city, the pulse, the vibrancy. The quirky atmosphere.

"So you're happy." The words were quiet, but Darcy recognized them as a minefield. No answer would be the right one. She swallowed hard.

"I am, yeah." She carefully washed the last plate and handed it over, mindful of his long fingers and the memories she had of them, both tender and erotic.

"I'm glad to hear it," he said quietly, and she looked up to catch his gaze. It was sincere and regretful at once. Her heart stuttered. Maybe she could get him to see what had been in her head and heart back then. Maybe she could apologize and he'd accept it. Maybe this was the opportunity she needed to finally move on and find peace.

"Thank you," she murmured, but couldn't look away, gripping the dishcloth because she was afraid she'd reach for him. Touch his face, with the faint shadow of whiskers on his strong jaw. Bury her hands in the longer length of his hair.

Or kiss him.

With a hard swallow, she turned back to the sink. None of those were options. Not a single one. To even think so was madness of a truly bittersweet kind.

He folded the towel and she drained the sink, bumping his arm with hers as he hung it up. She gritted her teeth against the little prickle of heat the contact generated. She didn't want this, but didn't know how to make it go away.

"How about you?" The question was more of a desperate deflection. "How's the vet practice? What else are you up to these days besides helping here?"

He leaned a hip on the counter and folded his arms across his chest. "I'm good. The practice is good. I've got another vet working with me now, too. We're a good team. The practice is expanding and we need more room, so that's why your aunt and uncle are selling to us."

She blinked and went cold. "I'm sorry. What did you say?"

He looked at her strangely, then comprehension dawned. "I'm buying the tree farm, Darce. With Chase. Didn't they tell you?"

She turned to the sink and swiped at it with the cloth,

fighting the sense of betrayal that flooded her. "It must have slipped their minds," she muttered.

What else hadn't she been told? Had things been so bad when her marriage ended they'd tried to shelter her to the point of simply not telling her anything?

He swore, then rubbed a hand over his face. "I'm sorry, I thought you knew. I wouldn't have—"

"Told me. I know. No one around here seems to think I need to know anything that's going on." She sounded put out but couldn't help it. What else didn't she know?

"You've been gone a long time," he pointed out, an edge creeping into his voice.

"I know." The words were bitter on her tongue, all the more so because he was right. "What are you going to do with it?" She wasn't sure she wanted to know.

He pushed off the counter. "Chase has an ecologically sound plan for the place, Darcy. If you stop by my office I'll show you—"

"Wait." She held up a hand. *Ecologically sound* were pretty words that hid a nasty truth. "Is he turning this into a subdivision?" The thought made her sick to her stomach. All the trees leveled, the ponds filled in, the buildings that had been here forever torn down.

"Not like you're thinking, I'm sure. The barn will hold my practice. The rest will be a sub, which will have large lots. The plan is to preserve as many of the trees as possible. It'll be natural, with trails and everything."

The roaring in her ears intensified. "You're taking my childhood home and tearing it down so you can build a subdivision."

Alarm crossed Mack's face as he narrowed his eyes. "You make it sound personal."

"Isn't it?" The bitterness spewed out of her now. "I

hurt you. Badly. I took everything from you and now here's your chance to hurt me back." This farm had always been here, always been a constant in her life. Now it'd be torn down and replaced with houses and people. And no longer part of her.

"Oh, come on, Darcy. It's been seven years! And you haven't been back since to the childhood home you love so much. Your aunt and uncle are important to me. This has nothing to do with you." His voice had risen to match hers, and she glanced at the living room, worried her aunt and uncle would overhear.

She stared at him, the final realization he'd truly moved on hitting her right in the heart. "You knew. And you're still going to destroy it."

"We gave them a fair price," he said simply. "They know my plans. They know Chase's plans. No one's destroying anything. It's why they agreed to sell to us. They had opportunities to turn us down. I'd never pressure them, Darcy. Give me some credit."

The tight edge of anger in his voice forced her to bring it down a few notches. "Right. It's not about me. As long as they are okay with selling the farm to you for a subdivision, it has nothing to do with me." Were her words for Mack, or for herself?

"No, it doesn't." There was a challenge in his eyes. "Because you'll leave. You claim to love it here, but you'll leave it without a second thought. And not ever look back." He snagged his jacket off the back of a chair. "Never mind, Darcy. I've got nothing to justify to you. It doesn't involve you."

His words followed him out the door and she resisted the urge to scream and throw something after him. Tears pricked her eyes and she swallowed hard. He had a point. She'd seen firsthand how little they needed her here, how they didn't see how much she'd loved it. How she'd dreamed of being back.

Whose fault was that? Her own. She'd needed to get away from Holden's Crossing so badly she hadn't thought about what it would mean to relationships with those she'd left behind. Even being in touch long-distance hadn't been enough, though she'd tried to convince herself it was.

It hurt they'd opted not to keep her in the loop. Worse that Mack had been the one to tell her.

Aunt Marla walked in. She looked around the kitchen. "Where's Mack?"

"Gone," Darcy said shortly. Marla frowned.

"Did you two have a fight?"

In spite of herself, she laughed. "Fight? That would imply there was something to fight over. No. He just—he told me he's buying you out."

"Oh." Marla sat down at the table. "Yes. He is."

Darcy didn't have the energy to pursue it further. Plus, it didn't matter, as Mack had made clear. "That's great."

Marla covered Darcy's hand with her own. "He and Chase will treat it with respect, Darce. It's a good choice for all of us."

Darcy's breath caught. *All of us* didn't include her, of course. And now it was too late to ask for a say. Besides, what could she do? She lived in Chicago, for Pete's sake. Her life was there. She'd spent the past seven years making sure everyone knew that. How happy she was, how successful she was, how busy she was.

It had all been a sham.

"Of course it is." She pushed back from the table. "I'm wiped. I think I'll go to bed."

Marla rose and gave her a quick hug. "I'm sorry, honey. We should have told you."

"Just out of curiosity, is there anything else I need to know?"

Marla shook her head. "No. Nothing. Darcy, I'm so sorry for how this has gone."

Being angry with them wouldn't serve anyone. Besides, the one she was mad at was herself. And Mack, no matter how unfair that was. "No harm done," she murmured and hurried up the stairs to her room.

A few minutes later there was a knock on the door. Darcy opened it to find her uncle standing there. "Can I come in?" His voice was quiet.

"Of course." She stepped back. The room was small, and he sat on the bed.

"Marla told me." He took a deep breath. "I know. We should have said something. We've really—we've really dropped the ball when it comes to all this. We thought—we thought we'd kind of ease you into it. That wasn't our intention, to shut you out."

Darcy's mind was whirling. It felt that way, but there was no point in going there. She was as much, if not more, to blame, letting them think she needed to be protected from all this. "I know. I understand." She stared out the window at the light snow that fell, dancing in the reflected light of the Christmas lights on the porch. "But—how can you sell it to them, Uncle Joe?" No matter what Mack said, that he and Chase would keep it intact and not level the whole thing to build wall-to-wall cookie-cutter houses, she couldn't believe him.

Didn't believe him. "It's just—always been here." But of course she could see the proof, that it needed more than Joe and Marla could give it.

"It's been in the family for a few generations now," Joe said. "But there's no one to carry on the farm. Unless…" His voice trailed off and Darcy, hearing the speculation in his tone, pivoted to face him.

"Unless what?"

"Unless you want to run it."

Darcy laughed and slapped her hand on her chest, incredulous. "Me? I couldn't possibly."

Joe's gaze was steady and her laughter died. "Why not?"

She scrambled for an answer. "My life. My job. It's all in Chicago." It seemed obvious. Didn't it?

"Are you happy there?"

She turned back to the window. What was up with that question? Mack had asked her the same thing. "Of course." Wasn't she happy? Was it her guilt that was eating at her?

She heard the creaking of Joe's knees as he rose off the bed and came to stand beside her. When he spoke, his voice was quiet. "As a child, you loved this place. Loved it, Darcy. Followed me and your daddy all over, helping. Even after he died, and you were so young, you kept on helping. With your PR skills, you could take this place and really turn it around. We have a verbal agreement only at this point. No papers have been signed yet."

She stared at his profile, her mind whirling. She had a closet full of stilettos, for God's sake. She'd never wear them here. She was a city girl now. And—Mack was here. Could she live in the same town and still move on with her life?

Joe looked over and slid his arm around her shoulders and pulled her into a hug. She breathed deeply of his outdoorsy, piney scent and squeezed her eyes shut. "Keep it in mind before you reject it totally, Darcy."

She hugged him back. "I can't make any promises, Uncle Joe." She didn't want them to pin their hopes on her. She just didn't see how it could ever work.

She'd worked so hard to make partner, a feat that was almost in her grasp. So hard to earn the respect of her coworkers. So hard to forget what had happened here, to move past it. To come home to stay would be like throwing away the past seven years of her life. Why would she want to undo everything she'd worked so hard for?

Why would she want to face, every day, what she'd tried too hard to forget?

Damn it. It hadn't gone away.

Mack walked into his office Monday morning in a foul mood thanks to his sleepless weekend. Ever since Darcy showed up, he'd been unable to sleep for the damn dreams.

Dreams of Darcy.

They'd managed to spend all weekend together, but not really. She spoke to him when necessary but no more than that. Eye contact was minimal but searing. Sometimes he'd catch her watching him, and he couldn't read her anymore. Wasn't sure he wanted to. It was driving him slowly insane.

Now he went into his office, tossed his coat on the coatrack and dropped in his chair to rub his forehead wearily. God help him, he'd never make it to Christmas this way. She'd kill him all over again and not even know it.

Even though Sherry would fuss at him, he went ahead and started coffee. Functioning on zero sleep required constant caffeine. Delivered by IV preferably. Since that wasn't an option, he headed for the coffeemaker.

There was a rhythm to the mornings. Check everyone, feed everyone, take out those who needed it. Medicine to those who needed it. He embraced the routine today, relieved for the constancy of it. Today he had no truly ill animals, which was always nice. By the time the coffee perked, he was feeling more relaxed.

Jennifer, another vet who worked with him, came in on a flurry of snow.

"Morning," she said, then looked at him hard. "Notice I didn't say 'Good morning,' because you look like hell."

He sputtered a laugh. He could always trust she'd get to the point. "Thanks, Jenn."

"This have anything to do with the return of the ex-wife?"

He shut his eyes for a second before reaching for a food bowl. "You heard."

"Of course. Small town means everyone eventually knows everything." She held up a hand before he could say anything. "You don't have to confirm or deny. Though one look at you is plenty of confirmation for me."

He replaced the bowl and ran his hand down the back of the cat gently. She didn't purr, but neither did she swipe at him. "There's not much to say." He knew his tone was curt but she didn't flinch.

"Maybe I'm not the one you need to talk to," she said softly.

He thought of Darcy, of her laugh, of her spill of hair, of her big brown eyes and smooth skin. Of her cute little body in worn jeans and a long-sleeved T-shirt. Of how he'd thought he was over her and somehow he wasn't.

Nope, no reason to say anything.

"I'm good," he said, and she rolled her eyes at him as Sherry entered the clinic.

The morning passed quickly. He managed to keep thoughts of Darcy to a minimum. He wasn't due to help at the Kramer farm till the weekend. With any luck he'd have this under control by then.

His last patient of the day was a cantankerous old cat. The owner, Mrs. Harris, had known him his whole life, and she still spent most of her days at the bakery she'd owned for as long as Mack could remember.

"Hello, Mrs. Harris," he greeted her as he entered the exam room. "Wolfie's not eating today?"

The older lady frowned. "No. He's just not himself."

An exam of the animal didn't reveal anything untoward, so Mack suggested a change of cat food and sent them on their way with a sample bag. He stood in the reception area, making his notes in Wolfie's chart. Afterward, he ran through the closing duties with his staff and headed out to meet his brother for dinner. It wasn't lost on him how his mother and brother checked up on him regularly. Even Katie had, all the way from California.

He tried to appreciate their concerns, but it was a little stifling.

"So. How's it going with Darcy?" Chase's question was casual, but Mack heard the concern under the words.

"There's nothing to report," he said drily. "I hardly

see her, much less talk to her." All true. She was avoiding him. He knew he should be grateful.

"Mmm. So that's why you look as if you haven't slept in a week," Chase observed, tilting his beer bottle toward Mack. "You want to try again?"

Unsure actually if that question meant change his answer or give it another go with Darcy, he gave the answer that covered both. "No."

Chase raised an eyebrow but said nothing else. Mack stared at the TV, pretending *Monday Night Football* was enthralling, even though he had no idea what the score was and the teams were just a blur, since Darcy's face kept floating through his brain. He rubbed his hand over his face.

"Have you talked to her?"

"Well, yeah. I have to work with her. I'm not going to be rude," Mack said, irritated.

"That's not what I meant."

Mack laughed. "Why would I do that, Chase? It's long over. There's nothing to say."

Other than ask questions. Like, *Why did you leave? Why didn't you love me as much as I loved you? Why wasn't I enough? Why couldn't we pull through our loss?*

And she might have one for him. Like, *Why weren't you there for me when I needed you?*

He had no answer for any of them.

"Nothing to say," he repeated flatly. "Chase. Drop it."

His brother looked at him hard and Mack managed not to flinch. Chase gave a short nod. "All right."

Mack let out a silent exhale. The only way he'd get through this was if people left him alone. All the well-meaning looks and questions were driving him crazy.

He wasn't going to self-destruct just because Darcy was home. Or because she'd leave again.

Because this time she wasn't leaving him behind. He'd walk away first.

Chapter Four

Darcy walked into Java, the local coffee shop, with her laptop bag on her shoulder. Internet at the farm was slow and spotty at best. She needed to check in at work, and this was the best way to do it. She stepped up to the counter, smiled at the barista she didn't recognize and ordered a latte. Then she settled in at a table by the window and booted up her computer.

She frowned at the sheer number of emails. It'd been only a few days since she left, and there were nearly a hundred of them. Many of them from her team on the Grant project. Her phone didn't work reliably up here, either. Apparently the farm was in a technological dead zone. With a sigh, she opened the first one, called her assistant and expected to be putting out fires.

So she didn't see Mack until he was right across from her. She looked up and her heart caught. She didn't hear what her assistant said and had to ask her to repeat. She pulled her computer closer, opening a space on the other side of the table, and gave him a nod. God only knew what this would do to gossip.

When she managed to hang up, he arched an eyebrow. "Problems?"

"I've got it under control," she said, and gave a sharp little laugh. "They take credit for the good stuff, but as soon as things turn into a flaming pile of poo they bail and blame me."

"Why do you put up with it?"

The question stopped her hand in midlift of her now cool latte. Why did she? "I don't know. It's just the way it is."

Mack shook his head. "Sounds as if you need a new team."

She set her cup down. "I've got it under control," she repeated. She wasn't sure why her temper was sparking. Why he'd touched a nerve with a simple observation. "I've worked very hard to get where I am. I'm not going to quit."

"No?" His voice was deadly soft. "Isn't that what you do?"

Her gaze snapped to his, but his was carefully blank. Temper surged, and she welcomed its heat because his words left her cold. "No. I don't. I didn't."

"Sure you did. You never gave us a chance, Darcy."

Darcy's jaw nearly hit the table. "This is not the place for this conversation." She snapped the laptop closed, hands shaking with fury. "In fact, there's no place for this conversation because that would imply we had something to talk about."

"Easy," he said softly. "We're being watched."

Of course they were. She bit back a sharp retort and

slid the laptop into her bag. She offered him a stiff smile. "Enjoy your coffee."

She stood and spun around. Her bag caught on the chair and sent it toppling to the floor. Every head turned, but Mack was off his chair before she could move. He picked up the chair and slid a hand under her elbow. "I'm sorry," he said in her ear as he guided her to the door. She just shook her head, because any words she had for him weren't fit for anyone to overhear. Outside she yanked her arm away and walked as fast as she could in the opposite direction of where he was. Which, she realized after about twenty steam-fueled steps, was away from her car. Which sat in front of the coffee shop. Where Mack stood.

She stopped, shut her eyes, then pivoted. He had his hands in his pockets. He tipped his head toward her car.

She lifted her chin and walked back. When she got close enough to kick him—which was awfully tempting—he caught her arm. "Darcy. I'm sorry."

She looked him in the eye and saw the remorse there. "It's too late, Mack. Sorry isn't enough."

She got in her car and managed to get onto the street with tears burning in her eyes. Oh, no, sorry wasn't enough. It'd never be enough. And she knew that from years of being sorry for how things ended with their marriage. From knowing she could never go back and fix it. Go back and handle it differently, right down to deciding to turn left instead of right.

To save the baby he'd wanted so desperately. When she hadn't been ready to be a mother. She'd barely been ready to be a wife. But she'd gotten pregnant and he'd insisted they marry.

As always, when it came to Mack, she'd been unable to say no.

A sob escaped her and she swiped at her eyes. He had every right to be angry—but she wasn't that young woman anymore. She hadn't been since she lost their baby. She'd grown up in those awful hours after the accident that had fractured their marriage. She hadn't needed him to take care of her. She'd just needed him to be there for her. And he hadn't been able to understand the difference.

He hadn't been wrong. She *had* quit. She'd run away because it was easier than facing everyone else's pain when she could barely tolerate her own.

So no, he hadn't been wrong.

But to hear it from him tore her up inside.

Later that afternoon, Darcy had managed to put the whole thing behind her. Mostly. Now she stood behind the cash register—an old one, nothing electric about it—and smiled at the young couple paying for the tree. They were probably a little older than she and Mack had been, but her heart tugged all the same. Had she ever been that young and in love?

She watched as the husband dropped a kiss on the woman's temple. Oh, yes. She had been. But she'd been uneasy in her marriage and Mack had been so confident. This couple didn't look unbalanced like that.

"This is our first tree together," the woman said, beaming at her husband, who gave her an indulgent smile, then left to talk to Mack, who had the tree. Darcy forced her gaze to stick to the woman in front of her.

"Congratulations," she said a little too cheerfully. "How long have you been married?"

"Eight months." The woman pulled out a check and when she stooped to write it Darcy saw the rounding of her stomach. She saw herself at the same time, the same place and the world tilted. In spite of her best efforts, her gaze shot to Mack, who had his back to her. *This is how we could have been, should have been.*

"Are you all right?" The woman frowned, tore off the check and held it out. "You look awfully pale."

Darcy forced a smile back on her face as she took the piece of paper. "Headaches. They come on fast."

The other woman's face cleared. "I'm sorry. Hope you feel better. Merry Christmas!"

"Merry Christmas," Darcy echoed and watched as she walked to her husband, who slipped a protective arm around her and dropped another kiss on her head. She tilted her chin up to him, love shining on her face.

Longing and sorrow swamped her, hard and fast, and she wrapped her arms around her middle, willing it all away. She'd been so good at not feeling anything for these past few years, and now one happy couple had undone all that hard work.

"Darce." Mack's voice, laced with concern. How had he seen? Where had he come from? She looked up at him, but his face was suspiciously blurry. She blinked.

"I need some air," she said. "Can you watch the register for me?"

Then she bolted.

Mack stood there, stunned as Darcy darted across the barn and into the back. Then he went after her, calling out to another employee to take the register. To hell with this not being his place. Something in her eyes tugged at him and he knew he was helpless to resist. Plus, he owed her after earlier, in the coffee shop.

When he came in the back room, Marla looked at him, then pointed at the door. "I'll get the front."

"Thanks," he said, and went outside.

The cold air hit him with a blast, after the warmth of the back room. She stood by the tree line, her back to him. He saw the defensiveness of her posture, her arms wrapped around herself, her head down.

The fierce need to draw her in, rest his chin on her head, to just hold her, nearly overwhelmed him. He shoved his hands into his pockets instead as he came up beside her. "What's going on? Did that woman upset you?"

Had she been thinking what he had? Seeing them as a young married couple? Wondering how their marriage had disintegrated so fast?

She went even stiffer than before, if that was possible. "Mack, why are you out here?"

"I don't know." It was God's honest truth. He came around to the front of her, but she wouldn't look up. "Darcy. Did she?"

She shook her head. "Of course not. She was very nice. Excited for their first Christmas together." Her voice cracked slightly. She cleared her throat. "I've just got a headache."

A headache. Right. And he'd just grown a third arm. "Okay. Can I get you anything?" Why had he thought she'd maybe confide? That maybe they'd seen the same thing and had the same regrets? Why would she tell him?

She lifted her gaze then, and the pain in her eyes

nearly brought him to his knees. "There's nothing you can do."

If that was the truth, then what the hell? He cupped her chin in his hand, saw her eyes widen. "I saw it, too. I felt it, too. Lie to me, but not yourself." His voice was rough in his throat. "Don't think this is easy on me, Darce. It's not." Then because he couldn't not, he bent forward and planted a soft kiss on her cold lips, lingering for a heartbeat, before he pulled away. Now there was surprise in her eyes, and that was better than pain. He ran his thumb over her lower lip, then turned to go back inside.

Because if he didn't, he'd kiss her again. For real. And once they started down that path, there'd be no going back.

"You going to turn the water off, dear?" Amusement filled Marla's voice as Darcy blinked, then yanked the handle down. *Mack kissed me.* That was a shock after the little scene in the coffee shop earlier. Marla hadn't asked any questions, and that led Darcy to believe Marla thought something had happened with her and Mack.

She wouldn't be wrong, exactly.

It had been a small kiss. A peck, really. But, oh, it—and the look in his eyes—had shot straight to her heart.

She managed a smile for her aunt's sake. "Just tired."

"Mmm-hmm." Marla folded the towel precisely and put it on the counter. "Darcy. What happened today?"

Darcy shut her eyes. She didn't want to relive it. If she'd been able to control the reaction, as she had the few times she was hit with it before, none of this would have happened. Of course, Mack hadn't been within touching distance. "I had a weak moment."

Marla sat down at the table, and the squeak of a second chair being nudged out was a clear hint that she wanted Darcy to have a seat, too. So she did, reluctantly. "Honey, this has been a shock for you. I'm not sure how much you've dealt with since you've been gone." She held up a hand as Darcy opened her mouth to deny it. "Please. Listen. Okay?" Darcy clamped her mouth shut and nodded. "Okay. You left but you never dealt with the pain. You suffered two incredibly hard losses in a short time. You wouldn't talk about it when we asked you. You kept insisting you were fine. And you were so very young to boot. You've thrown yourself into your new life, but reinventing yourself isn't any good if the foundation you've based it on isn't strong."

Tears pricked Darcy's eyes, but she folded her hands tightly in front of her on the table, not wanting to give in to the weakness. Again. Marla's gnarled hand found hers, closing tight over her own. Darcy focused on her aunt's neatly trimmed nails to try to keep the tears at bay.

"Honey. You are strong. You are one of the strongest people I know, and as stubborn as your uncle. You went through hell and back and it's okay to grieve. It's not weak. It's necessary."

Darcy shut her eyes. She appreciated this, she did, but Marla didn't know the whole story. No one did.

"Talk to Mack," Marla said gently. "You don't have to reconcile, but you do have some stuff to put behind you."

Darcy managed a smile. "I appreciate your concern. It has been a shock." That was the absolute truth. Seeing Mack had sent her off-kilter in so many ways. Knowing he was buying the farm had been the least of it. "But there's not much to say, Aunt Marla. It was a long time ago. I don't see what it would change."

Marla sat back and Darcy caught the look of disappointment that passed over her face. She swallowed hard. It was so important that she keep all this locked down. She'd worked so hard to get it to that point. She wasn't sure what would happen if she let it all out now.

The next night, she went upstairs to her room, but she wasn't sleepy, despite her restless nights and busy days. She looked out the window to see the snow had stopped. The moon was shining on the snow, gilding the trees with silver. It was still fairly early, only eight thirty.

She went back downstairs and outside. She needed more shampoo, so she'd run to Jim's to grab some. It'd get her out of her head and off the farm for a little bit.

Win-win.

She drove into town and parked in the half-empty parking lot of the grocery store. Inside, she got her shampoo but stopped dead when she saw who was in line in front of her.

Mack.

Knowing she couldn't turn and slip away once he spotted her, she lifted her chin and got in line.

"Evening," he said, and offered her a smile.

Her breath caught. The laugh lines that fanned out from his eyes added character and were surprisingly sexy. "Hi," she managed to return in a normal voice. Then, because she couldn't stand there and look at him, she dropped her attention to the items he'd put on the belt, including a garish box with a toucan on it.

"Kids' cereal?" A giggle escaped her. "Still?"

He looked sheepish. "Hey. I like them."

"I know." Now her gaze caught his and the weight of a shared past blanketed them for a heartbeat. For once, it wasn't fringed with pain. She swallowed hard.

"How are you tonight?" The cashier's chirpy voice cut through the moment and Darcy looked away, heart pounding, as Mack turned to address the young woman.

She kept her gaze fixed on the colorful box of cereal. Because then she wasn't looking at how those jeans hugged his perfect rear. If she didn't look, she didn't have to acknowledge how badly she wanted to slide her hands over it.

If she didn't acknowledge it, she could pretend everything was normal. That somehow she wasn't losing her tenuous grip on normal.

Oh, who was she kidding? He turned so his profile was to her and she couldn't help looking. He had a small scar on his jaw. That was new. Her fingers itched to touch it, to feel the roughness of the slight growth on his face. He turned to look at her then, and her face turned hot.

"See you, Darcy."

She managed a smile. "Bye."

He walked away, pushing his cart with his couple of grocery bags, and she could still see the box of cereal. It was bittersweet to know some things never changed.

She paid for her own purchase and walked out.

"Darce."

She jumped at his voice. "Mack. What are you doing?"

"Sorry. Didn't mean to scare you." He nodded to the Town Line Diner across the street. "Want to grab coffee? I'd like to make up for the other day."

Oh, yes, more than anything. Which was why, when

she opened her mouth, she fully intended to say no. "Sure."

Blame it on the darn cereal. He looked so relieved, she couldn't berate herself for her weakness. "Great. Let me just put these in the truck. I'll meet you over there."

"Okay." Darcy walked to her car, the butterflies in her midsection going full flutter. What had she done? This wasn't a good idea.

It was just coffee. Maybe a chance to smooth things over.

She sat in her car and waited until he got in his truck, then followed him to the diner. This was why Uncle Joe's suggestion she buy the tree farm was ridiculous. She couldn't imagine running into Mack all over the place. She'd never be able to breathe fully here.

Coward.

Well, yes. Yes, she was. She parked next to him, grabbed her purse and took a deep breath.

She got out of the car and walked in next to him, unable to suppress the little shiver of awareness when his arm brushed hers. Even through the thickness of their coats, she swore she could feel his heat. Neither of them spoke.

Unsettled, she followed him wordlessly to a booth in the corner. She remembered coming here as a teenager with her friends. It smelled the same, of coffee and bacon and burgers. She slipped her jacket off and tried not to look at him.

Which, as it turned out, was easier said than done.

The waitress, perky and young, came over. "Hi, Dr. Lawless. What can I get you?" Darcy swore the young woman batted her eyes at him.

"Hi, Michelle. I'll just have coffee. Darce?" He shifted

his smile from the waitress to her. She resisted the urge to bat her eyes, as well.

The waitress shifted her attention to Darcy and took her in. If she hadn't been already on the edge, she'd have found it amusing to be viewed this way by a girl who couldn't be more than twenty to Mack's thirty-two. Clearly she didn't know the story of Darcy and Mack. If she did, Darcy was willing to bet she'd find her coffee in her lap. "Same. Thanks."

Michelle pocketed her pad and headed off, a definite swing to her hips. Darcy looked back at Mack, whose gaze was on her, not the girl, and raised an eyebrow. "Still charming the ladies?"

"All but one, it seems," he said, and his tone was serious.

She dropped her gaze and toyed with her silverware. He didn't waste time getting to the point. "Why do you think charming her would work?" She meant to keep her tone light and failed.

"I don't. But nothing else does." The frankness of his words caught her. She sat back and regarded him with slightly narrowed eyes.

"What do you want, Mack?" It seemed best to just ask. Maybe they could just clear the air and move on.

He met her gaze as the waitress returned with the coffeepot. Darcy said nothing as she filled both cups, then reached for two creams when she left. "Nice to know some things don't change."

She emptied both in her cup. "Like what?"

"You've always taken your coffee the same way."

The reference to the past, which lately hovered too close to the surface, brought her up short. "I've changed a lot, Mack."

"I know."

"Do you?" She sipped the hot liquid, welcomed the burn. "I've been gone a long time."

"I know that, too." Now his gaze was steady on hers. "We've got a lot to talk about."

She shook her head. "No, not really. Nothing will change what happened and how it was handled. I will say I'm sorry." Damn it, now there were tears burning in her eyes. "I'm so sorry for how it all went down. But it's not all my fault."

He leaned forward. "You left, Darce. Just left."

"No, Mack. You let me go."

Chapter Five

He stared at her. "It was what you wanted."

No, it hadn't been. What she'd wanted was for him to want her—to want their marriage—enough to fight for her. Make her stay. Want her for more than just her role as mother of their child.

He hadn't. He'd just granted the divorce, no questions asked.

He'd never actually asked her why she'd left.

She pushed her cup aside. "It doesn't matter now, does it?"

Mack examined her, this woman who'd once been his wife. He'd so wanted to do right by her, but when it had come down to it, he'd failed her. Failed their baby. It wasn't any less bitter a revelation now than it had been then. He thought of when she'd bolted at the sight of the happy young couple. Clearly, it all mattered to her, too, even if he couldn't get her to admit it.

"It does matter." When she stared at him he cleared his throat. "It matters to me."

He saw regret and pain in her brown eyes. She dropped her gaze. "It was what I wanted."

Even as her words pierced him, he wondered if they were true. But this wasn't the place to push it. He reached over and took her hand, feeling its coldness in his own, but it did nothing to diminish the heat he felt when he touched her. "For what it's worth, I'm sorry, too." For all of it, even the way he'd sprung his plans for the farm on her.

She looked at their linked hands, then gave a nod. "Well, then. Friends?"

He squeezed her fingers before releasing her. "Friends." He didn't think this was settled, not by a long shot. But he'd take these first steps for what they were—a start. At least she wasn't running away in tears.

"So. Tell me about your practice," she invited, and he ran with the topic change, grateful for the chance to just be with her.

Nearly an hour later, he looked at his watch. Time to go back to the clinic. "I've got to go," he said, truly regretful. "I've got a patient to check on."

She looked at her phone, and seemed surprised at the time. "Wow. I didn't realize it was this late. Okay."

They paid the bill and walked out into the cold night. A light snow had moved in and it sparkled in the parking lot lights. Not wanting the evening to end, he turned to her. "Come with me?"

She blinked up at him, snow caught on her lashes. "Excuse me?"

"Do you want to see the clinic?"

He held his breath, not wanting to admit how important this was to him, as she clearly wrestled with the question. "Okay."

Relief flooded him, along with something else he couldn't name. "It's not far. Follow me."

She got in her SUV and followed him to the clinic. He had managed to get the Christmas lights up as well as the garland, and they were lit now—on a timer to go off at eleven, along with all the other businesses along Main Street. Darcy parked across the street and stood there, looking.

He came up next to her, closer than he knew he should. "What do you see?"

She gestured at the street. "It's so cheery. Especially in the snow. When I think of Christmas, this is the scene I picture. I've missed it."

He nearly pointed out she could have come back at any time—in fact, she'd never had to leave—but he didn't want to ruin their new truce. "It is charming." He swept his hand out. "Shall we?"

She gave a little giggle and stepped off the curb. God, how he'd missed her laugh. There hadn't been much laughter after they got married. Then the accident had happened only six months in.

Pushing that thought away, he unlocked the door and reset the alarm. She stepped in behind him, noting the neatness of the waiting room. A Christmas tree stood in one corner, tags hanging off it. "What's this?"

"A wish tree. For the humane society. Things like cat litter, dog food, towels and blankets, that kind of thing. People take a tag, drop off the items and one of us runs it out there."

Oh, yes, this was the man she'd so loved. "What a great idea." When he went in front of her, she took a tag off the tree. "Dry cat food," it read. She slipped it in her purse.

The waiting area had a hard floor, comfy chairs, a few magazines on a table. A bulletin board held pictures of lots of animals and their owners. Another framed picture said "Get to know Dr. Lawless" and had pictures of him and his pets. "This is sweet."

He glanced up from the chart he was looking over. "Oh. Well, people like to see my pets."

"How many?" she asked as she followed him back through a door.

"Two dogs, two cats," he said. "Sometimes more if I'm fostering somebody. Minnie is in here."

She heard the muffled barking behind another door and raised an eyebrow.

"Those are the boarders, or those that are recovering from less intense surgeries. In here I keep those who need a more relaxed environment. Trauma patients or riskier surgeries."

"And who's Minnie?" She followed him into the room, where a little beagle lay on a doggie bed. She thumped her tail when they walked up.

"Minnie was hit by a car. The guy who hit her brought her in. She was— It was touch-and-go. She needs more pain meds."

Darcy stared at the liquid brown eyes, so full of pain yet joy to see them. "Oh, what a sweet girl. Who's her owner?"

"We don't know yet. No collar, no tags, no microchip." He opened the cage door and murmured in a low voice to the dog while Darcy stood back, out of the way, watching. There was a little yelp as he gave her a shot.

Then he rubbed her head as she dozed off. "Here. You can pet her while she falls asleep."

Darcy stepped forward and rubbed the dog's head. Minnie tried to give her a little lick. "Oh, you poor sweet girl. You don't know who she belongs to?"

"No." His tone was grim.

A shudder ran through Darcy. "Abandoned?"

His face was grim. "Happens more than you'd care to know. Foreclosure, need to move, can't take care of the pets. Sometimes they just leave them in the house and walk away. Sometimes they just drop them off somewhere thinking, hey, it's an animal, it can fend for itself. They can't." Anger laced his voice. "I understand not being able to feed them. But I wish—I wish people would bring them to a shelter rather than just abandon them."

She touched his wrist with her free hand, thought of the wish tree in the lobby. "That's so sad. They've got you as an advocate, though. That counts as something."

He moved up next to her, and in the dim light she saw the weight of this on him. The grimness on his face was reflected in his tone. "It's not enough. It will never be enough. However." He reached in, his arm brushing hers, his hand touching hers as he rubbed the now sleeping Minnie's head. "We do what we can."

She looked up at him as he looked back down at her. The heat from the proximity of their bodies drowned out everything else. He was so close she could lay her head on his chest. If she angled her body slightly, she could fit against him, see if it was still as perfect as it had been all those years ago. His hand slid over hers on Minnie's head, and the rough warmth of his palm sent sparks across her skin. He withdrew both their hands together, and his hot gaze dropped to her mouth.

Minnie whimpered in her sleep and Darcy stepped back, her breath shaky, as he shifted his attention to the dog. She cleared her throat. "Will she be okay?" Her words were a little breathy.

"I hope so. So far so good." She heard the roughness of his voice and closed her eyes. This attraction wasn't welcome, yet she couldn't control her reaction to him any more than she could stop breathing.

He latched the cage and made a note in the chart. She stepped a little farther back. "Do you have to come back and check on her later?"

He shook his head. "Jennifer will check on her later tonight. There's an apartment upstairs. She lives there and usually when we have a case like this takes the middle of the night shift."

"Oh. Well. That's handy," she murmured, trying to ignore the completely irrational spurt of jealousy at the casual mention of the other woman. Stupid, and totally unwarranted.

"Yeah, it works well." He tipped his head toward the door. "I've done what I need to here. You ready?"

She followed him back out, noting the quiet with which he shut the door behind him. She nodded toward the other door. "Do they need to be taken out?"

"No, that's all been taken care of for the evening," he said, and set Minnie's chart on the front desk.

"You've done well, Mack." The observation slipped out and he turned to her with surprise. "You fit here."

He moved toward her, his gaze sharp. "As would you, Darcy."

She shook her head. "No, I'm good in Chicago. I love it there."

"Do you?" He moved closer still and she edged back, but the hallway wall stopped her. "Do you really?"

He wasn't holding her in place, but Darcy couldn't seem to move. It was as if her cells had missed him so much she needed to soak up his nearness, his heat, as if he were the sun. She swallowed. "Yes," she whispered.

He moved a little closer and braced one arm on the wall, his gaze never leaving hers, the heat and want there a mirror of her own. "Darcy," he murmured, then lowered his head to settle his mouth on hers.

Her eyes drifted closed and she savored the sweetness of the kiss, which quickly turned to fire as he nipped at her lip. She opened for him and the kiss went from sweet to spicy in a heartbeat.

She slid her arms around his neck and let her fingers play in the longer hair there. He plunged his fingers in her hair and deepened the kiss even more. Fire licked through her, and brought with it the roaring desire she'd always had with Mack.

All of a sudden he wrenched back and left her, nearly panting, against the wall. "God, Darcy, I'm sorry. I didn't mean— I overstepped."

Her face burned. Sorry. Of course he was. "Are you saying we need to just forget it happened?"

He didn't seem to sense the trap. "Yeah, I think that'd be best."

He couldn't have hurt her more if he'd physically struck her. She swallowed hard and lifted her chin. "Well. Consider it forgotten." She darted around him and he let her go.

He let out a curse as the door shut behind her. He'd made a royal mess of it. Not the first time. They'd been making strides toward a fragile peace and then he went and gave in to the need to push her, to touch her, to kiss her. To get her to admit she'd made a mistake. Now she'd be back to avoiding him.

Maybe that was for the best. Maybe they couldn't manage "friends" after all. Especially with kisses like that hanging between them.

He walked back to his office and looked out the window to confirm her car was gone. He didn't want to admit he was more than disappointed she'd left. He hadn't been able to give her a reason to stay when it mattered most, so why did he think it'd be different now?

He was a fool. A fool for Darcy Kramer. It seemed he'd learned nothing over the past several years.

She'd leave—again—and that'd be the end.

This time for good.

Mack had kissed her. Really kissed her.

And she'd melted all over.

The memory of it swirled through her system, like the snowflakes that danced in her headlights. A little shiver ran through her. No one had ever kissed like Mack did, made her feel like Mack did. Not that she had much experience outside of Mack. She'd shut that part of her down.

Of course, he'd also suggested it had been a mistake. So there was that. She tried to ignore the spike of disappointment and remind herself it was for the best.

She snapped out of her reverie when she pulled into the driveway and saw an ambulance parked there. In a heartbeat the panic set in. She threw the car in Park with a gasp and ran up to the door, where she saw her uncle strapped to the gurney and her aunt's ashen face.

"Uncle Joe! Aunt Marla, what happened?" She stood

to the side so the paramedics could load her uncle in the ambulance.

"His heart." Marla turned stricken eyes on Darcy. "He's having pain, shortness of breath, all of it."

Darcy inhaled deeply and took her aunt's arm. "I'll drive you up to the hospital," she said as the nearby paramedic nodded as they climbed into the vehicle. "Let's go."

They hurried back to her still warm car and Darcy bounced down the driveway behind the ambulance. Marla sat beside her and even in the dark, Darcy could feel the tension and fear rolling off her aunt.

Hours passed, and Marla looked up at Darcy. "You'd better call Mack. Let him know."

Darcy inhaled sharply. While she knew her aunt was right, the thought made her own heart beat irregularly. She kept her voice calm. "I don't have his number. If you can put it in my phone, I'll do that now."

Marla nodded, apparently not reading anything on her face, so Darcy pulled her phone out. It was late. Would he even answer? She'd left in such a hurry.

The phone rang twice. Then Mack's voice, low and calm. "Hello?"

Darcy took a deep breath. "It's me. Darcy," she added lamely, momentarily tangled up in the propriety of how to identify herself to the man she'd been married to yet hadn't spoken to for seven years until the past week or so.

"Darcy?" The question he didn't ask was clear in his tone. "Is everything okay?"

"Um, not really. Uncle Joe's in the hospital. Aunt Marla asked me to call you and let you know." She folded her free arm across her middle and stared out at the parking lot, at the snow sifting down on the cars parked there. The coldness of the scene reflected how she felt inside.

"What happened?" He sounded much more alert now.

Darcy explained what she knew. "So it's a waiting game now. I'm with Aunt Marla and some of her friends. They're knitting."

A little chuckle came over the line. "I'm sure they are. I'll be there in fifteen."

Darcy jumped and looked up to see Marla's gaze on her. "Um. That's not necessary. It's so late—"

"See you then."

The phone went dead in her hand and she pulled it away from her ear to stare at it, frustrated. There was no reason for him to be here. They weren't married. Joe was going to be fine.

She walked back over to her aunt, who had needles flying in her hands. She looked up, but the needles never slowed. "Did you talk to him, then?"

Darcy dropped in a chair. "Yep. He said he's on his way."

"That's good." Marla didn't miss a beat. "He'll be a good source of support for you."

"I don't need him," she said, too worried and too tired to care that this conversation had to take place in front of two of Marla's best friends, who knew what had happened with her and Mack. And she almost believed what she'd said. Almost. Truth was, she'd love to lean on him. But the price was more than she could ever pay.

Marla's needles clicked. "Maybe he needs to be here. He and Joe are close."

Of course. Now Darcy just felt foolish. Mack had relationships outside of and independent of her. One of those was with her uncle.

She fidgeted in her chair. The steady click of needles should be calming, but, God, she just hated hospitals. The smell. The feeling. The urgency, the waiting, the memories of a stay here in this hospital, where she'd lost her baby and the seeds of destruction for her marriage had begun to bloom.

Now it had Uncle Joe in its grasp.

She took a deep breath, tried to calm the nerves. Marla needed her to be strong. But it all felt like yesterday.

She laid a hand on her belly lightly, knowing no life beat there. That the last time it had beat there was seven years ago. By the time she'd gotten here after the accident, it had already been too late. And it was possible she'd never get pregnant again. And while she hadn't been ready at the time to be a mother, she'd had the opportunity ripped from her forever.

Of course, being a mother implied there was a man to get her pregnant. A marriage even. Someone who loved her and stood by her.

She thought she'd had a chance at that once, but she'd been wrong, as had the timing. Now that she was older and wiser, she was ready.

But she'd lost the only man she'd ever wanted to share the dream with. Now she was here and so was he and she needed to finally put it all behind her. And forget she was in a hospital and focus on her uncle, who'd need her help more than ever, since he'd be laid up for most of the Christmas season. Which meant what? She'd have to stay? She'd worry about that later.

She was thinking positive. He'd be okay. He was too tough not to be.

But it was so hard to beat back the fear.

Chapter Six

Mack made it to the hospital in under fifteen minutes. Darcy hadn't really said how Joe was, how Marla was. Equally important, how she was. He hurried in and up to the surgical waiting room. When he entered his gaze landed right on Darcy. She sat, arms folded over her middle, her face pinched and white, and stared at the TV, which ran a twenty-four-hour cable news show. Then he looked at Marla, whose expression was knowing despite the tension on her face.

Darcy looked over and he forgot to worry about what they thought.

She'd pulled her hair up in a clip, and pieces had slipped out and fallen all around her face. Memories of the last time they'd spent time in the hospital assaulted him, as they no doubt did her, as well. His gut twisted when she turned her pale face toward him and he saw etched on her face the pain and memories. Not to mention the fear for her uncle.

He crossed the floor but stopped short of pulling her in his arms, though every cell screamed that he needed to get closer, hold her, let her break down and get it all out.

She hadn't let him comfort her when they were married. Why would now, when they were virtually strangers, be any different?

"Mack. You came." It was Marla's voice. Not the one he wanted to hear, but he turned to her and hugged her instead. Darcy wouldn't meet his eyes over Marla's head. Marla hugged him fiercely.

"She needs you," she murmured in a low tone. "She'll never admit it. Thank you for coming," she added in a louder voice.

"Of course," he said, choosing to ignore Marla's words about Darcy. "Any news?"

Marla shook her head and he saw, with a pang, that she looked every one of her years. He'd always thought she was so strong, so youthful. Tonight, fear for her husband had aged her. "Not yet. They said hours, so—" She glanced at the clock.

Darcy came over and rubbed her aunt's back. "Time goes so slow, doesn't it?" He didn't know if Marla caught the undertone of deep sorrow, but he did. He remembered all too well.

"Can you ladies use something from the cafeteria?" He could at least be useful.

One of Marla's friends perked up. "That's a great idea, Mack. Why don't you and Darcy make a run?"

Mack turned to her. She wouldn't like that suggestion, he knew. "Darcy?"

She looked like the proverbial deer caught in headlights. Before she could say anything, Marla spoke up. "He'll need the extra set of hands, dear."

Darcy inclined her head and offered a stiff smile to him. More of a baring of teeth than a real smile. "Well, then. Let's hurry."

She strode away toward the elevator, and he couldn't help watching her slender hips sway. Jeez. What kind of guy stared at a woman's rear when she was worried and scared and suffering from memories better left buried? He tried not to think of her mouth, hot and mobile under his, just a couple hours ago.

He moved after her and stepped into the elevator as she jabbed the button for the basement and therefore the cafeteria. She leaned against the wall of the car, her arms folded tightly across her chest, her stance screaming "leave me alone."

He couldn't. "Darcy." He kept his tone gentle, his stance relaxed. Her gaze shifted to his, then away. "I know what you're going through."

At that her gaze shot to his and she straightened up. "I doubt it very much, Mack."

"You're thinking about that night. It's hard to be here."

"But yet you came," she said, and there was a thread of bitterness under her words.

"Of course I did. Joe and Marla are important to me."

Now her gaze was full of pain. "That's good," she murmured.

He moved closer, trapping her in the corner. "Am I wrong?"

She shook her head. "Not as long as you're here for them only. What went wrong with us can't be fixed, Mack."

"I lied."

She drew back, whether from the words or the heat in his tone, he wasn't sure. He forged on, pinning her in the corner with his gaze, careful not to touch her. "I'm not sorry I kissed you earlier."

She blinked and the elevator door opened. He turned and walked out, sure if he didn't get away right then, he'd give in and kiss her until the pain in her eyes went away. Until the past wouldn't wedge between them anymore.

Darcy followed him into the cafeteria, a little surprised at how busy it was for midnight. But far more shocked by Mack's arrival and his words in the elevator. She'd been working darn hard on a righteous anger and he'd just popped it like a balloon.

She needed the anger to keep her distance. To keep the fear for her uncle at bay.

Right now she was too wrung out to sulk about it.

Mack handed her a tray and proceeded to pile it with crackers, cookies and some fruit. Her hands trembled, but she managed to hold the tray.

He tipped her chin up with one finger. "Hey," he said softly. She blinked back the tears the gesture threatened to break loose. She would not cry, not here, not now, not ever…

He took the tray and set it down, then pulled her in as the dam broke. She couldn't help it, she burrowed in, and he wrapped her up tight, murmuring words she couldn't quite understand, but the tone was soothing. He pressed his lips to her hair. She felt the light kisses even as she sobbed out her fear and anger and regrets into the chest of the man she'd loved more than life itself and had lost.

Finally, she wasn't sure how long it took, but her sobs subsided into hiccups and it dawned on her where she was. She didn't have the energy to break away, even though she knew she needed to. They stood like that, the steady pound of his heart calming her, his heat seeping into places she hadn't known she was cold.

"Better?" His voice was a rumble under her ear. He didn't loosen his grip, but she nodded against his chest and pulled away slightly. He loosened his grip but didn't let her go.

"Oh, no." She touched his shirt lightly. It was wet and sported mascara smears. "I made a mess. I'm sorry." She must look a fright, but she couldn't bring herself to care, even if she was covered in snot, mascara and tears.

He ran his hands up her arms and she became aware they were in a public place, and even though it was late, they had an audience. Still, she couldn't bring herself to break the contact. "I don't care, Darce. It'll wash."

She stepped back and he let her go, with what looked like regret on his face. "Thank you," she whispered, feeling too emotionally flayed to pretend any different. It was the first time she'd cried over all this in seven years. Once she'd realized he was going to just let her walk away, she'd been unable to cry. To grieve what they'd lost. She'd locked it all down.

They paid for their purchases and headed back to the elevator. There she simply stood next to him and drew from his strength. Their arms touched, and the small contact was enough.

It felt good. She'd worry about how dangerous it was another day.

* * *

Back in the waiting room, Marla looked up when they walked in. Darcy knew her aunt took in her tear-ravaged face when her gaze softened. Mack held up the bag and inclined his head toward the cardboard container of drinks Darcy held.

"Food and coffee. Both hospital-grade, but that can't be helped."

Marla managed a small smile at his joke. "Thank you, you two." She glanced at the clock. "Shouldn't be long now."

Marla's friend Carol came over, snagged two coffees and handed one to Marla. "Not too long," she agreed.

Darcy took her aunt a cookie and set it on a napkin next to her. Marla's smile was faint but real. She reached forward and pulled Darcy into a hug.

"Oh, honey. You okay?" she whispered.

Darcy nodded. She needed to address this head-on. "I just had a moment. I'm fine now. You?"

Marla sat back. "I'm hanging in there," she said with a fierce nod. "He'll be okay."

"Yes, he will," Darcy agreed. It simply couldn't go any other way.

She couldn't sit, so she walked back to the window while Aunt Marla's needles clicked away. She held her cooling coffee in both hands and stared at the parking lot. A fine layer of snow coated all the vehicles in the lot. Mack came and stood beside her. He said nothing, just leaned against the wall near her. She decided to be grateful for that. She could allow the small chink in her armor.

As long as she fixed it tomorrow.

The phone rang and the nurse manning the station

answered, speaking in low tones. When she hung up, she said, "Family of Joe Kramer?"

Marla leaped up, Carol catching her knitting as it flew from her lap. Darcy hurried to her side, her heart pounding, her palms clammy. *Please, please, please let him be okay.* She slipped her arm around her aunt's shoulders, felt her take a deep breath. "That's us," she said.

"Come with me," the nurse said. "The doctor will talk to you back here."

They followed her wordlessly back to the room she indicated, where the surgeon was already waiting. He rose to his feet and extended his hand to Marla. "Mrs. Kramer. I'm Dr. Peterson. First of all, let me assure you your husband came through surgery just fine."

Darcy's breath whooshed out at the same time Marla said, "Oh, thank God." Darcy hugged her aunt hard, relief flooding her.

They sat and the doctor went over the details. The upshot was Uncle Joe would be sidelined for the next six to eight weeks. Darcy knew it would make him crazy.

They shook hands with the doctor and went back in the waiting room.

"He's okay," Marla said to Carol, and promptly burst into tears. Her friend opened her arms and hugged her close. Mack came over and stood next to Darcy, but didn't touch her.

"Good news," he said quietly.

She nodded and gave him a wan smile. "Very. A huge relief. They said Aunt Marla can see him soon, once he's out of recovery." She glanced at the clock. "Another forty-five minutes or so, I guess. He's got a long road in front of him, but the doctor was optimistic."

This would mean Joe couldn't work at the farm. They'd need full-time help. He'd check his schedule and see if Jennifer could take over a bit of his load, which would free him up to spend more time at the farm.

Near Darcy.

He wasn't sure yet if that was a good thing or not. Right now they were on fragile ground, because she was distracted—and because the memories that bound them were centered on this hospital. The real test would be when he spent more time at the farm.

"After I see him, you can go home," Marla said. "No point in both of us being here all night."

Darcy sent Marla a worried look. "You can come, too. Lie in your own bed, even if you can't sleep."

Marla shook her head. "I need to be here, Darcy. Please. You'll need to run the farm for now. Can you do that?"

"Of course." Her response was swift and sure.

"I'll help more," Mack said, and watched shock flit over Darcy's face. "I'll work my schedule around it as much as possible. You and Joe don't have to worry about anything but getting him well."

Marla squeezed his hands. "Thank you. I knew we could count on both of you. Don't let it get in the way of your practice, though."

"I won't," he assured her. Darcy looked less than pleased. He'd talk to her later, get her to see his point. They could work around each other just fine. He knew the peace they'd forged tonight was fragile, but they'd have to find a way to make it all work. Put aside the past for the sake of the couple they both loved.

His family would be fairly certain he'd lost his mind.

After Marla's visit, and she'd reassured Darcy she

was okay now and nearly shoved her to the elevator, she and Mack rode to the first floor in silence.

He saw the worry etched on her face and the exhaustion. "Do you want me to stay?"

Her shock showed he'd overstepped. "Excuse me?"

"At their house. I can sleep on the couch. Keep you company." Clearly, he was so tired his mouth had separated from his common sense. Still, in for a penny…

She blinked and shook her head. "No. I'm fine. I'll be fine," she amended, apparently seeing him forming a rebuttal. "Really."

He bit back a sigh. He had no grounds to push, wasn't sure he wanted to anyway. There were lines, and tonight they'd been grayed out a bit, smudged.

Darcy collapsed on her bed after a tense ride home. Mack had followed her, damn him, reminding her what a great guy he was. She didn't want to be reminded. It was hard enough with the past hovering between them, with the memories, with their loss. All of it combined into an overwhelming emotional morass that she could not deal with tonight on top of her worry about her uncle.

Mack had turned around in the driveway. She was grateful he hadn't tried to talk to her. "Do you want me to stay?" indeed.

Of course she didn't. Not after he'd kissed her and later, held her while she'd cried. He'd been so sweet. Dangerous.

She peeled her clothes off and crawled under the covers, fairly sure sleep would not come for her tonight.

She woke the next morning to light streaming through the window. With a gasp she sat up and grabbed her phone. It was nearly eight. She had to get to the hospital. Aunt Marla needed to come home and sleep and Darcy wanted to know how Uncle Joe was doing. Then she had a tree farm to run. A run through the shower was a necessity and she washed up quickly, ran downstairs as her phone rang.

"Hello?"

"Darcy, it's Aunt Marla."

Dread pooled in her stomach. "Is—"

"Everything is fine, honey. Joe is tough. He's doing exactly what he should be doing for someone postsurgery."

Relief had Darcy slumping against the wall. "Okay, then. That's good."

"It is. Carol and her husband are bringing me home. Did I catch you before you left?"

"Um, yeah. I overslept—"

"No, you didn't." Marla's voice was soothing. "Go back to bed if you can. It was a rough night for both of us."

Darcy looked at the coffee can in her hand. Not likely, but there was no point in saying so. Once she was up, she was up. "I'm good. So I'll see you soon."

"Yes. We're going to grab a little bite to eat and then I'll be there."

A few more words and Darcy hung up. Thankfully, Uncle Joe was okay. Should she tell Mack?

She stuffed the phone in her pocket. No. They'd already crossed too many lines. If he wanted to know he could call her. Or better yet, call Marla.

She started the coffee and poured a bowl of cereal, pulling the books out to peruse over breakfast. She was surprised Marla hadn't strong-armed him into computer records. The records were very complete and organized, but that would have to change— She stopped the thought. It didn't matter now. She wasn't going to use a computer when she'd only be here another week.

The schedule was spelled out in detail. Today she had to oversee the cutting of a fresh load for a big box retailer a couple towns to the south. If they'd had more of that kind of order, maybe the farm would have been okay.

The slam of a car door brought her head up for a moment from the books and her cereal. Must be Aunt Marla. When no one came in and a second door slam got her attention, she stood up and walked to the window.

Aunt Marla was just now being dropped off. So who had come before her?

Her gaze landed on the truck. Oh, no. That couldn't be—could it?

Marla and Carol came in before she could go stomping out in the snow to make sure it wasn't Mack, skipping work to help out here.

Her aunt enveloped her in a hug. Her skin was gray and she looked exhausted, but the little brackets of tension were gone around her eyes. "He'll be okay," she said, and Darcy squeezed her eyes shut against the sting of tears.

"Of course he will," she agreed. Those doctors had better be right. She didn't think her aunt could take losing her husband of so many years this early.

Marla gave her a little squeeze and stepped back. "I see Mack is out there."

Darcy sighed. "There's no need. I can handle it."

Marla exchanged a look with Carol and patted her

arm. "Accept his help, honey. The farm needs it. It's nice of him."

Nice. Darcy nearly snorted. He wanted this place for his own purposes, to expand his vet practice. His brother was going to build houses on it.

Marla slipped off her coat. "Besides, it's going to take some doing to convince Joe to relax and let the farm be managed by someone else. Mack will go a long way to easing his mind."

There was nothing to say to that, so Darcy didn't try. Instead, she pulled her aunt in for a hug. "Are you going to catch some sleep now?"

"She's going to try," Carol answered firmly, and shook her head when Marla opened her mouth. "The doc told you to get some sleep, Marla. Joe needs you to be strong. I promise I'll be back for you in a few hours."

Marla tugged at the hem of her shirt, which was wrinkled. Exhaustion was etched clearly on her face. "I'll try." Then she pointed at her friend. "You, too."

"Me, too," Carol agreed. "I'm going home now. I'll see you this afternoon."

She left and Darcy steered Marla toward the stairs. "Let's get you settled in," she said.

"Did you sleep?" Marla asked.

"I did. You will, too."

Marla paused in the bedroom doorway. "Accept Mack's help, okay, Darcy? I know you'd rather not be around him, but—"

"I'll be fine," Darcy said, and smiled at her aunt. "We'll make it work. Now go. Sleep."

Chapter Seven

Mack looked up from his conversation with one of the employees to see Darcy striding toward him, a frown on her face. He excused himself from the conversation, not missing the other man's interested expression. No doubt this was best done without anyone overhearing. He met her halfway.

"Why are you here?" The anger in her tone caught him off guard, as he took in her flushed face and fisted hands. She wore a green fleece and a red vest, with a red knit cap over her hair. She looked festive. And angry. And hot.

He took a second to focus on something other than the *hot* part of the equation.

"I'm here because your uncle needs help," he said carefully.

She narrowed her eyes and he resisted the urge to pull her in and kiss her. It wouldn't help things right now.

"I can handle it," she said, lifting her chin.

So she was feeling a little territorial about the farm. He got that. "I'm sure you can. But it'll be easier with more help. You've been gone a long time." She stiffened and he guessed that hadn't been the best choice of words. He caught her arm and she didn't pull away. "Darce. I don't mean that as a criticism. I mean that as a fact. You have. And you're leaving before the season is over." And once she left, the farm would be down two people.

Her shoulders slumped a bit, then she straightened back up. "You're right, of course." Her expression was a polite mask, but he caught a hint of pain in her eyes.

He hated to see all the fight go out of her, hated that he was the one who'd done the deflating. He resisted the urge to apologize—for what? For buying the place? For being available to help? "My schedule is pretty flexible. I'm happy to help you guys out. It's no trouble at all."

Her lips curved in a smile that still didn't reach her eyes. "I know my aunt and uncle appreciate it."

"If you are that unhappy about us buying it, you can always buy it yourself." The words slipped out before he could stop them.

She snapped her gaze to his, eyes wide. "No, I really can't, Mack. My life is in Chicago. I can't just—I can't just walk away and leave it behind."

He sent her a sideways look as he started back toward the barn. "Sure you can. If you want this bad enough." His point made, he walked off, leaving her fuming in his wake.

Darcy got the order filled and sent on its way. It was a good thing they had orders to fill. That people came out here to get their trees. It made her happy.

Or would have if Mack weren't about to take it all away. To be fair, yes, it was her aunt and uncle's farm. But how could Mack and his brother look at this place, look at the families, some of whom had been coming here for decades, and decide they could just build houses on it?

And how dare Mack hint that she had a choice? That she could leave her job, leave all she'd done, just walk away from it all?

So, okay, she hadn't been super happy at work lately. She was overworked and stressed, but that was normal for someone trying to make partner as she was. Right? And yes, she felt at home here, even more so than in the city she really did love, but she'd grown up here, so it made sense.

Didn't it?

Damn Mack for making her think. She just wanted to get through all this and back to Chicago. Okay, fine, they were going to tear apart her home. A home that would someday have been their son's—if their baby had lived.

Darcy stopped in her tracks at the thought. She'd never thought of it in those terms before. That the farm would have belonged to their child. That at seven, he'd be running all over, marveling at the magic of Christmas, doubly so on a farm that celebrated Christmas. Something warm hit her face and she realized she was crying. She dashed at the tears with her gloved hands, but they were already crusted with snow.

No. Why now? She'd worked so hard to keep the loss at bay, to lock the pain away. And she couldn't even rectify it—after the accident and the miscarriage, the doctors said she'd probably never have kids. Ever.

Just another reward for her selfishness, and something she'd learned after the fact. Another reason why she'd left. Mack had been so torn up over the loss, but he'd kept saying they could have more kids. Well, they couldn't.

"Darcy. Darcy?" Mack's concern cut through her fog. She tried to ignore him, but he came up behind her. "Darcy?" Now there was concern in his voice.

The snow fell around them, and not too far away, she could hear the happy calls of a family looking for the perfect tree.

"I'm sorry you're upset about the farm," he said, and sounded sincere. "It works well for all of us."

Except me.

Darcy kept the selfish thought to herself and dug though her pockets for a tissue of some kind to wipe her face. Would he think her red face was just from the cold? She could hope.

"Well," she managed in almost normal tones, "of course it does. I mean, you're right. I've been gone. I left. I made my choices."

How could one choice have so many consequences? Over so many years?

"Yes," Mack said carefully as if he sensed a trap. Smart man.

"Okay, then. I've got to—" she checked her watch as if it would give her the answers she needed "—run."

She scooted around him and sent him a wave over her shoulder as she trekked back the way she'd come, hoping he bought her line and left her alone.

Mack watched Darcy flee as if an army of rabid dogs was on her heels. Ah, well. It was better than having her fight with him.

On the other hand, when she was mad, at least she looked at him. And damn if she hadn't sounded as though she'd been crying. But since she'd been so clear on not letting him know he'd opted to honor her. Since his buying this place upset her so much.

Which he didn't want, either. But he couldn't tell her his reasoning. Owning it kept it near him. A piece of her.

Yeah, the fact Chase was going to develop it sucked a bit. But he'd be careful and tasteful. Chase's company specialized in green environmentally sound building practices. It was a big thing up here and, all told, it was much better than some other builder buying it and putting up cookie-cutter houses. Still, he knew it was cold comfort to Darcy.

That evening, he checked in on the animals, even though he didn't doubt for a minute Jennifer was doing a great job. Minnie was doing better, looking perkier and even filling out a little. He stroked her head a bit. When she was healed he'd either find her a new home or keep her himself.

Darcy had been very taken with Minnie that evening she was here. That evening he'd broken down and kissed her, which had been all kinds of stupid, but there it was. Would she like a dog? Or would that not fit in her big-city life?

The beagle licked his hand and he rubbed her ears.

"Everything look okay?"

There was only amusement in Jennifer's tone, and some surprise he'd stopped in here.

"Of course. I just— It's a habit."

"Like tucking in a child before bed, I would imagine." She pushed off the doorjamb as his gut knifed at her comparison.

I wouldn't know. The thought speared him. Jennifer didn't know he'd lost a child. "Most likely."

If she caught the odd tone in his voice, she gave no sign. "It's been as smooth as it always is, Mack."

"Are you saying you guys don't need me here?" he joked, hoping to dispel the tension in himself that had nothing to do with Jennifer and wasn't her fault.

"Of course not." She scratched behind Minnie's ears, as well. "There's always room for a token male."

Surprise huffed out in a laugh. "Damn, girl. You don't pull any punches."

"Nope. You should know that by now." She stepped away from the cage. "You going to fix things with Darcy?"

"What?" He wasn't sure what, if anything, to say.

Jennifer held up a hand. "I have eyes. I can see. The two of you have a lot of unfinished business. I hope she's smart enough to know what she's got in you."

What she had. Past tense. They were long past the point of being able to fix things. To pick up where they'd left off and move forward.

"We're very different people now," he said simply because it was the truth. "We want very different things." He shrugged.

Jennifer made a sympathetic sound in her throat. "Too bad." She turned to walk away. "I'll leave you to your tucking in, then."

"Thanks," he managed as she left. Why couldn't he be interested in *her*? She was smart, funny, cute and he enjoyed her company. She just wasn't Darcy. Not her fault.

He sighed and finished his rounds before heading

out to his house. The house he'd bought for his wife as a present, hoping to cheer her up, to give them a project to work on together.

Instead, she'd left and he'd signed the papers alone. And renovating it had been his therapy. Maybe someday he'd show her. But not tell her the whole story. It seemed cruel somehow, to tie it in with the past.

The house was a small one-story bungalow, white, with a very traditional front porch. He pulled into the drive and up to the garage—he rarely parked in there, since he had to shovel the snow somewhere and it ended up often as not in front of the garage—and got out. The motion light came on as he entered the kitchen. It took a few minutes of blessed busyness to take care of the animals' food, water and outside needs.

He had just finished when there was a knock at the front door. He could guess from all the joy coming from the dogs that it was his mom. She always had a treat for them.

He was right. She smiled at him when he answered the door and petted the dogs, giving them their treats before greeting him with a quick hug.

"Nice that I rate below the dogs," he said affectionately, and she patted his arm.

"Oh, don't be silly. But you don't slather attention on me the way they do."

"*Slather* is the key word there," he noted drily as Lilly attempted to lick his mother's hand while she walked toward the kitchen. She washed her hands and set another bag on the counter.

"So. How's Darcy?"

Mack winced at his mother's question. "Fine, as far as I can tell."

His mother made a harrumphing noise. "As far as you can tell? How can you not know?"

Floored Mack stared at his mother, whose narrowed gaze was lasered in on him. "Why would I know?"

Exasperation laced her tone. "Mack. Because you are working with her. Because you guys have a history—"

Mack held up a hand. "History or not, we're not chatty." He didn't want to explain how trying to reconnect, even tenuously, kept resulting in dead ends. It bothered him. A lot. "We're not—it's been a long time, Mom."

His mother opened the fridge and examined the contents as if all the answers to her confusing offspring resided inside, then turned and grabbed the bag she'd brought. "Maybe you can make it right with her."

Mack frowned. "I thought you didn't want her anywhere near me."

"Why would you think that?" Seeming truly shocked, his mother set the bag back down with a thump. "You and Darcy were perfect for each other. I don't think—" She stopped abruptly.

"Don't think what?" he asked softly.

She pulled out the first container, paused, then turned to him. "Honestly, I don't think she was ready to get married."

Mack's jaw dropped. "How can you say that? You were pushing me to do it!"

She nodded. "I was. But looking back, I see she wasn't ready for any of it. Not like you were. She loved you—I have no doubt about that—but she wasn't ready for the wife-and-motherhood thing."

"She kind of didn't have a choice," he pointed out, even as his stomach soured. Could his mother be right?

She looked at him, her gaze serious. "That's exactly my point, Mack. She didn't have a choice. And before she could even adjust to any of it, she lost all of it. I wish—" She stopped and pressed her fingers to her lips. "I wish I'd seen it then. I wish we hadn't pushed you to do right by her, when it was clearly not what she was ready for."

Mack sat there, stunned. "She could have said no, for God's sake. I didn't force her to marry me." Had he, inadvertently? He'd certainly worked to convince her. Maybe, in retrospect, that should have been his first clue.

She reached over and rubbed his arm. "She could have, you're right. And you were a wonderful husband. If there'd been no—accident, I think you'd have worked it all out and stayed together."

Would they have? As soon as the going got tough, she'd abandoned him emotionally, or so he'd always believed. Now it made sense, especially if his mom was right, and she hadn't been ready.

God, he was an idiot. Worse.

"I guess we'll never know," he said, and heard the note of sadness in his tone. His mother did, too, if the soft look she sent him was any indication.

"Maybe you can start again," she suggested.

"I don't think so." He thought of the pain in Darcy's eyes, and the fierce longing he had to hold her. It was a bad idea. Mack shook his head and pushed back from the counter. "It was a long time ago. We aren't the same people anymore."

"Exactly," she said, so soft he almost didn't catch it. In fact, he decided to pretend he hadn't heard her. Best that way.

Because if she was right, he had to rethink everything he thought he'd known.

Chapter Eight

Darcy ducked into the warm-up shack. Lori, the teenager working, gave her a smile. Christmas music played softly in the background and a fire crackled in the fireplace. The little building smelled of cider, coffee and hot chocolate.

"Hey, Lori. How's it going back here? You got enough cups and cocoa and coffee?"

Lori smiled. "Yep, all good. Been pretty steady back here."

"That's good." Darcy took a moment to check the supplies. "The snow brings people out."

"Yes, it does." The bell over the door jingled and a family came in. Lori greeted them with a smile, and Darcy slipped back out into the snow. It sifted lightly down, as if Mother Nature knew it was two weeks before Christmas and was giving her all to make some magic. Enough to be pretty, not enough to hinder anyone stomping around in it.

Perfect. She walked back up to the pole barn, hearing the roar of the baler, the laughter of kids, the notes of Christmas music here and there. Despite the snow, she wasn't cold. And if it weren't for the fact her uncle was in the hospital, her ex was about to buy her childhood farm—well, no, just for a heartbeat she was happy. In this moment, she was happy,

Her therapist would be so proud of her.

She skirted the busyness but noted the full parking lot as she made her way to the house. Uncle Joe was possibly to be released from the hospital today—seemed a little early to Darcy for someone who'd had heart surgery just a few days ago—but he was doing well and Marla didn't seem alarmed, so she'd go with it.

"Ready?" she asked as she came in the warm kitchen. Marla was seated at the table, tying her bootlaces.

"I am. Let's go."

They left the house and got in Darcy's car. She brushed the fluffy snow off quickly, and they were on their way. Darcy followed her aunt to the elevators and tried to breathe normally. The panic was there, pressing in her throat, but it didn't have claws today. Marla squeezed her arm. She followed her through the maze of corridors. Marla's stride was brisk and Darcy tried not to look at anything as they went. This was not the same floor she'd been on. It wasn't even the same wing.

But it was still the same building.

Marla stopped in front of room 527 and went in. "Good morning," she said, her voice quiet but cheery. Darcy followed her in, and her stomach clenched at the sight of her uncle.

He looked far more frail than he had a few days ago. His hair was mussed—he usually wore a hat from the time he got up until he went to bed—and his skin was pale. He had an IV running from one hand, and the skin around it was bruised and swollen. His eyes were tired, but he smiled at both of them.

"There's my ladies."

Marla went over and took his free hand, pressing a kiss to his forehead, and Darcy saw the look of relief that passed her uncle's face. She came up and kissed him, as well.

"Things okay at the farm?"

In spite of herself, Darcy smiled. He was all business. "Yes. We're moving along."

He quizzed her on a few things and she answered. Fortunately, correctly. She was lucky that she'd grown up on the farm and had retained most of the knowledge from way back when.

He sat back after a few minutes and sighed. Marla touched his hand. "If you overdo it before they even discharge you, they won't let you go today." Her tone was part affection, part exasperation, and he nodded.

"I know. It's just hard. To know I'm missing it."

There was more to that statement than just her uncle wanting the season to go smoothly—more than his need to oversee it. This was the last season and it had to be perfect. And he wasn't there to make sure it happened.

"Darcy and Mack know what they're doing. They've got it all under control." Marla looked at her for confirmation and she nodded.

"Absolutely." Too bad she felt anything but under control since she'd been back here and Mack had reentered her life.

* * *

Mack was already at the farm when she pulled back in. This was the second day in a row he'd been out here early. She got out of the car and slammed the door, stomping through the snow to the barn. Kelly, one of the wreath makers, looked up when she came in.

"Hey, Darce. How's Joe this morning?"

"Good. Ready to come home."

Kelly's smile was wry. "Marla will have her hands full when he does."

Darcy smiled back. "Yes. She will. Have you seen Mack?"

By now, everyone knew she and Mack had been married. While she didn't talk about it, it had made the rounds pretty quickly. But no one asked her about it, or pressed her. "Pretty sure he went to cut the trees for the delivery today."

Of course he had. "Okay. Thanks."

Kelly went back to work and Darcy went out back. She and Mack needed to have a little chat.

Sure enough, there he was, with four other guys, cutting the trees. She stood to the side for a moment, unable to take her eyes off Mack.

Dressed in old jeans and boots, with an insulated jacket and a hat, he looked right at home among the snowy trees. He didn't hear the approach of the ATV over the sharp whine of the chain saw that felled the trees as if their trunks were made of butter. She pulled her own hat down closer over her ears and came up behind him, the snow crunching under her boots as she picked her way over the drifts to where the men were working. One of the guys saw her and gave a little wave.

Mack turned. As soon as she caught his gaze, her insides heated up.

This was bad. A kiss, and now—now she was worried about being in over her head.

He strode through the snow toward her, his strides long and sure on the uneven path. “Hey,” he said when he reached her. She looked up at him, his face ruddy from the cold, and wondered what would happen if she kissed him.

No. She was here to ask him a tricky question. She needed to know. But shouting over the chain saw wasn’t the place for this conversation. She leaned in and he leaned down. “Why exactly are you here?” she said into his ear, trying not to breathe in his scent of spice and fresh air.

He turned his head, and his warm breath tickled her ear. She barely suppressed a shiver. “I’m getting the trees ready for the shipment.”

She shook her head and he straightened up. The chain saw had quit and the first few seconds of quiet after were almost more deafening in the ringing silence. “No. Mack, you’ve got a vet practice to run. Really, why are you here and not there?”

His expression turned cautious. “I told you before. Because your uncle needs the help, Darce. I’ve got my practice under control.”

She had to ask. “Are you trying to make up for what happened?”

He stared at her, then frowned. “What happened? With what?”

“You and me.”

Her words hung in the crystal-cold air for a second. The sounds of the guys dragging the trees to the wagon, their laughter and voices, all of it seemed to be coming through a kind of filter. Mack's eyes widened and then he frowned.

"What do I have to make up for, Darcy?" The words were clipped and colder than the air around them. She winced when they almost physically struck her, like shards of ice. But she couldn't say anything, because she could see she'd been wrong. Very wrong. "I'm not here for you, not in the way you seem to think. I'm here to help out, because I know your uncle is out of commission and this is important to him. He and your aunt are my friends, Darcy."

"Okay," she said, and turned to go back to the ATV. She'd read something very wrong there. But he caught her arm and, off balance in the snow, she teetered a little as she tried to turn to face him. He ended up with one hand on each of her upper arms.

"What do I need to make up for?" The intensity of his voice made her breath catch.

She blinked at him, the lump in her throat making it hard to breathe. "Nothing." He didn't get it, didn't understand what she'd been through. He didn't see his part in it. She'd made a mistake bringing it up. When his eyes narrowed she pulled away and he let her go. "I'm sorry. I was wrong."

This time when she turned and walked away he let her go.

What the hell had that been all about?

All day the odd encounter with Darcy played through Mack's mind. Over and over. He'd blamed himself for a lot that had happened with them, more maybe than he should have. He'd never viewed working with her uncle as atonement. Joe had never hinted he felt that way, either, so it caught him off guard that Darcy apparently did.

And the upshot seemed to be, it wouldn't be enough to fix—it. Whatever exactly she blamed him for. Looking back, he could see any number of things. He'd failed her in almost every possible way, and no doubt there were more he didn't even know about.

So, no. He wasn't doing this for her. Or for him. He was doing it because it was the right thing, to help out a friend who needed it. It wasn't that he didn't feel the need to make things right for her, as much as he could, but this wasn't the way he'd do it.

He let himself in the house and absorbed the dogs' ardent greeting.

He took care of the drying of paws and dishing out of food, then wandered into his bedroom to take a shower before he scrounged up something to eat. The bedroom he'd have shared with Darcy, if she were still his wife.

That wasn't a line of thought he wanted to follow.

Bone tired, he showered and dressed in sweats and a long-sleeved T-shirt. He waded through the animals to get a container of frozen stew from the freezer and popped it in the microwave. There was a knock at the front door and he frowned, glancing at the time.

He walked through the living room and opened the door to see Darcy standing there, in the dark on his porch. She gave him a tremulous smile and he shoved a hand through his hair before stepping aside. "Darcy. What brings you here? Is Joe okay?"

"Fine," she assured him as she entered, her arm brushing him as she moved past him. "And I won't stay long. I just wanted to apologize."

He closed the door behind her. "For what?"

She shoved her hands into her coat pockets. Her cheeks were pink. He didn't know if it was nerves, the cold or the fact she was too warm in her down jacket. "For my behavior earlier. I was wrong to come after you like that."

The microwave dinged behind him, but he didn't turn around, even when her gaze slid in that direction and back to him. "Bad time?"

"No. Just dinner. Darce. There's no need—no need for apologies." He wanted her to smile, to see her relax. One of the dogs came out and shoved his head against her leg. She patted him with her bare left hand and he wondered what she'd done with her rings. Did she still have them? He had his, wrapped in a plastic bag in the bottom of his underwear drawer. Classy all the way. "That's Sadie."

"Hi, Sadie," she said, her gaze still on the dog, who sat down and looked up at her adoringly.

"Do you want to stay?" The words slipped out before he could stop them. And now it was too late to call them back. "I just reheated some stew, if you're hungry. Otherwise you can just keep me company."

She hesitated. "I'm not hungry. But I can stay a little bit."

After he took her coat, she followed him through the house to the kitchen. He wondered what she thought of it, if he should tell her why he'd bought it. Seeing her wary expression as she seated herself at the breakfast bar, he decided not to.

She looked around and he saw the frank curiosity on her face. "This is really nice, Mack. I like it."

The words fill him with a silly gratitude. “Thanks. I do, too. Chase and I worked on it together.”

“How long have you lived here?” She nodded when he held up a bottle of wine. He opened a cupboard and took out a glass, then met her gaze and decided he couldn’t do it. Couldn’t tell her the whole truth.

“A while now. Long enough to be settled in, I guess.” The evasive answer was kinder. If he told her, she’d do the math and realize when he’d bought the house. That might open up more guilt, and there was no point in either of them going there.

He slid the wineglass across the counter and watched as she fingered the stem. Nervous. He seated himself near her and started in on the stew.

“Do you cook?” The surprise in her voice made him laugh around a forkful.

“God, no,” he said when he’d swallowed. “My mom makes extra and drops it off. She caught me buying a TV dinner once when I ran into her at the grocery store.” He grinned at the memory. Her reaction hadn’t been much different than if she’d caught him buying condoms. “She was horrified. And then I started getting containers.”

Darcy gave a little laugh. “I bet.”

He forked up another bite. “I know I’m too old for my mother to be cooking for me. But she enjoys it. I guess it benefits both of us.”

“I guess so,” Darcy agreed, a slightly wistful look in her eyes.

“You should come to dinner sometime,” he said, and she drew back, already shaking her head.

“Oh, no. After everything…” Her voice trailed off.

“They’d love to see you.” That might be a bit of a

stretch when it came to Chase, but after what his mom had said earlier, he knew she would be welcoming.

He wanted to ask her if it was true, if she'd felt rushed into their marriage, then decided now wasn't the time. Besides, Darcy had always been straightforward. They'd talked about it at length when they found out she was pregnant. She'd never expressed any reservations about any of it at all.

She smiled at him then. "Maybe. We'll see."

No, he decided, his mother had been wrong.

The next morning, Marla sat at the table with Darcy. "I need to ask you something."

"Okay," Darcy said carefully, her pulse kicking up.

"I know you only planned to stay a few days." Marla drew in a deep breath and Darcy's heart sank. She knew what was coming. "But. We could really use your help now that Joe is out of commission. Mack can't do it all, since he's got his vet practice. I know he's putting a lot of it on Jennifer, but he can't just leave it. I can't do it all with Joe, and the farm needs someone who can give it attention full-time." Her voice trailed off and Darcy saw the misery on her aunt's face and knew how hard it had been to even ask her.

"Of course I'll stay. I'll make it work," she said with far more confidence than she actually felt. They needed her here, far more than they needed her at work. What did that say about her career? "I need to call my boss and make some arrangements."

Marla grabbed her hands and squeezed tightly. There were tears in her eyes. "Thank you, Darcy. I know—I know there are parts of this that aren't easy for you."

Darcy squeezed back. "You're welcome. It'll be fine.

You don't need to worry about anything but getting Joe back on his feet." She glanced at the clock. "I'm going to give my boss a call and get this all arranged." She had several weeks of vacation. Sad to say, she almost never used any of it. She'd convinced herself she loved her job, and she was pretty sure that was true. But more than that, she didn't have anyone to share the time off with. So really, why bother?

Somehow she'd convinced herself that was okay.

She pulled on her jacket and shoes and grabbed her bag. It'd be easier to do this in the car, without anyone overhearing. She pulled out of the tree farm and drove the little way into town, where she parked in the diner parking lot—she'd noticed earlier her phone signal was strongest there—and hit Ross's number on her phone. It was six o'clock in Chicago, an hour behind, but she knew that he'd be there. Sure enough, he answered on the third ring.

"Darcy. Please tell me you are coming back early." His voice was tense.

Darcy's heart plummeted and she gripped the phone tightly. "What's going on?"

He launched into an explanation of how one of her accounts, the one she'd worked so hard to bring in to the company, was teetering on the edge of disaster. Darcy propped her arm on the steering wheel and rested her head on her hand, the urge to scream building like a head of steam. Why hadn't she been apprised of any of this? Her team was in contact with her, but hadn't said a word. She cut Ross off. "I'll call Mally and talk to her," she said with a calmness she didn't feel. Ross could be an excellent boss, but if he sensed weakness, you'd be out on your tail before you could blink. She'd seen it happen before. And this was why what she was about to ask was risky. "I need the month of December off, Ross."

Silence. Darcy stared at the lit windows of the diner. A couple was laughing, framed by Christmas lights. The woman leaned forward to accept a forkful of something from the man. A simple scene. Why couldn't things in her life be simple? How had she gotten so far off track that she'd lost the simple things?

"You're joking." It wasn't a question. "Your account is going to hell and you're asking for a month off?"

They got the week between Christmas and New Year's off anyway, but Darcy wasn't going to point that out. She kept her voice soothing. The best way to deal with Ross was to stay calm. "My family needs me. I wouldn't ask if it wasn't an emergency."

"Your family needs you," he repeated, and laughed. "Darcy, you never talk about your family. I didn't know you had one. It's why you are the perfect employee. You give me—this company—100 percent. Without fail. There's never any drama with you. It's as if you are married to the company."

Tears stung Darcy's eyes because he was right. It wasn't a compliment. She'd given far more of herself than she'd ever get back. And Ross would take as much as she'd give and come back for more. She knew this, had always known this. But she'd managed to convince herself it was a good thing.

"I need the time off, Ross. My uncle had a serious heart attack and I need to run the business."

"What kind of business is that?"

"A Christmas-tree farm."

A pause, then a bark of laughter exploded in her ear. “A Christmas-tree farm? What the hell do they need you for? Are you going to chop trees in a suit and heels?”

Chapter Nine

Darcy was taken aback by this view of her. Clearly, she'd been good at hiding her past, at making herself over—too good. Not that her boss should necessarily be her friend, but the whole idea that he thought it was ridiculous nettled her. "Of course not. That's ridiculous. I grew up here, Ross. I know what I'm doing and they need me to run it." It was more than a business. It was about traditions, for her family and the families that came to the farm every year. "I wouldn't ask if it wasn't important."

She heard the squeak of Ross's desk chair as he dropped into it. It drove all the employees crazy, that squeaky chair. It was the only thing not full-on chic in her boss's office. Hearing it now, she realized he must have been pacing in front of the windows overlooking Michigan Avenue. She'd bet he hadn't noticed any of the Christmas cheer that Chicago put on, or the beauty of the falling snow. She herself hadn't, not for years, and on purpose. "Darcy. I need you here."

"I can manage my team from here," she said, wishing she had room to pace herself, but the wind outside would make conversation difficult. And stomping around in the slushy mess in the parking lot would ruin her shoes. "I've been checking in with them periodically. And really, Mally is perfectly capable of handling this on her own, Ross. You know she is." Darcy had spent much of her professional life putting out fires before they even reached Ross's radar. Mally needed to do that. Darcy was betting that the account wasn't that bad at all. Now he was seeing just how valuable Darcy was—in time for her to step away. She couldn't help wincing. "I've got plenty of time to take off. This isn't a hugely busy time for us."

It took the better part of an hour, but she got Ross to agree to her time off. She called Mally next and filled her in. Thankfully, the woman was calm and unflappable and very good at what she did. She and Darcy made an excellent team. Mally sounded surprised when Darcy told her she was taking an entire month off, but she didn't make a big deal of it. "Good for you, showing him work isn't the only thing you've got in your life. He tends to think that's how it should be. Probably because it is for him."

Darcy didn't want to be like Ross, so tied to his company he couldn't separate out his real life from his work life. But she was well on her way. It made her wonder—for the first time—if something had happened to send him to seek solace in his work. Like what she had done.

She drove back to the house and sat in the driveway for a minute, just looking. The Christmas lights were on, outlining the house and blanketing the bushes. A huge lit wreath glowed on the side of the barn. The tree dazzled in the living room windows. The whole scene was cozy and familiar and Darcy realized how much she'd missed it. Missed being here.

She thought of Mack's house, the charming bungalow that he'd restored so beautifully. But he had no Christmas decorations up, save a small tabletop tree on the dining room table she'd bet he never used…and she'd double down on the bet that the little tree was his mother's doing.

They'd lost so much, at the time of year when families were supposed to be celebrating.

They'd lost everything.

Darcy swallowed and gathered up her stuff. She'd assumed Mack would move on. That he, wrapped in the Lawless name and family, would be able to grieve and let go and start his life over, without the specter of his very short marriage and almost parenthood hanging over him. It was a huge part of why she'd run.

No, not run. Running implied she'd been unable or unwilling to deal with things as they'd been. But they'd been too much of a mess to fix. She'd seen that clearly. Leaving had been her last gift to Mack, the only way she could see to make it all up to him. Setting him free of all of it.

But—maybe she hadn't. And the thought that she'd given up so much for nothing made her feel ill.

Mack knew he was burning the candle at both ends. Which was why he knew it was a waste of time to stop and grab a beer with Chase. Except Chase was insisting on it and Mack had finally given in.

So he parked in the icy gravel lot of Sloan's Bar and got out, noting he'd beaten his brother here. He pushed through the heavy door and headed up to the bar, where they always sat. This late on a Tuesday, the place was fairly empty. He sat and smiled at Sally, the bartender tonight.

"What'll it be, hon?" was Sally's cheerful greeting. She called everyone hon. He ordered from the tap and waited for Chase. She set the glass in front of him. "You alone or are you meeting someone?"

"Chase," he answered drily. "He asked me to come."

"And now he's late." Sally smiled. "Big brothers, huh?"

"Yeah."

He and Sally had graduated together. She had an older brother, too, but he was in and out of jail. Not really the same.

Chase slid next to him then. "Sorry I'm late." He gave Sally his order and dropped his keys on the bar. "Hell of a day."

"Yeah?" Mack was more than happy to listen to someone else's problems. Anything but his own.

Chase explained how he had a supplier that had first sent the wrong kind of shingles, then the correct ones only to realize they had a major defect. Each delay was more of a setback on a project that was running perilously close to being late as well as over budget.

Mack listened sympathetically. Until Chase cut himself off and said, "What's going on with the tree farm?"

"Going on?" If he played a little dumb, maybe Chase would let him off the hook.

Chase gave him a look and Mack nearly groaned. He wasn't off the hook.

"Come on, Mack. You're spending more time there than at your practice."

Mack folded his arms on the bar and fixed his gaze on the hockey game on the TV across the room. How the hell did he know that? "Joe had a heart attack. You know that."

"Yeah. And you told me he'll be okay."

"He will," Mack agreed. "But not in time to finish out the season. So I'm stepping in."

"Stepping in," Chase repeated. "How does Darcy feel about that?"

Mack took a sip of his beer. "She's not thrilled."

"I bet." Chase dug into the bowl of peanuts that Sally had placed in front of them. "How's it going? Is she speaking to you?"

"Fine. And yeah. We're adults, Chase. All that was a long time ago."

"Mmm-hmm. That's why you've been seen with her around town."

Mack opened his mouth, then shut it and shook his head. "That's not your business."

"When it comes to her, yeah, it is." Chase's tone hardened. "She left you. She wrecked your marriage. She wrecked *you*. There's no way you can go through that again. Hell. No way we can watch you go through it."

Mack rubbed his unpeanutty hand on his face. "Chase. Let it go. Please. She did what she needed to do." The words were low in his throat, almost a growl.

"What she needed to do was stick around and see it through." When Mack's head snapped around, Chase held up a hand. "She never gave you a chance to see if you could go on. To grieve together."

No, she hadn't. And that was something that had

bothered Mack for years. Why hadn't she? Why had she shut down and run? He'd never been able to figure out the answer. "Not your business," he ground out, and Chase gave him a hard look, then sighed.

"I know. But after last time—"

"She'll go back after Christmas," Mack said tightly, and Chase gave a hard nod.

They spent the rest of the time talking about nothing and Mack relaxed. When he went home, he went through the ritual with the dogs and headed for bed, for dreams of Darcy, where she came to him willingly.

But he knew that was all it was—a dream.

Darcy spent a good chunk of the next day on the phone with her team. The good thing was, Ross's interpretation of the situation was wrong, which relieved Darcy. Mally had it all well in hand, which she'd already determined from their conversation yesterday. They agreed to stay in touch with emails and calls every other day, unless Mally needed more. Darcy didn't think she would.

Mack's truck, which had been there earlier in the day, was gone when she got back to the farm. No doubt he'd gone to his real job.

She wished she could make him see that she had this under control. That while his help was appreciated, she didn't need him to come every day for ten hours. He didn't have to give anything up for her. For them. For whoever.

He was stubborn. She knew this all too well.

She dropped her laptop off in the house, got her winter stuff on and trudged over to the barn. They didn't open until three on weekdays, so she had a little time.

She checked the wreath orders when she was in there, and started making another one. They had four due to be picked up today, and a few more the next day. This was a part she'd like to expand. The wreath making, the grave blankets, the garlands, all the piney decorations.

Of course, it didn't matter now. This was the end of the road for the tree farm, and thinking of ideas now didn't help. Why hadn't she made the suggestions before now?

Because you hadn't known. You should have known.

And that was a loop that had played in her mind over and over since she came back. It was pointless and frustrating. And maybe wouldn't have made any difference after all. Her aunt and uncle were selling because it was time to move on. Not because of anything she'd done, or not. She couldn't prevent them from aging or retiring.

But the guilt sat heavily in her chest as she went through the motions of making a wreath.

You should have known.

"Darcy." Marla looked up with a smile when she came into the house. Joe sat at the table, still looking pale, but far better than he had been. Recovery was taking a while, but he was getting there.

"How's it going out there?" Joe's question was casual, but the slight tension in his body gave away how much he missed being in the action.

"Just fine," Darcy said. She put the paper with the notes she took in front of him. It had the sales on it and other information he just devoured. It was a kind of unspoken compromise. He'd stay in the house and she'd give him the information he wanted.

Marla held out a carefully packed casserole. "Can

you take this to Mack? I told him I'd be by but—" she glanced at the clock "—I'm not going to get over there before my book club comes over."

Caught, Darcy took the pan. There was no way to say no. "Of course. I'll get right on that."

"Thanks," Marla said gratefully, and untied her apron. "I've got about fifteen minutes."

Darcy was about to ask why she was hosting it, at this time of year, but then she realized of course Marla wasn't going to leave Joe alone. And her friends would understand that.

She went back out the door to her car and drove to Mack's. This time, the porch light was on. She parked on the street and went up the front walk. She knocked and realized that she hadn't asked if Mack knew she was coming.

When he answered the door, his warm smile slipping into clear shock that she was standing there, she had her answer. "Marla couldn't make it," she said, holding out the packages. "She ran out of time. So she sent me instead." This was stating the obvious and she felt a little silly. She was always so off-kilter around him.

He stepped back. "Come on in."

"Oh, I can't stay," she said, and found herself stepping into the warm house anyway.

"I'm sure there's enough for both of us," he said wryly. She wondered if it was what Marla had in mind. Now that she thought about it, she wouldn't put it past her aunt. "Sure," she said, and took off her coat, then followed him into the kitchen. This house was big for a bachelor. Unless—

"Mack, do you have a girlfriend?"

The question was out before she could stop it. He

dropped the silverware he'd just pulled out of the drawer. "What the hell kind of question is that?" He stepped over the pieces on the floor and came over to her, the look on his face completely predatory. "Do you think, if I had a girlfriend, I'd do this with you?" And his mouth came down on hers.

It wasn't a gentle kiss. It was an angry kiss, a punishing kiss. A kiss that shot to her soul and flared to life.

She needed to stop it, to push him away. Instead, she wound her arms around his neck and kissed him back, all the hunger and need she'd felt since she came home—probably well before that—pouring out of her. When he backed her into the fridge, she welcomed the hard press of his body, the way his hands fisted in her hair and his mouth plundered hers.

When he pulled back, the loudest sound in the room was that of their ragged breathing. "Does that answer your question?" His voice was rough, and the sound made shivers skip over her skin.

For a moment, she couldn't recall the question.

"Yes," she managed, when the fog cleared enough for her to think. "It does." But it opened up more questions, the biggest one of which was *why?* Why had he kissed her? Why did he still care? Why did she?

Those weren't questions she could answer. That she *wanted* to answer.

"So I guess I'll leave you to dinner," she said, and edged for the door.

He looked at her, his eyes still smoky with desire and want and need. "Running away?"

She stopped, affronted, but couldn't make herself meet his gaze. "What? No, of course not."

"Are you sure?" He stepped closer. "You were willing to stay until I kissed you."

Caught, she just looked at him, afraid of what he might see, of what she wasn't ready for him to see. Of what she wasn't ready to admit to herself. She tucked her hair behind her ear.

"I'll behave," he said, and the wicked tilt to his mouth made her raise an eyebrow. "Scout's honor."

Now she lifted both eyebrows. "Were you ever a Scout?"

"No," he admitted. "But Chase was."

"All right," she relented, and moved back toward the island. She didn't really want to leave. "Anything I can do?"

He directed her to the glasses and she got out new silverware, placing the pieces that had been on the floor in the sink. It didn't take long to get the simple meal on the table—and Darcy would bet that her aunt had planned this. Book club, dinner, send her out to run the errand—it had Marla's fingerprints all over it.

Darcy couldn't be mad.

They sat at the table, and she refrained from asking him how often he used it. There was a cozy bay window overlooking the backyard, and while it was too dark to really see anything out there, she could tell it had begun to snow. "That's a real tree?" she asked, nodding toward the one on the table.

"It is," he agreed, and took a bite of his dinner.

"Why not have a full-size tree?"

He looked at her as if she'd grown an extra head. "Why would I do that?"

"You work at a Christmas-tree farm," she pointed out. "Surely you could get one there."

He gave her a wry, almost sad, smile. “No need. It’s just me. I don’t get trees anymore.”

Anymore. The implication of that hit her hard. Of course he didn’t. When was the last time she’d gotten one? Her last tree, other than a little halfhearted, fake formal tree she did just because she felt she had to, had been here. With Mack.

Oh, no.

“We need to fix that.” She couldn’t do much to fix the past or her mistakes, but she could give him this. It was a little thing, a small thing, but a start.

“We do? Why?” He sounded truly puzzled.

“Because it’s not right. You should have a tree. This house should have a tree.”

“Darcy—”

“I happen to know the owner of a tree farm.” She offered him a crooked smile. “I think I can get you in.”

Damn if he could resist her. “Darce. I don’t have any ornaments.” That wasn’t completely true. He had the boxes of the ones they’d picked out together, all those years ago. His mother had packed them up for him, when he was unable to face anything, much less packing up a Christmas tree. He’d never touched them since. They were in her attic. That wouldn’t work.

“That’s okay. We can get some. I’m sure there are extras in Marla and Joe’s attic.”

He carried his plate to the sink and she followed. “When did you want to do this?”

“Now?”

He looked over her head at the microwave clock. “It’s eight thirty. The farm’s closed.”

She shrugged. “That’s what flashlights are for.”

What the hell? “All right. Let me get my stuff on.”

He followed her to the farm. The snow was coming down lightly, a sifting that glittered in the headlights. They both parked by the barn, not the house. She already had on her boots and parka and hat and gloves. She gave him a smile in the light of the big wreath on the front of the barn. “Ready?”

For a guy who hadn’t bothered with Christmas since his wife left him—a wife who was standing in front of him now—he was remarkably ready. “Let’s go.”

He grabbed a saw and she got the flashlight and a cart to haul the tree up to his truck. They walked down the lane, the silence broken by the creak of the wagon wheels, the crunch of their boots on the packed snow and, if they stopped moving, the sound of the snow collecting on the branches around them.

“Spruce?” she asked as they stopped at a fork in the lane. Her breath puffed out in front of her in the cold.

“What else?”

She inclined her head in acknowledgment and turned to the left. She stopped a few feet down and dropped the handle of the wagon. Trying to drag it through the snow would be too much work. “How big?”

He followed her, amused, and still able to pick out the sway of her hips even in the dark. The metallic finish of her blue coat caught the beam of the flashlight. “Six feet or so. Pretty full.”

She aimed the light at him, momentarily blinding him. “Oh, sorry! Are you okay? And have a little faith, okay?”

He’d lost what little faith he had left when she left him. But now wasn’t the time to tell her that. Not when things were going well with them. Whatever *things* were.

It took some time, and he enjoyed stomping around

in the dark with her. She finally settled on a tree that was tall enough and fairly full. "This one okay?"

He took the light from her and flashed it over it. He couldn't resist teasing her a little bit. "Looks good to me. But of course, it's dark out, Darce."

She snatched the light back. "It's fine."

He caught her chin in his hand and pressed a kiss to her cold lips. He couldn't help it. Being out here in the dark and cold, with the sharp scent of pine and the softly sifting snow, made him miss her more. Want her more. When he pulled back, looking in her eyes, even in the dark he could see the desire there. When she breathed his name on puff of peppermint-scented air, he was lost.

This kiss was sweet, bittersweet. He knew they were going down a path that was going to end up in heartbreak for both of them—well, him for sure. Then she dropped the heavy metal flashlight on the top of his foot.

"Sorry," she said sheepishly. "I forgot I had it."

He kissed her forehead. "Good thing my boots are thick. Next time you want me to stop kissing you, just tell me instead of trying to hurt me, okay?"

He was teasing, but only sort of. She fished the light out of the snow and he went over to saw the tree down.

By the time they got it back to his truck, he was cold and wet, but it was worth every minute of her company. "Do you want to come in?" She jerked her head toward the house. "Get something to warm you up?"

Tempting as it was— "No. I'm going to go home and change out of these wet clothes. I'll see you tomorrow."

Disappointment flashed over her face. "All right. Tomorrow we'll get the lights on it."

"Sounds good."

He drove away, seeing her in the red glow of his taillights as he went back up the lane to the main road, the tree bouncing in the bed of the truck.

Chapter Ten

Darcy wasn't sure what had come over her the night before. Mack's kisses were seared in her brain, and about all she could come up with was she had somehow fallen back into the past. A time warp of sorts, triggered somehow by being in his presence. For a few minutes it'd almost been as if nothing had happened.

In the early days of their marriage, there'd been no hot kisses like that. Oh, they'd been the ones that had gotten them in trouble. Her pregnancy had meant they'd had to get married. He'd insisted on doing the right thing, and since she couldn't see herself with anyone else—even if she wasn't totally sure she wanted to get married yet—she'd gone along. He'd been happy.

But she hadn't been.

How bad was that? He'd been so sure. She'd allowed him to sweep her off her feet. But then her worst fears had been realized. He only wanted her as long as the baby was in the picture. She, by herself, hadn't been enough. So how had she gotten all caught up in it again?

Her phone rang and Darcy tucked the phone on her shoulder as she answered. "Hi, Corrie."

"Darcy! I miss you, girl. How is it way up there?"

Darcy curled up in the chair and smiled at her best friend's exuberant greeting. "Same as it always is. Cold." Her hands and lips were a little chapped.

"Mmm. How's the ex-husband?"

Just like Corrie to cut right to the heart of the matter. Darcy stared into the flames, which crackled cheerily around the logs she'd added just before the phone rang. "Fine."

"Fine," Corrie repeated. "That tells me nothing."

"That's because there's nothing to tell," Darcy said, trying to keep her voice light. She knew she'd failed when she heard Corrie's sigh.

"Darcy. Come on. Is he hot? Or did he get sloppy?"

"Hot," she answered before she could stop herself.

A long pause. Darcy shut her eyes. She'd stepped in it now.

"Really?" Corrie drew out the word. "That's pretty definitive, Darce. You still have feelings for him."

It wasn't a question, but Darcy chose to treat it as one. "No. No more than nostalgia. We were married, Corrie. That carries some weight, even after all these years." Or so she'd been trying to convince herself. That it was all just based on where they'd been.

"Would it be so bad? If there were feelings between you two? You've shut yourself down pretty tight, Darce. Seems like getting the opportunity to move on would be good for you. Even if it's moving on with him."

She laughed, because if she didn't, she'd cry. "It'd be

awful. I can't stay here. You know that. There's nothing for me here. And Mack—well, he was pretty clear all those years ago it was over. I'm not willing to give it a shot. Plus, there's no time." And thank God for it. She wasn't risking her heart, not with the guy who'd broken it in the first place.

"If you say so," Corrie said softly. "But, Darcy. Promise me you'll keep your options open. Just in case."

Darcy shook her head and pressed her fingers to her lips, even though her friend couldn't see her. "I can't. You of all people know that." Mack hadn't understood then. Why would he now? She wasn't going to risk her heart on that. She'd do what she could to make things right, but she wouldn't give him a chance to steal her heart. It was too risky. She wasn't sure she could take another blow like that.

"You deserve love," Corrie said firmly. "If it's not Mack, well, that's okay. You'd know better than I would. I don't know him. But at some point you need to let *someone* in. You don't want to miss out on the perfect guy for you."

Darcy *did* know the perfect guy for her. But thanks to their past and her choices, they were stuck apart. Mack had kissed her, but how did she know that wasn't based on the old Darcy? The one he'd married? The one he'd made—and lost—a baby with. The one he'd let go.

He didn't know her now. That mattered. And in the three weeks she had left on the farm, there was no real way to get to know him again.

Mack had tried to figure out a way to frame the request. In seven years, he'd never asked about the Christmas ornaments he and Darcy had had on their first—and only—tree together. He wasn't going to go in his mother's house without her knowledge, and he for damn sure wasn't going to ask Chase.

So it looked as though he had to suck it up and face his demons and his mother's questions.

He stopped in on his lunch, which was what he framed the time between leaving his vet practice and getting out to the farm. Mom was there, of course, and she brightened right up when she saw him.

"Mack." She stepped out of the doorway and gestured him in. Little flurries of snow accompanied him and she shut the door quickly. "What's going on? We don't usually see you in the middle of the day."

He dropped a kiss on his mother's head. "Hi, Mom." He raised his voice so his father could hear him over the TV in the den. "Hey, Dad."

His father's reply carried over the noise of the television. Mom rolled her eyes. "This one's about how Sumatrans made their pottery." Mack had to grin despite the nerves in his belly. Dad loved history programs. In the winter, the off-season, he had them on almost nonstop and was enthralled by all of it. Mack had asked once why they just didn't go visit the places he was so interested in, and Dad had just looked at him and said, "I'm an armchair traveler."

Fair enough.

Mom led him into the kitchen, where she had something in the oven that smelled fantastic. "Lasagna," she said with a faint smile as she caught him sniffing the air the way a hound might scent a bird. "There will be extra for you."

"Do you take extras to Chase?" He knew the answer but was trying to stall on his actual request.

"Sometimes. But that boy can cook. He even likes it." She gave him an amused look, then got out a mug. "Coffee?"

"Sure," he murmured, taking in the scene as she poured the mug from the pot that always seemed to be at the ready. He'd always pictured himself in the same kind of marriage his parents had. In terms of the affection, the love, the way they still enjoyed each other's company. He'd thought he'd found that in Darcy. But he'd been wrong.

He accepted the mug she held out. She'd let him sit and stew as long as he needed to spit out what he needed to say. It was a time-honed technique that had worked way too well when he was a kid.

Still worked now as an adult.

They made small talk for a few minutes when he finally blurted out, "I need the Christmas stuff Darcy and I had."

She set her mug on the table and leveled a serious gaze on him. "What are you going to do with it?"

"Put it on a tree," he said, and she nodded, pushed back from the table and started toward the back bedroom. He rose and followed her.

"Do you know what you're doing, Mack?" she asked as she flicked on the light and gestured to the two cardboard boxes sitting on the floor by the bed. Not in the attic? *Mack and Darcy, Christmas* was written in his mother's neat hand in black marker on the lids of both.

I don't have a clue, he wanted to say. *No. Freaking. Clue.* But instead he asked, staring at the boxes, "How did you know?"

She gave him a tiny smile. "Helen's daughter saw you

driving home last night with a big old tree in the bed of your truck. Helen called me as soon as she heard."

Mack opened his mouth, then snapped it shut. There wasn't much to say to that. He should have known his mother would hear about it from one of her friends. Her social network was impressive. He shook his head. "I see. Well. Thanks."

She shrugged. "I hope you know what you're doing, Mack. Not only for your sake, but for hers. Darcy is so fragile."

He almost laughed as he lifted one of the boxes. Darcy was anything but fragile. She was tough, far tougher than she probably knew. "I'll be careful."

She picked up the other box and followed him down the hall lined with family pictures. He was careful not to knock any off with the big box. He put the first one in the truck and came back for the second.

"See that you are," she said quietly, and he didn't even pretend to misunderstand what she meant.

Mack wasn't sure what to do with the boxes, so he put them in his own spare bedroom—not the one he used as a weight room, but the back one he almost never went in. The one that would have been the baby's room. The one that, in the back of the closet, still had a crib in its box. It also had a box of stuff Darcy had left when she split. He wasn't sure why he kept any of it. After several months of no contact, he'd realized she wasn't coming back.

He didn't open the closet.

Apparently, he could have saved himself the trouble of quasi hiding the tree on the back deck and just left it on the front porch. He should have known someone would see and report it to his mother.

He propped his hands on his hips and surveyed the tree. It wasn't bad, considering they'd chopped it down in the dark. There was a fairly sizable hole on one side, but if he angled the tree a little to the left, it was facing the wall.

Better.

He peeled off his gloves and dropped them on the coffee table. Trees like that tore you to pieces if you weren't careful. He poured water in the stand and left the house for the tree farm.

Darcy had spent the better part of the day throwing herself into her work, making wreaths with the team and filling orders. It kept thoughts of Mack at bay. Thoughts of how she had to finish what she'd started with her impulsive Christmas-tree idea.

She mentally kicked herself for the zillionth time. It had been a stupid idea, an uncharacteristically impulsive thing that she never did anymore. Impulsiveness led to mistakes. Mistakes couldn't be undone. She was very careful not to make them, much less ones like this.

She wired the spruce boughs into the large wreath she was making for the wall of the Methodist church. This one would be three feet across, but fairly simple. It would have a huge red bow that'd she make next. It was a good way to stay occupied.

Until her thoughts slipped back to Mack's mouth on hers.

She stabbed herself with the wire and it went through her glove. She pulled the glove off with a muttered curse and Wendy, one of the longtime employees, sent her an amused look.

"Mack on the brain?"

Darcy shut her eyes and then opened them to examine her finger. "No more than usual," she muttered, which could have meant anything.

"He's quite a catch," Wendy said, all seriousness now.

Darcy felt her back go up. "Of course he is."

"But so are you," she said quietly. Darcy could only blink at her as she went on, "I don't know what went wrong, but he sure looks at you like you matter to him."

Like you matter to him. Those words echoed in her brain as they got through the evening, as she sold trees and decorations and poured hot chocolate and made sure the Christmas station was playing at the proper volume.

He hadn't said anything to her about the tree. She had a trunkful of lights at the ready, thinking he might need them. Since it'd been her idea and all and she'd practically forced him to get the tree.

He looked up then, across the cold barn, and his gaze locked right on hers. As if he'd known she was looking at him. The corner of his mouth quirked up in an almost smile. Then someone said something to him and he turned around and disappeared from her vision.

They closed the place down at seven. It didn't take long. Darcy locked the money in the safe and waved to the departing workers.

Except Mack, of course. He was at his truck. Waiting for her.

"So," he said as she approached. "I've got this tree. It needs some love." He arched an eyebrow at her and she suppressed a smile.

"Does it, now?" she said. "I need to eat first and give Uncle Joe a report. I can be at your place in—" she looked at her phone "—less than an hour."

"Sounds good," he said.

She didn't watch him leave. She walked back to the house and it took more willpower than it should have to not look back.

She was at his house, as she'd said, in less than an hour. As she did every night now, she'd delivered her report, her handwritten notes, all the receipts to Uncle Joe so he could pore over them. It made him happy and helped him feel as though he was still a part of everything. She ate a quick dinner, showered and changed, then drove into town.

She pulled the bags with the lights out of her trunk. Their first tree had had multicolor lights on it. She'd bought the same for him.

He opened the door almost as soon as she knocked. "Hey," he said, stepping out of the way.

"Hey," she echoed, surprised to realize she was a little shy. She brushed past him, smelling his soap or shampoo. He smelled yummy enough to make the heat begin to rise in her, just a little.

Even a little was too much.

She gave him her coat when he reached for it and toed off her boots. She saw bags on the coffee table, too. He'd been shopping. Or maybe his mom had.

She mentally winced. What did Mack's mom think of Darcy now? Of her being back in town and even remotely in Mack's life? His mom hadn't been thrilled with the marriage—that had been clear from the start.

It didn't matter. Darcy wasn't staying.

She pushed aside the thoughts and stepped into the living room. He'd lit a fire, she noted. She looked at the tree and then at him, a small smile tugging at her mouth.

"Not too bad for being dark," she said cheerfully, walking over to inspect it. "And you didn't—" She turned around and found him right behind her.

"Didn't what?" His voice was low.

"Trust me," she whispered, and almost closed her eyes, the fragrant tree at her back, the man at her front.

But he stepped back and the moment shattered at her feet like a glass ornament handled carelessly. She swallowed hard and turned back toward the tree.

"It's got a big hole," he said, and his voice was a little rough. So she hadn't imagined the charged moment they'd just shared. "But not too bad for being in the dark."

She smiled and fingered the tip of a branch. If you smoothed the needles right on a spruce tree, they wouldn't draw blood. "I brought lights."

"I got some ornaments." He paused for a moment, a faraway expression on his face. "Nothing fancy."

She shrugged. "It's your tree, Mack."

Not theirs. *His*. Her observation wasn't lost on her, and she tried to ignore the little stab of pain it brought.

He didn't correct her and she started unloading the boxes of lights while he put on the leather gloves and started winding them, tucking them in the branches. The radio played softly in the background from somewhere—the kitchen, maybe—and she found it soothing to work with him like this, companionable. The past seemed to have receded somewhat as she realized she liked Mack. Not as the man she remembered, but as the man he was now.

That was every bit as dangerous as the memories.

She handed him the last string and he hooked it up, then wrapped it around the tree. He stepped back and she leaned over to click off the light on the end table. He peeled the gloves off and nodded as they both took it in. Transformed, it glowed bight and Darcy sighed. "It's beautiful. You did a good job."

"Thanks." He tossed the gloves on the floor and reached for a bag. "Let's see what we've got here."

He'd bought a mishmash of brightly colored ornaments. Nothing real personal. She didn't ask where their stuff was. She wasn't sure she could handle seeing it, even after all this time.

"Plastic," he explained as the smaller dog—Lilly—demonstrated the reason why glass would have been bad. Her tail slapped several on the floor and as they rolled away a calico cat leaped out from under a chair to chase them.

Darcy had to laugh. "Maybe they should go up. Out of tail range," she added doubtfully. "I've seen parents with little kids do that."

Then she froze at her own stupid, thoughtless words. The past came roaring back and sat right down in the living room with them, making itself comfortable in the sharpness of the silence. She opened her mouth again, but for the life of her couldn't think of anything to say that would make it better, so she clamped it shut again.

"Yes," he agreed quietly, and she heard the threads of pain in his tone, even in that one word. "They do. So should pet owners." When she turned to look at him—

Is he really going to let me off that easy?—he gave her a small smile.

He was.

"Want something to drink?" he asked, heading for the kitchen. "I've got beer. No wine, I'm afraid," he said, "but there's some diet Mountain Dew in here, too."

She should go. Before all this became too much and something happened. Something that even now she could feel tugging at her. "Beer's fine."

He held up two different kinds, and she pointed at her choice. He poured them each a glass and handed her one before going back in the living room. Which was far too cozy with the fire crackling, and the lights from the tree sending out a soft light. The dogs were asleep on the hearth, and a wave of longing hit her hard. This was all she'd ever wanted. And someday he'd share it with someone else. She took a drink of her beer and sat down on the couch. He did, too, and she sent him a sideways look as he turned on the TV.

What she should do was go home. There was no reason not to. The night was clear as a bell, if cold. No snow, no ice, no excuses to stay.

He put on a movie, a recent action flick. "Did you see this one?"

She shook her head. She hadn't been to see a movie in ages. "Nope. Missed it."

"Me, too. We can watch it while we decorate."

He got up and went to make popcorn and she tried really hard to make herself leave. Listing all the reasons this was a bad idea. Why it was always a bad idea to get attached.

But when he came back, set the bowl on the table and handed her a paper towel for her fingers, she knew she wasn't fooling even herself anymore. They shared the bowl, sipped beer, hung ornaments and laughed at the antics on-screen.

And Darcy found herself tipping toward him a little more.

Chapter Eleven

This was how it'd always been with them, and there was a time Mack would have given anything for one more night like this.

Be careful what you wish for. He could hear his mother's voice in his head, same as when he was a kid. There was always a price. No doubt. But Darcy was here now, her fingers bumping his in the popcorn bowl, her knee touching his thigh when she tucked her feet under her on the couch after they'd finished the tree. He didn't look at her, or pull away, and neither did she.

Finally, he'd had as much as he could take. The next time their fingers brushed, he twined hers in his. Her head snapped around, her eyes wide and luminous in the soft light of the tree and the TV. He pulled her in and kissed her. Her mouth was a little slick from the butter. He tasted the beer, the saltiness of the popcorn and the sweetness of the butter. She opened to him right away, as though maybe she'd been waiting for this, too.

It felt like a first kiss.

He sank deeper and pulled her in. She turned her body so she folded right into him, her arms around his neck. When he lowered her to the couch, his mouth still on hers, she didn't protest.

He pressed a kiss into her neck, feeling the flutter of her pulse there. It kept pace with his own. She ran her hands down his back and turned her face back to his when he slid a hand under her sweater. Her skin was so soft, so smooth, and he felt her inhale sharply at his touch. He lifted his head and looked her in the eye, seeing the desire and heat there, and the uncertainty, too. "You okay?" he asked, his voice a rasp in his throat. He didn't bother to shift away from her, so he knew she felt the hard length of him pressed into her thigh. Her eyes were molten, and he held still, wanting this so badly.

She lifted up and nipped his bottom lip, but he didn't lower back down. "Darce. I need to hear you say it." He was about to lose his mind, but he'd walk away if he had to, if it was what she needed.

"Yes," she whispered, and there was a small wobble in her voice. She lifted her eyes and met his and he saw the uncertainty was gone. "Yes," she repeated. "I'm okay, Mack." Then she smiled that smile, the one that always made his blood go hot, and he dropped his forehead to hers, relief flooding him, along with something much hotter, and much more intense.

Since he knew where this was heading, he stood up and held out a hand. They'd be better off in his bed than on this slippery leather couch. She took it and walked with him the short steps to his room. There was a slight tremor in her fingers, and when he drew her over to the bed, she laid a hand on his chest. In the faint moonlight that came through the window, he saw the intensity on her face. “What is it, Darce?”

She pleated his shirt in her fingers, then looked back up. “It’s been a long time for me, Mack.”

“Yeah?” He tugged her sweater up and she lifted her arms for him to slide it off. Her skin was creamy in the pale light. “Me, too, honey.”

She seemed to relax then, and reached for the hem of his shirt, which he stripped off and tossed, then pulled her in, feeling the heat of her skin and the raspy lace of her bra on his skin. He closed his eyes, buried his face in her hair and groaned. “Darcy.” There were no more words, and yet too many to say. She ran her hands up his arms to his face, which she pulled down to hers, and kissed him. Heat, passion, sweetness, all in one kiss.

He was a goner.

He reached behind her and unhooked the bra, which she shrugged off her shoulders and let it fall. She let out a laughing little “Eep!” when he bent and took those rosy, luscious nipples in his mouth. They were already peaked for him and he played with them both, with his tongue and his fingers, until she was gasping.

He kissed her throat, that sweet little pulse jumping even more now, and reached for the snap of her jeans as she reached for his. It took a little fumbling to get things down—her leg got stuck and she was hopping around trying to kick her pants off until he finally grabbed it and yanked and she went back on the bed with a giggle and a bounce of those glorious breasts. He landed beside her, his own grin so wide he was pretty sure his face was going to split in two. No matter. He'd be a damn happy man.

"Hey," she said softly, and he traced a line with one finger down her chest—a slight detour each way for her nipples—over her smooth belly and the scar there. He stopped there, running his fingers over the roughness of the scar. She reached for his hand and he shook his head.

"Mack—don't—"

"It's part of you, Darcy." It was part of him, too, but he didn't say that. He did lean down and kiss it before slipping farther to the curls at the juncture of her thighs, into the damp heat he found there. She gave a little gasp and he shifted his body. "While I'm here…"

Her legs fell open and he settled in. She grasped his head as he rolled his tongue and fingers around in the sweetness that had always been Darcy.

Darcy was losing her mind. Oh, Mack had always been good at this, so good, so very good. She bucked and he threaded his arms through her legs, resting his hands on her belly, a gentle pressure to hold her in place as he worked his magic. The pressure built like a wave and crashed over her just as fast as she gasped his name. Then his big body was covering hers as he held her through the tremors. She heard the crinkle of the condom package and he was inside her. A shudder racked his body as he held himself still, and pushed up on his forearms.

"Darcy—I'm not going to last long—" he gritted out, and she smiled and started moving against him. Turnabout was fair play and if he was going to make her lose her mind, well, she was going to return the favor.

The joke was on her. She matched him stroke for stroke and held on as he loved her, as the sweet pressure built, and he threw his head back as his whole body strained and shuddered. She followed him right over, the shock and pleasure of the second orgasm floating her gently to the ground.

He lay on her for a minute, breathing hard. "Wow."

She laughed and ran her hands up his sweaty back. "Yeah. Wow." But under all the sweetness was a bit of panic. Nothing had changed. Or rather, it'd gotten better, and it had been fantastic all those years ago. If it had been because they were so in love the first time around, what did that mean now?

She pushed the thoughts away. This might be her only chance to be like this with Mack, when she'd thought it was over for good. This was a gift, even if she'd pay for it later.

He rolled off her, onto his back, and his fingers found hers. They lay in the dark, and Darcy felt the dampness of tears leaking from her eyes.

"Stay," he said quietly, and she wasn't sure if he meant forever, or just tonight.

She wanted to, but her aunt and uncle— "I'm not sure, Mack."

He turned his head to look at her, then shifted and ran his thumb over the moisture at her eyes. "Please." Then, in a lighter tone, he added, "We never actually made it into the bed. We're on the covers." In the dark she saw his grin, and she was lost.

She sat up and scooted back toward the pillows, peeling the covers back, a wicked smile on her gorgeous face. "Well. Can't have that, can we?"

He followed her.

Darcy cracked one eye the next morning. The sky was barely light and Mack was still sleeping, one arm thrown over her like the way he used to sleep. The way they'd slipped into this so easily scared her. She knew why it could never be casual with them, and it made her heart hurt. He didn't stir as she slipped out from under his arm and tiptoed around and gathered up her clothes. She dressed quickly and quietly and let herself out into the cold predawn stillness. She shivered the whole drive home, not so much from the freezing temps but from the loss of the heat she'd shared with Mack. He wouldn't be happy she'd left. But she knew it was for the best. They'd crossed too many lines, and while she couldn't undo that, she could try to draw new ones.

She parked at the house and saw the kitchen light was on. Left on? Or was Marla up?

Darcy rested her head on the steering wheel. She was an adult. No one was going to say anything to her.

She let herself in the side door and saw that it had been left on. It wasn't quite time for Marla to be up yet. Darcy crawled back under the cold blankets of her childhood bed and stared at the ceiling, trying not to relive the night before and finding it impossible.

Marla gave her a knowing smile when she walked in the kitchen a couple of hours later. "So. Did you and Mack have a nice time?"

Darcy's face heated in spite of herself. "Yes. The tree looks nice."

"Mmm-hmm. Took all night to decorate, huh?" There was no censorship in her tone, but Darcy felt slapped down anyway.

"Something like that," she murmured, and grabbed a mug. Thank God there was coffee. She'd had very little sleep, thanks to what had turned out to be a very active night. As if they'd been making up for lost time. But Darcy knew better. There was no way to make it up, to recover what they'd lost. Or to start over and make something new.

Marla laid her hand on Darcy's arm. "Darcy. Be careful. If you're going to leave again, don't set yourself up for heartbreak."

She gave Marla a smile that was more a curving of her lips than a real smile. "I know. I'll be careful. I don't want to go through that again." That was God's honest truth.

As her aunt walked away, Darcy tried to ignore the little voice that told her it was already too late, that she was going to hurt like crazy when she left. That all her hard work, all her careful defenses had been for nothing when the man could strip her bare with just a look. She'd destroyed the last of them herself when she'd fallen apart in his arms last night.

Seemed she'd never learn.

Despite Darcy's predawn exit, Mack was in a good mood the next morning. Oh, he knew this didn't really change anything—no way it really could—but damn. Having her in his bed again was like an early Christmas gift to himself. To both of them.

He hoped this maybe meant they could put the past behind them, where it belonged.

He came into work, actually whistling, and Jennifer narrowed her eyes at him. "You got some, didn't you?"

He did a double take. "What?"

She sighed. "I recognize the signs. The loose walk. The perma-grin. You're whistling, for Pete's sake. Yeah. I'm hoping it was Darcy, otherwise you're a fool."

"Ah." He took a moment to think it through.

"I won't say anything," she added. "You know that. But, Mack… Is it a good idea?"

He rubbed his hand between his eyes. "Doesn't matter now, does it, Jenn?"

She shook her head. "Sure it does. She's leaving. You're taking away her reason to stay."

I should be her reason to stay. But he didn't say that. "What reason is that?"

Jenn looked at him as if he were nuts. "Her farm, dimwit. Why should she stay? Why will she ever come back? You guys are turning it into a subdivision and her family's moving to Arizona. If you think you're going to win her back this way, you're going about it all wrong."

Mack's head spun. "She didn't want the farm."

Jenn smacked his arm. Hard. "You're an idiot, Mack. Really. I expected better from you. You figure it out. I can't tell you what to do. I don't know Darcy. But I do know that if a man wanted me as bad as you want her, he'd damn well better put forth some effort to make me stay."

She was right. Of course she was right.

He was an idiot. And he'd overlooked one very important detail. He wasn't going to get her to stay *for him.* She needed a reason to leave Chicago, something that mattered to her. And Jenn was right—he and Chase were destroying the one place she loved more than anything.

"I don't have a lot of time," he said more to himself than to her. And really, did he want her to stay? Did he want her to be part of his life? Was he ready to go there again?

He wasn't sure.

Jenn had moved on to the end of the row, and the cacophony of hungry dogs and cats allowed him the luxury of no conversation. His thoughts bounced back and forth between his night with Darcy and Jenn's words.

When Mack arrived at the farm, Darcy had hoped that she'd be out on the back forty somewhere, but of course that wasn't the case. He walked right up to her, in front of all the other people that were milling around, and said, very quietly, "Hi."

"Hi," she said back, more of a breath than a vocalization.

There was an awkward moment while they looked at each other, then away. *Crap.* She felt her face burn.

"You okay?"

She looked at him almost shyly. "Yeah."

Then he stepped back and gave her a little smile before heading around back. Darcy took a breath and the cold air burned her lungs. Well. Anyone watching knew exactly what had happened with them. Wonderful. She took a quick look around, but it was hard to tell with so many people moving around who had noticed and who hadn't.

She threw herself into the work, trying not to cue in to him in the most primal way possible. He seemed to be everywhere she was. Or maybe she was just hyperaware of him.

That was probably it.

She smiled at the couple in front of her, and it took her a minute to realize the woman was looking at her with a bemused smile.

Recognition clicked in. "Oh, my gosh. Cheryl?"

The other woman smiled. "I didn't think you recognized me." She laughed.

"No, I—I was distracted, I guess," she admitted, and

came around the table to hug her former friend, whom she hadn't seen in ages. Since before she'd left for good.

"I bet I know why," Cheryl said with a low laugh. "I see Mack here."

"Ah." She darted a quick glance in the direction he'd been, and saw he had his head bent in conversation with a gorgeous black-haired woman. She tore her eyes away and ignored the sharp stab of jealousy. "Yes, well, he's been helping Uncle Joe."

Cheryl raised an eyebrow but didn't say anything else. She gestured to a tall man who was holding a little girl on his hip. She couldn't be more than three, as blond as her mother, wearing an adorable red velvet beret. Darcy couldn't stop her smile.

"Oh, Cheryl. She's gorgeous. She looks just like you!"

"Thanks, Darce. This is my husband, Jake, and daughter, Olivia. We met at college. Been married five years."

Yes, Darcy knew that. Marla had told her, had sent the invite on, and of course Darcy had sent her regrets. "I remember."

Cheryl let it go. "Can I have your number? I'd love to get together for coffee if you've got time."

Darcy's first instinct was to say no, as much as she wanted to reconnect with her old friend. All these connections were like a vine, binding her to this place, holding her back when she knew she had to leave. But at the same time— She pulled out her phone. "Sure. I'd like that."

Mack caught her eye over Cheryl's head as Darcy slid her phone back in her pocket. He'd seen. He'd know what it cost her to connect. He gave her a private little smile and her heart flipped.

She got through the rest of the day and headed up to the house after. It was cold, colder than it'd been yet.

It made the air dry, and the snow was squeaky under her boots. She'd managed to avoid Mack, but she was pretty sure it wouldn't last for long.

He could be determined.

She went in the kitchen and peeled off her layers. She usually just wore a thermal undershirt, a fleece jacket and a vest. Today it'd been cold enough for the full-on parka, even in the shelter of the barn. She unlaced her boots and left them at the door, and peeled out of her wool socks. She had cotton ones on under them, and long underwear under her jeans.

In the kitchen, her aunt and uncle smiled at her, and she pushed down thoughts of Mack and all the stupid feelings he invoked in her.

"Pretty cold," Joe commented, and she plopped into the seat opposite him, handing the papers to him over the cracked and worn linoleum table.

"Yes, but it didn't keep people away," she said simply. "They're just more likely to choose a precut tree rather than go tromping around in the woods."

He grunted. "Mack had extra cut?"

"Of course," she said, getting up to pour a cup of coffee. Decaf, of course, but it smelled good enough she didn't care.

Another grunt, this one of approval. "Smart boy, that one."

In some things, maybe. But Darcy wasn't going to go there. "You trained him, Uncle Joe."

Her uncle laughed, and she smiled back. He was looking better. His color was better, and while still he tired easily, he was coming back pretty good. Marla set a steaming plate in front of her. Chicken, sure, but also mashed potatoes and gravy. Her mouth watered.

Darcy knew if she kept eating like this, she'd need a whole new wardrobe come the first of the year, but she couldn't bring herself to care when she was this hungry.

"How is Mack?" Marla's question was conversational, but Darcy sensed the potential minefield.

"Fine," she said as she dredged a bite of chicken through the potatoes and gravy. "This is excellent, Aunt Marla." She popped the bite in her mouth, hoping her dodge worked.

"Thank you, dear," Marla said. Joe had retired to the living room and his favorite chair and was poring over the records. It appeared he'd pulled out last year's, as well. He was oblivious to the twist in conversation. Marla folded her arms on the table and leaned forward earnestly. "I have to ask. Are you and Mack considering reconciliation?"

Darcy opened her mouth, then shut it again. She pushed a few peas out of the gravy river on her plate. "No. I don't believe we are, Aunt Marla." The words were surprisingly hard to say. Because she wanted it to be true? Or because it hadn't occurred to her?

Who was she kidding? Of course it had occurred to her. How could it not?

Marla sat back. "I will say that's too bad. He's a great guy and you deserve the happiness you had with him."

Darcy shoved her plate away, all appetite gone. No, she didn't. She'd tossed it away as if it didn't matter. Made no difference at this point if it was true or not—he believed it was. "It's a little more complicated than that, Aunt Marla. You, of all people—you know that." She'd been the one to pick up the pieces. Or as many pieces as Darcy had allowed.

Compassion softened her aunt's features. "I do know

that, honey. I know that very well. But a lot of things brought you back here. If there's a chance, an opportunity, why not take it?"

It wasn't too far from what Darcy had been thinking, yet worlds away. She hadn't been thinking in terms of reconciliation. She'd been thinking of apologizing, maybe getting him to understand where she'd been coming from. Somewhere along the line that had changed. And she hadn't even realized it until now.

"Too much time has gone by," she said simply. "We're different people now. That's not a bad thing."

Marla shook her head. "No, it's not, that's true. But you've locked yourself down so tight, you won't let anyone in. How is that a good thing? You're so young."

Darcy gave a little shrug, as she had done when she was a teenager and pinned in the corner by her aunt. She didn't like being cornered. But she wasn't going to explain herself. She didn't think she'd shut herself down that tightly. She was practical, sure, but that wasn't a bad thing. It'd gotten her this far in life.

In her bed that night, she listened to the wind howl. It battered snow against the window—in this kind of temperature, it was little more than hard kernels of snow—and just seemed to underscore her loneliness. She was under the quilt in her old bedroom in her childhood home, instead of in the bed of the man who'd loved her. Who'd married her and done right by her when she got pregnant.

And she'd left him.

She curled onto her side and slipped into dreams of what could have been.

Chapter Twelve

The next couple of days were busy. She and Mack had fallen into a kind of truce. She didn't know what he wanted, but he wasn't pushing her. He was friendly, sometimes flirty, and every time he gave her that slow smile, her insides turned into a total puddle. Was he waiting for her to come to him? That didn't seem likely. Mack wasn't a game player. He was straightforward and solid. But he was clearly holding back. Waiting for her to make the next move?

Racking her brain meant she wasn't paying attention. And not paying attention meant she was recruited to go with Mack out to the far field to check one of the warming stations.

"I can just go," she offered, and saw him cock his eyebrow. "I mean, I'm sure you've got other things to do."

"Let's go," he said, and walked to the ATV. She trotted behind, mentally kicking herself for thinking she could get away from him.

They got in, and while she was grateful for the roar of the engine, she was pressed right up against him in the little vehicle. This was really a one-person ride, not for two, especially when the past of those two people crowded in and seemed to both shove them apart while cementing them together.

She tucked her face in the neck of her zipped-up parka, trying to protect against the stinging wind.

At the station he cut the engine and got out almost before it came to a stop. She hopped after him, feeling resentful and angry and knowing it wasn't his fault.

No, she wanted more and was angry with herself for wanting it.

She restocked while he checked the errant coffeemaker. She loved that he was so handy, had always been, and that didn't appear to have changed at all.

By the time he'd finished she was done. "Why am I here?"

"That's a good question," he said mildly, and all it did was make her madder.

"Mack. You didn't need me out here. And you won't talk to me—"

He was in front of her in about two strides. She gasped and backed up, but the wall was behind her and he'd planted both arms on either side of her, caging her in but not actually touching her. The look in his eyes was molten and she swallowed hard. He didn't say a word, just kept his eyes on hers until the last moment when his mouth came down on hers. Hard. There was no mercy in his kiss. He didn't touch her, but she felt the tension and hardness of his body even without the contact. She fisted her hands at her sides and kissed him back, giving as good as she got. Then she stopped thinking altogether.

He pulled away and the only sound other than the blood roaring in her ears was the rasp of their breathing in the quiet of the cabin. She lifted her fingers to touch her mouth, realized they were shaking and dropped her hand again.

"Damn it, Darcy," he said, but there wasn't any heat in the words. "You've got it all wrong." He stepped back, his eyes still on hers, and she could barely breathe. "All wrong," he repeated, and turned away.

She moved quickly and grabbed his arm. "What? What do I have wrong, Mack?" If he could tell her, if she could know, it would make all this so much easier.

He shook his head. "I just wanted to love you. But you wouldn't let me, then or now. Why is that?"

She stared up at him. It had never been that easy. "Because that's not how it worked for us. And, Mack, come on. We have too much baggage to make anything work. It's better left behind."

"Not a day goes by, Darcy, that I don't think of you. Of the baby. That I don't wonder what if. If we'd stayed together, would we have more? What would they look like?" His voice was so raw tears burned in her eyes and she knew what she had to do.

"I can answer part of that. No. There wouldn't be any more." Her voice was shaky and the words almost stuck in her throat. But it had to be said and it had to be said now.

"Because you didn't want them?" There was bitterness in his tone, and it made her heart ache even more that he'd think that of her, even if it was in anger.

She took a deep breath and looked him in the eye. "No. Because I can't have any more. I can't get pregnant, Mack."

Mack's ears were ringing. Darcy stood in front of him. Her mouth was still forming words, but he wasn't hearing any of them. *Can't get pregnant.* "What do you mean, you can't get pregnant?"

She lifted her chin. "From the damage of the miscarriage and the accident, the odds of me ever conceiving again are nearly zero. I'm more likely to be struck by lightning." Her tone was nearly expressionless.

Shock was reverberating around in him, making her words bounce around in his brain like a bunch of loose Ping-Pong balls. He moved away from her and she stayed where she was.

"Mack. I'm so sorry." Now there was pain in her words, regret and sorrow. She'd known this for how long?

"How long?" The words ripped from his throat. "How long have you known?"

Her eyes widened, but she said nothing. And he knew.

"You've known since you left," he said, almost wonderingly. "And you never said one word. Not one." And hell if he'd ever thought to ask her. He'd said, over and over, they could have another baby. How much he wanted to have a baby with her.

And she'd said nothing. Why not? If she hadn't been able to tell him, why hadn't the doctors told him?

She looked away and he saw her visibly fighting for control of her emotions. Then she looked back at him. "Yes. I knew the possibility was there. And it was confirmed later."

"After you'd already left."

"Mack, the doctor said there was a chance I couldn't get pregnant again! Remember? But you were so dead set on having another one, when I wasn't even out of the hospital yet."

She was already moving toward the door. "I'm walking back up. There's nothing more to say about this. I'm sorry. I really am. But I didn't see any reason to tell you when it was clearly over with us."

It wasn't until she'd left and the swirl of snow she'd let in on her exit had settled that he realized what she'd said.

It'd been a long time since Mack drank enough to, well, get drunk. And he was only half surprised when Chase showed up on his doorstep, grim-faced and tense.

Mack let his brother in and went back and collapsed on the couch. He could still feel, damn it. There wasn't enough alcohol in the world to fill the hole Darcy's words had made in his heart.

"Why are you here?" Or at least that was what he meant to say. It seemed to come out a little slurred.

"Darcy called me. Told me I should check on you." Even in his state, Mack could hear the bitterness in his brother's voice. "What the hell did she do to you?"

He let his head loll back on the couch. Closing his eyes was bad. Things started to spin. Maybe he'd had a little more than he thought. "Nothing."

The crash and clink of glass pierced his mental fog. "All these say otherwise," Chase said as he left the room, the bottles clinking in his hands. "Tell me," he said quietly when he came back in. "It must have been bad if she called me."

Something seemed off about that, but Mack wasn't

quite tracking well enough to get it. Wait. There it was. "Darcy called *you*?" Wow. Cold day in hell, and all that.

"Yeah," he said. "She asked me to check on you. Why?"

"She told me she can't have any more babies," he blurted, then winced. Even in this condition, he didn't want to talk about it. It wasn't Chase's business. He wasn't sure it was even his own. Not anymore.

"Okay," Chase said, his voice level. "But you're not together."

Nope, he wasn't far enough gone to muffle the pain of those words. Damn it. "No."

Chase didn't say anything else. He got up, and when he came back he had a sandwich, which he handed to Mack. "You need this more than another beer."

Mack took it, but he wasn't so sure. What he really needed he was afraid he'd never have again.

His wife back.

The next morning Mack's head pounded. He'd earned the headache. He dragged himself through his day at his vet practice, and while he was perfectly pleasant to his staff, his patients and their owners, his office staff had clearly caught his underlying mood and were handling him with kid gloves.

He went out to the tree farm because it wasn't in his nature to shirk his duties just because it was awkward. He could handle it. Unless it came to his ex-wife, of course. It was becoming crystal clear he had no idea how to handle her.

He didn't see her when he first pulled in. Then he spotted her in her navy fleece jacket and red vest, a bright red hat covering her copper hair. He swallowed hard. She looked up then, spotted him and said something to Wendy, who laughed as she walked away.

Now she was walking toward him, her stride long and purposeful. He didn't move, just shoved his hands in his pockets and let her come, let her make the move. It wasn't in his court. This was all her.

"Can we talk?" Her brown eyes searched his and he saw the shadows on the fine skin under her eyes. She hadn't slept any better than he had.

He was tempted to say no way, but he didn't want to hurt her more. There'd been too much pain between them already. "Sure."

She turned and headed out the door, toward the house. He caught up with her and they walked, wordlessly, through the dark to the house.

Darcy was nervous. Her fingers shook as she unzipped her fleece jacket. She went into the kitchen. "Coffee?"

"Sure," he said, and his voice was quiet and cautious. She didn't blame him. She'd undone everything they'd rebuilt in the space of a few minutes last night. Again. Clearly, this was not meant to work out. Not ever.

She prepared the mugs and handed him one, unable to hide the fact her hands were shaking. The coffee sloshed in the mug but didn't spill. He took it with no comment other than a murmured "Thanks."

The best way out is through. She'd always loved the line from Whitman and it steadied her now. She sat and gestured for him to do the same.

"I'm sorry I sprang that on you like I did last night," she said. This needed to come from the heart, for her sake and his. "And I'm even more sorry I didn't tell you what the doctor said all those years ago."

Maybe it would have been easier for him if he'd known they could never be what he wanted so badly. Help him understand why she'd left. Tears burned her eyes. She'd thought she was done crying over this. But the magnitude of their loss hung between them now and she finally saw it differently. She'd held on to it as *hers* for so long she'd forgotten it was really *theirs*.

He sat back, his expression shuttered, his untouched coffee steaming on the table between them. She couldn't read him, wasn't sure what was going on in his head. "It was a lot to take in," she said quietly. "And I handled it all badly."

He rubbed his hand over his face. "Yeah, we both did." He sat forward, and rested his arms on the table, gaze on his fingers. She wanted to take his hand in hers, but instead threaded her fingers together tightly in her lap, so tightly it hurt. "Darce. I just wish you'd have told me. Let me carry some of it with you."

The dark thing, the deepest secret she held, battered against her chest. She wasn't going to tell him all of it. They had a chance to make a fragile peace. Telling him it had all been her fault wasn't going to help that, help him. And she owed him the chance to move on. So she said simply, "Me, too."

Because that was true. If she'd let him take some of it from her, would she have been able to stay? Hard to tell. She'd been a physical and emotional wreck at the time. She'd come back here, to the farm, to recuperate. He'd tried to get her to come home, but she'd refused. And he had eventually stopped arguing with her. Her physical injuries had healed, but her emotional ones ran much deeper. So deep, she didn't think she'd ever get around them. It was an ache she doubted would ever go away.

They sat for another few minutes and Darcy would have given almost anything to know what he was thinking. Then he said, "We need to get back."

Relieved it was over, she pushed back from the table and stood, reaching for his mug. But he caught her hand as he rose from his chair and tugged her around the table toward him. She stood in front of him, inhaling his scent, close but not close enough. She knew it'd never be close enough. Not now. He bent and pressed a soft kiss to her mouth. Then he dropped her hand and stepped back.

She put the mugs in the sink and they walked, wordless, back to the farm. The cheery, noisy bustle of happy families and Christmas music carried down the lane and for a minute Darcy felt suspended between two worlds—the one she had and the one she could have had if she'd stayed.

It was an eerie, unsettling feeling.

They managed to work around each other, but Darcy found the fragile peace they'd forged exhausting. She just wanted to curl up in bed and sleep. Until the day after Christmas, when she could finally go back to Chicago. *Home.*

Or was it?

She missed Chicago, but she'd begun to realize it wasn't quite home. Not the way this place was. Was that because she'd grown up here? Or because she still had some kind of feelings for Mack?

It seemed best to just admit it. That there were clearly lingering feelings, but it was in no way enough to move forward on. If either of them had wanted to. And she did not. There was too much pain in the past that would bleed through to their present.

"It's not enough," she said out loud to the spruce tree in front of her. *There, I said it.* Now all she had to do was hang on to that for the rest of her stay and she could escape mostly unscathed.

Some things just couldn't be fixed, no matter how much you wished otherwise.

The next morning, Darcy disconnected her phone and set it on the table in Java, the coffee shop that had become her closest thing to a home office.

So far, things were moving fairly smoothly in Chicago. Mally had things well in hand, which didn't surprise Darcy. She opened her laptop to check for the file Mally had emailed during their conversation. Perusing her assistant's work, she realized that Mally didn't need Darcy's direction. She knew exactly what she was doing and was in fact fully qualified to take over Darcy's position if she wanted to step down.

She could step right in and Darcy could—what? Leave? And do what? Ross wouldn't give Mally Darcy's job, of course. Not right away. But Ross would move on, fill her position.

Darcy put the thoughts aside. No point in going there when it wasn't going to happen. She'd worked long and hard to get where she was and she wasn't going to throw it all over for—what? Definitely not for something she couldn't even define. That was reckless. And stupid. And so very un-Darcylike.

"Darcy. How are you?"

She looked up at the friendly voice to see Cheryl.

"Hi, Cheryl." She pulled her papers and laptop over so the other woman could sit if she wanted to.

Cheryl hesitated. "Are you sure? I don't want to bother you if you're working."

Darcy closed the laptop and gestured for her to sit down. "I'm completely sure. I could use a break anyway. I'm sorry we haven't been able to get together yet. How are you?"

Cheryl smiled. "Good. Busy. Decided to treat myself to a latte today since we got word that we're being considered as adoptive parents for a teenage mother's baby."

Darcy's heart stuttered. "Wow, Cheryl, that's wonderful. When will you know?"

"Soon. She's about seven months along. She's a good girl, got in a tough situation and wants to give her baby the best life she can. It's not a done deal, but I hope..." She trailed off and took a sip of the latte.

Darcy reached over and touched her hand. "I hope so, too, Cheryl."

"There's something I've been wondering," Cheryl said quietly, her hands closed around her cup. She leveled her gaze at Darcy. "Why did you leave without saying goodbye? And why did you cut off all contact with me?"

Darcy sucked in a breath. There was pain in her old friend's voice, but no censure. She slid her laptop in her bag to give herself a second to regroup. Then she folded her arms on the table and looked right at Cheryl. "I'm not really sure. It hurt too much to be here, and everything was a reminder of what—of what I'd lost. I was just trying to move forward and I know I did a bad job of it." She'd rejected Cheryl's support, everyone's support. How stupid she'd been. "I was just so lost, I guess. In the grief. I'm so sorry I cut you off."

Cheryl nodded. "I figured that was what happened, but I needed to hear it for sure. I would have been there. I wanted to be there, Darce. A lot of people did."

So she was learning. All the bitterness she'd carried like a shield was withering away. She'd erected the shield as a defense to keep herself in, not to protect herself from people who cared. But that was exactly what had ended up happening.

"I wish you'd let me in," Cheryl said quietly now. "And I wish I'd tried harder to reach you. I didn't know what to do and I didn't try as hard as I could have."

Darcy's head came up sharply. "What? No, Cheryl, that's not what happened. You were there. That's all you needed to do, was to *be there*. And you were. I was the one who didn't know how to handle it. Or how to let anyone help me handle it. I just wanted it all to go away."

Cheryl cocked her head. "Did it?"

"No," Darcy admitted now. "Not really. I got good at kind of locking it away. Until I came back here."

A small smile ghosted across Cheryl's mouth. "I bet. There's something I need to tell you."

"What's that?"

"Olivia's middle name is Darcy."

Darcy's breath jammed in her throat. Cheryl couldn't have surprised her more if she'd hit Darcy with a hammer. "You—really? Oh," she said, and the word kind of fell from her lips. "Cheryl—"

"Yes, really." Cheryl's smile was looking decidedly damp around the edges, which was okay because Darcy knew hers was, too. "I just wanted you to know."

The lump in Darcy's throat was almost too big to breathe around. She reached for Cheryl's hand and held on tight, a connection she wished she'd accepted when it was offered all those years ago. "Thank you, Cheryl."

Chapter Thirteen

Mack showed up late at the tree farm. He looked a little ragged, and despite her best intentions to stay away, she went up to him. He gave her a tired smile that didn't reach his eyes. Concerned, she touched his arm. "Are you okay?"

He rubbed his hand over his eyes. "Yeah. No. Rough day."

Which told her nothing, since she could already see that. "We can get by without you tonight if you need to go home, Mack. Don't feel you need to stay."

He dropped his hand. "Thanks, but I need to stay."

Since he wasn't going to confide in her—why would he?—she nodded. "Your call. Let me know if you change your mind, though."

He said nothing as she walked away. Then—

"Darcy."

She stopped and turned. "Yes?"

He drew in a shaky breath. "It was an abuse case. Worst one I've seen yet. Dog beaten within an inch of his life and left out to die in the cold. He was frozen to the ground. I don't know if he'll survive, or if he'll ever be able to go to a new home." His voice was low, and the pain in his words fell heavily on her heart. Horror and anger fired there, too, that someone would treat an animal that way. Any living being.

She walked back toward him. "Oh, Mack. Do they know who did it?"

He shook his head. "No. Not yet. I hope they find the son of a bitch. Because it's more than the dog, Darce. What if this guy's doing this to his family? There's something wrong with a person who can hurt an animal this way."

She gave up and wrapped her arms around him, laid her head on his chest. His jacket was cold under her cheek. He wrapped his around her, too, and they stood there, by the side of his truck, Darcy feeling his warm breath on her hair. This was what they should have had. This was one of those moments that was out of time, from a life she didn't live but could have.

"He's got you," she said finally as she stepped back and looked up to meet his eyes. "And we'll hope the person who did this gets found soon."

"Thanks," he said quietly. "I see a lot in my job. A lot of broken animals, sick ones, too. But almost never something like this. I don't know how he survived as long as he did. I really don't. So I'll cut out early tonight, if it looks like things are under control, to go check on him. Jennifer's with him now."

"It's a Wednesday," Darcy said. "Our slowest day. It'll be fine, whenever you're ready to head out."

They walked to the barn in silence and he gave her hand a quick squeeze before heading the opposite way. Warmth fizzled through her, a little burst of surprise and happiness. He'd never touched her like that in public. She didn't know if anyone had seen.

She kept an eye on him through the evening, and he did leave early. That night, after she'd closed everything down and chatted with her aunt and uncle, she went up to her room and called Mack to check on the dog. She felt a little bit like a teenager as she lay flopped on her back across the bed, knees up. She almost wished for the days when there was a long phone cord to wrap around her finger.

"Hello?"

His voice was just as sexy over the phone as it was in person. Despite the reason for her call, her lady parts gave a little shimmy. She cleared her throat. "Hi. It's Darcy."

He gave what sounded like a pained chuckle. "I know. Everything okay out there?"

"Yeah. I just wanted to see how the dog is. If he's—well, if he's okay."

Mack sighed. "He's not okay, but he's holding. At this point, that's about all I can expect. Still touch-and-go. If he makes it through the night, his chances will be better."

"Poor guy," she said quietly.

"Yeah. I'm going to check him every hour until five, then I'll go home and catch a few hours of sleep while Jenn checks him."

"So you're staying at the clinic?" She knew Jennifer lived above the clinic. Maybe he stayed with her. And it was completely none of her business. Still, an odd twist slipped through her chest.

There was a rustling, as though he was moving around. "Yeah. I keep a cot here. I'll sleep in my office. Grabbed a pillow and blanket from home. I don't have to do it too often."

"That's good," she said.

There was a pause, but it wasn't uncomfortable. They were just quiet. Together.

"Darcy?"

"Yeah?" Why was she whispering?

"Thanks for calling."

"You're welcome."

She disconnected the call and stared up at the dark ceiling, feeling all kinds of fluttery and weird. Truth was, she could have waited until tomorrow to find out about the dog. She'd been concerned, yes, and saddened. But she'd wanted to check on Mack, too, and this had been a convenient excuse.

She rolled over and put the phone on the bedside table. She already missed his voice. Missed him. How sad was that?

"Two weeks until Christmas Eve," Joe announced at breakfast. "This upcoming Saturday will be almost as busy as the day after Thanksgiving. I'm going to meet with you and Mack to discuss a game plan."

Darcy spooned up more oatmeal. She had no idea what her aunt put in it, but it was good. It didn't matter if she didn't need the meeting. Uncle Joe did. "When?"

"Tonight. He'll come to the house when he gets here. We'll have it here, in the kitchen."

"I'll have pie," Marla broke in with a smile.

"Sounds good." If it hadn't been the last season, it would have been a different sort of meeting. Darcy wanted to ask why they'd never branched out into more sales, why they hadn't expanded the tours, why more promotion hadn't been done. Yes, some of that cost money, but they'd have earned it all back and then some. But she wasn't going to ask now. It was too late.

The farm had two weeks left. Then, after the new year, it'd be turned over to Mack and his brother to bulldoze. Appetite gone, she slid her chair back to carry her bowl to the sink. For all Mack still tugged at her heart, he was taking away the one thing that had always been a constant in her life. She needed to remember that.

"I'm so sad this place is closing," one woman said to Darcy later that evening after the meeting with Uncle Joe. "I've come out here since I was a little girl. Now I bring my kids. We look forward to it every year." The kids in question looked to be around five and nine, and happily sucking on the mini–candy canes Darcy had given them from her stash by the register.

"Me, too. We all are. But my aunt and uncle are going to retire. A tree farm is a lot of work." She'd said the same thing many times over the past couple weeks. But now she added, "It's been a wonderful experience, being a part of all these Christmases for all of these years."

The woman handed over the cash for the tree. "So much better than grabbing a tree at a big box store," she agreed. "I wish your aunt and uncle all the best in their retirement. Maybe they'll get lucky and find someone to take it over."

Darcy couldn't bring herself to say it'd been sold and would be parceled off into home lots. "Maybe," she said noncommittally, and smiled as she gave the woman her change.

As she watched them go, Wendy came up to her. "I heard her. Tough, isn't it?"

Darcy sighed. "She's not the only one. I've heard some variation of that several times each week. Some people aren't invested, you know? They'll just get a tree and move on. For others, it's a tradition. I never realized or appreciated how much that matters."

How shameful was that? She'd grown up in a business that catered to people's traditions and she'd still missed the point. Until now.

When it was too late.

Wendy nodded. "It is hard. I've made the same wreaths for a decade for the same people. I know who likes a little more spruce, and who to give the most juniper berries to. Who likes a bigger bow, who prefers flatter. I love to see their faces light up when they come pick them up. It's all part of the package of tradition. I'll miss it." She held out her hands and gave a little laugh. "I won't miss being stabbed fifty times a day by needles, though. Or getting pitch on my clothes."

Darcy smiled and shook her head ruefully. "No. I guess not."

Wendy went outside to check the wreaths and grave blankets—Darcy had sold a few—and it was quiet for a moment in the barn.

Until Mack walked in.

She'd asked him earlier about the dog, whom he'd named Fraser. He'd made it through the night. Mack was cautiously optimistic he'd pull through physically. Emotionally, he couldn't say.

She gave him a little smile. "Hey. Staying warm?"

He walked over and snitched a candy cane from her bowl. “Yep.”

She frowned at him and teased, “Hey. Those are for paying customers only.”

He arched an eyebrow and the look in his eyes went hot. Oh, my. An answering heat tugged low in her belly. “What’s your price?”

Her mind went unhelpfully blank. “Um, well.”

“How about I suggest one?” He moved behind the register and the plastic wrapper of the candy cane crinkled loudly as he put his hands on her shoulders. She licked her lips and could say nothing as he lowered his mouth to hers. “This okay?” he whispered, so close but still too far. In response, she pressed her mouth to his.

“Oops,” Wendy’s voice, and laughter, carried through the little cocoon that had woven around them. “Sorry to interrupt you kids.”

He made a hungry sound in his throat and she pulled away, breathing hard, feeling her face flame. He pressed his lips to her forehead and gave a little chuckle.

“What’s so funny?” she asked, not seeing anything humorous in the way her body revved and ached for his. For him. Plus, Wendy had caught them, even if she had stepped back out of the room.

“I don’t know.” He released her and stepped back. “We’re just like a couple of teenagers sometimes.”

She closed her eyes. “We’re at work. This is a family place. When you and I kiss…” She trailed off.

There was a predatory light in his eyes now. “When you and I kiss, what?” he prompted.

She lifted her chin. “It gets out of control, okay? And this isn’t the place for that.” There. She’d said it.

He caught her chin. "You're right. It's not. Come to my place after we're done here."

He was completely serious. A thrill shivered down her spine. "I don't know."

He leaned down and gave her another quick kiss, and filched another candy cane. "The offer stands," he said, and sauntered out as another family made their way in. He sent her a wink over their heads and Darcy wasn't sure if she wanted to laugh or scream.

Or risk going over to his place. She knew exactly what was being offered there. But she wasn't sure she could spend the time with him and walk away whole when it was time for her to go.

Darcy went home afterward, gave her report to her uncle and headed upstairs to shower. As she stood under the steaming water, she wrestled with herself over Mack's invitation. It wasn't that she didn't want to go. She did. It was that she was afraid she was getting in too deep already.

Maybe it didn't even matter anymore. It was going to hurt when she left either way. This time, though, she could control it. And maybe minimize the regrets.

She turned off the water and toweled off quickly. In the steamy mirror she couldn't see the jagged scar on her abdomen, but she was aware it was there. Mack hadn't been put off by it. In her two sexual encounters in the seven years since her marriage ended, the room had been dark and it had been only one time. Each.

She dressed and dried her hair, combing it into place and securing it with a clip. A little mascara and she was good to go. She took a deep breath. From the time, she knew Uncle Joe and Aunt Marla would have retired to their room. She tossed a few necessities into a small bag she pulled from the closet and headed out before she lost her nerve.

Except Marla was in the kitchen.

Darcy froze, feeling for all the world like a teenager caught sneaking out when Marla's gaze fell to the bag, then up to Darcy's face. She surprised Darcy by laughing.

"Don't look so guilty, honey. No one here is surprised to see this rekindle with you and Mack." Then she sobered. "Is it serious, Darcy?"

Darcy sank down in the chair across from her and let her bag slide to the floor at her feet. "I don't know, Aunt Marla. There are so many reasons why it can't be, and yet…" She left the words unsaid.

"And yet it is anyway," Marla finished softly. Darcy could only nod. "Tell me again why you are fighting this?"

"You mean other than the fact that my life is in Chicago?" Was that her only reason?

Marla nodded. "Where's your heart?" She held up a hand before Darcy could speak, not that she had any answer for that question. "You don't have to tell *me*. You have to be honest with yourself. Go to him. Take some of that pie. And don't come home until morning."

Darcy was pretty sure her face was as red as the flaming red teakettle on the stove. "Yes, ma'am."

Marla drew her in for a hug when they both stood up. "We just want you happy, honey. That's all."

Mack had half expected Darcy not to show up. As it got later, and he looked at the damn clock every two minutes, he tried to convince himself he didn't care.

It wasn't true.

He'd checked on Fraser, who looked to be out of immediate danger but not out of the woods by a long shot. Jenn would check on him a couple more times before morning.

Another look at the clock. The cat sat on the back of the couch and cracked one eye halfway open when Mack leaned forward to check the time on his phone. Again. In case it was different than the time on the wall clock.

It wasn't.

He sat back with a *thump*, which finally dislodged the cat, who stomped over his lap on her way to the floor, where she sauntered off with a baleful flick of her tail.

This was stupid. He stared at the game on TV, not even caring what the score was, and usually he was glued to his alma mater's basketball games.

It didn't mean anything if she didn't come. It meant she didn't come and that was that. He was a big boy and could handle it. He knew she was wavering on the edge and so was he. Just because things had been good in the past didn't mean they'd be good now and all that. After all, they'd never dealt with the things in the past.

He almost had himself convinced she'd done them both a favor by not showing up when there was a knock on the door. He got off the couch as if he were rocket propelled, then forced himself to walk slowly to the door and ignored his stupid racing pulse.

It was Darcy, looking a little nervous as she worried her lower lip between her teeth. A lip he had every intention of kissing in the next few minutes. "Hi," he managed.

"Hi," she said, almost shy. She lifted a container.

"Marla sent pie. She caught me on my way out." Then she blushed.

Mack took the container and Darcy's arm and drew her inside. Something about the way she'd phrased that bothered him. "Caught you?"

The blush deepened as she unzipped her coat. "I went in the kitchen and she was there. I was hoping…" She trailed off and Mack's stomach dropped.

"You were hoping to avoid anyone knowing you are here?"

Her eyes widened. "No. I was hoping to avoid acknowledging what was going to happen when I came here. Even as an adult, it's an awkward thing to share with your relatives."

He pulled her in and kissed her, long and slow and deep. "And what's going to happen now that you're here?"

She plucked the container out of his hand with trembling fingers. "We're going to eat pie, of course."

With a laugh he followed her into the kitchen, watching as she greeted the dogs, who wagged at her as if she were a long-lost friend, before setting the dish down. He came up behind her and slipped his arms around her from behind and buried his face in her hair, like he used to do when they were dating, then married. She wrapped her arms around his and tilted her head so he could kiss her neck.

"Can the pie wait?" he whispered, and pressed against her backside, letting her feel his erection. She made him crazy and hungry and it wasn't for pie. She pressed back, making him groan her name, then turned in his arms.

"Make love to me," she whispered, and he had her

mouth, kissing her as if the whole world depended on it, before she could finish the last word.

They didn't make it very far, just out to the couch by the Christmas tree, and he'd managed to divest them each of their shirts and her bra by the time they got there.

With his hands full of Darcy's glorious breasts, he couldn't get her pants off, but that was okay because right now these needed his attention. He alternated between each sweet nipple with his tongue and his thumb, feeling her rise beneath him as she fumbled for the snap on his jeans. "Mack," she pleaded, and he shifted so she could get where they both wanted her to go.

When she tugged the zipper down and slid her hand into his boxers, closing around him, he groaned. "Darce," he panted.

A wicked smile curved her lips as her hand started to move up and down his length. "What?"

He'd forgotten. "Hell, honey—"

Her hand moved away and she started tugging on his jeans. "Off," she commanded, and he was more than happy to oblige. "Now sit and let me," she whispered. His erection throbbed and jumped and he fisted his hands in her hair as her hot mouth took him to the point the stars exploded around him.

It took him a minute to refocus and when he did, the only thing he saw was Darcy, kneeling between his legs, a smile on her face. Her breasts brushed the inside of his thighs as she leaned forward to get up. He caught her arms. "Your turn."

He had her pants down around her ankles and his mouth on her before she could do much more than gasp. She managed to get one foot out of her jeans and he lifted that leg up on his own thigh so he had better access to her. He wrapped his arm around her rear and held on as she braced her arms on his shoulders. She was so ready for him, so wet and hot, and she tasted like his own personal heaven. Her whimpers turned to cries as she reached her peak, and when she came apart he lowered her into his lap and drove himself home.

"Darcy," he growled, and she wrapped her arms around him, her breasts rubbing on his chest, and all that glorious friction and wetness and heat sent him right over the edge again, and by the contractions around him she was right there with him.

Spent, he lay back on the couch and arranged her next to him. "Wow," she breathed.

He pressed a kiss to her head. "Yeah. Wow." Clearly, they had no problems in the sex department. They never had. But it had never been that—explosive before. And it'd been plenty hot.

Chapter Fourteen

Sometime later, Darcy woke to feel Mack's fingers lightly stroking her flank. She blinked and lifted her head. He chuckled.

"Hey, sleepyhead."

She started to sit up and his hand came up to cup her breast. "Did I doze off?"

"We both did." He pulled her on top of him and took a nipple in his mouth, giving it a slow, lazy circle with his tongue. The tip of his erection pressed against her thigh. She adjusted so she could slide right down and take him all in. His hips rose to meet her and he let out a low groan.

This time they moved slow and sweet, and when the climax broke over her, he followed her over and held her while they floated back down, their bodies still joined. This wasn't sex. This was intimacy. That meant there were feelings involved.

Her stomach growled and he laughed. She lifted her head off his chest and managed a grin. "I guess it's time for pie."

It was a wonderful evening. They ate pie naked and talked—not about the past—and made love one last time, in his bed, before falling asleep. Her last thought, before she drifted off, was this was how it was supposed to be, all those years ago.

In the morning when she woke, Mack was gone, but she smelled coffee. Her clothes were neatly folded on top of the dresser, and her bag was on the floor in front of it. She stretched and couldn't help smiling at the slight soreness. They'd been busy and she'd loved every minute of it.

She got out of bed, took a quick shower, dressed and went in search of the coffee. There was a note on the counter.

Good morning, sexy. Had to go check on Fraser. See you soon.

Not a lot, but it made her smile.

She poured the coffee into the mug he'd left out for her and patted the dogs, who seemed quizzical as to why she was still there. "It's okay, girls. I'll be on my way soon."

That was true in more ways than one, she knew. She'd be out of Holden's Crossing in a couple of weeks. And this would all be a wonderful memory. Much better than her last memories of her and Mack. They both deserved better.

It still meant she had to leave.

* * *

"Did you have a nice time, dear?" was all Marla asked when Darcy walked in the kitchen.

She held out the pie plate, trying not to picture her and Mack eating from it naked, feeding each other straight from the dish. Seemed very inappropriate here in her aunt's kitchen. "Yes."

"That's good." Marla turned to the chicken she was preparing. "Joe's going to go out to the barn tonight with you guys for a bit. Will you help me make sure he stays put and doesn't wander off to overdo it? You know your uncle. He'll want to 'check'—" here she used air quotes "—everything."

Darcy smiled, grateful the topic of her and Mack had been dropped. "Oh, yes. He will. Of course. We'll find a way to keep him busy." Her phone rang. A local number, but not one she knew. "Hello?" she said as she left the kitchen.

"It's Cheryl. Are you free for lunch today? I know it's short notice."

"I'd love that. When and where?"

Cheryl named a new café Darcy wasn't familiar with and they agreed to meet just before noon. That would give Darcy enough time to do some catching up with work emails and then be back in time for the evening's shift at the farm.

"So nice that you and Cheryl are reconnecting," Marla commented when Darcy told her her plans. "I was always so sad you let all those friendships go. Wasn't healthy for you to be so alone."

Darcy stood in the kitchen, her briefcase in one hand and her phone in the other. A stab of regret hit her hard. "I know. I just—couldn't do it. Be reminded." She'd had to bury her son and her marriage, too. It had been too much to hold. She'd been afraid that someone would tell her how Mack was doing and she'd never been sure what she'd been more worried about—that he'd be fine, or that he wouldn't be. Either one made no sense.

Marta laid her knife on the counter and wiped her hands on the dishrag. "I know. But you never allowed yourself to heal, Darcy. You closed it all off, but never let yourself work through the pain. It was too much for one person."

She didn't want to do this. Not now, not ever. "I'm fine."

Marla sighed and nodded. "I won't push. But let yourself feel, Darcy. You deserve to be happy. So does Mack."

Darcy slipped on her boots and walked out into the falling snow. Of course he did. They both did. But the only way she'd ever been able to really make him happy had been in bed. That hadn't changed, clearly, as they were combustible together. But didn't that mean they hadn't changed in other ways—and she hadn't been enough for him then. Why would now be any different?

Darcy pulled into the café's parking lot with five minutes to spare. She was looking forward to this, but a little nervous, too. She didn't want to blow it. She'd love to leave here with her friendship with Cheryl back on track.

Of course, she might have to come back sometimes for visits. But she wouldn't let that stop her. She could probably manage to avoid Mack, if it came to that.

They placed their orders with the cheerful girl behind the counter once Cheryl came in and greeted Darcy with a hug, as if they hadn't been apart for years. They chatted for a few minutes while waiting for their food, and once they were seated Cheryl asked the question that Darcy had been trying to figure out if she was going to bring up. "So. Tell me about Mack. Are you back together with him?"

"Ah." Darcy gave a little laugh and set her sandwich down. She hadn't even managed a bite. "No. Not really."

"*Not really* isn't an answer," Cheryl said slowly. Her expression was sympathetic. "What's going on, Darce? You don't have to tell me," she added quickly. "I understand."

Darcy gave up and filled her in, sparing no details except those of their actual lovemaking and ending with, "I'm not sure what to do. This isn't what I thought."

"No?"

She shook her head. "No. It's different this time. Not like, 'Oh, okay, we shared a past,' but more like—" She stopped, unsure of exactly what she wanted to say. Of what it meant.

"More like you share a future?" Cheryl said softly.

Darcy pressed her free hand to her eyes. "Yes." The word was a whisper.

"Oh, Darcy." There was a world of sympathy in Cheryl's voice. "What are you going to do about it? How can you make it work?"

Darcy thought of her job, her life in Chicago. That promotion was poised to take her to the next level, one she'd been working toward since she got there. How could she give that up? What would she do for income? She had savings, sure, but not enough to make that kind of life change. Did she even want to? "I don't know how. Or if it can be done."

"You love him." It wasn't a question.

"Yes." There was no point in denying it. "But what if it's left over from before, when we were married? How can I know it's real?" It felt real enough. But she just couldn't be sure.

"You know," Cheryl said simply. "You know you do. Trust yourself."

"There's one more thing," Darcy said quietly. "I didn't want to get married the first time. I was pregnant and he insisted. Not in a bad way or a mean way, just he really wanted to be married and start a family and all that. And I wasn't ready. I know it was too late to not be ready, cart before the horse and all that, but, Cheryl, I wasn't happy. I was freaking out and he thought it all was fine and wonderful." Now the tears were flowing, right there in the café, but she couldn't stop the words. "I didn't want any of it. Now, when I can't have any of it, I want it so badly it's tearing me up inside."

"Oh, honey," Cheryl said. She reached over and took Darcy's hand. "Did you tell him? Does he know that's how you felt, either then or now?"

"No," Darcy whispered. "I couldn't. He was so sure. I thought maybe there was something wrong with me, that I didn't want it, you know?" Mack hadn't known. He'd never guessed. Probably foolishly, she'd hid the truth from him instead of giving him the chance to help her. And he would have. He'd have moved heaven and earth for her if she'd allowed him the chance. But she hadn't.

"You need to tell him," Cheryl said firmly. "He needs to know, because that's a big part of why you left, correct? You have to set him straight because that's the only way you can really move on and start over. You both deserve the chance to know the truth and decide where to go from there. Don't make this decision for him, Darcy. It's not fair."

Even though her friend's words were spoken in a gentle tone, they still stung, because Cheryl was right. She'd made that decision for him, for them, once. She couldn't do it again.

She took a deep breath. "Okay. You're right. I will. Soon."

"Saw Darcy's car in front of your place yesterday," Chase said, and Mack rolled his eyes. "I'm not going to tell what I'm supposed to ask you. But I will ask—have you lost your mind?"

"No," Mack said, taking the phone off speaker. This wasn't going to be a good conversation for his staff to overhear. "I haven't." But he had had his mind blown several times last night with the incredible sex he'd shared with Darcy. That wasn't a detail he planned to share with anybody, especially not his big brother.

Chase blew out a breath. "You are a glutton for punishment, little bro. I can't save you from yourself."

"No, you can't," Mack agreed. "So back off and don't try. Let me do this."

"She'll hurt you."

No doubt. "I can handle myself, Chase. I know she's leaving. She does, too. It's fine." But deep down he knew that wasn't quite true. It wasn't that easy. It never had been easy with Darcy, and it hadn't changed. There was too much history between them, history they hadn't touched, to be anything more than temporary. Because then they'd have to really examine the past and frankly, Mack couldn't see that going anywhere good.

He also knew it'd have to be dealt with sometime.

He owed her a lot, and as much as he wanted her in his bed, he didn't want to be destroyed by her all over again.

He hung up after promising he'd meet Chase for lunch tomorrow and exacted a promise from Chase that he'd drop this thing with Mack and Darcy. It had been grudgingly given, and had taken some minor threats, but his brother had agreed.

He didn't want to be reminded it would end again. That she'd leave again. He knew this, felt the time slipping past him like water in a fast-moving stream and every bit as impossible to hold on to. But it made it awfully hard to stay in denial—his current happy place, though he wasn't stupid, knew he'd have to deal with it sooner rather than later—when people kept waving her leaving in front of his face.

Even though their intentions were good.

He couldn't help but hope that somehow they'd be wrong. And that was why this was so dangerous.

On impulse, Darcy stopped at the vet clinic after her lunch with Cheryl. She wanted to check on Fraser and frankly, see Mack. She called him from the parking lot, hoping she'd caught him at a good time.

"Hello?"

"Hi, Mack, it's Darcy."

"I know." There was a smile in his voice and she heard barking in the background. "What's up?"

"Are you on lunch? I was wondering if I could see Fraser. If it's no trouble." She held her breath. If he said no and saw her car out here, she'd feel silly.

"Sure. I don't really take a lunch, but I've got a few minutes. Are you close?"

"Yeah," she said. "I'll be there in a couple minutes."

When she walked in, he was behind the counter. Her heart gave a jump and she felt a bit of a blush as their night together flashed before her eyes. He wore jeans and a light blue button-down and she just wanted to melt into him.

This was bad. Even knowing what she did—that she loved him, still—it scared her.

He gave her a smile and she was glad there was no one in the waiting area to see her blush. "Hey," he said, and came around the end to drop a kiss on her mouth. Brief, but hot and way too public.

"Hey," she said back. She loved the kisses, darn it.

A tall blond-haired woman strode in from the back, looking at some papers in her hand. "Mack, are we out of the purple packages of the dog flea treatments? I thought— Oh," she said as she looked up, drawing out the word, her gaze flying to Mack, then settling on Darcy. "Hello."

"Jenn, this is Darcy. Darcy, Jenn. She's the other vet here. And yes, we're out of that for now. Sherry said they called this morning and are back-ordered. They can deliver Monday, I think it was. The notes are on the desk there."

Jennifer came forward, hand extended, papers tucked under her opposite arm. "Good to know. Thanks. So nice to finally meet you, Darcy. Mack talks about you a lot. Or as much as a guy will talk."

Darcy couldn't help smiling as Mack shifted uncomfortably beside her. "Jennifer."

She looked at him innocently. "What?"

He just shook his head.

"It's nice to meet you, too," Darcy said, and meant it.

Mack rested his hand on the small of her back and

steered her toward a door. “We’re going to check on Fraser.”

“All right. He told you about that?” Jenn said to Darcy, and she nodded. “It was awful. Just—awful.”

“You told her about me?” Darcy asked once he’d closed the door behind them.

His jaw tightened. “She’d heard some rumors. She made some guesses.”

She stopped and laid a hand on his arm. His muscles flexed under her touch and she slid her hand down to grab his hand. “Mack. Is that okay?”

He paused at another set of doors. “Yeah. I just don’t want you to think I go around talking about you. Or us. Or our past. It’s private.”

“I know,” she said. “I wasn’t worried or mad.” But he seemed embarrassed. A light went off in her head. “Did you date her, Mack?”

He pushed open the door. “No. Not really. We’d hang out, I guess you could say, but it was never a date situation.”

She followed him through the doors. The light was dimmer here and the smell was defiantly hospital-like. She swallowed hard. He stopped at a cage where a big dog lay under a blanket.

Even in this light, and when it was clear the animal was asleep, she gasped. She could see the scars and cuts and what looked like burns on his head. Tears burned her throat. “Oh, Mack.”

His face was grim. “You should see the rest of him. He’s in bad shape. He’s going to lose a front leg. I was hopeful, but it’s not going to heal right. But I couldn’t do it at the first round of surgery.”

She touched the cage quietly, not sure if she’d wake

him if she made too much noise. He was sleeping, breathing even. Mack noticed. "You won't wake him. He's under right now. Helps with the healing and the pain."

"Who pays for his care?"

"There's a fund that people donate to for situations like this, when an animal needs serious help or when an owner can't pay the bill. Same with Minnie. We do fund-raisers to keep it going. That will cover some of it."

And he'd pay the rest. He didn't say it, but he didn't have to. She knew. She tucked herself into his side and wrapped her arms around his waist. He slid an arm around her and squeezed. She could hear the steady beat of his heart under her cheek and felt the warmth of his skin through his shirt. "You're a good man, Mack."

He went still. "Anyone would help out, Darce."

No, they wouldn't. But she let it go. And she knew now what she'd given up when she walked away. She'd been so, so shortsighted. Stupid. So she held on while she could, knowing she'd have to leave again, and they stood there, in the dimness, and watched Fraser sleep.

A *clang* from inside the clinic broke the spell. She stepped away and he let her go. She cleared her throat. "Well. I guess I'll let you get back to work. I'd like to see him when he's awake, if you think that'd be okay."

He slid his hands in his pockets and started walking toward the door. "Should be. Starting tomorrow, I'll keep him on pain meds, but not keep him under. I'll let you know."

"Thanks." Darcy hitched the strap of her purse up, but before she could take a step, he turned her to face him and kissed her. A real kiss, hot and deep. He pulled away.

"That's the greeting I wanted to give you," he whispered.

She blinked at him. “Well, hello, then.”

A slow, sexy grin spread over his face. “Hi.”

“Thanks for the coffee this morning, by the way.”

“You’re welcome. Last night was amazing. Hands down the hottest night I’ve ever had.”

Darcy was pretty sure her blush had spread to her toes. She swallowed hard. “Yeah. Me, too.”

He kissed her again, a gentle one this time. “Thank you.”

“For what?”

“For taking the chance to come over. I know it wasn’t easy for you.”

His gaze was gentle and saw too much. She wasn’t ready to face that, to let him all the way in. So she just smiled back and followed him out of the ward and back into the clinic, where an older man sat with a cat carrier. The occupant was yowling with displeasure.

“Ah, Doc,” the man said with a wry smile. “Yoda is awfully excited to see you.” He winked at Darcy and she couldn’t help smiling.

“I can hear that,” Mack said drily. “I’ll be ready for him a few.”

“No problem. We’re early.” The man went back to his magazine.

Mindful of all the ears that were suddenly around them—she’d seen Jenn in one of the offices when they came back out, and voices came from somewhere she couldn’t see—she turned to Mack and gave him a quick smile. “Thanks for letting me see him.”

“You’re welcome. See you at the farm later.”

Darcy nodded and walked out into the bright sun, which reflected off the snow and made her sneeze. He’d always teased her about her sneezing in the sun.

Chapter Fifteen

Jenn was waiting for him when he went back to his office to grab a fast bite to eat. Mr. Franklin was early, and while Mack would get to him as soon as possible, he needed three minutes to wolf down a sandwich.

"Not now," he said as he pulled the sandwich from the bag he'd retrieved from the office fridge. "Please."

Jenn shook her head and ignored him as he'd known she would. "Mack. It's serious, isn't it." Not a question. A statement.

He chewed his ham sandwich, not tasting it. He swallowed and reached for the water bottle on his desk. "Just a lot of history."

She shook her head. "More than that. Lots of people have history. You've got chemistry and clearly the two of you still have feelings for each other."

Now he choked on the bread. "You got all that from a one-minute introduction?"

She looked at him straight on. "Yes. It's obvious, Mack. Not only from seeing you together, but the way you talk about her. Do something about it, even if it's just settle the past so you can move on. You're not over her."

"I'm over her." The denial was quick and sure. He was. He had to be. It'd been a long time. "But what happened was really awful, Jenn. For both of us."

"It must have been," she said quietly. "I know you lost a child."

So she did know. His child and his wife. His family. His future. He wasn't interested in replacing them. He couldn't. He threw the last of the sandwich away, his appetite gone. Jenn was right. Things from the past needed to be settled before Darcy left again.

He finished out the afternoon at the clinic, ran home to take care of his pets and change his clothes as well as grab another bite to eat. He drove out to the tree farm, anticipation building in his chest. Jenn wasn't too far off. He'd fallen right back into this. It had been way too easy.

Sure enough, Darcy was there. She turned when he came in and gave him a smile. Things were growing there, no doubt about it. What they were exactly was a whole nother story.

"Mack." Joe's voice caught him off guard and he looked over to see the older man sitting on a stool behind the register, Marla smiling behind him.

"Joe. Good to see you out here. Feeling better?"

"Yep. I can be out here for a while. Can't do the heavy lifting, though. Doc won't let me, and my girls are keeping a close eye on me." The words were grumpy, but there was a twinkle in his eye.

Marla patted his shoulder. “That’s ’cause we want you around for a good long time, dear.”

Mack chatted with them for a couple more minutes, then excused himself to go outside, pulling his gloves on as he went. He wanted to talk to Darcy, but didn’t think she’d want him hunting her down under the watchful eyes of her aunt and uncle. Not that they weren’t adults. But he knew she was a little nervous about all this, and bringing them into it wasn’t going to help matters.

Marla caught Darcy as she was walking past the register. “As soon as Mack came in, he looked for you.” Marla’s voice was gentle. “As soon as he saw you, he relaxed. Darcy, that man is in love with you. What are you going to do about it?”

Her heart pinged painfully in her chest. What was she going to do? She was going to leave because there was no other option. “It’s been a long time, Aunt Marla. Too long. And we never talked about our past.”

“Then, you need to do that. Work it out and see where it goes.”

Darcy shut her eyes. She already knew she had to do that. Her conversation with Cheryl had driven that home. “I know we need to talk. But there’s nowhere it can really actually go.”

Marla reached for the box of mini–candy canes. She scooped a handful into the bowl that sat next to the register. “That’s just an excuse, honey. You can make this work if you want it to. So I guess the question is, do you want it to?” She held up a hand. “You don’t have to tell me the answer. It’s between you and him. I’m just trying to make sure you don’t make a big mistake you’ll regret.”

Another big mistake, Darcy amended silently. She'd made a lot in a short time, and no matter how casual she'd kept it, or tried to, the fact was it was going to hurt when she left. But was it a mistake to leave? That was what she wasn't sure of.

"I'll keep it in mind," she said finally. "I understand and appreciate your concerns. I really do." She stopped short of saying she knew what she was doing, because frankly, it wasn't true. The whole thing had gotten away from her as soon as Mack kissed her the first time.

Marla gave her a quick one-armed hug, the bowl of candy canes in her other hand. "We love you. We want you to be happy. That's all."

Darcy managed a smile as Marla hurried away to get Uncle Joe back to the house. She put the box of candy away and took a couple of deep breaths, trying to get her bearings. *That man is in love with you.*

She shook off the thrill the words gave her. No, he was in love with who she'd been years ago. He didn't really know her now. She'd changed. *So has he.* They were getting to know each other now, too, but how could it be enough? Could she be sure?

He was buying this farm. Once she left it, there was no coming back to it. Not like this. Marla and Joe were heading to warmer pastures. There'd be nothing here for her, nothing but memories. The physical places would be gone. That meant there was no reason to come back, to be here.

If she walked away from Mack, it would be for good. She wasn't foolish enough to think they could stay in touch. The contact would open old wounds each time. She knew that for a fact. But after she talked to him, would he want to be with her?

* * *

Darcy went out and filled in in one of the warming sheds. She kept the fire going, and the coffee and hot cocoa ready. She answered questions about trees, and directed people to the proper areas for the type of tree they were looking for. At the end of the evening she banked the fire, cleaned the pots, swept the little cabin and set everything up to go the next day.

It was snowing pretty good when she came out, the kind that had been sifting for a few hours and had piled up about three inches. Then Mack came around the curve. He stopped in front of her and cocked an eyebrow. "Want a ride?"

"Sure." She walked around and climbed onto the ATV, and he executed a three-point turn to head back in. The rough ride jostled them together and she couldn't even pretend she didn't mind the press of his arm on hers, even if she couldn't feel his heat.

"Your aunt and uncle went back to the house already," Mack said. "He looked happy, Darce. It was a good thing for him to be out here."

"That's good." She brushed the snow off her arms and looked up as Mack pulled her in for a kiss.

"I've been waiting for that all evening," he said, resting his head on hers. She leaned into him, even knowing it wasn't a good idea. She just couldn't help it.

"Me, too," she admitted.

"Come home with me tonight," he said, then the corner of his mouth quirked up. "I can't cook you dinner, but I can spring for takeout."

She should say no. There were so many reasons why this was a bad idea. Too bad she couldn't remember them at the moment. "That sounds wonderful."

But the truth was she couldn't bring herself to stay away. One more night wouldn't hurt, right? One more night before she had to tell him the truth.

"Excellent. Will you ride with me or bring your car?"

She hesitated, but only for a second. "I'll follow you."

They went up to the house and Darcy went to pack a bag while Mack talked to Marla and Joe. She tried not to dwell on the weirdness of it all, but failed. She threw in a change of clothes and her toothbrush, then sat on the bed and took a deep breath.

Things had shifted. How, exactly, she wasn't sure. But she had the feeling she'd finally reached the point where she couldn't go back.

And that scared her.

The snow had picked up and the plows hadn't been out yet—four inches or so wasn't much in terms of a northern snowfall—but it was coming down pretty hard and the wind had picked up. She kept her eyes on the taillights of Mack's truck and both hands on the wheel.

The trip took twenty minutes instead of the usual ten, but she gave a sigh of relief when they parked at his house.

He got out and came over to her. "We can ride together to the diner," he said.

"Okay." She gathered her keys and purse and left her bag on the backseat.

His truck was warm and smelled spicy, like him. Wonderful, like him. She buckled in and pulled her gloves off. He put it in Reverse and they drove the few minutes to the diner in silence. The lot was nearly empty, and they hurried in, the snow falling fast and hard.

"What can I get you?" The waitress wasn't the same one they'd had before. She was older, but friendly.

"Looking to place a take-out order," Mack said while Darcy scanned the menu quickly.

"Are you closing early?" she asked.

The waitress, whose name tag said Denise, nodded. "Night like this, we don't get much business."

They placed their orders and waited for the food. It didn't take long. Even in the fifteen minutes they'd been inside, there was significant snow to brush off the truck.

He pulled in the driveway next to her car, since with the plows it wasn't a good idea to park in the street. She opened the back door, got a bunch of snow dumped on her for her efforts and pulled out her bag. Inside she stomped off her feet and laughed. "Wow. It's quite a night out there."

He kissed her, a hungry openmouthed kiss that had her dropping her purse on the floor to hang on to him. "Yeah. Hopefully, in here, too."

She gave him a smile, her body tingling all over.

He built a fire and she set the food out on plates she found in the kitchen. They sat on the couch and ate, the dogs looking on hopefully.

"Wow, I didn't realize how hungry I was until I started eating," she admitted, reaching for the ketchup for her fries, a treat she almost never had. And the ones from the Town Line Diner were still the best.

"I knew I was starving," he said cheerfully as he polished off another bite of his burger.

"Your mom not cook for you lately?" she teased, and took another fry. Heaven.

"It's all good," he said. "She brought a potpie the

other day. It's in the freezer. It makes her happy and saves me time. Win-win for both of us."

Darcy didn't remember her own mother. She'd left not long after Darcy was born and died a few years after that. She'd been raised by her father, and her aunt and uncle. She didn't think her mother would have been the type to fill her freezer with leftovers. But Marla was. So she didn't feel left out. But there was the occasional pang of sadness that she'd never know the woman who gave birth to her.

"I can see that" was all she said, and took a bite of her own burger, another splurge. "Mmm. So good. It'll be so hard—" She stopped, as she'd been about to say *when I go back.* But she could tell from the way Mack stiffened that he knew what she hadn't said.

"Hard to what?" His attention was on her now, not on the food.

So he wasn't going to let her off easy. "To go back to Chicago."

"Then, why are you going?"

She stared at her burger, so good a moment ago. "Because it's where my life is." That was true. But she was starting to worry it wasn't where her heart was. How did she reconcile those things? Could she?

"Is it?" he murmured. "Darcy. Why did you leave?"

She froze. "You know why I left. After—after everything it was pretty clear we weren't going to make it." Which was true, and had played a big role in her leaving. But it wasn't all of it.

"You didn't give us a chance," he said quietly, but there was a hard note in his voice.

She slapped her hand on her chest. "I didn't?" Then

she pointed at him. "You didn't, Mack. You went to your family and left me alone."

"You wouldn't let me in," he said. "You wouldn't talk to me or let me see you. You shut me right down."

She shook her head. "That's not what I did, Mack. It's not."

He looked at her over the plates and stood up. He walked away, down the hall, and she heard him open a door. Should she leave? A glance out the patio doors showed the snow still coming down pretty hard.

Mack came back out in the living room with two boxes stacked in his arms. Darcy put her wineglass down and stood. "What are those?" She asked the question, but she knew the answer already. *Mack and Darcy, Christmas* was written on the tops in his mother's neat script.

He set them down carefully and looked at her solemnly. "My mom kept these. She packed it all up. After—after everything." Her heart started up as he opened the first one. "Look."

She set the glass down and the liquid sloshed around because her hand was so unsteady. She came over near him and saw ornaments from their first tree. Her breath caught. "Oh. Oh, Mack."

She touched the glass balls on top. The memories hit her hard, ones she'd tried so hard to keep at bay. She and Mack choosing these ornaments—none of them particularly special or expensive, but they'd had fun picking them out. That trip had, of course, ended in the bedroom and they'd wound up decorating the little tree in their apartment nearly naked, with Mack constantly touching her pregnant belly. She'd been six months along and had enough of a bump she'd just started wearing maternity clothes. He'd loved her pregnant body.

He'd loved her.

She swallowed. "What do you want to do with them?"

"We can put them on the tree," he said quietly. "Or we can divide them up and you can take them home."

Tears blurred her vision. That had been such a magical time. Not that they could ever really re-create it, but maybe they could use it as a new start. For something.

"Let's put them on the tree," she said when she found her voice. "They should be used."

He put on a Christmas station, and the festive tunes helped alleviate the pain she held in her heart. This would be fun, but bittersweet. Because he'd have to take them off the tree. Alone. After she'd gone. Like he'd had to the first time she'd left.

She pushed the thoughts aside and lifted out the first box. These were four chili peppers, because he loved spicy salsa. She couldn't hide her smile. "Remember these?"

He looked up from the other box and smiled. "Yeah."

It was easier than Darcy had thought to go through the boxes. Mack kept her laughing and sometimes he kissed her. But she caught him looking at her in that way, the way he used to, back when he loved her.

Marla's words echoed in her head. *That man's still in love with you.*

It wasn't possible. Was it? How could that be, after all this time?

She picked up a glass ball, hand-painted with the words *Darcy and Mack, First Christmas* with a heart and the year of their marriage. She froze, and held it in her hand. Did this go on the tree? Or did she try to bury it in the box?

She sent a furtive glance at Mack. He was looking in the other box, not paying attention. She could just tuck it in the tree, where it wouldn't be visible. She slipped it around the side and hung it deep in the branches, where it couldn't be seen if you were just walking by or sitting on the couch. When she came back over, he'd returned from the other side of the tree.

Mack's phone rang and he answered it with an apologetic look at Darcy. She smiled at him to let him know it was okay, and wandered over to check out the snow. The wind was howling now, banging against the windows. Peeking out the door, Darcy could see by the porch light the snow was really piling up. Several inches were on the porch, and her car was a white lump. She clearly wasn't leaving tonight. Not that she'd planned to, but it was always in the back of her mind. An escape plan in case things got to be too much, she supposed.

She went back to the tree and sat on the couch, just looking at it, now that it held their ornaments. It made the tree more theirs. She could hear Mack's voice in the kitchen. The dogs snored in front of the fire. The cat was asleep on the couch, too. It was cozy. Comfy. And she was content. This could have been her life. So different from her life in Chicago.

Mack came back and sank down next to her. "Sorry about that. Jenn was checking in. Normally, we don't do that unless there's a patient we are watching closely. In this case, Fraser."

"And how is he?" She didn't protest when Mack took her feet, one at a time, and pulled them into his lap.

"Making progress. He's got a long way to go, but

he is healing. Barring a serious infection, I think he'll make it. And I'm doing my damnedest to keep infection at bay. He doesn't deserve any less."

"I agree," she said softly. "What will you do with him when he's healed?"

He started to massage her foot. She scooted down a little closer. "When he's well enough he'll go to the shelter. They'll take care of him and see if he's adoptable. There's a list of people who will take him, but if any of them are suitable or if he's going to be able to be adopted is another matter."

"If he's not?"

Mack sighed. "I'll take him. Or find a home. He's terrified of people, thinks we're going to hurt him."

Her heart caught. "Of course he is. Poor guy. Any luck on finding who did it?"

"Actually, yeah. There's a promising tip that came in they are checking out. Hopefully, it pans out and they can make an arrest." He tugged her socks off and dropped them on the floor. She flexed her toes and propped a pillow under her head. They said nothing for a long while as they sat there in the light of the tree and listened to the crackling of the fire. Darcy found herself dozing. She couldn't shake the feeling that she was home.

Chapter Sixteen

When Darcy nodded off, Mack just sat and watched her for a few minutes. He wanted her, to be sure. But right now what he felt was more tender. He just wanted to keep her here, in this house he'd bought for them, in the little cocoon they'd spun tonight. Sure, it wasn't reality and he knew that all too well. But damn if she hadn't slipped right back in his life, as if she'd never been gone.

She stirred and he squeezed her leg. "Hey, sexy. Let's go to bed."

She sat up, sleepy eyed, and gave a big yawn. "Okay."

She got her bag and he heard her in the bathroom, as he banked the fire and unplugged the tree. It looked right now, with their ornaments on it. Then he went into the bedroom as she came out of the bathroom. Flannel bottoms, a long-sleeve T-shirt. No bra, as he could see her breasts sway gently as she moved. He gave her a slow smile. "Flannel? I'll keep you warm."

Her nipples peaked against the shirt and he took that as a yes. "Unless you're too tired."

She shook her head and he kissed her, long and slow. He was in no hurry. None at all.

It didn't take long to get her out of her pajamas—she was bare under the bottoms, too—and he took his sweet time with her body before finally sinking into her. They moved slowly and he never took his eyes off hers, even when her eyes blurred and she rose with her climax. When he followed her and collapsed on top of her, he knew this had been different. Something had changed. He rolled off her, then tucked her against him. She kissed his arm and he buried his nose in her hair as he pulled the blankets over them both.

Something had changed, all right. He was afraid he knew exactly what it was.

They made love once more in the night, and in the morning before he went to the clinic. Mack figured it was a great way to spend the night and start the day. In fact, he'd happily do it every day.

The snow hadn't stopped, but it had tapered off. There was a good foot of new stuff on the ground. Their vehicles were just white mounds. He went out through the garage and shoveled quickly—it was light and fluffy, so it didn't take too long to get it out of the way. Then he brushed off both his truck and her car and got in. This was why he had a four-wheel drive truck, he thought as he plowed his way down the street. They were last in line for the plows, being a residential neighborhood, so if he wanted to get anywhere on days like this, it was four-wheel drive and a steady hand.

It took him nearly three times as long as usual to

make the trip to the clinic, but he got there. He figured there'd be plenty of canceled appointments today.

Jenn was in the back when he walked in. "You made it" was her greeting.

"Ha. Yeah. No school today, I take it."

"Not according to the news, no. Do we want to call off any of the techs for today?"

Mack hesitated. "No, but tell them there's no rush. If they can't get here safely, then tell them not to risk it. We'll be okay today."

"All right." She gave him the report on the animals and went to call the techs while he went to see Fraser.

He looked at the big dog in the cage, who looked back at him with pain and fear and suspicion. He talked to him quietly. Jenn had already done the morning's meds. He'd change the bandages later when the meds had a chance to take effect. He made a point of talking to him quietly several times a day to try to win the dog's trust, or at least let him know Mack wasn't going to hurt him. He was very careful to avoid sudden moves and loud noises, as well.

It'd take time.

He went back up front as Jenn was hanging up the phone. "All done. They both said they'll try it but promised not to take chances. I don't think either of them will be here before ten."

"That's fine." He wondered when Darcy would attempt to go home. Would she stay? He hadn't asked her to, but not because he didn't want her to. It was because he wondered what she'd say.

Plus, asking her to stay sounded needy. He wanted her to do it—or not—because it was what she wanted.

Sure enough, almost all of the patients canceled. But

they still had a couple discharges to do today, and those people came in for their animals. Jenn went home for lunch and Mack sat behind the desk, looking over supply orders. This was the techs' job and they did it well, but since they weren't here, he figured he'd do it. When the bell on the door jingled, he looked up.

It was Darcy.

He rose as she plopped a huge bag of cat food on the floor at her feet and slapped one of the tags from his tree on the counter. Then she smiled. "Here you go."

He came around the counter and pulled her into his arms, allowing himself a deep kiss, which she happily gave. "Thanks," he said.

She stood there for a minute in his embrace. "I've got lunch, too. Let me go get it."

"You didn't have to—"

"It's not fancy," she laughed. "Hold on."

He transferred the cat food bag to the room he kept that stuff in. They made regular runs to the shelter and dropped items off. She came back in, a whirl of snow coming with her, and held up a bag. "Where do you want this?"

"Let's go in my office." He led the way and she followed. When she opened the bag, she pulled out sandwiches and fruit and chips. From another bag she took out two pops and offered him one.

"This is a nice surprise," he said. It was. It was wonderful to see her in his space, spending time with him. Just being together.

She gave a little shrug. "I just thought it'd be nice to have lunch together."

They chatted and finished. Then he asked her if she wanted to see Fraser and she said yes.

The dog gave a thump of his tail when he saw them, which was the first time he'd done that. She gave a little inhale. This time there was no blanket covering him. All his cuts and scars were out in the open. "Oh, Mack. Oh. You poor thing," she said to the dog, who shut his eyes and gave a little huff. She turned to look at Mack. "He looks awful."

"He's had it rough," he agreed, and that was an understatement.

"Are the circles cigarette burns?" she asked, and there was anger in her tone.

Fraser whimpered.

"Easy," Mack said to both of them. "Watch your tone. He's really sensitive to tone." No surprise given the abuse.

"Of course. Sorry, puppy," she said to the dog, who relaxed again, apparently not sensing any danger from them. "Heartbreaking. Sickening, too," she said to Mack, who nodded.

"That pretty much sums it up." He just hoped they'd find who did it, and soon. Fraser deserved nothing less than justice and a good home. A lot of animals in his situation got neither.

Darcy left for her aunt and uncle's after promising she'd be careful.

"I drive in snow," she pointed out. "We get our fair share in Chicago."

He knew that. But the accident still lingered with him after all these years. He'd never forget seeing her, banged up and bleeding and broken in that hospital. Ever. It was the moment his heart had stopped. "Just be careful. Please."

She gave him a kiss as Jenn walked into the room. With a quick greeting to Jenn, she was out the door.

"You have to tell her if you haven't already, Mack," Jenn said quietly. "She deserves to know."

"Tell her what?" Mack wasn't keeping anything from her.

"That you love her."

Mack shook his head, but he was afraid Jenn was right. "Jenn."

"Mack. You let her go once. Are you going to do it again? Because she's going to leave without knowing. How can you do that?"

Easy. If she left without knowing how he felt about her, he didn't have to run the risk of having his heart punted back at him. Again. The first time had been hard enough. He wasn't going to risk it again.

So he said nothing and Jenn sighed. "Mack. Don't be stupid."

"I'm not," he said. "I'm smart enough to know how this ends."

"Do you?" Her voice was quiet. "How can you be sure, if you haven't asked her?"

I don't have to ask her. No, she'd left once. That was enough for him. If she wanted to stay, she would. She'd find a way. But he couldn't risk rejection anymore. This time would kill him for sure. He just shook his head.

She sighed but left it alone. For that he was grateful.

Darcy made it to the farm. It took a while, but she got there, snow and all. The main roads had been plowed but were still tricky. The lane to the farm had been plowed as well, but the packed snow was still slippery. Her SUV was designed for this. Probably why she'd bought it, even in Chicago where she relied mostly on mass transit—she'd gotten so used to vehicles with four-wheel drive that it hadn't occurred her not to purchase one for herself.

Ironic that back here was where she needed it the most.

She parked and hauled her bag out of the backseat. Joe had a checkup with the heart doctor today, so her aunt and uncle weren't there. Luckily, they didn't have to drive far for it. She was kind of relieved that she didn't have to come in with her bag after an overnight at Mack's.

But last night had been different.

She was trying not to dwell on it, but something had shifted. What that was, she couldn't quite pinpoint. She did know she needed to tell him what had really happened, and she needed to tell him tonight.

The nerves wouldn't quit.

The farm was open, even in the snow, and Mack was everywhere. Darcy was jumpy and distracted all evening. Marla kept giving her strange looks, but she managed to stave off any questions because they were so busy. She kept rehearsing what she wanted to say in her head. Running through it over and over.

It didn't help.

Finally, when it was all said and done, she went up to Mack, whom she'd been somewhat avoiding all evening, torn up by guilt and nerves. "Do you have time to talk?"

Clearly, he'd picked up on her tension, because he looked at her closely. "Darcy. Are you okay?"

She hesitated, then nodded. "But we need to talk," she repeated.

"All right. Can we go back to my place? I need to check on the dog." He was looking at her with concern.

It took about fifteen more minutes to close down, say good-night and get everyone out the door. Darcy's nerves had taken the form of huge angry butterflies in her stomach. She followed him to the clinic, where she stayed in her car, then to the house. By the time they got there, she was ready to explode. Was it the right thing? To tell him, after all these years? Did it matter anymore?

Yes. It did matter.

"What's going on?" His voice was quiet once they got in the house and the dogs were wagging around them. She saw the concern in his eyes, but he didn't reach for her. Clearly she was giving off stand-back vibes. "Darcy."

She took a deep breath and looked at him, at this man she loved so much. Always had and, she suspected, always would. "I wasn't ready to get married," she blurted. "I wasn't ready for any of it." She put her hands over her eyes. That was the easy part of the truth.

He moved closer but still didn't touch her. "What do you mean?"

It was so important she make him see. "You were so sure. *So sure*, Mack. Of yourself. Of us. Of everything. And I went along because I wanted to be sure, too."

"Why didn't you say anything?" He sounded shocked, as if it had never occurred to him. Maybe he hadn't noticed the change in their relationship after they'd gotten married. She'd tried so hard to hide it.

She laughed, but it was more of a sharp bark than a joyful sound. "I was pregnant, remember? We had to get married. I thought maybe some of your optimism would rub off on me, too."

He just looked at her, his face unreadable. She forged on. "And again, you are so damn sure you know what's best here, too. Buying the farm, making it into something you know I'd never want it to be."

She drew a shaky breath. "I loved you then, Mack. So much. But you didn't feel the same, after all that sureness. You let me walk away."

"Come with me." He didn't offer her a hand, but stalked off down the hall, and she followed after a moment. He went into the room that usually had the door shut. It had some boxes stacked up. Clearly, he used this one for storage. He opened the closet door and took out a couple of boxes labeled—

Oh, God.

Labeled *Baby.*

She wanted to back away, but couldn't make herself move, much less look away. "Where have those been?"

"My mom held on to them."

Of course she had. If she'd held on to the ornaments, she'd hold on to the baby stuff. Behind him, in the closet, she saw a long box. Her heart stopped. "Mack. What is that?"

He moved out of the way, his jaw set, his arms crossed over his chest. "Look. Look at all of it, Darcy."

It was the crib. They'd bought it two days before the accident. Had never had the chance to open it, much less set it up. He didn't move when she pressed her hand to her mouth and laid the other on the box. She couldn't speak.

"Look in the others," he said, his voice rough.

She did. She moved from the crib, her hands shaking so badly she almost couldn't open the next box. But she managed and couldn't stop the tears. More baby stuff. Things they'd picked out together. Blankets, onesies, the changing table. Crib bedding, printed with trains. Not to mention their wedding china and other assorted gifts that he'd never used. All of it, he'd held on to for all these years. She finally sank to the floor and sobbed. All of it, the pain, the regrets, the truth spilled free. And then Mack was behind her, pulling her in and she felt his own tears on her hair. She wrapped around him and burrowed in, the sobs shaking them both. He stroked her hair and finally her sobs reduced to hiccups.

He just rested his head on hers and held on. He didn't ask if she felt better, which was good because no, she didn't. She really, really didn't. She felt worse. She'd assumed he'd gotten rid of all this stuff. Let it all go, the pieces of their old life that never really got started. But here it was, their old life, real and tangible and oh-so-painful.

"Mack," she whispered finally, and he said, "What?"

She pulled away and looked at him. His eyes were red rimmed and her heart ached because she wasn't done delivering the blows. "I'm so sorry. For all of it. For causing the accident—"

"It was an accident, Darce. You didn't do anything."

She lifted her chin. It was time he knew. "I did. I turned left instead of right because I was delaying coming home." At his confused look she faltered, her stomach twisting in knots, then forced herself to continue. He deserved to know the truth. "I can't stress this enough. You were so sure, Mack. So sure of us, of the baby, of our future. Everything. But I wasn't. We got married because of the baby. And then it was gone and with it, the whole reason for our marriage."

He sat there, stunned, and stared at her tearstained face. "What do you mean, the whole reason for our marriage?"

"I wasn't ready to get married, much less be a parent. I thought maybe it'd get better. I knew I was going to have to figure out parenting. But the marriage…" She trailed off, looking lost.

"But the marriage, what?" His voice didn't sound like his own. It seemed to come from far away.

She swallowed hard. "I was going to see if we could separate."

Her words couldn't have hit him any harder if she'd shot him. He gaped at her. "Separate? You wanted to leave me? While you were pregnant?" What the hell was this? How had he missed it?

Her face was ghostly pale and her eyes were full of pain. And guilt. "Yes. I wasn't thinking straight and it was an impulsive decision. So I turned left and—" Her voice caught, and then she continued, "And the other car was there. I didn't see it because I was trying to make the light."

Which had been yellow and she'd broken no laws. The other car had run the light and hit her broadside. He wasn't fully tracking here. She'd wanted to leave him. That had been her plan all along.

Then it hit him. "You had no intention of ever staying," he said slowly. "Not then. Not now. All this was just for, what? Show? Pity?" Anger filled him, white hot, and that was better than the equally strong pain that was trying to push through.

She touched his leg and he pulled back. He couldn't have her touch him. She affected him in ways—still—that wouldn't help him get over her. "Mack. Please understand. We were so young and I was scared and confused." There was a plea in her voice. He couldn't understand.

He looked away. She couldn't have talked to him about it? Was he that awful? Had he been that bad a husband? He didn't remember their marriage being awful. Yeah, she'd been a little nervous, but weren't all new parents-to-be? Clearly, he hadn't known her as well as he'd thought.

"And now?" He waited for her answer, knowing he wouldn't like it.

There was a long pause and he heard her breathing, which seemed so loud in the quiet room, almost as loud as the blood rushing in his ears. "Now I know better," she said finally, her voice sad and low.

He couldn't move. She'd left him once, and it had nearly killed him. And here she was, leaving again, without giving their future any thought.

He hadn't learned. All these years, and he hadn't freaking *learned.*

After a moment, she stood up and left the room without a word. He was pretty sure there was nothing left to say. He heard the front door close shortly after that. It was pretty clear—she'd never felt for him what he had for her. He remembered his mother's words—she hadn't been ready. He'd waved her off, but it seemed she'd been right after all. Darcy would never be ready. Not for what he had to offer.

He got up off the floor and left the room and pulled the door shut, not bothering to close the boxes that were open and all over the floor. They didn't matter now. They were part of a life that hadn't ever really existed, apparently.

What a fool he'd been.

Chapter Seventeen

Mack moved through the next day in a fog. Jenn gave him worried looks, but didn't ask any questions. He didn't go out to the tree farm. He wasn't sure he had it in him to act as if everything was okay. So when his brother showed up to take him to grab a beer, he didn't have the energy to turn him down.

Chase booted up his laptop once they were seated. "Been making plans for the new sub. Want to see?"

He really didn't want to see it, or have anything to do with anything Darcy related right now. Mack stared at the screen when Chase turned it to face him. "This is Darcy's farm?"

"No," Chase said slowly. "Darcy left. This is Joe and Marla's farm. That they are going to sell to us after the holidays. Remember?" He looked at Mack. "Ah, shoot. You did it, didn't you?" He swore.

"Did what?" Mack asked, his gaze back on the computer screen. Chase had left a lot of trees and had carved out large home sites. It'd be gorgeous. Darcy would hate it. The thought gave him no pleasure.

"You fell in love with her."

His gaze flew to Chase's. Actually, it was more accurate to say he'd never stopped loving her. "She's out of here in a few days." She'd been crystal clear there was no hope of a future. She hadn't wanted one back then. She didn't want one now. Then again, he hadn't asked her, had he? He'd been more than happy to have her company, both in bed and out of it. He'd been afraid if he'd asked for more, she'd bolt.

Of course, as it turned out, she was going to bolt anyway, so it wasn't as if he'd saved himself any grief, now, had he?

"Clearly, that doesn't matter." Chase took the laptop back and closed it, slipping it into his bag. "I noticed you didn't deny it. So. What are you going to do now?"

"Nothing. Like I said, she's leaving." The words were bitter in his mouth. He took a deep draw of his beer to try to erase the picture of her tearstained face.

"You're a coward," Chase said flatly.

Mack's head snapped up and he barked out a laugh. "What? Why? You've been telling me all along to let her go. To not get involved." He could not win.

"And you did neither of those things," Chase pointed out. "You *can't* let her go and you *are* involved and not in the kind of way that will allow her to walk away from you without ripping out your heart. So." He leaned on the table, looked Mack in the eye and threw down the gauntlet. "I repeat. You're a coward. What the hell are you gonna do about it?"

Mack opened his mouth, then shut it again. "You're an ass. You know that, right?"

"Yeah, thanks. But it doesn't solve your problem."

Chase was right. Mack didn't really want to acknowledge it to his brother, much less himself. Still, denial hadn't served him so well. He let out a breath. "I'm not being a coward if I let her go. She wants to go. Why would I fight that?"

"But you want her to stay," Chase pointed out quietly. "And you're going to let her walk. That's gonna suck for you. So why not try? At this point, what do you have to lose?"

A lot, actually. If he took a stand and she left anyway, it'd be too damn hard. Chase was right. He wasn't willing to risk the pain. "She's going to leave anyway."

Chase shook his head. "How do you know? Have you given her a reason to stay? No," he answered himself. "You haven't. I don't get this. I understand not wanting to get hurt, because that sucks. But you've got a second chance with the woman you love and you are letting her go without a fight."

Mack hadn't been enough the first time around. Why would now be any different?

He rubbed his hand over his face. "I can't explain it, okay? She hasn't given me any hint she's willing to give it another shot."

"No? She's in your bed, am I right? You rearranged your whole schedule to be out at the farm more. She looks at you the same way you look at her, with that sappiness couples in love have. It's all there, Mack. If I can see it, you damn well should be able to." Chase leaned forward. "Go. Talk to her. Fix this, Mack. For both of your sakes."

Mack just stared at his brother. He wasn't sure what to say. Chase had been so adamant that he stay away from Darcy. Not that Chase had any control over Mack's life, but he knew how bad it had been for Mack in the aftermath and had been trying to keep that from happening again. "Why are you doing this?"

Chase rose from the table and picked up his laptop bag. He put money on the table to cover his bill. "Because you should be happy. Think about it," he said, and slapped Mack on the shoulder as he went past him.

Happy. Darcy had made him very happy, until she'd left him. But he hadn't made her happy. Was Chase right? He hadn't tried hard enough to see what she was feeling? She'd lost so much—they both had. He didn't even care if she was infertile. There were lots of ways to make a family. In retrospect he could see that he hadn't handled everything so well. All he'd wanted was for them to be happy. In trying to give her space, he'd pushed her away.

They'd both made mistakes. But the question was—was it too late to fix them?

Marla called up the stairs, "There's someone here to see you, Darcy."

Darcy frowned at the laundry she was folding. "Be right down," she called back. If it'd been Mack, Marla would have said so. But it wouldn't be him, not now. Not since she'd told him the ugly truth. She'd handled it poorly, to be sure. She'd run when she should have tried to make him see. The look on his face when he'd shut down—she shivered at the memory. He'd never looked at her like that. As if she were a stranger.

She came downstairs and stared at the man in the

kitchen. Chase. She hadn't been expecting to see him, either.

Marla folded the dish towel and hung it over the stove handle. "Nice to see you again, Chase." She gave Darcy's arm a little squeeze as she left the room.

"Um, hi," she managed. Chase had been decidedly unfriendly to her over the past weeks, clear in his anger over her treatment of Mack all those years ago. She'd never blamed him, had accepted it as her due. "Have a seat," she suggested, and started toward the table. Chase shook his head.

"No, thanks. This will only take a minute." He looked at her, and she could see his mistrust of her hadn't abated, but there was resignation in there, too.

"Okay," she said slowly, curiosity almost getting the better of her. But she waited for him to speak.

"Are you leaving?"

"Yes," she said slowly.

He nodded. "Mack is in love with you. Still. Hell, he'd kill me if he knew I was here. I don't know what you feel for him, if you ever loved him. You left him behind awfully easily."

"It wasn't easy," she shot back. It'd been so hard. So. Hard.

"You left him," Chase repeated. "Is this time going to be different?"

"What do you mean?" His words were starting to sink in. *Mack is in love with you.* Chase would probably know that. More than anyone else. He and Mack had always been close. Her heart gave a little flutter.

He looked her in the eye. "You know what I mean," he said quietly.

She lifted her chin. "That's my business."

"I disagree. It's Mack's, too. Fix this for both of you or he'll be the wreck he was when you left the first time."

"Wreck?" He hadn't tried to contact her after the divorce. They'd communicated only through lawyers. It had only served, at the time, to reinforce she'd done the right thing.

"Yes. A wreck. Now you're going to walk away. Again. And leave him to pick up all the pieces. Why?" He turned to go. "I'm not the one who needs the answer to that question. But if you love my brother, you'd better figure this out quick. I don't think you'll get a third chance."

She didn't want a third chance. She hadn't been sure she should have a second chance. She stood for a moment, heard the door close, then an engine start.

Chase was right. She had to do something, something to fix this.

She hurried out into the living room, where her aunt and uncle were watching a Christmas movie on TV and Marla was knitting. "I'm going into town."

Marla frowned in concern. "Now? It's so late."

"I know. It's important." More important than anything.

"All right," Marla said. "Are you going to see Mack?"

She didn't hesitate. "Yes. Yes, I am."

Her aunt and uncle exchanged smiles. "Good for you," Marla said at the same time Joe said, "'Bout time."

Darcy took the stairs two at a time, grabbing her purse and keys and running back down. She didn't know what kind of reception she'd get. Or if he'd even be home, actually.

She knew exactly what she was going to do. It was all so clear, and felt completely right.

* * *

She drove as fast as the conditions allowed, but once she got there and parked in front of the house, she sat for a moment. She'd been trying to rehearse what to say to him, but nothing really stuck. Now, in front of the house, seeing the dark shape of the tree they'd picked out and decorated, her heart squeezed.

She'd been so wrong. So afraid. And she'd taken it out on him.

She got out of her car and took a deep lungful of the cold, still air. All around were houses all decked out for the holidays—trees in windows, twinkle lights on trees and houses and bushes. But this one—this one was dark.

She walked up the drive to the front door and knocked.

After a moment the door opened. Mack stood there, silhouetted against the frame. She linked her fingers to keep them from shaking. "Can I come in?"

In answer, he stepped out of the way and she came in, closing the door behind her. He went and sat back on the couch, arms crossed. So he wasn't going to make this easy. That was okay. It shouldn't be easy.

She perched opposite him on a chair, her back to the tree and the window. She unzipped her coat but didn't take it off. He muted the TV and gave her his full attention, but she couldn't read his expression. She took a deep breath. "Mack. I'm so sorry. I really handled this wrong." It was an understatement and didn't really cover the depth of her feelings.

He leaned forward and rested his forearms on his knees. He was wearing gym shorts despite the cold temperature outside. "Me, too."

That stopped her in her tracks. She frowned. "You? How did you?"

"I didn't pay close enough attention, then or now. You weren't wrong. I was pretty sure of myself. Of us. Too sure." He gave her a pained grin. "I didn't mean to be overbearing, Darce. I just thought—I just thought it'd all kind of work out on its own."

That little flutter of hope grew into a flare. She took a chance and moved next to him on the couch. He didn't move away. "I should have talked to you, told you what I was feeling, instead of hiding it from you. And I should have come home long before now to apologize." Of all of it, that was what she regretted the most. She'd let so much go—not just Mack, but her friendships here in town, and let her aunt and uncle down, too. All because she'd been unable to face her feelings.

"Darce." There was a tenderness in his voice now that made her eyes burn. He ran his hand along her jaw and she turned her face into his palm. The heat of his touch made her want to burrow into him and never let go. Ever. "No apologies. We both screwed up. If I could go back, I'd ask you what was wrong and pester you until you told me. I won't make that mistake again."

She opened her eyes and looked at him, almost afraid to breathe. "What are you saying?"

"I love you. That's what I'm saying. I never stopped. I was going to ask you to stay, but I realized that's not fair. Jenn can run this practice with one hand tied behind her back. I can find a place in Chicago—"

"Wait." Her heart leaped with joy. In all that was one important point she needed to hear again. "You love me? Really?"

"Really." He pressed a kiss to her mouth.

"I love you, too," she whispered, and kissed him back, trying to pour all she felt into the kiss so he would know she'd never leave again. Just as his hands came up under her shirt, she eased back. "But. There's one thing you should know."

He eased back but kept his arms around her. "What's that?"

She took a deep breath. "I'm not leaving. I'm not going back to Chicago. Well, not for long anyway. I'm going to quit my job and move up here to run the tree farm."

Mack stared at her. "You what? You are?"

She nodded. "I haven't been happy there since I left here. Coming back here was coming home. You're here. My roots are here. And I want to make all that work." It had taken losing him—again—to make her see it and realize it.

He sat back. "Wow. Do your aunt and uncle know?"

She shook her head. "No. Not yet. I just decided. I know you guys wanted to buy it—"

"I think your aunt and uncle will be thrilled to sell it to you. I think that's part of why they wouldn't finalize the sale until after you left. They were hoping you'd take it over."

Sneaky of them, too. "I don't know how it all will work. You've got this adorable little house. I'd hate to move you out to the farm—I mean, if this is going anywhere..." She faltered. Was she getting ahead of herself? He pulled her in for another kiss.

"Oh, it's going, sweetheart. As soon as you're willing, I'm ready. I bought this house for us. Well, I found it and before I could tell you about it, the accident happened. But this is where I wanted to raise our son, and any brothers and sisters he might have had. After you left, I went ahead and finalized the sale and remodeled it. It's what saved my sanity."

Darcy stared at him, her jaw on the floor. She hadn't known he'd bought a house at that time. Or even that he'd been looking. She'd shut down at any mention of Mack and her aunt had eventually stopped bringing him up. It had been too hard.

"I— Wow. Mack. You bought this house for us?" Was that why it'd felt so homey to her? Tears gathered in her eyes, but this time they were happy tears. "Then, let's stay here."

"No rush to figure it out," he whispered against her neck. She laid a hand on his chest. He stopped and looked up at her, heat and exasperation in his gaze. "We're still talking?"

She had to laugh. "Yes. We are still talking. There's one more thing."

He sighed and trailed his hand up her side, over her breast, clearly with something else on his mind. "Okay. What's that?"

She hesitated. "I know you wanted more kids. And you know I most likely can't have them."

"Yeah."

"And?" She held her breath.

"And what?" He sat up and looked at her steadily. "There are lots of ways to make a family, Darce. We can adopt. Try fertility treatments if you want. Be foster parents. I'm open to anything."

The love she felt for him rose and nearly swamped her. She couldn't say anything, so she just nodded.

He kissed her again and pulled her in close. "Now are we done talking?" The words were a playful growl.

She laughed and wrapped her arms around his neck as he scooped her off the couch and started toward his bedroom. She pressed her face into his shoulder, closed her eyes and held on tight.

Oh, yes. She was definitely home.

* * * * *

SLOW BURN

JANICE MAYNARD

This book is dedicated to my wonderful readers.

2020 hasn't been the year we all envisioned for ourselves. In the midst of uncertainty and change, I am so grateful for your love of books, and I'm thankful that we take this journey together!

One

Jake Lowell had circumnavigated the globe more than once in the last fifteen years. He'd traveled everywhere and seen everything. Well, except for Antarctica. That continent was still on his bucket list. But of all the cities and countries he'd visited and/or put down temporary roots, the one place he *absolutely* thought he'd never return to again was Falling Brook, New Jersey.

The town's name was idyllic. Jake's memories weren't.

He'd left his birthplace at twenty-two, in the midst of scandal and tragedy. And he'd never returned. Until today. Under duress.

When his stomach growled for the third time, he pulled into a gas station and topped off his tank. The credit-card machine on the pump was out of paper, so he wandered inside for his receipt and to grab a very late lunch. In the end, he decided a candy bar would do for now. He'd always had a sweet tooth.

As he paid for his purchases, the stack of newspapers near the checkout stand caught his eye. The usual suspects were there. *New York Times. Wall Street Journal.* But it was the small-town paper that gave him heartburn. The headline screamed, "Vernon Lowell Lives! Black Crescent Fugitive Located in Remote Caribbean Location."

Jake's stomach churned. The story had broken over a week ago, but the local news outlets were milking it daily. He'd had time to get used to the incredibly upsetting news, but he was still in shock. For a decade and a half, he had known his father was gone. Probably living it up in the bowels of hell. Now the dead had come to life.

When the cashier handed Jake his receipt, she gave him a curious look. Too late for him to realize he should have paid cash. Would the woman see the name on his card and put two and two together? Was she part of the always speedy Falling Brook grapevine?

The name *Lowell* wasn't all that unusual, but here in Falling Brook it was radioactive. Fifteen years ago, Jake's father, Vernon Lowell, had absconded with an enormous sum of money—the assets belonging to some of Falling Brook's most high-profile citizens. A dozen or more elite clients had entrusted Black Crescent Hedge Fund with their fortunes and their futures. Vernon, along with his CFO and best friend, Everett Reardon, were financial wizards who founded Black Crescent and made piles of cash for everyone involved.

But, inexplicably, something went very wrong. The money evaporated. Everett Reardon was killed in a car crash while fleeing police. And Jake's father disappeared from the face of the earth, presumably dead.

The living were left to clean up the mess. And what a mess it was.

Jake drove aimlessly, tormented by the memories even now.

Falling Brook was a small enclave, still not much more than two thousand residents. Jake had done his due diligence before returning home. He'd waded through enough online research to know that not much had changed. This town with the rarefied air and high-dollar real estate still protected the famous from the outside world.

For a few moments, Jake parked across the street from Nikki Reardon's old house—a mansion, really—letting the engine idle. Nikki's world, like Jake's, had been destroyed by her father's misdeeds. Fifteen years ago she'd fled town with her mother, their lives also in ruins.

When Jake allowed himself to remember Nikki, he experienced the strangest mix of yearning and uneasiness. Because his father and Nikki's had been business partners and best friends, it was inevitable that the two families spent a considerable amount of time together while Jake was growing up. But what he remembered most about Nikki was his one wild night with her in Atlantic City five years ago.

Though she was four years younger than he was, she had always been mature for her age. Eons ago, she had been his first real girlfriend. Despite all that, the alluring woman he'd hooked up with in a brief, unexpected, passionate reunion in a casino hotel was far different from the redheaded, pale-skinned beauty he had known as a very young man.

That new Nikki had dazzled him. And scared him.

Muttering under his breath, Jake made himself set the car in motion. Nikki's ghost might still wander the halls of that glamorous house, but she was long gone.

His immediate destination was a small boutique hotel known for its discreetness and luxury. Jake needed the first and would enjoy the second. Though he possessed the skills to live off the land, these days he much preferred a comfortable bed at the end of the day.

Once he checked into his spacious, beautifully appointed room, he sat on the edge of the mattress and stared at his phone. He needed to let Joshua know he had arrived. Joshua Lowell. Jake's brother, his twin. The only characteristics they shared were dirty blond hair, their six-foot-two-inch height and eyes that were a mix of hazel and green.

When Josh had called to say their father had been found, Josh asked Jake to come back to Falling Brook, and had invited him to stay in his home. But the invitation was obviously issued out of duty. The brothers hadn't been face-to-face in fifteen years. Other than the occasional stilted text or email on birthdays and Christmases, or the very recent phone call, they might as well have been strangers.

Over the years, Jake had made himself hard to track down. On purpose. He had cut ties with his siblings, and now he knew little of their personal lives. When he was twenty-two, he hadn't fully understood that family was family, no matter what. He also hadn't realized that being a footloose, rolling stone would eventually lose its appeal.

Now that he was a seasoned man of thirty-seven, he was hoping to mend fences, especially since Joshua wanted Jake's input on the CEO search at Black Crescent. It felt good to be consulted.

Joshua had agreed to meet in the hotel restaurant at seven. The entire place was dark and intimate, but even so, Jake offered the hostess a fifty to seat him and his prospective dinner date at an inconspicuous table. If anyone saw two of the three Lowell brothers together again, tongues would wag.

Jake hated the paparazzi. In the aftermath of his father's disappearance, reporters had hounded every member of the Lowell and Reardon families. In fact, *any* family connected to the scandal was targeted. Jake, a newly minted university grad at the time, had already been planning to backpack around Europe, so he simply moved up his timetable and fled.

Josh—good old dependable Josh—had been left to clean up the mess. The guilt from that one decision hounded Jake to this day. His brother had rebuilt Black Crescent bit by agonizing bit. Joshua had stayed the course, faced the accusers and cooperated with the police. Despite having incredible artistic talent, he had put his dreams on hold and tried to make up for their father's despicable deeds.

Jake had done nothing but pursue a selfish agenda.

Sometimes, the truth sucked.

When Joshua arrived, Jake leaped to his feet and hugged his brother awkwardly, feeling a tsunami of emotional baggage threaten to pull him under. "Long time no see." He winced inwardly at what must have sounded like a flippant comment at best.

The two men sat, and a hovering sommelier poured two glasses of a rare burgundy that Jake remembered his brother enjoying. Although, who knew? Fifteen years was a long time. Tastes changed.

Josh downed half the glass, leaned back in his chair and managed a small smile. It seemed genuine enough. "You look good, Jake."

"So do you."

A few seconds of silence ticked by.

"This is weird." Joshua raked a hand through his hair. He wore an expensive sport coat, dress pants and a crimson necktie. Jake, in jeans and a rugby shirt, felt scruffy in comparison. But that had always been the difference between them. Josh dressed the part of a wealthy man. Jake preferred to be unfettered by society's dictates.

He straightened his spine as tension tightened his jaw. "Here's the thing," he said abruptly. "I might as well get this off my chest. I'm sorry, Josh. I'm sorry Dad screwed us over, and I'm sorry I let you do the heavy lifting. I abandoned you. But I'm here now. For what it's worth."

His brother's smile was strained. Born first by three minutes, Josh had often taken the role of "older" brother seriously. He sighed, the sound a mix of resignation and something else. "I quit being mad at you a long time ago, Jake. We all choose our own path in life. Nobody made me stay and sort through Dad's screwups."

"But we both thought he was dead." It was true. Their mother, Eve, had hired private detectives fifteen years ago. The feds had searched for months. No sign of Vernon Lowell anywhere.

Joshua's gaze was bleak. "It would have been easier if he *was* dead, wouldn't it?"

The harsh truth hung between them. Jake's stomach clenched. Authorities had recently located Vernon Lowell on a remote Bahamian island and extradited him to the United States. Currently, the patriarch was languishing in federal custody. And he wanted to see his two oldest sons.

Oliver, their younger brother, had made the pilgrimage recently. It hadn't gone well.

"We have to go, don't we?" Jake said.

Josh shrugged. "He can't make us."

"On the other hand, telling him to go to hell might give us closure."

His brother's lips twitched. "You have a valid point."

"I guess these last six months haven't been easy for you after that damn reporter wrote an anniversary piece about the Black Crescent debacle. I didn't see it until recently."

Joshua's smile broadened. "Actually, I have no complaints. I'm now *engaged* to that damn reporter."

Jake's jaw dropped. "Seriously? Why didn't you tell me that when you called?"

"You and I hadn't spoken in forever. I wanted to give you the news in person. We're planning a wedding very soon. Sophie is great. You'll like her. And you might as well know, she's the one who encouraged me to resurrect my art career. That's why I'm giving up the helm of Black Crescent."

"That explains the CEO search. I was wondering why now." If anybody deserved to follow his dreams, it was Josh. "I'm happy for you. What will happen to the company, though?"

Joshua didn't answer immediately, because a waiter dropped off their appetizers. A few moments later, Josh drummed his fingers on the table, his unease palpable. "You've played the part of a dilettante well over the years. No one realized you were a financial wunderkind." Joshua's smile was wry.

Jake tried not to squirm. "Why would you say that?"

"I've been doing some digging, baby brother. You're an uncannily successful day trader. Probably richer than I am. At the risk of insulting you, I'd say you've inherited some of Dad's business savvy. But not his morals," Josh said hastily.

Jake told himself not to overreact. "I've had some success," he said mildly. "And I'm *not* your baby brother."

Joshua stared at him, gaze clear, jaw firm. "I want you to take over Black Crescent."

What? "Oh, no," Jake said. "Oh, *hell* no." His hand fisted on the table. "Surely, you have other possibilities."

"We do, actually. I've been interviewing candidates for some time now. But I don't know that any of them are exactly right."

"Well, you're dead *wrong* if you think I'm the man."

"Maybe." Joshua's expression was hard to read.

"What about Oliver? I'm guessing he doesn't want to give up his photography?" The youngest Lowell brother had been affected deeply by their father's betrayal, perhaps even more than Josh and Jake. His anger and despair had led him into addiction. Fortunately, he'd been clean for a very long time now.

"Oliver is finally in a good place. Finding out Dad is alive has been hard for him. He's dealing with a lot of the old anger. But he's handling it well."

Eventually, the meal came to an end and Joshua insisted on picking up the tab. A nice gesture, but unnecessary. Awkwardness returned.

Joshua frowned as he slid his credit card back into his billfold. "I need to talk to you about something important," he said. "Something I didn't want to say over the phone. But not here."

"More important than the fact our father has returned from the dead?"

Jake expected at least a smile for his snarky question. But Joshua was serious. "Perhaps. How 'bout we walk while we talk?"

With his mind spinning, Jake followed his brother through the restaurant and outside onto the sidewalk. The air was crisp, though not unpleasant. It was early November. A few businesses had already begun to decorate for the holidays, getting a jump on the busiest season of the year.

For fifteen Decembers, Christmas had been a painful season for Jake, presumably for the rest of his family, too. It was a reminder of all he had lost. The memories of happy times with the Lowell family of five gathered around the tree had faded beyond repair. In the golden years of Jake's childhood, there had been spectacular gifts: ponies, guitars, racing bikes. Everything a kid could want.

And then it was all gone. Even worse, other families, innocent families, had been hurt. Jake and his siblings and his mother had been innocent, too, but no one had wanted to believe that. They were vilified, scorned. Hated.

Jake hunched his shoulders in his jacket and matched his brother's stride as they set off down the street. He didn't want to think about the bad times, but the memories clung to him like cobwebs. There was no peace to be had in Falling Brook.

Even so, it felt good to get some exercise. For three blocks, Joshua didn't say a word. Jake tried to wait him out, but his patience evaporated quickly. "Why are you being so mysterious?"

Joshua halted suddenly, beneath the soft illumination of a streetlight. "I don't know how to tell you this."

"What? Am I dying?"

"This isn't funny."

"How am I supposed to know that? You haven't said anything yet."

Josh leaned against the light pole, his features betraying tension and exhaustion. For a man in love, he didn't look all that carefree.

He shrugged. "When that article came out back in the spring, the story omitted one very big bombshell."

"Oh?" Jake shoved his hands in his pockets, trying not to react to the gravity in his brother's voice.

"Sophie had DNA evidence proving that I had fathered a child."

"Hell, Joshua. Why didn't you tell me?"

"At first, she wouldn't reveal her source, but when she and I got closer, she finally admitted that Zane Patterson had given her the DNA analysis."

Jake was more than shocked—he was suspicious. "Zane Patterson from prep school? He was a year behind Oliver, right? What would he have to do with any of this?"

"Zane received the report from an anonymous source. He was still angry about everything his family lost when Dad disappeared with the money. So Zane saw this as a chance to stick it to me and Black Crescent. Only Sophie decided not to include Zane's info in the article."

"But surely, you've had time to prove it's a hoax. That's been, what? Six months ago? It's bogus, right?"

Joshua shook his head slowly, his jaw tight. "The report wasn't fabricated. It was the real deal. Somewhere out there is a four-year-old girl who shares my DNA. So I discreetly began investigating any woman from my past who might have matched the timing of this pregnancy. The list wasn't that big. I came up with nothing."

"So it *is* a fake report then." Jake was starting to feel as if he had walked into an alternate universe. Joshua wasn't making sense.

His twin straightened, giving Jake a look that made his stomach clench and his skin crawl with an atavistic recognition of danger.

Joshua's expression finally softened, revealing the oddest mix of sympathy and determination. "The report is legit, Jake. But I'm not the kid's father. You are."

Nikki Reardon glanced at her watch. In half an hour she would have to pick up her daughter, Emma, from

Mom's Day Out at a local church in their tiny town of Poplar Ridge, New Jersey. Emma loved her twice-a-week preschool and had made several sweet friends.

The classes had also given Nikki some valuable alone time. Between her job as assistant manager at the diner four days a week, caring for her daughter and dealing with her mother's needs, it was hard not to feel stretched thin. When Nikki worked the overnight shift, her mother came and stayed.

It wasn't the best arrangement in the world, but it sufficed for now. Sometimes Nikki felt guilty about using her mother for a babysitter so much of the time, but she also believed that being with Emma gave her mom a healthy focus in a life that was empty.

Nikki's attention returned to her iPad, where she was reading a story that brought up too many bad memories. A few days ago she'd discovered that Vernon Lowell wasn't dead. Today's front-page article claimed he'd been found hiding out in the Bahamas. After a speedy extradition, Vernon now waited in federal custody for his trial.

She wanted to talk to him. He was the only person who knew the truth. Vernon and her father, Everett, had been best friends and business partners. But her father was dead. She had seen the body, suffered through the funeral. The world thought Vernon was dead, as well. But now he was back.

Thinking about the Black Crescent scandal inevitably made her think of Jake. Beautiful, stubborn, wandering Jake. Her first boyfriend. She understood why he left. Reporters had made his life miserable. She had only seen him once in the intervening years.

It had been both the best and worst night of her life.

A loud knock at the door demanded her attention.

Sometimes the UPS guy did that. But this knock sounded more peremptory than a package delivery.

Cautiously, she peered through a crack in the inexpensive drapes. *Dear God.* It was Jake. In the flesh. Why was he here? His family still lived in Falling Brook, but that was over an hour away. Why had he come? Her secret threatened to choke her with anxiety.

She opened the door slowly, trying to project mild curiosity even though her heart nearly beat out of her chest. "Jake," she said. "What a surprise."

His greenish-hazel eyes bored into her. "Is it true?"

Her brain processed a million reasons why he might be on her doorstep. "Is what true? Why don't you come in and have something to drink?"

As she stepped back and opened the door wider, Jake entered her small living room and paced, his furious gaze cataloging and dismissing the contents of her modest home. "I want to know why you sent Zane Patterson anonymous information claiming Joshua was the father of your baby."

All the blood drained from her head, and she forgot about offering Jake a cup of coffee. She sat down hard on the sofa. "My baby?" She hated the quavering tone in her voice. She had done nothing wrong.

"Don't give me that." Jake shook his head, scowling. "I know it's true. What did you hope to gain by blackmailing my brother?"

Nikki straightened her spine and glared. "If you want to sit down and discuss this civilly, I'll listen. But you're way off base. I've never had any contact with your brother or Zane, not since we were teenagers. I don't know what you're talking about."

At last, Jake plopped down in a chair and drummed his fingers on the arms. His whole body radiated strong emotion. As she tried to catch her breath, she absorbed the look of him. He was a beautiful man. Always had been. Today he wore a scuffed leather bomber jacket and jeans so old and faded they molded to his legs, and other parts, as if they had been made just for him. His soft cotton button-down shirt was pale green, the color of vintage glass bottles. Deck shoes with no socks exposed his tanned ankles.

He was tanned all over, in fact. The man had spent his life outdoors. Or much of it. His streaky blond hair needed a cut. In the summers when they were kids, the sun would bleach Jake's hair gold. Now it was more subdued.

She glanced at her watch, trying not to panic. Did he know the truth about Emma, or was he fishing? She wouldn't lie about her daughter, but she wasn't going to volunteer any unnecessary information at this point. "I have an errand to run," she said calmly. "This will have to wait."

His jaw tightened. "Then I'm coming with you."

Her stomach clenched. Having him close made her senses go haywire. Why was it so hard to be sensible when Jake Lowell was around? "It won't take me long. I could meet you for dinner later."

"I'm not letting you out of my sight, Nikki Reardon." His gaze was grim. Implacable. As if he was the hunter, and she was the prey.

"Fine," she said. She stood and retrieved her purse and keys. She had no idea what he would think when he saw Emma, but she would put one foot in front of the other until she figured it out. Her mother had pressed her to contact Jake and ask for child support, but Nikki had been too proud to beg. When Jake walked away from her five years ago without a word, she had known he was still running from his past. And that he was never going to be the man she needed him to be.

Outside, she grimaced when she saw his fancy black sports car, a rental no doubt, parked at the curb. The sleek vehicle looked wildly out of place on this middle-class street. Her own mode of transportation was a fifteen-year-old compact model with a car seat in the back.

She unlocked her car and watched as Jake folded his body into the passenger seat. He was a couple of inches over six feet, so he was not going to be entirely comfortable.

Good.

"Where are we going?" he asked.

"I have to pick up Emma from preschool."

"Emma?" The word sounded strangled.

She shot him a sideways glance, noting his sudden pallor.

"Yes. Emma. My daughter."

Two

Jake watched through the windshield as the gorgeous redhead and the bouncy little girl walked toward the car. He felt queasy. A host of other emotions swirled in his chest.

The brief ride from Nikki's house to this pleasantly ordinary brick building had been silent. Nikki's knuckles were white as she gripped the steering wheel.

Now he tried to study her dispassionately. In the midst of his clinical visual survey, the memories hit him hard and fast. Nikki naked. Sprawled across his hotel bed. Smiling. Warm and sated from their lovemaking. Her pale, pale skin like porcelain.

It had been one night. One extraordinary night almost five years ago. And now he was a father? Why hadn't Nikki told him? Or was this all just a misunderstanding? Even as he tried to rationalize her behavior, he couldn't get past the anonymous emails that were eventually passed on to his brother.

Despite Joshua's insistence that a baby existed with Lowell blood, Jake was by nature a suspicious man. Being betrayed by his father had taught him not to trust easily.

The rear car door opened, and Nikki helped the child into her car seat. Though Emma had been chattering excitedly, she fell silent when she spotted the stranger up front. Her eyes were green. That meant nothing. The color could have been from her mother as easily as from Jake's DNA. But the girl's blond hair was nothing like her mother's.

Jake wanted to say hello. The word stuck in his throat. Instead, he gave the kid a quick nod and turned back toward the front. He wanted to stare at Emma. To examine her from head to toe. To see if there was anything of him in her. But he didn't want to make the child uncomfortable. No point in both of them feeling weird.

Back at Nikki's house, Nikki lowered her voice as she parked the car. "I usually give her a snack, and then she'll go play in her room for half an hour or so. You and I can talk then."

Jake nodded brusquely, not entirely sure what he wanted to say. Crazy revelations were popping up in his life like rodents in an upsetting game of whack-a-mole. His father was alive. Nikki had a kid. The child was Jake's? It was too much to process.

He shoved his hands in his pockets as the unlikely threesome walked across the lawn into the house. Once inside, Jake escaped into the small living room with a muttered excuse. Even at this distance, he could hear mother and daughter in the kitchen debriefing Emma's day at school. When Nikki finally returned, she looked tired, but resigned.

She took a chair across from him and gracefully curled

her legs beneath her. Her steady green-eyed gaze and long, wavy red hair made him clench his fists as an unwelcome wave of desire swept through him. He remembered burying his face in that hair. Inhaling the scent of her shampoo. Feeling for a brief moment in time as if everything in his world had finally popped into sharp focus.

In his early twenties, he had loved her with a ferocity that was equal parts lust and devotion. He'd been waiting for her to grow up. His nightly fantasies had featured Nikki, and no one else. But just when his desire had almost come to fruition, both of their worlds had been torn apart.

Running into each other in Atlantic City a decade later had been a shock to his system. The very best kind of shock. Even now, his hands tingled with the need to touch her. But, in the end, he had been wary of the new Nikki, unable to handle how *together* she was, how grown up. She hadn't been a frightened teenager anymore. She had moved on. And she knew exactly who she was.

The new Nikki had been even more appealing than the girl he remembered. But the changes spooked him, as did the depth of his feelings, so he ran. The same way he had so many times before.

He cleared his throat. "I'll ask you again. Is it true? Is Emma my daughter?"

Nikki paled, making her skin almost translucent. "You weren't making sense earlier. I don't know why you're here. What does your brother have to do with this?"

"Don't be coy, Nikki. You sent Zane DNA results and notes that threatened Joshua. But Josh eventually concluded that he couldn't possibly have fathered a four-year-old child. So that left me. His twin. Why did you try to blackmail my brother and not me?"

As he watched, Nikki's lower lip trembled, and her

eyes glistened with tears. "I have no clue what you're talking about, and I don't appreciate your accusations. If that's all you have to say, Jake Lowell, you can get the hell out of my house."

A tiny voice intruded. "You told me not to say that word, Mommy."

Both adults jumped. Emma stood in the doorway, visibly distressed.

Nikki swiped a hand across her face, drying her eyes. "You're right, baby. Mommy goofed. I'm sorry."

Jake left his seat and crouched beside Nikki's daughter. "Hi, Emma. I'm Jake…a friend of your mother's."

Emma stared at him solemnly, her gaze filled with suspicion. "Then why did she tell you to leave?"

The irony didn't escape Jake. Were all four-year-old kids this aware of social cues? He cleared his throat. "We were having an argu—"

Nikki stood abruptly, halting his explanation with a chopping motion of her hand. She ruffled her daughter's hair. "Em, would you like to watch a *Peppa Pig* episode on my phone?" Nikki gave him an exasperated look. "I don't allow her much screen time, but it would give us a chance to finish this conversation."

Emma's face lit up. She smiled at Jake, distracted by the promised treat. "They're called 'Peppasodes.' Get it?"

Jake grinned for the first time, his mood lifting despite the situation. The child's charm and obvious intelligence delighted him. "I get it, munchkin."

He stood and gave Nikki a measured glance, trying not to notice the way her soft, fuzzy sweater delineated her breasts. He wanted to hold her, to relearn the contours of her body. The sexual awareness threatened his focus. "I have another idea. If you can get a babysitter on such short notice, I'll take you to dinner."

Now Nikki's face showed no emotion at all. Her gaze was level, and her arms wrapped around her waist in a defensive posture. After a couple of heartbeats, she took her phone from her pocket, tapped a few icons and handed it to Emma. "You may take it to your room, sweetheart. Fifteen minutes. No more. I set the timer."

When Emma was gone, Nikki sighed. "The truth is, Jake, I can't afford a babysitter right now. The holidays are coming, and I'm saving every penny for Emma's gifts from me and from Santa. Can't we just wrap this up? I honestly have no clue what you're talking about. I've never been in contact with your brother about *anything*."

Jake pulled a sheet of paper from his pocket. Earlier, Joshua had printed out one of the incriminating emails. "So you deny sending this?"

Their fingers brushed when Nikki took the note. She glanced down, read the contents and moaned. If she had been pale before, she was ashen now. "Oh, my God."

Her obvious distress convinced Jake she was telling the truth. But that only deepened the mystery. "Let me pay for a sitter," he said urgently. "We need to clear the air." He pulled a business card from his wallet and gave it to her. "This is my cell number. I'll grab coffee somewhere and return a few phone calls. Let me know when you work it out. I can pick you up at seven."

She shook her head vehemently. "No. If we do this, I want to be back home to do the bed-and-bath routine with Emma. We would have to eat early. Five thirty."

He blinked. "Ah. Okay. Call me."

That beautiful bottom lip trembled again. "I'll see what I can do," she whispered.

He was incredulous to realize that he was aroused, hard and ready. It had been five years since he had made love to her, but it might as well have been yesterday. It was difficult to cast Nikki as the villain when he wanted her even now. Was he so besotted that he could ignore her lies?

Her anguish touched him despite the turmoil she had caused his family. He brushed her soft cheek with a single fingertip. “It’s not the end of the world, Nik. But I do want answers. Don’t try an end run. I’m not leaving town until you and I get a few things straight.”

Once Jake said goodbye, Nikki made the necessary phone call and fretted. She knew a threat when she heard one. Even if it *was* couched in seeming cordiality. Jake was not a man who bluffed.

She remembered watching him play poker with other guys in high school—*after* class mostly, but whenever they could elude faculty detection. All the parties involved had been highly privileged teenagers with virtually unlimited resources.

Jake had taken bragging rights as top dog, and he loved it. People *thought* he bluffed…and would bet against him time and again. But his lazy, chilled attitude concealed an amazing skill with numbers.

Was that why he had been in Atlantic City? To gamble? If so, he would have won. She knew that much.

But gambling had been the last thing on his mind the night the two of them had gone up to his hotel room. When a hot shiver worked its way down her spine, she knew she was in trouble.

Reluctantly, she dragged her attention back to the present. Emma was bouncing with glee that her favorite babysitter was coming over. Nella was a college-aged woman who lived just down the street. She had five brothers and sisters and was no stranger to caring for little ones. Nella adored Emma and the feeling was mutual, so Nikki was free to have dinner with Jake.

Despite the gravity of the situation, she couldn't squelch a little flutter of anticipation. As she showered and changed, she vacillated between fear and excitement.

She had known this day would come eventually. But not like this.

Since giving birth four years ago, her social life had been mostly nonexistent. The only remotely suitable outfit she owned for having dinner with Jake Lowell was a sophisticated black pantsuit that she paired with an emerald silk chemise and spiky black heels. She left her hair down and added a spritz of her favorite perfume. She probably shouldn't be dressing up at all, but maybe deep down inside she wanted Jake to see what he was missing.

The scent was for *her* benefit, not his. She needed a confidence boost.

He arrived at five thirty on the dot. Nikki didn't give him a chance to come inside. She hurried out to the car, almost tripping on the sidewalk in her haste to keep him from seeing Emma again. She would protect her baby girl at all costs.

Jake hopped out and opened the passenger door of the sinfully luxurious roadster he was driving while in New Jersey. When he helped Nikki in with a hand under her elbow, she was wrapped in the smells of soft leather and warm male.

She was glad when Jake closed the door and went around to the driver's side, though it wasn't much of a reprieve. The car's interior was intimate. With every breath, she inhaled him. Not that his aftershave was overpowering. In fact, she wasn't sure he wore any. She might only be smelling soap on his skin.

Either way, she was susceptible to his considerable appeal.

"Why did you change clothes?" she asked. He now wore a conservative dark suit, though most restaurants seldom enforced any kind of dress code these days.

He shot her a cautious grin. "Because I knew you would look nice. You always did enjoy sprucing up for an evening out."

What could she say? He was right about the old Nicole Reardon. That teenager had owned two closets full of designer clothes. Nikki had lived in a pampered world that seemed a lifetime away.

Intentionally, she drew his attention to the night that had gone so well and ended so badly. "Things are different now. In Atlantic City I was wearing a cocktail waitress uniform when I ran in to you. Not exactly haute couture."

He shrugged, his sideways glance filled with dark male interest. "I can't say that I noticed. I was more interested in getting you out of *whatever* you were wearing."

That shut her up. He was right. They had both been intent on one thing. The results had been spectacular.

Tonight, Jake had made reservations at an upscale seafood restaurant with white linen tablecloths and plenty of candlelight. The ambiance made Nikki the slightest bit uncomfortable. She and Jake weren't a typical couple. And they certainly weren't celebrating anything.

Once they were seated at a table overlooking a small manmade lake, Jake gave her his undivided attention. But his face was hard to read. "Thank you for coming. I know this was last-minute."

"My sitter was available. It worked out."

"Good."

The conversation was painfully stilted. Memories of

the last time they had been together swirled beneath the words. "Do you think about Atlantic City?" she asked quietly.

His jaw tightened. "Don't be coy, Nik. Of course I do. We hadn't seen each other in a decade, and there you were. Wearing one of those provocative outfits. Your legs were about a million miles long."

The flash of heat in his eyes told her he remembered *everything*. She hadn't been sure until right now. For her, the night had been a watershed moment, the culmination of all her girlish fantasies. But Jake was a man of the world. She had assumed their tryst was another notch on his bedpost.

"It seemed to embarrass you," she said hesitantly. "That I was working as a waitress in a casino. You acted very odd at first."

He nodded slowly. "I was startled. I'll admit it. I went to Atlantic City for some fun. Just a quick flight in and out. Seeing you was a punch to the gut. The girl I used to date was wealthy and pampered. I was aware that you and your mom lost everything. But witnessing the personal cost of your father's deceit stunned me. I didn't know what to do with that information or how to relate to you."

Nikki shrugged and snagged a fat boiled shrimp from the appetizer plate. "You don't have to feel sorry for me, Jake. No one *wants* to be poor, but the rapid fall in my social position taught me a lot."

"Like what?"

He seemed genuinely interested.

"Well…" She paused, thinking back. "I learned there are many very nice people in the world. And a few jerks, of course. I learned how hard a person has to work to earn five hundred dollars a week after taxes. I learned how scary it is not to have a safety net."

His gaze darkened. "Those are some damn serious lessons."

"Maybe. But I also learned my own resilience. I discovered that although I had been a pampered princess, it felt good to be responsible for myself… To know I was stronger than I knew."

Their meals arrived, momentarily interrupting her self-analysis. Despite the gravity of this encounter with Jake, she spared a moment to appreciate the quality of the food. Her scallops were plump and perfectly grilled. She enjoyed every bite. Jake would probably be astounded if he knew how many nights she shared boxed macaroni and cheese with her daughter.

Over coffee and dessert, Jake pressed for more. "When I showed you that email, you were clearly shocked. No one is that good an actress. So, if you didn't send it, who did?"

Nikki's cheeks heated with embarrassment. "Possibly my mother."

"Why?"

"About a year ago I lost my job. I was unemployed for almost ten weeks. Money was tight. Mom kept pressing me to ask for child support from Emma's father. I put her off and put her off, but she wouldn't let it go. Finally, after she had badgered me incessantly, I told her that Joshua was the father. Your brother. That he and I weren't ever a couple, but we had been intimate for a brief period. I said he didn't know about the baby. I thought that would be the end of it."

"But it wasn't."

"Obviously not."

"Why would you lie to her?"

"Because I didn't want her to know the truth."

"And that was?"

Nikki inhaled sharply. "That *you* are Emma's father."

* * *

Jake had heard the truth from his own brother. He'd had a little time to get used to the idea. But in this moment, he realized it had all seemed like a remarkable fiction until Nikki told him straight out. He felt sick and angry and everything in between.

"Damn you, Nikki. How could you not tell me I had a child?"

If he'd been expecting her to look guilty, he was way off base.

His dinner companion stared at him with cool hauteur reminiscent of the old society princess she'd been. "A little while ago you told me you still remember our night in Atlantic City. If you'll recall, you disappeared afterward. I woke up in your hotel room *alone*. The only thing missing from that scenario was a stack of hundreds on the nightstand to make me feel like a hooker you hired for the evening."

"I had a very early flight," he muttered, guilt making him ashamed. He'd acknowledged to himself at the time that he was behaving badly, but he hadn't known how to deal with the all-grown-up Nikki, so he had left her sleeping, her vibrant red hair spread across his pillow. The provocative image had almost been enough to make him stay and miss his flight.

But he had left her, anyway.

Nikki shrugged. "It doesn't matter. That night was a long time ago. I've moved on, believe me."

Something struck him. "We used protection," he said, feeling suspicion creep back in. How could he trust her? Did he know her at all after fifteen years? If he was really the father, why the secrecy?

"Not every time." She stared him down. "It doesn't matter if you believe me or not. Emma is the result of our reckless reunion. You and I were both curious, weren't we? And blindsided by sexual attraction. A decade before that night in the casino, we had been on the verge of a physical relationship. But then your father and mine destroyed everything. I suppose Atlantic City was closure, in a way. We came full circle."

They finished their meal in silence, the mountain of regrets and what-ifs too tall to climb. Jake was achingly aware of Nikki's beauty, her poise, her intense femininity.

When Nikki was almost eighteen, Jake had fled Falling Brook never to return. Even then, he had understood what he was giving up, but his father's actions had made staying impossible. The closest Jake had come to Falling Brook in the intervening years was a visit to Atlantic City five years ago. Running into Nikki had knocked him off balance. The long-ago feelings, the yearning and the need for her, had come roaring back to life.

He and Nikki had reminisced. When Nikki finished her shift, she went to his room at his invitation. They had showered together, tumbled into bed and screwed each other until dawn. Even now, the memories made him hard.

He cleared his throat. "I'm sorry I left without saying goodbye."

She grimaced. "You're forgiven." Her gaze was filled with something he couldn't decipher. "It would have been a very awkward morning after if you had stayed," she said.

"And then you found out you were pregnant. That must have been a shock."

Her face flushed. She nodded slowly. "You have no idea. Telling my mother was hard. After Daddy died in the car crash, she imploded emotionally. Our roles reversed. She has helped me enormously with Emma, of course, but Mom leans on me."

"It makes sense. She lost her whole world and way of life. Except for her daughter." He paused, swallowing hard. "You and I didn't do much talking that night in Atlantic City. What happened to you after you left Falling Brook? Before I met up with you again?"

"Nothing earth-shattering. I made it through four years at a state school. Got my degree. Mom and I worked multiple jobs to cover tuition and to handle our living expenses."

He had a gut feeling there was more to the story. So he pushed.

"And after you finished school? I count at least five or six missing years until I ran into you in Atlantic City."

"I got married."

"Married?" He parroted the word, feeling like somebody had punched him in the belly. "Married?" So Emma did have a dad after all. Anger returned, mixed with an emotion he didn't want to examine too closely. "I'm surprised your husband is so open-minded. Letting you go out to dinner with another man..."

His sarcasm didn't even make her blink. Nikki Reardon was a cool customer. "The marriage didn't last long," she said. "Two years. He resented my privileged past. Had a chip on his shoulder about my upbringing. I realized I had said 'I do' because I was lonely. Our relationship was doomed from the start."

"I'm sorry," Jake said stiffly. He was still coping with the fact that he was *jealous*. Jealous of a faceless man who had slept with Nikki. Since when did Jake get jealous about *any* woman? He was a love-'em-and-leave-'em kind of guy.

She cocked her head. "And what about you, Jake? All I

know is that you travel the world. I'm not sure how that's a full-time occupation, but it sounds like fun."

The note of criticism stung. "I'm lucky," he said lightly. "I learned about day-trading early in my life. And I have a knack for it. In among my many adventures, I made a few bucks here and there. Enough to eat and hit the road whenever the mood strikes me."

Nikki's smile mocked his statement. "You're wearing a limited-edition Rolex. I may not have money anymore, but I haven't lost the ability to recognize luxury when I see it."

"Being comfortable isn't a crime. I like to think I'm generous with my money. I don't maintain a huge house. So I wander. I value experiences. Learning my way around the planet has changed me and made me a better person. At least I hope so."

The way Nikki stared at him made him itchy and uncomfortable. It was as if she could see through to his soul. When was the last time he had ever articulated so honestly what he wanted from life? Never?

"You're fortunate," she said slowly. "And I don't blame you a bit. You're still a young man. Healthy. Wealthy. Unattached. Why not enjoy what the world has to offer?"

Something about her response bothered him, but he couldn't pinpoint his unease.

"We need to make some plans," he said.

Nikki lowered her fork, her expression wary. "Plans?"

"Plans for integrating my life with Emma's. I've missed four years. I won't miss any more. She's a part of me."

Every bit of color leached from Nikki's porcelain complexion. Now he could almost count the smattering of freckles on the bridge of her nose. "Absolutely not," she said, her tone fierce. "I won't have you playing at fatherhood and then walking away. Emma is happy and well-adjusted. She doesn't need you, Jake."

Perhaps Nikki realized her rejection was harsh. She circled back to the beginning. "You're a good man, but you're not father material. Emma is better off having *no* father than one who flits in and out whenever the wind blows."

He ground his jaw, trying to control his temper. "You're making a lot of assumptions about me, Nik."

"It's been fifteen years since you walked away from Falling Brook. From your family. From me. You've never been back. Not once. You juggle demons, Jake."

He felt raw. Only someone who had known him so well would dare to diagnose his behavior. "At least I don't keep secrets," he muttered.

She stood abruptly and gathered her coat and clutch purse. "Take me home, please. I want to go now."

Three

Nikki was angry. And scared. Once upon a time Jake had held her entire heart in his hands. She had adored him. They had been friends forever, and then, just as she began to grow into her feelings for him in a very adult way, their fathers had ruined everything. Jake fled, and Nikki and her mom had fled, too.

But not in the same direction.

As they walked outside, Nikki barely felt the cold. At least not on her face, hands or feet. Her chest felt frozen from the inside out. How dare he blame her? Didn't he know how many times she had cried herself to sleep, wondering again and again if she had made the right choice for her daughter? For the absent Jake…

Jake started the car but left it in Park. He reached for her wrist, not letting go even when she jerked backward. "I don't want to fight with you, Nikki." He rubbed his thumb over the back of her hand with a mesmerizing stroke. "The past is the past. We can't change any of it."

In the dimly lit interior, his face was hard to read. "But your father is back," she said quietly. "That's why you're here. In New Jersey, I mean. To see him?"

Jake shrugged, his posture and expression moody. "Joshua and I are being summoned to the prison tomorrow. But to be clear, I came back because Josh asked, not for my rat bastard of a father."

His palpable misery twisted her heart and dissolved some of her animosity. She flipped her hand over and twined her fingers with his. "I'm sorry you have to see him. But maybe it will help. For closure, I mean."

"He won't answer our questions. We'll never know why he did it or what happened to the money. I can tell you that right now. My father never let us boys talk back to him…ever. He was always king. Arrogant. Proud. The worst part is, he turned his back on our mother, and for that alone, I'll never forgive him."

Nikki cupped his cheek with her free hand, feeling the late-day stubble. "Forever is a long time. Bitterness and anger poison your soul. I want you to be happy, Jake."

It was true. Despite everything that had happened, Nikki didn't want Jake Lowell to suffer. She could have found him when she turned up pregnant after their night in Atlantic City. Possibly. And told him he was a father. But he had hurt her so badly once in her life, she had been reluctant to trust him with the truth. Instinctively, she had known he could hurt her again. And she knew it now.

Jake sucked in a sharp breath. Audible. Ragged. "You're right. It's time to take you home." He released her, so she was no longer touching him.

Something shimmered in the air between them. Was

it sexual chemistry that refused to die? Nostalgia, grief and hormones were a dangerous combination.

Nikki cleared her throat. "Sure," she said.

Jake put the car in motion. Traffic was only now beginning to taper off as commuters found their way home. Nikki stared out the window, searching for answers. Was she wrong to keep Jake away from his daughter?

When he parked in front of her house, she bit her lip and stayed put. "I'll have to think about it," she said. "You and Emma. I need time. Please."

"Okay." His voice was quiet. "I don't blame you for not telling me earlier. But I know *now*, and we'll start from here."

The following morning, after a sleepless night, Nikki drove to Falling Brook. The small community where she and her mother lived was about an hour's drive away. Her mother was with Emma at the moment. Nikki's shift at the diner didn't start until eight tonight, and it was a short one. She felt the tiniest bit guilty about leaving her daughter. But this errand was important.

At ten to nine, she pulled up in front of Black Crescent headquarters. The building had been a source of conflict over the years for the way its modern architecture stuck out jarringly in the midst of Falling Brook's mostly traditional landscape.

Nevertheless, it was an impressive structure.

Nikki had dressed in the same black pantsuit from last night. But she had exchanged the sexy stiletto heels for espadrilles, and her sleeveless blouse underneath the jacket was simple white cotton.

There would be two obstacles between her and her destination. The first was a young receptionist at the front desk.

Nikki gave the barely twentysomething kid a confident smile. "I have an appointment with Mr. Lowell at nine. Is it okay if I go on up?"

The smile faltered. "His assistant will have to okay you."

"No worries. They're expecting me."

It was only partly a lie. She *had* called Joshua to tell him she needed fifteen minutes of his time. If he wasn't in, his assistant would surely have listened to his messages. So either way, Nikki wouldn't be a total surprise.

She climbed the stairs to the second floor. The executive assistant at the desk outside Joshua's office was familiar. Nikki smiled. "Haley Shaw? You're still here?"

Haley was only a couple of years older than Nikki. She had been working at Black Crescent as a college intern when Vernon and Nikki's dad, Everett Reardon, had disappeared. Well, Nikki's dad had *tried* to disappear. He'd fatally crashed his car into a tree while fleeing the police.

Nikki hadn't been inside Black Crescent headquarters since she was a senior in high school. Nothing much had changed. Her father's old office was at the opposite end of the hallway. She didn't look in that direction. Her heart was already beating too rapidly. Being inside this building brought up painful memories.

Haley had a puzzled frown between her eyebrows. "I'm sorry, I—"

"It's me. Nikki Reardon. I'm here to see Joshua. Very briefly."

The other woman's face lightened. "Nikki, of course. How nice to see you again." Her gaze went to the computer screen at her elbow. "I don't have you on his calendar..."

The door behind the desk opened, and Joshua Lowell poked out his head. “Thanks, Haley. Please hold my calls. Nikki, it’s good to see you after all these years.”

Nikki entered Joshua’s office and waited as he closed the door. “I won’t take much of your time, Josh,” she said quietly, conscious of the gatekeeper just outside the door.

Joshua waved her to a comfortable seat in front of his massive desk. “No worries. Let me have your coat. What can I do for you?”

She shrugged out of her thigh-length parka, handed it to him and sat down. Joshua was Jake’s twin. By all accounts, she should be feeling the tug of sexual attraction. But despite the fact that both men shared an unmistakable physical similarity, they projected a different vibe.

Josh was very handsome, confident and appealing. But he projected authority and a no-nonsense air of being all business. Where Jake was funny, and at times outrageous, Joshua was more reserved.

Nikki folded her shaky hands in her lap. “I’m sure Jake has already talked to you since last night. I owe you an apology,” she said bluntly. “He showed me one of the emails my mother sent. I knew nothing about them, and I am so very sorry. I’m going to speak to her firmly and warn her never to do anything like this again. She was trying to help me, but it was wrong. I hope you can forgive me.”

Joshua leaned back in his chair and smiled wearily. “I think you and I both know that parents don’t always make good choices.”

“Touché.”

“How did my brother react when you told him he’s the father? He wasn’t forthcoming about that part of the evening.”

Nikki tried not to fidget. Joshua Lowell was a powerful man. “Well, you had already given him a heads-up.

I suppose me telling him wasn't news. He says he wants to be part of Emma's life."

"And?"

"And I'm not sure. You know your brother, Josh. What your father did—what my father did—sent Jake running fifteen years ago. As far as I can tell, the only reason he's back at the moment is because you asked him to go with you to see Vernon. I don't think he's father material."

"You could give the guy a chance."

The suggestion was couched in mild tones, but Nikki felt the unspoken edge of criticism. Her defenses went up. "I have to protect Emma. She's my first priority."

"I understand."

"May I ask you a personal question?" she said, taking a deep breath.

His eyes widened fractionally, but he nodded. "Yes."

"Is it true that you're giving up your position here at Black Crescent? That you've been interviewing potential replacement candidates?"

Joshua nodded slowly. His gaze narrowed. "Yes. I have."

Nikki leaned forward, feeling an urgency that was perhaps not hers to feel. "Have you thought about asking Jake to replace you? I know he likes to pretend he has no depth, but he's whip-smart. Especially with finances. He could do this job and do it well. Maybe the challenge would be enough to make him stay. To put down roots."

Jake's twin sighed, and his expression filled with sympathy. "I get where you're coming from, Nikki. And, yes. That would be a great plan. But I already offered him the helm of Black Crescent, and he turned me down flat."

"Oh." The bottom fell out of her stomach. Suddenly, she realized she had been naive. She knew it was stupid to think she and Jake could have a relationship after all this time, but her need for him continued to sabotage good sense. Clearly, Jake only wanted to leave. Again.

She stood abruptly, near tears. Her sleepless night was catching up with her. “I should go. Thank you for your time.”

Before Nikki could move, the door burst open and Jake strode into the room. He pulled up short when he saw her, his gaze narrowing. “What are you doing here?” The question was just short of rude.

Nikki hitched her purse on her shoulder. “I wanted to talk to Joshua. Don’t worry—we’re done. I’m leaving—”

Josh interrupted before Jake could speak. “It’s my turn to ask *you* something, Nikki. Jake is here now, because he and I are headed into the city to see our father. It occurs to me that you might want to ask a few questions, too. Since your own father can’t answer them. My dad owes you that much.”

Jake’s face had frozen in stone. “I don’t think that’s appropriate. Vernon asked to see us. No one else.”

Nikki flushed, mortified. “Thank you, Josh, but Jake is right. This will be a family moment. I don’t want to intrude.” She scooted toward the door.

Josh snorted. “We’re going to see the worthless son of a bitch who for a decade and a half let his own wife and kids think he was dead. I doubt we’ll share any Hallmark moments today. You’re welcome to come.”

Nikki was torn. She did have questions. A million of them. Why did the two partners steal from their clients? Why did they run? Why did Vernon never come home? Why did he and Everett think it was okay to destroy dozens of lives? And for what?

Jake sighed. “Come if you want. I doubt he’ll talk, anyway. He won’t want to incriminate himself.”

The cynicism in Jake’s voice didn’t entirely conceal

a son's pain. Vernon Lowell had betrayed his own flesh and blood. How could he have been so selfishly cruel?

"My mother is with Emma. Let me see if she can stay." Nikki stepped out into the hallway and called her mom's cell. It wasn't hard to fabricate an excuse. Besides, Roberta loved spending time with her granddaughter. Not to mention the fact that Nikki partially supported her mother. Other than a small government retirement check, Roberta had no income. The woman who had once been a society maven and influencer now shopped for groceries at a discount store and drove a ten-year-old car.

Nikki liked to think her mother had adapted to their new reality, but the truth was, Roberta never gave up hope that one day she might reclaim what she considered to be her rightful place in the social scene.

When Nikki returned to Josh's office, the two brothers had their heads together and were talking in low tones. They both jerked upright with identical guilty expressions on their faces.

"Am I interrupting?" she asked wryly.

"Of course not." Jake gave nothing away. "We're ready to head out. You okay with the plan?"

He didn't mention Emma's name. The oblique question was odd. "I'm good," she said.

Downstairs in the employee parking garage, Joshua motioned to a large black SUV. "We're taking mine. Jake is leaving his car here. He spoke to our security guard and asked him to feed your parking meter. I hope that's okay."

"I appreciate it." She wasn't going to jockey for shotgun position. Before either man could say a word, she climbed into the back seat. The interior was nice. It reminded her of a Secret Service vehicle. Nothing wrong with that.

Falling Brook was an hour from New York City, depending on traffic and the destination. Once Joshua put the SUV in motion, Nikki fell dead asleep…

She roused as the car slowed and turned a corner. Up ahead, she saw a sign for the correctional facility.

Jake shot her a glance over his shoulder. "You okay back there?"

She nodded, rubbing her eyes and smoothing her hair. "Yes. I can't help thinking about all the times my mother and I came to the city for a play. Or shopping. Those days seem like another lifetime, another person. I was spoiled and naive."

He frowned. "Don't beat yourself up. You were the only child of wealthy parents. Of course they gave you the best of everything."

Until they didn't.

This prison, among others, made the news now and again for overcrowding and poor treatment of inmates. Nikki shivered. Her own father could have landed here before his certain conviction. Maybe death had been a kinder sentence.

When the three of them exited the parking garage a short time later, Nikki huddled into her coat. The wind whistled through the streets between tall buildings. The sun was out, but it shone hazily behind a thin veil of clouds.

Once inside they had to go through a security checkpoint with a metal detector. She began to wish she hadn't come, but it was too late to back out now.

Joshua signed a visitor log for the three of them, and then they sat in a waiting room. About fifteen minutes later, a uniformed security officer appeared in the doorway and called Joshua's name. Jake and Nikki stood, too. Her stomach fell to her feet.

Without overthinking it, she slid her hand into Jake's. He was about to see his father for the first time in a decade and a half. What was he thinking? His fingers gripped hers tightly.

The officer's face was stoic. "Mr. Lowell has changed his mind. He doesn't want visitors today."

After a moment of silence, Josh cursed beneath his breath. He and Jake had both gone pale. Joshua straightened his shoulders. "Perhaps you misunderstood. My father *asked* us to come today. We're here as a courtesy to him."

The man shrugged. "I don't know what to tell you. Mr. Lowell was perfectly clear. He's in his cell, and he doesn't want to be disturbed."

Nikki could feel the tension in Jake's body. "Well," he said, his tone gruff. "I guess that's it." He turned on his heel, dragging Nikki in his wake.

Joshua followed them out onto the street. They all stood on the sidewalk, stunned. Nikki let go of Jake's hand, self-conscious now that Joshua might notice.

Jake exhaled and stared at the ground. "I'm not sure why we're surprised. The old man is a class-A bastard. We've done our duty. Now we're off the hook."

Joshua shook his head slowly. "I can't believe it. Why would he ask us to come and then refuse to see us?"

"Maybe he's ashamed," Nikki said. She tried to put herself in Vernon's shoes, but couldn't imagine it. What kind of parent abandoned his family?

Jake made a face that could have meant anything. "It's freezing out here, and I'm starving." He gave Nikki a quick glance. "You up for walking a couple of blocks?"

"Of course."

They ended up at a little hole-in-the-wall place the Lowell brothers remembered from their teen years. Jake actually smiled when they entered. "We used to come here on the weekends and eat pizza and play pool. We felt like such rebels."

"Why was that?" she asked.

"Because it was a million miles from Falling Brook," Josh answered. He looked around the crowded, dimly lit room with a grin. The booths were covered in faux green leather. The wooden floor was scarred. The dartboards on the far back wall might have been relics from the Second World War.

There was an awkward moment as they were being seated. A booth for three meant that two people were cozy. In this case, Jake and Nikki. She squeezed toward the wall and tried to pretend she wasn't freaked out by the fact that his leg touched hers.

He helped her take off her coat.

Though Joshua seemed oblivious to any undercurrents, Jake's gaze, intense and warm, held Nikki's for long moments. Thankfully, the waitress came, and Nikki was able to catch her breath.

It occurred to her that the three of them had been frozen in time. Jake and Nikki had left Falling Brook fifteen years ago, headed in opposite directions. Joshua had stayed behind, the dutiful son, though Nikki had to wonder if his sacrifice had been worth it.

And now, here was Nikki, pressed up against the man who made her quiver with awareness and need. She'd had a taste of intimacy with Jake…in Atlantic City. Though she didn't want to admit weakness—even to herself—the truth was, she wanted more, even if her brain was shouting *danger, danger, danger.*

"This is a weird reunion, isn't it?" she said, clearing her throat. They had finished ordering, and now her stomach growled as they waited for their meal.

Joshua nodded. He gazed at his brother. "Weird, but satisfying. I'm sorry it's taken us this long to reconnect."

Nikki hesitated and then decided to indulge her curiosity. "Tell me, Josh. How have the finances at Black Crescent recovered? I felt so guilty for years that those families lost everything."

Jake slid an arm around her shoulders, resting it on the back of the booth. "My saint of a brother has been able to repay a lot of the money."

Her eyes widened. "Really?"

Joshua grimaced. "Well, not at first. Although I wasn't implicated in the crime, the feds were all over me for several years."

Jake nodded. "Everything was liquidated, including your home, as you know, Nikki. Our cars, yachts, vacation properties. Oliver's remaining tuition for Harvard was canceled. Luckily for our mother, our home was in her name, since it had been in her family for generations. There were some Black Crescent assets liquidated, too, but not enough to cripple the company. It was in everyone's best interest to keep things afloat so Josh could start rebuilding."

"I'm glad to know that you were able to make at least *some* reparations," she said.

The food arrived, and serious talk was sidelined in favor of hot pizza.

Eventually, Joshua picked up the earlier thread. "Because of the nature of the crime, Black Crescent has been bound by some pretty stringent rules. Thankfully, I've been able to pay all the people our father cheated at least eighty or eighty-five cents on the dollar. It's not everything, but our clients signed off on the agreement. They were thrilled, actually, to know that they would recoup most of their investments over the long haul."

Jake's expression darkened. "I still want to know what happened to the money."

"Living off the grid for fifteen years isn't cheap," Nikki said.

"But he took millions." Jake shook his head slowly. "I doubt we'll ever know."

A silence fell, rife with unspoken emotions. Nikki wondered what Jake was thinking. Perhaps he was deciding how soon he could get back to his travels. Suddenly, her throat was tight. "I hate to break up the party, but I need to get back to Emma."

"Of course." Joshua raised his hand for the check, and then pinned Nikki with a determined gaze. "I was glad you turned up in my office today. I'd been planning to talk to you, anyway. Now that I have finally fulfilled all the company's legal obligations, Black Crescent will begin paying you and your mother a monthly stipend. You were victims, too."

She opened her mouth, stunned. "Oh, no. My father was one of the perpetrators. Mom and I are fine. Don't be ridiculous. We don't need the money."

Jake's eyes snapped with displeasure. "You're working in a diner, and you can't afford a babysitter. You are definitely *not* fine. My brother is doing the right thing."

Nikki straightened her spine, her cheeks burning with humiliation. "My life may not look like much to you, Jake Lowell, but I'm proud of what I've accomplished. The good things in life aren't always measured by dollars and cents."

Both Lowell twins were formidable when they put their minds to it. Joshua wouldn't be moved. "What you do with the money is up to you, Nikki. Put it away for Emma's college, if you want. But you deserve to regain what you lost."

Four

Nikki didn't sleep on the way back home, but this time, she sat quietly, listening to the two brothers' conversation. It had been a strange and unsettling day. She wanted to spend time with Jake, but she was confused and worried. If she let him come around to see his daughter, Nikki might be tempted to sleep with him again.

Joshua had offered his brother a permanent, full-time, challenging opportunity, but Jake had turned him down. Wanderlust. That's what it was. Jake didn't know how to stay in one place, and he was far too old to learn new tricks now.

In the parking garage at Black Crescent, Joshua said a quick goodbye and ran upstairs. He was late for a meeting. That left Jake and Nikki standing awkwardly.

"Let me take you to dinner tonight," Jake said. "We still have plenty to talk about. And I've missed you, Nikki."

The raw honesty in his words seduced her more than anything. “I’m sorry,” she said. “I have to work.”

He scowled. “Are you blowing me off?”

She lifted her chin. “I’ll spend a couple of hours with Emma, and then I have to go straight to the diner.”

“I see.”

“How soon will you be leaving?”

His face reflected shock. “What do you mean?”

“You came home to see your father. That didn’t work out. I assumed you’ll be heading out again soon.”

“No.” He leaned back against a concrete pillar. “Are you trying to get rid of me, Nik? Is that what this is about? Are you afraid of what I make you feel?”

“I’m not afraid of you,” she said, the lie sticking in her throat.

He stared at her so long she began to get fidgety. “I’m staying for my brother’s wedding and my father’s trial. Both of those are soon. In the meantime, maybe you and I could reconnect.”

“Reconnect?” She parsed the word for meaning.

He straightened and took the few steps that separated them. “I want to touch you. Kiss you. Get to know you again. Atlantic City was only a start.”

When his lips settled on hers, warm and firm, her legs threatened to buckle. Just like five years ago, this sexy, desirable man knew how to cut the ground from under her feet.

She pulled away, wiping her mouth with the back of her hand. Words came tumbling out. Words she should have censored but didn’t. “I missed you so much, Jake. I fantasized about you. Wanted you. But you left me twice. Once fifteen years ago, and again in Atlantic City. Only a foolish woman would place a bet on a man who flits around the globe.”

He shoved his hands in his pockets, his expression stormy. “I couldn’t save you, Nikki. I couldn’t save *us* back then, so I ran. I couldn’t bear to stay in Falling Brook one more day. Everywhere I turned, there was another damn reporter. Digging. Poking. Prodding. Wanting every detail of our bleeding lives.”

“And yet you abandoned me to the wolves.”

He blinked. “Ouch. The old Nikki I knew wasn’t so harsh.”

“The old Nikki was a child, Jake. I had to grow up fast. It wasn’t fun, and it wasn’t easy. I survived, though.”

“Yes, you did. You’re an extraordinary woman.”

Something pulsed between them. Awareness. Need. He looked so sexy she wanted to climb him like a tree and never let go. If it had been only her, perhaps she would have rolled the dice. Taken a walk on the wild side.

The kind of selfish pleasure she had embraced in Atlantic City was not a choice now. She had her mother to look out for, and she had Emma to raise. Nikki’s wants and needs had to come in dead last.

“I should go,” she muttered, looking at her watch. “I’m sorry your father wouldn’t see you today.”

“Like I said, I’m not surprised.” He reached for her hand and squeezed her fingers.

“Think about it, Nikki. Not just me and Emma, but you and me. I want to spend time with both of you.”

“Because you’re bored and at loose ends?”

His eyes flashed. “Because she’s my daughter, and you’re my past.”

Nikki played Barbies with Emma, started dinner and then dashed to work, leaving her mother in charge. Roberta Reardon wasn’t incompetent. She was merely fragile. As Nikki poured coffee and took orders—because one of her best waitresses was out—she chatted with regulars. Half of her brain was occupied, trying to cope with the ramifications of the email she had seen on her phone just before she left the house.

It was from Black Crescent Hedge Fund—from Joshua Lowell, in particular. As he had promised, the attachment to the email was a very official-looking document. Beginning January first, Nikki and her mother would both be receiving checks for ten thousand dollars a month for a period of ten years.

The math was staggering. In the first twelve months alone, the two women together would have just shy of a quarter of a million dollars. There would be money for her mom to have almost anything she wanted, within reason. Nikki would be able to quit her job and spend these last precious months before kindergarten with Emma.

They would have financial freedom.

Why did the prospect seem so threatening? Perhaps because Nikki knew what it felt like to lose everything. She was superstitious about this extraordinary windfall. It was great that Black Crescent had recovered enough to restore much of what was lost. But Nikki's father had participated in the con, the scam.

She felt guilty.

It was late when Nikki got home, so her mom was sleeping over. That was often their pattern. Even though Roberta spent a lot of time with Emma, it was healthier for the two grown women to maintain separate residences. That hadn't always been possible in the beginning. Back when their lives had fallen apart, and Nikki had barely been an adult, they had needed to save every penny.

Eventually, things had changed.

And now, they were about to change again.

Nikki wanted desperately to go to bed, but she knew she would toss and turn if she didn't tell her mother what was about to happen. "Mom," she said. "Can I talk to you for a minute?"

Her mother raised an eyebrow. "So serious, sweetheart. What's up?"

"I had lunch with Joshua and Jake Lowell today."

Her mother paled. "Oh?"

"I found out about the emails. Your emails. And I apologized to Joshua."

Roberta Reardon went on the attack. "Well, I *won't* apologize for wanting to protect my daughter and granddaughter. Joshua Lowell is a scoundrel. He should be supporting his baby girl."

"Mom…" Nikki rubbed her temple, where a sledgehammer pounded. "Joshua is not Emma's father."

"Of course he is. Don't try to cover for him. You told me the truth."

"I lied."

Roberta Reardon stared at her daughter. "I don't understand."

"You kept badgering me when I lost my job. Trying to get me to ask Emma's father for child support. I didn't want you to know the truth, so I finally told you what you wanted to hear. I never dreamed you would try to blackmail him."

Her mother was visibly offended. "It wasn't blackmail. I never *asked* for money. I just wanted him to know he had a child."

"But he didn't."

"So, who *is* the father?"

Nikki felt her face heat. She was a grown woman, but this wasn't an easy topic to talk about with her mother. "Jake," she said quietly. "*Jake* Lowell. Not Joshua."

Roberta put her hands to her cheeks. “Well, that makes a lot more sense. You always did love that boy. He left Falling Brook, though. He’s never been back. Right?”

“That’s true. But about five years ago I ran into him when I was working at the casino in Atlantic City.”

Her mother looked shocked. “A one-night stand? Oh, Nikki.”

“I couldn’t resist him, Mom. I made a mistake. But trust me, Jake hasn’t changed. He’s still the proverbial rolling stone. I can’t risk being with a man like that.”

She was strong. She could let Jake come over, let him spend time with Emma, but Nikki wouldn’t risk her heart. She wouldn’t give in to sexual attraction. Not this time. The stakes were too high.

Her mother’s gaze judged her. “Emma deserves a father. Even one who’s not around much. He’s her blood kin. What did he say when you told him?”

“Not much. I only confirmed what Jake had already heard from his brother. But Jake is only here for the trial. Then he’ll be gone again.”

“Life is never easy, is it?” Her mother’s eyes were filled with resignation.

“It felt easy when I was a kid. You and Daddy gave me a perfect childhood.”

“Nothing is perfect, Nikki. I thought I had a perfect marriage, but look how that turned out. It’s hard to know what’s inside a person’s heart.”

“I’m sorry, Mom. You deserved better.”

“And so do you, my dearest girl. So do you.”

Jake was answering emails in his hotel room when his phone dinged. It had been twenty-four hours since he had seen Nikki. Now she was texting him.

If you don't have plans, you're welcome to come over for dinner. Maybe even read Emma a bedtime story. As a friend.

Jake shook his head wryly. He did have plans, but he would cancel them. Nikki had made an overture. He wouldn't miss this chance.

When he showed up at her house at five o'clock, he saw neighborhood kids playing outside. The weather had shifted, and the late-afternoon temps were in the upper fifties. He reached into the back seat and grabbed a shopping bag. He had bought Emma a treat for just such an occasion.

Nikki opened the door before he could ring the bell. Her face was flushed, her fiery red hair pulled up in a ponytail. Wispy curls escaped around her forehead and cheeks. Those emerald eyes searched his soul.

"Hi," she said, giving him a wary look.

Emotion gut-punched him. This woman. What was it about this woman? She was dangerous to him, to his emotions, his good sense, his need for self-preservation.

As Nikki stepped back to let him in, he saw Emma, half hiding behind her mother's leg. He squatted, greeting her at eye level. "Hey, there," he said. "I'm Jake."

Her eyes were big, her gaze solemn. "I remember. Is my mommy gonna be mad at you again?"

Jake glanced up at Nikki. "I hope not."

Nikki shook her head ruefully. "I have to finish dinner. Why don't you two get acquainted?"

Jake rattled the shopping bag. "Would it be okay if we played outside? I hate to miss this weather. And I brought Emma a ring-toss game."

Emma's face lit up. "It *is* okay." She took his hand. "We have to go to the backyard, 'cause there's a fence."

"Presents, Jake?" Nikki's expression said she disapproved.

"Relax. It was less than fifteen bucks. I have a few friends with kids. They always tell me simple toys are the best."

Nikki spied unashamedly out the window over the sink. Emma didn't always warm up to strangers, but perhaps Jake's thoughtful gift had lowered her defenses. Nikki wouldn't be so easily convinced. Jake was a loner, a man who deliberately stayed away from any kind of home base, any kind of tie. She wouldn't let him hurt her or her daughter.

Even so, Nikki had to admit he was good with the little girl. Patient. Kind. Time and again, he showed her how to position the ring horizontally and how to hold her hand sideways to fling it. Emma got closer and closer. When she finally landed the first one, father and daughter did a spontaneous victory dance.

Moments later the duo came inside, their body language relaxed. Nikki was bemused by the way her daughter had taken to Jake. Did Emma feel some mystical bond? Did she recognize her father on some visceral level?

Nikki tried to swallow her misgivings. "Wash up, please. This will be ready soon."

Jake gave her an odd glance. "Emma wants to show me the butterflies in her room. We won't take long."

Nikki followed them, unable to squash her anxiety about seeing Jake inside her house. Emma loved butterflies. Always had, even as a toddler. On her fourth birthday, Nikki had let Emma redo her room. Bedspread, posters, mobiles hanging from the ceiling.

Jake whistled long and low. "This is amazing, Em."

Nikki waited for Emma to correct him. No one shortened her daughter's name. But Emma simply beamed. "I can name fifteen different species on flash cards," she said, "and I'm working on the others. Some of the words are hard."

Jake seemed surprised. "You're reading already?"

Emma gave him the kind of eye-rolling look that precocious kids have been giving parents since the beginning of time. "I started reading when I was three. It's easy, Jake. Don't you love books?"

He nodded. "I do, at that. And I'm glad you do, too." He stared around the room, taking in every bit of it. "Emma," he said, "I have something to show you." He sat in the rocking chair, the one Nikki had bought at a thrift store when Emma was an infant. He lifted Emma onto his lap.

She squirmed and got comfortable. "What is it?"

He pulled his phone out of his pocket. "You know the monarchs, right?"

"Of course. They're the easiest ones."

"Last year, just about this time, I was in Mexico." He pointed to the large map on her wall. "It's that pink country under the United States."

"I know," she said. "There's a kid at my preschool named Matias. He and his mom moved here from Mexico when he was a baby."

"Ah. So you know geography, too." The expression on his face when he glanced over at Nikki made her shrug and grin. Emma was very bright. And endlessly curious.

"What's jog-raphy?" Emma asked, perplexed.

"Never mind, kiddo. Here. Look at this." He cued up a video and Emma zeroed in.

"Wow," she said.

"It's part of the monarch-butterfly migration. People come from all over the world to see it."

Emma's intense absorption tugged at Nikki's conscience. Travel was something she hadn't been able to afford. At least not anywhere out of state.

Her daughter looked up at Jake, wonder in her eyes. "Do they really fill up the whole sky?"

"It seems that way. It's so beautiful, your heart wants to dance."

"And maybe you wished you could be a butterfly, too?"

His voice got all low and gravelly. "Maybe I did."

Nikki tried to swallow the lump in her throat. "Will you help her wash her hands? I've put pasta in the pot. We'll eat in five."

In the kitchen, she concentrated on her task, but her brain raced like a hamster in a wheel. Jake had so much world experience to share with his daughter. Nikki had traveled as a teenager, but taking trips had ground to a halt when she and her mother had been sent away from the only home Nikki had ever known.

Her father had cleaned almost everything out of the checking and savings accounts. Her mother had been forced, by necessity, to sell most of her jewelry that first year so she and Nikki wouldn't starve.

When Nikki's two dinner companions returned to the kitchen, they were discussing the merits of brownies versus cupcakes.

Emma took her usual seat at one end of the table. "Mommy makes both of them good. You'll see."

"No pressure," Nikki muttered. Her daughter wouldn't understand that a man like Jake had dined on the world's finest cuisine in dozens of the most cosmopolitan cities.

But Jake was unfazed. "Comfort food is the best,"

he said, digging into his spaghetti as soon as Nikki was seated. "This is amazing, Nikki."

"I'm glad you like it." She had set the table so that Emma was between her two parents. Maybe Emma didn't feel the weight of the moment, but Nikki definitely did. Judging by the look on Jake's face, he did, too.

During the entire meal, he watched Emma with a combination of pride and wonder that would have been adorably macho if Nikki hadn't been so torn about the future.

When the meal was over, Nikki put on her stern-mommy look. "Into the shower with you, ladybug. And don't forget to brush your teeth."

When Emma disappeared, Jake raised an eyebrow. "Isn't she a little young for that?"

Nikki picked up the plates while Jake gathered the silverware. "Three months ago, she informed me that baths were for babies. She's trying her best to grow up as fast as she can, and I'm trying my best to slow her down."

Jake watched Nikki put the dishes in the sink, then he dropped the silverware and pulled her close, tucking a stray strand of hair behind her ear. "You've done a great job with her, Nikki. She's smart and funny."

"I'm glad you think so." Nikki backed away. She was supposed to be focusing on her daughter, but with Jake this close, all she could feel were her wobbly knees and sweaty palms. After fifteen years, she should have developed some kind of immunity, but whatever pheromones he'd been blessed with made her crazy.

They weren't touching. Not really. Not anymore. But the eight inches of air between them vibrated with deep emotion. She wanted him.

Did he feel the same urgency?

"I need to check on Emma," she croaked. "Don't

worry about the kitchen. Make yourself comfortable in the living room. I have basic cable."

His lips twitched. "Go, little mama. Look after your chick."

The whole time Nikki supervised Emma's drying off and choosing clean pajamas and picking a bedtime book, her skin quivered. Jake was in the next room. Waiting. He was staying to talk about Emma. She knew that.

Maybe Nikki was the only one in this house acting immature.

When Emma was completely ready for bed, Nikki kissed the top of her head. "Would you like Mr. Jake to read your bedtime story tonight?"

The little girl's face brightened. "Sure. But I need to get a different book."

Nikki glanced at the picture book in her daughter's hands. It was a Caldecott Medal winner about Irish fairies and sliding down rainbows—one of Emma's favorites.

"I don't understand, sweetie. You love this book."

"Yeah, Mommy. But it's kind of *girly.* Mr. Jake is a boy, and he's real smart. I've got other books he'll like better." Before Nikki could stop her, Emma was tearing through her bookcase, moving and tossing and stacking until she found what she wanted. "Here it is."

Nikki frowned. "I thought we agreed that book was a little too hard for you to read right now. Maybe next year, Emma." It was a thick, several-hundred-page volume about the solar system.

"But I'm *not* reading it, Mommy. Mr. Jake is."

"It's far too long, baby."

"He can do just a few pages."

Nikki knew when she was beaten. She followed her daughter to the front part of the house where Jake was sprawled on the sofa resembling the dangerous male animal he was. He hadn't bothered turning on the TV. Instead, he was staring at his cell screen.

When they walked into the room, he immediately dropped the phone. "Hey, there."

Emma walked right up to him and handed over the book. "Will you read me a story? I picked this one for you," she said, beaming. "Because you told me you liked zubzertories."

Nikki shot Jake a puzzled glance.

He smiled. "Observatories. And I'd love to read this to Emma."

"Ah. Well, twenty minutes, no more, please." Nikki needed to get Jake out of her house before her resolve cracked.

Even when she left the room, Jake's low, masculine voice carried in the small house. It was impossible to ignore him, impossible to pretend she didn't react to him strongly.

Fifteen minutes later, Nikki returned to her daughter's room. "Time for bed, Emma."

"Just one more chapter, please, Mommy."

Nikki had played this game far too many times. "Now means now. Tell Mr. Jake thank you."

Emma slid off Jake's lap. "Thank you, Mr. Jake," she said, her expression doleful. The sad-little-girl act sometimes won her five extra minutes, but Nikki held firm this time.

Nikki managed a smile for Jake, though she was nervous and jittery. "There's beer and wine in the fridge. Help yourself."

He gave her a slow, sleepy smile. "I'm good. Take your time."

Emma yawned. "Can Mr. Jake tuck me in?"

Nikki froze. She was pretty sure Jake did, too. It was one thing for a visitor to read a book. Tucking in was for family members. "Um, no, sweetheart. That's for mommies and little girls." She picked up her *baby*, who was getting almost too heavy to carry like this. "I'll be back, Jake."

Five

Jake stood and paced. Suddenly, this small house felt stifling. The home-cooked meal. The cute kid. The beautiful mother. All the things he had managed to avoid in his life.

In Atlantic City five years ago, Nikki had appeared as a sexy woman from his past. A chance to indulge in some hot and heavy no-strings sex. But now, Nikki had changed. She had moved on. She had grown up and matured. Or maybe she had already changed five years ago, and he hadn't seen it.

Though Jake admired her for the life she had created despite her father's deeds, he was wary. He'd been on the run for far too long to be seriously tempted by the idea of *settling down.* It would be unfair to let Nikki think that he might. Better to keep his distance and fight the sexual hunger that consumed him.

Maybe Nikki was right. He had no business playing "Daddy" unless he was ready to go all in. And he wasn't.

Returning to Falling Brook had been hard enough.

This little blue-collar town where Nikki lived, Poplar Ridge, was less than an hour away from where she had grown up, but by every other measure, it might as well have been on a different planet. Jake had hung his hat in all kinds of communities over the years. He'd enjoyed luxury, and he had found meaning in testing himself with deprivation. But all the while, he had known he had a safety net. He always had money.

Even when he fled Falling Brook and the reporters that were hounding him, he'd had secret money saved from playing poker. Jake had used his skills in day-trading and gradually built his fortune.

But Nikki and her mother had been left with virtually nothing.

Roberta Reardon had come from a social background and a generation where trophy spouses entertained and visited the spa but weren't employed. Nikki had been seventeen, almost eighteen, when her father disappeared. Not a child, but certainly not a full-grown adult. In the midst of grief, her whole world had imploded. At the time, Jake had insisted she was partly to blame. Even now, he regretted that.

He had lashed out at his teenage girlfriend, because the truth was too much to bear. Vernon and Everett had embezzled money and left their families behind. In search of what? If Everett Reardon hadn't been killed, if he had joined his partner in the Bahamas, what were the two men hoping to accomplish?

That unanswered question had shaped Jake's life. Bitterness and angry regret kept him on the run. Or maybe it was the memory of the woman he had lost that locked him in a lonely cage of his own making.

Thinking about the past was never fruitful. Jake

shoved aside the baggage and sprawled in a chair, his focus returning to the present. What would Nikki and Roberta do with their windfall from Black Crescent? Jake had thought about asking if Joshua could add Nikki and her mom to the list of people Black Crescent was repaying, but Josh had beaten him to the punch.

Would Nikki and Roberta want to return to Falling Brook?

His turbulent thoughts were eventually interrupted when Nikki appeared in the doorway. Her ponytail was mussed from being in bed with her daughter.

"Is she asleep?" he asked.

"Close," Nikki said. "She played hard today."

Jake patted the sofa beside him. "Come sit with me."

Nikki hesitated, but did as he asked. It didn't escape his notice that she left a good four feet between them.

Didn't matter. He felt connected to her and drunk with wanting her. He didn't know what to do about that.

"Emma is delightful," he said gruffly.

"Thank you." Nikki's response was subdued. In fact, she seemed to be having trouble looking at him.

He sighed. "You're right about me. I don't know that I'm father material. I'd still like to hang out with her now and then while I'm here. But I won't cross any boundaries, I swear. I would never tell her she's mine. That would be cruel."

Finally, Nikki lifted her head. "I don't know if you saw it, but what happened between you two tonight was extraordinary. She's usually shy with strangers, especially men. But with you, she was happy. Excited. How can I *not* tell her the truth?"

Now the roles were reversed. Nikki wanted full disclosure, and Jake was uncertain about the future. "Let's give ourselves time," he said, feeling some unseen noose tighten around his neck.

"So, what? You'll just stay away until we figure it out?"

"Do you have a better idea? If our goal is not to hurt our daughter, we both have some thinking to do."

She nodded thoughtfully. "I suppose you're right."

"But let me be clear about one thing."

Her eyes widened. "Oh?"

He reached for her hand, stroking the back of it with his thumb. "I don't think I can stay away from *you*. I'm feeling the same things I felt five years ago. Seeing you face-to-face destroys me. Everything inside me says, 'Hell yeah!' I want to make love to you, Nikki. Rather desperately, in fact."

Her eyes flashed with anger. "Those feelings in Atlantic City didn't last 'til morning, Jake. You're a flight risk."

"What does that have to do with me wanting you? Besides, I don't think this attraction is one-sided…is it?"

Tears sheened her eyes. Her chin wobbled. Her fingers curled around his. "No. But at what cost?"

"It will be our little secret. Just the two of us."

"We both know that secrets can tear a family apart." Her gaze clung to his, begging for assurance.

"Not this one. I give you my word. Come here, Nik. Let me show you."

They met in the middle of the sofa, a ragged curse from him, a low moan from her. He wrapped his arms around her and pulled her close, kissing her recklessly, telling himself there was no danger. Sex was good. Sex was healthy.

Her body was soft, pliant. Her scent tantalizing.

She was perfection in his arms. That one night in Atlantic City had haunted his dreams. He told himself he had embellished the memories…the way their bodies seemed to recognize each other. But something had been different that night, and it was different still.

He wanted Nikki to be his teenage sweetheart, but she was not the same woman now. She had made a life for herself. What had Jake ever done but run?

Despite his unease, he couldn't walk away. Touching her, kissing her, needing her. It was as simple and perfect as falling asleep in a feather bed. But the dark edge of lust was something more. Dangerous. Powerful. He was a man who respected women, yet in this fraught moment, he felt capable of behavior that frightened him.

Why, after so many years, did Nikki still have the power to push him beyond all reasonable boundaries?

When she put a hand to his chest and shoved, he was almost relieved.

"Wait, Jake. Please."

He released her instantly, still recognizing the beast inside him. "You changed your mind." His tone was low and flat, his mood mercurial.

She met his stormy eyes bravely. "I want you every bit as much as you want me. But I don't have the same freedom you do. Every choice I make, every road I take, affects at least two other people. My life is inextricably tied to my mother's and to Emma's. I don't have the luxury of spontaneity or reckless pleasure. As much as I wish things were different, I have to face the truth."

"So you *won't* make love to me?" He was frustrated now and trying to pretend this conflict wasn't proof of all his misgivings.

"I don't know," she said, the words taut with misery.

"That's no answer, Nik."

"Then how about this? Not now. It's too risky."

"Does Emma wake up during the night? Is that it?"

"Not usually. But it feels wrong with her in the next room."

"How can it be wrong if our being together created that perfect little girl?" Nikki was pale, obviously distressed. It was all he could do to keep his distance.

"Jake," she said quietly. "This thing between us is like sitting in front of a fireplace on a cold night. Even though we scattered the logs years ago, and the blaze went out, somehow, a couple of small embers stayed close enough to create danger. I can't explain it. We're a weird paradox. Virtual strangers who somehow know each other very well."

"You don't feel like a stranger to me." It was the God's honest truth. One encounter in fifteen years? They should be awkward together. Instead, touching her was the easiest thing he had ever done. He wanted to drown in her.

"Maybe we need to back up. Spend some time talking. Getting reacquainted."

"Talking?" He clenched his fists. "What will that accomplish?"

She lifted her chin. "You think you know me, but you don't, Jake. We can't pick up where we left off fifteen years ago. And not even where we were in Atlantic City. Time changes people. I've changed."

His body vibrated with sexual tension. He was hard and desperate—a toxic combination. There was the tiniest possibility she was right. Only in Jake's case, he had dealt with the tragedy in his past by moving slowly through the years. He'd made plenty of money. But he lived from day to day. Alone. Sometimes in the midst of a sea of people, but alone.

Now he was back in New Jersey. What was his next step?

Emma complicated the outcome. Enormously.

Maybe Jake could be a lover, but not a dad. It was painful to admit.

He exhaled and told himself no man ever died from unfulfilled lust. "What do you want to talk about?"

"Would popcorn make you feel better?"

His nose twitched, already imagining the scent. "With real butter?"

"Sure."

He followed her into the kitchen. Nikki's body language was wary, as if she knew he was on a short fuse. As he watched, she pulled out an old-fashioned aluminum popper. She added oil, seasoning and kernels, then put a chunk of butter in a tiny pan and set it to low.

Her small dinette chair was barely big enough to support his weight. He sat, anyway, his knee bouncing under the table with nervous energy.

When there was nothing to do but wait, she joined him, her body language guarded.

Jake plowed ahead. "What shall we talk about?"

Nikki shrugged. "You first."

"Will your mom want to go back to Falling Brook now that money won't be an issue?"

"Honestly? I don't know."

"I guess she's made friends here."

"Not really. We've moved around a lot, at least we did before Emma was born. For years, we used my mother's maiden name. A dozen different apartments. A dozen not-so-legal leases. She was terrified that someone would recognize her from the news."

"That's understandable." Wasn't that why Jake, himself, had fled?

The sound of the first pops ricocheted in the small room.

Nikki jumped to her feet. "You want wine?"

"Coke goes with popcorn. If you have any..."

She cocked her head. "Jake Lowell is asking for a sugary soft drink?"

He crossed his arms over his chest. "It's been a stressful week. I think I'm entitled."

"That's an understatement, for sure. Here you go." She got a can and handed it to him, then reached up into the cabinet for bowls. "I'll let you salt yours how you like it."

"Thanks." The fact that Nikki's brief, light touch affected him so deeply meant he was in real trouble.

Moments later they were enjoying their snack in silence.

His throat tightened. "Your turn," he said gruffly.

"I'm surprised you're willing to answer questions."

He frowned. "What does that mean?"

"Fifteen years ago, it was like you disappeared off the face of the earth."

The tops of his ears got hot. "It wasn't that extreme," he said, feeling guilty all over again. "I sent the occasional text or email to my brothers. First question, please."

"I know you're good at playing the stock market. But day-trading isn't a full-time occupation, at least not in your situation. What else have you done for the past fifteen years? I wanted to write to you, but I never worked up the nerve to contact Joshua and ask for your addresses, snail mail or otherwise."

"Why would you have to 'work up the nerve'?"

She gnawed her bottom lip. "You blamed me for what happened. I thought Josh might, too. Believe me, I've wished a million times that I could turn back the clock and beg my father not to get involved with yours."

Jake's chest was tight. Mostly because he knew Nikki was right. Even as a twenty-two-year-old, Jake had known that his dad must have orchestrated whatever convoluted plan led to the painful implosion of Black Crescent. With Vernon Lowell missing and presumed dead, and Everett killed in a car chase, the details weren't all that important.

"I can't believe I'm saying this," he muttered, "but I'd rather talk about me than what happened fifteen years ago."

Nikki nodded. "Fair enough." She poked at the unpopped kernels at the bottom of her bowl. "You can hit the high spots. What does a twentysomething do when he sets out to seek his fortune?"

Jake leaned his chair back on two legs, completely willing to narrate a travelogue. That was a hell of a lot easier than dealing with messy emotions. "Everyone expected me to head to Europe, so I started out in Wyoming instead," he said simply. "Working for a mountain-climbing school. Teaching inexperienced tourists the basics, so they could climb Grand Teton. It was a dangerous job at times. And I pushed the edge more than I should have. I wasn't suicidal. But I didn't really care what happened to me at that point."

"How long were you there?"

"About eighteen months. One day I heard some guys whispering and snickering. They shut up when I walked by. I found out later that one of our climbing school pupils was from Jersey and recognized my face and my name from the news."

"That must have been awful."

"It was shocking. Humiliating. So I decided that North America was too close. I set out for Australia. I always wanted to travel more, so that's what I did. A couple of weeks here. A month there. Gradually, I worked my way around the globe."

"Sounds like fun."

"It was. Mostly. Still, there were days I was so homesick I could hardly stand it. It was as if I was living life in slow motion. But that slow pace was the only way I knew how to handle the upheaval. Every time I thought about flying back to New Jersey, I remembered there was nothing left to return to."

"How can you say that? Joshua and Oliver were here… and your mom."

"I sent Oliver a few texts over the years, but he never answered. I thought he was still angry with me for leaving, but now I know he was busy partying, doing drugs. And I couldn't face Joshua. I had run out on my twin… Left him to clean up my father's mess."

"My father's mess, too…"

"Yes."

"What about your mom?"

"She was in deep denial when I left. The few times I called home it was the same. 'Vernon will be back. This is just one of his stunts.' After six months, I still called her occasionally, but I quit talking about anything that happened at Black Crescent. I didn't mention my dad's name. It was too damn sad."

"I'm sorry, Jake."

"She and Oliver went to see him recently. Before I got back. Joshua couldn't get any details out of them."

"In a way, your mom was right. Vernon *did* come back. Don't you wonder what happened to the money?"

"Every damn day."

After a heartbeat of silence, Nikki smiled. "Still my turn," she said. "What about you, Jake? Did *you* ever get married?"

The question stopped him dead in his tracks. "No," he said bluntly.

"Any close calls?"

The expression on her face reflected mild curiosity, but he suspected she was hiding her true feelings. "None. I like my freedom too much."

Nikki surprised him when she reached across the table and squeezed his arm briefly. "We have to get past this and move on. We've both played the hands we were dealt. I don't hold any grudges, Jake. You are who you are. Maybe we could tell Emma the truth when she turns eighteen."

"And have her resent me for missing her childhood?"

"You can't have it both ways."

He had to get out of this house. His head threatened to explode with a million unanswered questions, and his libido wanted to get laid.

Not with just any woman. With Nikki. Nikki of the pale white skin and the fiery hair and the eyes that went moss green or forest green depending on her mood. She was a fascinating, desirable female.

Even though he had gone an entire decade without seeing her, he could have used the encounter in Atlantic City to build something new, something more than his vagabond existence offered him. But he hadn't had the guts to try again.

His own lazy, selfish choices had brought him to this point.

Jake had run away fifteen years ago. He had wanted to be left alone, and he had succeeded in his quest. As he wandered the globe, he'd kept his friendships and his sexual relationships on a shallow plane. Expedient. Disposable. Forgettable.

The one woman he had never been able to forget was Nikki Reardon.

Now it was too late.

He stood up abruptly, nearly tumbling the chair. "I need to go," he said. "I'll call you later."

Nikki stood, too, seeming hurt or relieved or maybe both. "Okay."

"Joshua is getting married soon. I'll need a plus-one."

She gave him a loaded look. "Is that an invitation?"

"You know it is," he said, feeling more irritated by the minute.

Nikki shook her head slowly. "Charming. You sure know how to make a girl feel wanted. I'll think about it."

"What's to think about? Who else would I take?"

Nikki poked her finger in the center of his chest. "You need to learn some manners, Jake Lowell. I don't know what kind of women you've been hanging around with, but I'm not some floozy you can pick up and put down when the mood strikes you."

"Floozy?" He laughed out loud despite his uncertain temper. "This is the twenty-first century, Ms. Reardon. Women aren't judged for their romantic entanglements anymore. Haven't you heard?"

She poked him a second time, eyes flashing. "You know what I mean. You're the absolute definition of a man who keeps a woman in every port. Just because you and I share a history doesn't mean I'm going to let you push me around. Are we clear?"

They were toe-to-toe now. He could feel her breath on his skin, hear the uneven hitch in her angry words. "Poke me one more time, Nik. I dare you."

Her chest heaved as she sucked in a breath and exhaled. "I'm not scared of you." One feminine finger prodded his sternum.

"Well, you should be, you frustrating woman." He groaned the words and snatched her up in his arms, backing her into the refrigerator. "Because you make me insane."

Six

Nikki was a rule follower, a straight arrow.

Even as she recognized that Jake was neither of those things, she was drawn to him inescapably.

He hitched her legs around his waist and buried his face in the curve of her neck. "You smell good, Nik."

As he nibbled the sensitive skin below her ear, she shuddered. "You like the scent of tomato sauce?"

"On you I do." He caught her earlobe between his teeth. "Tell me to go home." He begged her with as much sincerity as she had ever heard from him.

She smoothed his hair. "You told me you don't have a home."

"You know what I mean."

He let her slide to her feet, but where their bodies were pressed together, she could feel the hard length of him. Her memories of Atlantic City undermined her good sense. "I've dreamed of you holding me like this, Jake."

"I did more than hold you five years ago," he said huskily.

She unbuttoned two buttons of his shirt and slipped her hand inside to test the warm contours of his chest. "Yes, you did. I was there, remember?"

Sexual tension pulsed between them.

Jake shifted his feet. "At the risk of jumping the gun, are there any condoms in this house?"

"What do *you* think?" She kissed his chin and tasted his lips, loving the way he shuddered at her touch. "Don't you have one or two?"

"Not on me."

His disgruntled response might have been funny if Nikki wasn't so wound up. Being a single mom for the past four years had been a monastic existence. Life was hard. Busy and good, but hard. Not much time for a woman to indulge her sexual needs. And now here was Jake—sexy, gorgeous, every inch the man of her dreams.

She wanted badly to undress him and explore his taut, hard body. But if she wasn't going to have sex with him, there were rules to follow. Fair play. Self-denial.

Though it took remarkable willpower on her part, she moved away. "Would you like some coffee?" she asked, trying to pretend as if everything was normal.

Her kitchen looked the same as always, despite Jake's presence. Pine cabinets. Faded Formica countertops. Beige walls. This little house was dated and homely, but the community was friendly, and crime was low. Nikki's neighbors were Black and white and Hispanic. Young and old.

The man with the laser gaze stared at her, his jaw rigid. "Coffee? That's your answer?"

"I don't want to fight with you, Jake."

"And you don't want to have sex with me."

She shook her head slowly. "Not like this." She dealt with the coffeepot and turned it on. When she faced him again, he was leaning in the doorway, arms crossed over his broad chest, a dark scowl doing nothing to diminish his sexual pull. "Have you bought a return airline ticket?" she asked. No point in pretending.

"I have an open-ended one. Because the judge has fast-tracked the trial, I want to catch the opening arguments. Apparently, my father is planning to make a statement. Given the nature of the case, the judge is also allowing wronged parties to face the man who stole from them. Perhaps even let them speak."

"Poor Vernon."

Jake raised an eyebrow. "You have more charity than I do. My father *deserves* public condemnation. In fact, that's the tip of the iceberg. He should be—"

Nikki held up her hand, halting the flow of angry words. "Stop." She poured a cup of coffee and handed it to him. "Bitterness will destroy you. Mom and I spent the first several years of our exile constantly in the midst of grief and emotional upheaval. It was only when we decided to forgive my father that we were finally able to move on."

"I've moved on," he said, his tone defensive.

"You moved *away*," Nikki said. "Ran away. By your own admission. It's not the same thing. I know you're in Falling Brook for a brief time, but why don't you use these weeks to find closure with your dad? Actually, closure with the whole dismal experience?"

He stared down at his coffee, his expression moody. "Can we take this outside? I need some air. It's not all that cold."

"Sure." She grabbed a coat and the baby monitor. Jake retrieved his jacket from the living room.

"A baby monitor?" he said. "Still?"

"It gives me peace of mind."

"I can understand that."

They settled on the porch, skipping the swing in favor of sitting on the top step. Nikki didn't bother with the light. Because the stoop was narrow, she and Jake were hip-to-hip. She wanted badly to lean her head on his shoulder and dream of a future that included everything she wanted.

But that was futile. She sipped her coffee in silence. They weren't the only people taking advantage of the unexpectedly mild evening. Older kids still played up and down the street.

Without warning, Jake put a hand on her knee, making her jump.

"Why don't you and Emma come to Switzerland with me when this is all over?" he said. "For a visit," he clarified, as if wanting to make sure she understood. "The mountains are magnificent, and I think Emma would like it."

"What's in Switzerland?" Nikki kept the question light and casual, though her guts were in a knot.

"I own a small house there. I have a great housekeeper who handles things when I travel."

When I travel. There it was. The truth of Jake Lowell.

Nikki clenched the handle of her cup. "I have a job," she said evenly. "And other responsibilities."

"Emma's not in regular school yet. Besides, with the money from Black Crescent, you could quit the diner, right? I'll cover all the Europe expenses."

She sucked in a breath. "Being poor is not as bad as you think it is, Jake. But even if I decide to take the money from Black Crescent, it's a long time until January. Besides, I think Emma is a little young for a trip like that. I appreciate the offer."

They were both being so damn polite. As if roiling currents of emotion and discord didn't threaten the foundation beneath their feet.

Jake stood abruptly and set his empty coffee cup on the porch railing. "When can I swing by tomorrow?"

Nikki stood, too. The night was cloudy. She couldn't read his expression. "Tomorrow is not good. I work a double shift. Maybe you could come to a movie with Emma and me late Friday afternoon."

"Joshua's bachelor party is Friday night."

"The wedding's so soon?" The prospect of seeing people from her old life sent anxiety coursing through her veins.

"The actual ceremony is a week from Saturday. You never answered me. Will you be my date?"

She saw a challenge in his eyes, a dare. She weighed the prospect of attending a romantic wedding with Jake against her very real concerns. "I will," she said. "But I'll be nervous about seeing Falling Brook folks."

"You didn't do anything wrong. We'll face them together."

"Okay." It might be the only carefree time she had with Jake. An evening that would have to sustain her for the long, lonely years to come. "Good night," she muttered. Jake was too tempting. Too everything.

He cupped her neck in his big, warm hands and pulled her head to his. "I'll dream about you, Nik."

This kiss was lazy and slow. As if he had all the time in the world.

She put her hands on his shoulders to steady herself when her knees went weak. He tasted like coffee and dreams. Her dreams. All the ones that shattered when Black Crescent imploded, and Jake left her.

For long seconds, she let herself kiss him back. It was exhilarating. Toe curling. She felt like a princess at the end of a fairy tale. A very hot, flustered, needy princess. Only this particular prince was never going to stick around for the happily-ever-after.

When she realized she was running her fingers through his hair, she made herself step back. Take a breath. Reach for reason. "I should go in," she said. "I have a few mommy jobs to accomplish before I head to bed."

"I'll pay child support," he said gruffly. "Even if we decide not to tell her."

Nikki's temper flared, but she held her tongue. He was trying to do the right thing. "I don't need your money, Jake. Emma and I are fine. A child is a huge responsibility, but money is the least of it."

"You're saying you want emotional support?"

Is that what she was saying? She honestly didn't know. Having Jake around as a part-time dad would be awkward and painful. Maybe it *would* be better if he simply went away. She was convinced he still saw her as a version of her teenage self. He didn't understand or want to admit how much she had changed. "I only meant that it's eighteen years of hard work."

"Longer for some families whose kids never move out."

"I suppose so. Either way, I need you to know that you're off the hook. Your life doesn't accommodate fatherhood. Let's think about it. Maybe we can come up with a solution that suits us both."

"And Emma."

"Of course."

He moved toward the sidewalk. When a streetlight illuminated his features, she saw that Jake looked tired, sad. Maybe even uncertain. She had never seen him so vulnerable. Her heart squeezed. "You're good with her," Nikki said. "Truly, you are. She's lucky to have your brains and your fearlessness."

"You're wrong about one thing, Nik."

"Oh?"

He shoved his hands in his pockets and kicked at one of the small rocks Emma loved to collect. "I'm not fearless at all right now. Falling Brook. My father. My brothers. You. I feel like I'm stumbling around in a fog. I'm not even sure if I should have come back."

This time, her heart hurt when it pinched. "I'm glad you came, Jake. Really glad."

Jake always slept with the drapes open in a hotel room. In big cities, he liked seeing the array of colored lights on decked-out skyscrapers. Here in Falling Brook, the lights were fewer and less impressive, but they still lit the night with a comforting glow.

He was lying on his back with his hands behind his head. It was three in the morning. He'd barely slept. A few days ago, when he was flying across the ocean, he'd worried about reuniting with his twin. But the thing with Joshua had gone well.

The two brothers had fallen into their old relationship without drama.

Jake still had to face his mother and Oliver. Those reunions weren't something to dread, not really. The harder encounter had been finding out that he and Nikki had created a child, a daughter.

Suddenly, unable to be still a moment longer, he rolled out of bed, threw on some clothes and went down to the twenty-four-hour fitness center. On the treadmill, he set a punishing pace. If he ran hard enough and long enough, maybe he could outrun the demons at his heels.

At last, exhaustion claimed him. Back in his room, he showered and tumbled into bed, comatose almost instantly. When the alarm went off at eight, he opened his eyes and groaned. Insomnia had rarely been a problem in his adult life, except for the occasional bout of jet lag. Clearly, being back in Falling Brook was bad for his health.

He sat up on the side of the bed and reached for his phone. If peace and closure were his aims, he needed to work his list. Oliver was Jake's next priority. After thinking for a moment, he sent a text asking if his younger sibling could meet him at the Drayhill Quarry at ten thirty. It was a spot where the three Lowell brothers had often hiked and played around.

On one memorable hot summer day, they had even taken a dip despite the warning signs posted everywhere. Their mother had found out and grounded them for a month. After that, they still returned now and again to the abandoned quarry, but not to swim.

What appealed most was the isolation. At the quarry, they were free to be on their own. No parents breathing down their necks. No teachers demanding excellence.

But that was a long time ago.

Jake dragged his attention back to the present. While he was brushing his teeth, the text *ding* came through. Oliver would be there.

Jake was nervous. Once upon a time, the three brothers had been tight. But Jake had let his father's actions drive him away. He'd lost Nikki, his brothers, everything. Now a chance for reconciliation beckoned. Jake knew he didn't deserve anyone's forgiveness—least of all, his baby brother's.

After a few sprinkles of rain overnight, the mild weather had continued today. A weak sun shone down, making the morning slightly more cheerful. The drive out to the quarry was familiar but different. The old rutted road was worse now. Jake's fancy rental car took a beating. He parked by the gated fence and waited.

Soon, Oliver showed up in a late-model sedan. When the other man climbed out, Jake felt a wave of emotion he rarely allowed himself to acknowledge. This was his sibling, the man who was part of him. His blood and kin.

The two men embraced without speaking. Jake's eyes were damp when he pulled back. "Good to see you, Ol."

Oliver's brilliant blue eyes twinkled with happiness. "Took you long enough to contact me. I started to think you hadn't really come home at all."

"Sorry about that. I had to deal with some urgent business first."

"Yeah. Joshua told me. You have a baby. Right?"

"Well, Emma is four. But yes."

"Must have been quite a shock." Oliver's eyes held empathy.

Again, Jake's throat was tight. "On a scale of one to ten, I'd say a fifty. I don't know what I'm going to do about it."

"Joshua told me Nikki Reardon is the mother?"

Jake nodded. "I assume you remember her?"

Oliver snorted. "Are you kidding me? Of course I remember Nikki. You panted after her for years. It was painfully obvious that you were a one-woman kind of guy."

"Well, I screwed that up, too. I abandoned her just like I abandoned my brothers. I'm sorry, Oliver. Sorry for what happened to you."

"I doubt you could have done anything. Josh tried to

reach me. Mom did, too. But I was so damn angry. The anger ate me alive."

"Will you tell me what happened? If you want to," Jake said quickly. "I only had snippets from Josh."

"Sure," Oliver said. "But do you mind if we walk out to the falcon? I need to stretch my legs."

They climbed the fence and set off, striding along the makeshift trail that wound around the quarry. The underbrush was heavy. At times they had to scale fallen trees. After three quarters of a mile, they reached their destination. The falcon was an enormous boulder, shaped vaguely like Han Solo's famous spaceship. The broad, flat surface was perfect for hanging out, drinking beer or simply enjoying the summer sun.

Today, the November water below wasn't blue. It was murky and threatening. No temptation at all to chance a swim.

They sat down and got comfortable.

Oliver pitched a pebble into the quarry, his expression pensive. "I headed out for Harvard just a few weeks after you left. I was glad to leave Falling Brook, even though my tuition was only paid up for a year. I was furious with Dad. That anger moved with me, fueling the usual freshman-year screwing around. But I couldn't let it go, even though those feelings were poisoning me. Drugs and alcohol dulled the pain."

Jake's stomach twisted with guilt. He was silent for a moment. Stunned. "I'm sorry I wasn't there for you."

Oliver shrugged. "I needed to sort myself out. Things are good for me now, and I've been sober for years. I'm finally happy. But our father still has a lot to answer for."

"Josh said you went to visit him?"

"I did. He looked old, Jake. Old and pitiful. But when I saw him, all that anger came back, and it scared the hell out of me. He immediately criticized me for being a photographer. Same old crap. I asked about the stolen money. He said it was his. At that point, I knew he'd never change. I walked out. I won't let him destroy me a second time."

"I'm really proud of you, you know. You're very good at what you do. Our father is an asshole. Josh and I went, too," Jake said slowly, remembering and sorting through his own emotions. "Actually, we were summoned. But when we got there, the old man apparently changed his mind. Sent us away."

"What a bastard. But then again, perhaps you were lucky. Did you really want to talk to him?"

"Maybe. I don't know. I became a man without a country because of him. Falling Brook was unbearable. I went on my graduation trip and just never came back. Because of him, I've lived my life in slow motion. Slow to forgive, slow to process my feelings. Slow to mend the rift with you and Joshua."

"And Nikki?"

"Her most of all. I ran into her five years ago in Atlantic City. We had a…thing. But I let her slip through my fingers again. When Josh called and said Dad had been found, I took it as a sign that maybe it was time to deal with my own failures."

They sat there in silence. Although Jake couldn't speak for Oliver, he suspected the two of them were juggling the same mishmash of regrets.

Finally, Jake exhaled. "So, are there any women in *your* life?"

Oliver's broad grin caught Jake off guard. "As a matter of fact, there *is* a woman. Samantha. We just got engaged. And we're expecting a baby."

"Well, hell, man. You buried the lead. Congratulations."

Jake envied the fact that his brother was clearly thrilled about fatherhood. Oliver wasn't conflicted, like Jake.

"Sammi is a firecracker. You'll love her. She's had a tough life, but she's one of the strongest women I know."

"How did you meet?"

Oliver ducked his head, his expression sheepish. "A one-night stand. But it turned into something more, really fast."

Jake winced inwardly. His one-night stand with Nikki was at the root of his troubles. Did he regret it? How could he? It was arguably the best night of his life. But he'd been terrified by what he felt for her after a decade of nothing. She had changed, grown up. Though he wouldn't have thought it possible, she'd been even more intensely appealing than the teenage girl he had known all those years ago.

The tsunami of feelings had swept him under, drowned him. And so he had run.

Was he any better equipped to deal with her now?

Since there were no clear answers to his current dilemma, he changed the subject. "I assume you're going to the bachelor party tomorrow night?" One of Joshua's friends had put together a fun evening in Atlantic City.

"I'll be there," Oliver said. "It's not every day a Lowell man gets married. How about you?"

"Yep. I'm coming. Have you bought him any kind of gift?"

"No. Damn. I'll get something tomorrow."

"Well, here's the thing. When I was in Paris earlier this fall, I stumbled on a small Matisse at auction. It's a window scene from Morocco. I immediately thought of Joshua. You know how much he always loved Matisse. Of course, I had no idea Josh was going to get married soon, but when he told me, I had my assistant package the painting and send it to me. I should have it at the hotel tomorrow morning. I'd like to put your name and mine on the gift. You know, to acknowledge the fact that Josh is starting a new career, a new life. We left him to clean up the mess fifteen years ago. I know he didn't have to do it, but he did. What do you think?"

The words had tumbled out in a rush.

Oliver nodded. "That's perfect."

"Good. I want this gift to come from both of us. Together. I want to mend fences. To heal our family. We used to be the three Lowell brothers, unbreakable, unshakable. I'm sorry for my part in breaking us up. This is a gesture. A peace offering. Are you in?"

"I'm in."

Oliver ran a hand through his hair, his profile stark as he stared out across the quarry. Jake felt the coals of guilt burn hotter. Oliver had been a teenager when Jake left. Jake had failed him. Had failed Joshua. And Nikki. And his mother.

Could he ever do penance for his neglect? Sometimes he thought he'd simply been too lazy to look for a reason to return home. The truth was...he'd been scared. Scared that the people he loved would judge him. Or turn their backs on him.

Now it seemed that both of his brothers were willing to forgive and forget. That realization filled him with quiet satisfaction.

But what about Nikki? He had wronged her, most of all.

Would the mother of his child be willing to accept his regrets and his determination to do better?

And, if she did, was Jake willing to deal with the consequences?

Seven

It had been a very long time since Nikki shopped the designers on Fifth Avenue or Madison Avenue. But some memories never faded.

If she was going to Joshua's wedding—as Jake's date—nothing in her closet was remotely suitable. She had a credit card for emergencies. This didn't qualify. But even if the promised payments from Black Crescent didn't come through, Nikki could pay off a purchase over the coming months.

She had trained herself, out of necessity, not to live on credit. Today, she was going to break her own rule. A woman deserved the occasional fantasy, and this was hers.

After working the very early morning shift at the diner and then spending time with her daughter, Nikki changed clothes and said goodbye to her mom and Emma. Because the wedding was close, she decided to postpone the movie date with her daughter. Catching a train into the city at one o'clock didn't leave Nikki much time for shopping.

She dozed en route, exhausted. Yesterday's double shift, followed by a 4:00 a.m. alarm this morning, had drained her. Even so, adrenaline pumped in her veins when she arrived at Grand Central.

In better days, Roberta Reardon had employed a full-time chauffeur. Now, Nikki was happy to use the subway. It was cheap and easy and took her where she wanted to go.

The first two stores she tried were a bust. Her mother had shopped with her at both when Nikki was a teenage girl. But Nikki's tastes had changed.

She was getting discouraged when she spotted a small boutique wedged in between two well-known fashion houses that took up most of the block. The modest shop had a name on the glass door that Nikki didn't recognize. The items in the window told her to go in and take a look.

Inside, a pleasant saleswoman honored Nikki's intent to browse undisturbed. There were casual outfits aplenty. Deeper into the salon, Nikki found what she was looking for. Jake had told her the wedding would be in the early afternoon. Which meant tea-length was perfectly appropriate. The dress she spotted was a beautiful shade of ivory. Strapless. With a ballerina skirt that frothed out in layers of soft tulle.

"I'd like to try this one," she said impulsively, although the price tag made her gulp.

"I'll put it in a changing room for you," the woman said. "And if you're interested, that small rack over there is marked down. Last year's items. You know the drill."

Nikki wondered if the clerk had scoped out her customer and noted the inexpensive jeans and generic top. It didn't matter. False pride was a commodity Nikki couldn't afford. Though she had planned only to flip through the discounted items, her hand landed on a scoop-neck red cashmere sweater that might or might not clash with her hair. The black wool pencil skirt was a no-brainer. It would go with everything.

In the curtained cubicle, she tried the sweater and skirt first. They fit perfectly. A small pulled thread on the sleeve of the sweater and a missing button on the skirt explained another reason the items were on sale. The small imperfections didn't daunt Nikki. She had learned to be handy with a needle. Jake wanted to see her again. If that involved a night out, this outfit would bolster her confidence.

Her choice for the wedding was even better. She smoothed her hands over the skirt and tugged at the bodice. The only thing holding her back was the color. Some people insisted that only a bride should wear white to a wedding.

The saleslady knocked on the door frame. "Any luck?"

Nikki held back the curtain. "I love this, but I don't know if I can wear it to a wedding. You know, because of the color."

The woman tilted her head and studied Nikki. "It fits you like a dream. And I don't think most people care anymore. Besides, it's a deep, rich ivory, not white. What if you add a pop of color? Hold on."

When the woman returned moments later, Nikki nodded. "That might work." She took the proffered scarf and draped it around her shoulders. It was soft, watered silk in pale, pale pink. When Nikki looked in the mirror, she smiled. "Thank you. I'll take it."

As the clerk rang up the purchases, Nikki battled her conscience. Any extra money she made over and above her household expenses went to doing things with her daughter and her mother. Movies. Meals out. This self-indulgence was hard to justify.

The saleswoman excused herself for a moment to deal with a call on the store's landline. While Nikki waited perched on the edge of a chair, her cell phone dinged. Her heart gave a funny little jump. It was a text from Jake…

Dinner tomorrow night? Just us? Let me know…

There was no reason to get flustered. Jake wasn't making a romantic overture. He clearly wanted to speak with Nikki about the future and how he would be a part of Emma's life. Or how he might not. Nikki knew it was an important conversation. One she needed to have with Jake alone. She would have to act like a mature thirty-something single mother and not the giddy cocktail waitress who had still adored Jake Lowell and let him coax her into bed.

Even more importantly, she absolutely *had* to decide what it was she wanted from him. She needed his body, his intense lovemaking. His rakish charm. But common sense said she couldn't sleep with him and still make smart decisions about Emma.

What happened if Nikki didn't make the right choice?

If she agreed to this dinner, she had little more than twenty-four hours to figure it out.

Other customers entered the store, and Nikki got up, rattled by the unexpected text. When the employee handed over two lilac-and-navy shopping bags, Nikki winced inwardly. On the other hand, a little part of her was already thinking about how perfect her new sweater and skirt would be for a night out with her daughter's father.

Elegant. Not too fussy. Nothing that would suggest

Nikki misunderstood Jake's motives. But definitely flattering.

Outside, the wind had picked up, and the sky was gray. The pleasant temperatures were gone, replaced by a bone-chilling cold. Nikki leaned against the building only long enough to answer the text.

She dithered over what to say, even as her fingers began to freeze. Finally, she pecked out a response…

Dinner is fine. Can we do seven?

Her phone dinged again…

Works for me. I'll pick you up then.

She gnawed her lip. But decided to add one more note…

Have fun at Joshua's bachelor party!

After a long silence, all she got was the thumbs-up emoji. Jake could be busy. Or he wasn't interested in a long text exchange.

No need to feel rejected.

When she glanced at her watch, she saw that she had a little time to kill before she caught the train. Too bad the Rockefeller Center tree wasn't up yet. Maybe she could bring Emma in a few weeks. At four, her precocious daughter was more than old enough to enjoy the treat.

Since Nikki's shopping errand had been accomplished with time to spare, she decided to walk despite the gloomy weather. She could definitely use more exercise. Everywhere she looked, retail establishments were beginning to deck the halls for the holiday season.

Thanksgiving was the weekend after Joshua's wedding. Barely two weeks away. Nikki and Roberta never made a big deal about the holiday. Nikki often baked a pumpkin pie. And sometimes they cooked a small turkey breast. But the celebration was low-key.

When Nikki was in high school, she remembered huge Thanksgiving spreads, mostly put together by the Lowell cook and housekeeper. As a kid, Nikki had never really thought about the work it took to pull off something like that. Or the expense.

Vernon Lowell had loved hosting lavish celebrations and inviting fifteen or twenty of his friends and business associates. The enormous cherry dining-room table could seat two dozen. The chandelier was actual Venetian glass. The priceless Persian silk rug and the enormous sets of china, crystal and heavy silver had all been sold off after the patriarch's disappearance.

Nikki had nothing of that era to pass down to her own daughter.

It didn't matter, she told herself firmly. Emma knew she was loved, and that's what mattered.

Eventually, Nikki made her way back to Grand Central and caught the train home. This time she didn't sleep. She worried. Did she and Jake have anything in common anymore? Could she step back into his world even temporarily? Could she sleep with him and let it be no more than that? And what about the fact that he didn't understand how much she had changed?

She knew he wasn't staying. But she badly wanted him to acknowledge all the ways she had survived and thrived. Something deep inside her craved his approval and his love.

And if that wasn't the most dismal admission a woman had ever made, she didn't know what was.

Arriving on the doorstep of her familiar small house calmed some of Nikki's nerves. She and Emma had made it this far and had a good life. Whatever came next, they would handle.

When Nikki opened the front door, the aroma of homemade chicken-noodle soup wafted out. Though her mom and Emma had finished eating, the soup was still warming on the stove.

Nikki shrugged out of her coat and hung it up on a hook near the door. Her shopping bags went in a nearby closet. Then she hugged Emma and smiled at her mom. "Thanks for keeping her this afternoon." She tried never to take her mother's help for granted, even though Roberta enjoyed time with Emma.

Emma demanded to be picked up. Nikki nuzzled her daughter's hair. "You smell like dessert," she teased.

The routine of the next hour and a half was comfortable and familiar. At Nikki's request, Roberta stayed. When Nikki told her mother they needed *to talk*, Roberta raised an eyebrow, but nodded.

At last, Emma was asleep. The two women made their way to the tiny living room, turned on the gas logs and put up their feet.

Roberta sighed. "This is nice. Did you find a dress for the wedding?"

"I did," Nikki said. "I'll try it on for you sometime soon. Thanks again for keeping Emma. I tried to get back as quickly as I could."

Roberta cocked her head. "You said we needed to talk. Is this about Jake?"

"Not directly. He and I are having dinner tomorrow night to discuss Emma and the future."

"What's to talk about? He's her father."

"Jake being Emma's daddy isn't what I wanted to talk to you about, Mom."

"Oh?"

Carefully, and as calmly as possible, Nikki shared what Joshua had told her about his plan to compensate Roberta and Nikki for all they had lost. She went on to explain that all of the Black Crescent clients who lost money fifteen years ago had received payments at an agreed-upon rate. It had taken Joshua a very long time, but the ethical and legal obligations had been met.

Roberta listened in silence, though her eyes widened, and her cheeks flushed.

When Nikki finished, Roberta sat up on the edge of her seat, clearly agitated. "Vernon stole that money. Why should you and I get anything?"

"That's what I told Joshua, Mom. But he says Dad stole from us, too. Joshua wants to do this."

"Dear Lord." Roberta seemed dazed.

"The payments will begin January first. It's a lot of money. Not like what you had before, but plenty if we're careful. We'll need to invest some and save some. You don't want to get to the end of the ten years and find yourself right back where you are now."

Roberta nodded. "I didn't know a single thing about finances when I married your father. I've regretted that more than once since he left us."

"I'll help you. And I suspect Joshua will be willing to advise us."

"And Jake, too. If he's such a financial genius."

"Yes," Nikki said hesitantly. She'd told her mom how Jake had supported himself for years by day-trading. "Jake, too. Think about it, Mom. You can go back to your old friends. Pick up the good pieces of your old life."

Roberta's face hardened. "They turned their backs on me."

"No. To be fair, you and I disappeared. We didn't give anyone a chance to help us. We were embarrassed and too humiliated to show our faces. I'm sure there were a few of your friends who might have shunned you for what Daddy did, but I have to believe that at least some of them would be glad to reconnect. I think that's true even now. But we haven't wanted any contact. Maybe we were wrong, Mom."

"I suppose."

It was a lot to digest. Nikki was glad her mother didn't turn the tables and ask what Nikki wanted to do. Life was comfortable now. Hard and demanding, but comfortable in its predictability.

Did Nikki want to uproot all she had worked for and return to the town of her childhood? Emma could attend the same Falling Brook prep school where her mother got a good education. Nikki could be a stay-at-home mom for a few years. Volunteer at school. Pay attention to her physical and mental health. Not be so exhausted all the time.

Maybe see Jake when he came home to visit his mother and brothers.

Nikki yawned. "We've got a lot to think about. Thankfully, nothing has to be decided tonight."

The more important questions surrounded Jake. Despite the changes happening all around her, Nikki was most conflicted about Jake. Fascinating, sexy, unpredictable Jake Lowell. What would tomorrow night bring?

Jake sipped his scotch and loosened his tie. Joshua's bachelor party was proving to be a good distraction from thinking about Nikki. A friend of Joshua's had reserved a large room on the top floor of one of Atlantic City's glitziest casinos. Jake didn't know the man. It was someone Josh had become friends with after college—a relationship that began after Jake had left Falling Brook.

The dress code tonight was upscale, but Jake noticed that several guys had already shed their jackets. Enormous flat-screen TVs covered the walls, tuned to various sports channels. The open bar was stocked with top-shelf booze. Three beautiful pool tables were busy. Half a dozen female servers wandered among the partygoers handing out delicious hors d'oeuvres and smiles.

At the far end of the room, elegant tables were set for the steak dinner to come. Jake sat in a bubble of quiet at the moment, observing. He knew most of the men in the room, or he had at one time. Many of them had greeted him cordially tonight. They were understandably curious about Joshua's absent twin. When Jake left Falling Brook, he had cut all ties with surgical precision, preferring to look forward rather than dwell on the past.

That recollection brought him right back to Nikki. She, like Jake, had abdicated her place in Falling Brook society and had gone into hiding. Maybe that was a dramatic way of phrasing it, but the result was the same.

A waitress stopped at his elbow. "Would you like anything, sir?"

He looked up, noticing the woman's surgically enhanced breasts and the flirtatious look in her eyes. At one time, he wouldn't have thought twice about getting her number and hooking up after the party was over.

"Thanks, I'm good," he said, giving the woman his best noncommittal smile. Despite the fact that he was in the midst of a dry spell, sexually speaking, he wasn't interested. Nobody but Nikki pushed his buttons. Knowing that she was so close and yet so far away made him grumpy. Their brief text exchange had revved his motor to an embarrassing degree.

He found himself obsessing about tomorrow night's date. Clearly, he and Nikki had to come to a decision about Emma. Maybe Jake was a total jerk to think so, but dealing with his small daughter wasn't nearly as worrisome as understanding his feelings for Nikki.

Seeing her in Atlantic City five years ago had been both exhilarating and unsettling. He hadn't stuck around long enough to find out what was going on in her world. Despite the incredible sex, he'd been afraid to hear that she had a life that didn't include him, which was stupid, because of course she did.

His stomach tightened unpleasantly as he finally admitted the truth to himself. One reason he had stayed away from Falling Brook for so long—among many—was that he'd been afraid to come back and see that Nikki had moved on with another man.

And she had. By her own admission. She had married and divorced.

That was more of a relationship than Jake could claim. His hopscotching travels had, by design, left him little opportunity to get attached to any one place or person. He had anesthetized his pain over his father's betrayal with new experiences, fresh vistas.

For a very long time, he had been satisfied with the status quo. Or, at least, he had convinced himself he was. When Joshua's phone call came out of the blue saying that Vernon was alive, it had been an electric shock to the system.

The Jake who lived day by day and never worried about anything was suddenly jerked back into the truth that he was indeed tied to other people. Despite time and distance, he was still a son, a brother. And now, a father, too.

What he was to Nikki remained to be seen…

Oliver approached him and bumped his knee. “Play me some pool?”

Jake finished his drink and set it aside. “I’d be happy to kick your ass. Lead the way.”

It wasn’t as easy as he had imagined. Though Jake was a shark when it came to the pool table, his baby brother was a different kind of wizard. Jake lined up his shots with cool precision, sinking ball after ball.

Oliver, on the other hand, played wildly, taking dumb chances that paid off. After four games, they had each won twice. Both men had shed their sport coats and rolled up their shirtsleeves. Jake raised an eyebrow. “Best three out of five?”

“Nope.”

“Nope?”

Oliver wiped his forehead with the back of his hand. “I learned in recovery to be satisfied with ‘enough.’ That who I am is sufficient. Now, when those competitive rushes try to drag me into deep water, I step away.”

Jake frowned. “You know we weren’t playing for money, right?”

“Doesn’t matter. I still have that killer instinct. And it can get me in trouble. So I stop and take a breath and ask myself what’s really important. You should try it, Jake. It’s good for the soul.”

Oliver excused himself, leaving Jake a lot unsettled and a little bit pissed. He was damn glad his sibling had beaten addiction, but Jake didn’t have similar problems. He didn’t drink to excess. He’d never done drugs. Why did Oliver’s implication sound so judgmental?

Maybe Jake was making a big deal out of nothing. So Oliver didn't want to play the tiebreaker. So what?

Jake was leaning against the momentarily empty pool table, brooding and watching the nearest TV screen, when the man of the hour crossed the room in his direction. Joshua looked relaxed and happy. For a split second, Jake was jealous. Jealous that his twin had found love and challenges and purpose in his life.

The truth was, if anybody deserved that trifecta, it was Josh.

Jake grinned at him. "I still can't believe you're getting married. And leaving Black Crescent."

Joshua lifted an eyebrow. "The job is still yours if you want it."

The urge to say yes came out of nowhere. Jake quaked inside. Here was an opportunity to fit back into the fabric of Falling Brook, to grow close to his family again, to build a bond with his daughter. To make Nikki proud. The temptation dangled. But it would require stepping up to the plate. Changing. Growing.

His gut clenched. *Back away.*

"Lord, no," he said, managing a chuckle. "I'd be terrible at it. It's one thing to take risks with my own cash. I wouldn't want the responsibility of handling other people's money, but I don't mind helping you with the CEO search."

"Then what *do* you want to do, Jake?"

The serious question caught Jake off guard. He hadn't expected to be grilled in the middle of a party. "Same thing I always do, I guess. Be me."

Joshua's gaze showed concern. "We all have to move forward. Whether we want to or not. Don't let Dad control your life."

The expression in his twin's eyes baffled and bothered Jake as much as Oliver's pseudo lecture about being *enough.* "That's bullshit," Jake said angrily, keeping his voice low. "Dad doesn't control me. I haven't seen the man in fifteen years. Are you nuts?"

"He casts a long shadow. And now even more. He's going to spend the rest of his life in prison, by all accounts. It would be foolish of us to let him affect our choices. I'll admit that I'm being selfish. I lost you for a decade and a half. I don't want to lose you again."

Joshua bumped Jake's shoulder with an affectionate fist and walked off, leaving Jake with the strongest urge to run out the door and keep on running. That's what he did when things got tough. But this was his brother's bachelor party. His twin. His other half. He couldn't bail on Joshua. Not tonight. He'd done it too often already. He owed Josh.

He certainly didn't *deserve* Josh's goodwill and forgiveness. Jake had left his brother holding the proverbial bag. When Vernon disappeared, Joshua had dealt with the feds and the insurance companies and their mother and everything else in the midst of panic and grief and confusion.

What had Jake done to help? Nothing. Nothing at all… He had disappeared, severing the ties that might have sustained him in his grief. He might be slow, but he was finally beginning to understand how much he had lost.

Eight

The bachelor party was a huge success. Even the guys who imbibed heavily were classy enough not to get falling-down drunk. Or maybe Joshua picked his friends carefully. Maybe he surrounded himself with men of depth.

Whatever the reason, the evening was going well.

When it was time for dinner, the men moved as one to the tables, where shrimp cocktails and Caesar salads sat waiting. As everyone dug in, Jake noted that Joshua had perhaps intentionally *not* set up a head table. In most families, the groom-to-be might be flanked by his two brothers. But the Lowell relationships, though cordial, were strained by the events of the past.

Jake sat with Oliver to his right and a Black Crescent employee he had just met on his left. The meal was fabulous. And it must have cost a fortune. Again, Jake felt guilty. *He* should have been the one paying for this spread. He could certainly afford it. But, heck. He hadn't even known his brother was getting married.

Jake had kept himself out of the loop.

When the steaks and potatoes were only a memory, and there was a brief lull before dessert was served, Jake seized the moment to say a few words. He stood and cleared his throat. "As the twin brother of the groom, I believe it's my duty to make a toast."

Joshua grinned, his expression a mixture of surprise and pleasure. "By all means," he said. "But if you start telling childhood stories, I'll plead the Fifth."

Ignoring laughter and a few catcalls, Jake began his spiel. "Joshua…you were known as the good kid, and I was the bad apple. I guess some things never change."

A titter of laughter went around the room.

Jake continued. "For a decade and a half, you've managed to find the best in a really crappy situation. Now, although I've only met Sophie briefly, I can already tell that the two of you are a perfect match."

"Thanks," Joshua said, his posture slightly guarded as if he didn't know what was coming next.

Jake reached beneath the dinner table and picked up the small package that was loosely wrapped in brown butcher paper. "Oliver and I want to give you something to mark this occasion. It's not exactly a wedding gift. It's more of a thank-you for being a damn good human being, and our steady-as-a-rock brother. We love you, man."

Jake walked past several people and handed over the small package, then returned to his seat.

Joshua stood and carefully peeled back the paper. He examined the painting intently, his fingers clenched on the frame. His face went pale. He looked up, startled, staring at his two brothers. "My God. Is this really a…" He trailed off, his expression gobsmacked.

"It's a Matisse," Jake said quietly. Joshua's reaction made him damn glad he'd come up with this idea.

Oliver, shoulder-to-shoulder with Jake, spoke up. "We're pumped as hell that you're jump-starting your art career, and I hope you know we'll both be first in line to hang a few Josh Lowell masterpieces on our walls."

Jake lifted his glass of champagne. "To Josh. May your marriage be as long lasting as this old master."

"To Josh." The chorus rose around the tables.

Amid the laughter and applause, Joshua stood and hugged each of his brothers tightly, then pulled them both in for a triple embrace. "Thanks, guys. This means the world to me."

Oliver held up his hands. "We're heading for the mushy zone. Time for more red meat and male bonding." He returned to his seat with a chuckle.

Joshua kept his hand firm on Jake's shoulder. "I'm not letting you hold me at arm's length ever again. You got that?"

The words were low, only loud enough for Jake to hear. But they packed a punch. Jake nodded, his throat tight. "Understood."

The remainder of the evening passed in a haze for Jake. He was more of a watcher than an active participant. The men in this room admired Joshua. It was evident in the way they joked with him and laughed with him and thanked him for inviting them to be part of his bachelor celebration.

Oliver was equally popular and social, though he drank nothing stronger than sparkling water. Jake wondered how his brother felt being present at an event where the alcohol flowed freely, but Oliver never seemed tempted.

The room was booked until midnight. Gradually, the

guests began making their goodbyes. Oliver had come with a trio of guys and was the designated driver. Eventually, quiet fell. Only Joshua and Jake remained.

Joshua yawned. "That was fun. But I sure as hell am glad the wedding is not tomorrow. I'm going to go home and crash hard."

"Sounds like a plan," Jake said. "You want me to drive you? I switched to coffee a couple of hours ago."

"Sure. I'd like that. My driver is waiting, but I'll send him on."

In the car, Jake adjusted the heat and made his way out of the crowded parking garage. "This may take a while," he said, grimacing at the line of cars.

Joshua took off his tie, reclined his seat a few inches and sighed deeply as he stretched out his legs. "If you had told me six months ago that I'd be getting married soon, I'd have said you were crazy." He shook his head, but he seemed more smug than reflective.

Jake swiped his credit card and waited for the arm to raise. "What does it feel like?" he asked, easing out into the traffic. "Knowing that you've found someone for a life partner? Isn't it scary? What if you've made a mistake?"

"I know the statistics. But I also know Sophie. I didn't even realize I had been waiting for someone like her. She argues with me and pushes me and makes me a better person. Plus, she's hot as hell. Not that I'm bragging."

Jake horse laughed, wiping his eyes with one hand. "Of *course* you're bragging. That's what a groom is expected to do."

"And what about you and Nikki and Emma?"

Josh shrugged, keeping his eyes on the road. "Nikki and I are having dinner tomorrow night to talk about the situation."

"A date?"

"Not a date." The clarification was irritating, mostly because he had asked himself the same question a dozen times.

"What are you going to say? About the daddy thing, I mean."

Jake rotated his shoulders. He felt as tight as if he had been driving for hours. "I'm not sure. I don't think I can walk away from my own flesh and blood."

Several seconds passed. Long, suddenly awkward seconds.

Joshua ran a hand across the back of his neck. "Not to belabor the point, bro, but you did before. I can understand where Nikki is coming from. She wants to protect her daughter from getting hurt."

Suddenly, all the warm fuzzies Jake had been feeling as he reconnected with his twin evaporated. Was he always going to be the bad guy? Was there nothing he could do to make up for his fifteen-year hiatus? Nikki insisted she had changed, but did no one entertain the possibility that Jake might be changing, too?

He reached for the radio and tuned it to a station that played current music. It wasn't long before Joshua was snoring.

It was just as well. Jake knew where he stood now. He was always going to be on the outside looking in, wishing for something he couldn't even name…

Nikki worked the eight-to-four shift on Saturday, then rushed home to shower and change. Emma was pouty because her mom was leaving again, but it couldn't be helped. And, honestly, except for work, Nikki seldom left her daughter to go out. Mommies had needs, too.

She gave herself a mental slap. Tonight wasn't about a

single mother's *needs*. She and Jake were getting together to discuss his role in Emma's life, her future.

The red sweater and black skirt, both newly mended, gave Nikki's confidence a boost. She paired the outfit with spiky black heels and silver snowflake earrings. Her black wool coat was at least seven years old, but it had classic lines. The forecast called for spitting snow, so she had no choice but to dress for the cold.

Roberta had been with Emma during the day, but Nella came over at five thirty to help with Emma's dinner and stay until Nikki returned.

"Enjoy yourself, Ms. Reardon," she said. "I brought stuff to do when Emma is in bed. If you're late, it won't matter. I'll doze on the sofa."

"Thanks," Nikki said, hoping her cheeks weren't as red as her sweater. "Text me if you need anything. And I'll check in with you a time or two." When the doorbell rang, Nikki kissed her daughter. "Be good, sweetheart. You and I will spend the day together tomorrow, I promise. Bye, Emma."

When she went through the house to the front door, she slipped her arms into her coat, then picked up her cell phone and purse. Jake wasn't coming in. Not with a babysitter who might or might not gossip.

As she pulled open the door, she smoothed a flyaway strand of hair. "Hi, there. I'm ready." Though she thought she was prepared, the sight of him made her weak. Those beautiful greenish-hazel eyes. The tousled hair. Broad shoulders. Flat belly. She felt the zing between them and forced herself not to react.

He blinked when he saw her, as if he, too, felt something. She saw the muscles in his throat work. "You look nice, Nik. I hope I didn't rush you too much."

"Not at all. Actually, I'm starving." They were back

to being polite again. She hated it. At least when they fought, they were honest with each other. Now she felt the need to guard her words to preserve the peace.

Jake had suggested eating at the restaurant in his hotel. Nikki looked it up online while she was getting ready. It was one of the top-rated eateries in Falling Brook. Upscale. Jackets and ties required.

The fact that Jake had a king-size bed a few floors above was incidental.

"How was the bachelor party?" she asked when they were in the car.

Watching Jake's capable hands on the wheel made her tummy feel funny. *Sexual attraction. Animal attraction.* She recognized it for what it was, just like she had recognized it that night in Atlantic City. No point in denying the truth. But her physical response to Jake complicated the conversation about Emma.

When he helped her out of the car at the hotel, he put his hand under her arm momentarily. She came close to leaning into him the way she used to when they were together as teenagers, but she stopped herself.

He smelled warm and spicy and masculine. As they walked quickly toward the building, icy snow pellets dotted her coat. She turned up her collar and shivered. Neither of them was wearing gloves. When they entered the lobby and were enfolded in warm air, she inhaled the scents of fresh gardenias and furniture polish.

They bypassed the registration desk and walked down a long, carpeted hallway. The decor was understated and elegant, with no expense spared. It had been a very, very long time since Nikki had found herself in such sophisticated surroundings.

Their table was waiting for them. A single white orchid bloomed alongside a lit hurricane lamp. The restaurant was already swathed in holly and gold ribbons. The smells wafting from the kitchen promised culinary delights.

When Jake helped Nikki out of her coat, the warmth of his breath on the back of her neck made her shiver. He draped the coat over one of the extra seats and held her chair as she sat down. Then he took his place on the opposite side of the table and stared, his gaze hot and hungry.

"Don't," she said.

"Don't what?" His eyes danced, though he didn't smile.

"Don't look like you're going to gobble me up. It's disconcerting."

"I'd forgotten how beautiful you really are."

"I'm older and five pounds heavier, and I have stretch marks."

Now his beautiful lips curled upward in a sexy grin. He shrugged. "I know what I see, Nik."

"Can we eat right away?" she asked, unable to look straight at him. It was as dangerous as peering at the sun. Everything inside her heated and churned. "I don't want to be out too late." Was she reminding herself or him?

"Of course." Jake lifted a hand and summoned the waiter. "My friend is famished. We'd like to order, please."

"Yes, sir. As you wish."

Nikki glanced blindly at the specials. "I'll have the prix fixe menu," she said. "Bruschetta. Shrimp bisque. The chicken piccata."

The dignified older man nodded. "And for dessert?"

"I'll decide later if that's okay."

The server turned to Jake. "And you, sir?"

"I'll order the other choices, so we can try them all. A house salad, the sweet-potato puree and the pork tenderloin."

Soon, Nikki and Jake were alone. Again. She worried her bottom lip with her teeth. "This feels awkward."

Jake nodded solemnly. "Very. Shall we discuss Emma now or later?"

"Let's get it over with." She clasped her hands on the table and took a deep breath. "Have you thought about who you want to be in her life?"

His response was instantaneous. "I'm her father," he said firmly. The possessive words sent a thrill through Nikki. They had made a baby together. "That's who I am and who I want to be," he said. "But I understand that I'm new to this game. I don't want to step on your toes or cause a problem for you."

Too late. Nikki kept her dark humor to herself. She cleared her throat, acknowledging the butterflies in her stomach. Though she spoke prosaically, she wanted to crawl across the table and drag his lips to hers. "I'm glad. A girl needs her father. How often do you think you might be available? I know you live a long way from here, and you have a busy travel schedule."

"It's the twenty-first century. We have jets and Wi-Fi conversations. I'll make time for Emma, I promise. I want to know her. I want to know her well."

Nikki found herself on the brink of tears. She realized in that moment that she hadn't known for sure Jake would claim his fatherhood. The fact that he had made her wildly emotional. "I'm so glad," she said, her throat tight. "I suppose we can work out the details later."

"I suppose we can." He reached across the table and took one of her hands, stroking his thumb across the back of it, giving her goose bumps. "Now that we've settled the big topic, let's talk about us."

"Us?" Her heart raced.

His tight smile held a hint of determination. "I ran away from you twice, Nikki. Once in Atlantic City, but even worse when you were almost eighteen."

They both winced. By the time Nikki's birthday rolled around that June, she had lost her innocence, but not because of Jake. Her world had been in ashes. Law-enforcement vehicles in her driveway. Uniformed men and women inside her house, boxing up her father's office. Opening the safe. Confiscating computers.

"I wish I could have spared you all the awfulness," he said, the words gruff and raw. "You were in so much pain. It broke my heart."

"You stayed for the funeral before you took off. I always appreciated that."

"It was a circus, as I recall. Paparazzi everywhere we turned. My mother and your mother weeping in a corner. I still get nauseous when I smell carnations."

"It was all a long time ago," she said softly. "We're different people now."

Suddenly, their food arrived, and the intimate conversation was shelved. Though Nikki was the furthest thing from calm, she ate, anyway. Soon, the flavors and textures of the various dishes coaxed her into enjoying the meal.

Beneath their conversation, a current of heated lust ran strong. She saw it in Jake's laser gaze, recognized it in her trembling body. They laughed and flirted and shared something rare and wonderful.

But Nikki knew in her heart it was temporary. Ephemeral.

Jake seemed relaxed, more relaxed than she had seen

him since he had returned to Falling Brook. She asked the question she had been avoiding. "What did you do Thursday when I was working? I felt bad about turning you down."

"You have a job, Nik. I understand that. Oliver drove in from Manhattan, and we reconnected. Then we went to my mom's."

"How did that go?"

"Mom hugged me. Cried a little. I'm worried about her, Nik. A few years back, my father was declared legally dead. Mom took off her wedding ring. Thank God she didn't date anyone seriously. It would have killed her, I think, to know she had committed adultery."

"Is she glad your father is alive?"

"I'm not sure. It's a devil of a mess. The hell of it is, there's not much my brothers and I can do for her."

"Except be there."

"I suppose."

"Sorry," Nikki said. "I didn't mean to ruin the mood."

Jake's face lightened. "Well, that's promising. I didn't even know we had a mood," he said, teasing. "Have I told you that your very lovely red sweater gives me all sorts of naughty ideas?"

"It's new," she admitted. "I bought it even though I shouldn't have, because I wanted to look good for you."

"Mission accomplished." The words were intense. Now he had both of her hands in his.

"Seeing you again after all this time has surprised me, Jake."

"How so?"

"You know the phrase *slow burn*?"

"Of course."

Her bottom lip trembled. "You severed our relationship. But the burn didn't end. I used to fantasize about you sometimes when I was having sex with my husband. How awful is that?"

He went pale. His pupils dilated. "Why are you telling me this? The truth, please."

She pulled her hands away and wrapped her arms around her waist, trying not to fall apart. "I know there's nothing between us, Jake. You've been gone almost half my life. Fifteen years. We've lived apart. Separate. No connection at all except for that one insane night in Atlantic City five years ago. But that slow burn rekindled when I saw you again. And I have to know. Do you feel it, too?"

Now his face was grim, almost angry. "You know I do."

She swallowed hard, wondering if she was making a huge mistake, but feeling the urgency of the moment. "I'd like to sleep with you again. I'm living like a nun. I miss physical intimacy. I miss you."

The server brought dessert. For a moment, Nikki thought Jake might come unglued. The glare he gave the poor man sent him scuttling away.

"This looks good," Nikki said inanely.

Jake's jaw was hard as iron. "Please tell me you don't really expect me to eat anything right now."

"Shall I ask for to-go boxes?"

The sexual frustration and hunger rolled off him in waves. She had unleashed a sleeping dragon. A beautiful creature capable of creating great destruction.

He stared at her, his gaze hot. "Fine."

This time, Nikki was the one to summon the waiter. Soon, the check was taken care of, and Nikki had a paper bag in front of her. It was imprinted with the restaurant's name and held two clear plastic boxes, one with tiramisu, the other pecan pie.

She stood up on shaky legs. “Are we done?”

Jake stood, as well. His feral smile made the hair rise on the back of her neck. “We’re *not* done, Nikki. Not even close.”

Nine

Jake wondered if he was dreaming. He'd had a number of vivid dreams about Nikki Reardon over the years. With color and sound and all the visuals he could handle. But tonight was different. She stood at his elbow in the elevator, her gaze downcast, her fair skin tinted with a noticeable flush.

When the elevator stopped on his floor, they both got out, but still he didn't touch her. His hand shook as he tapped his key card on the electronic panel and waited for the tiny light to turn green.

Inside, he turned on lamps and kicked up the heat a couple of notches.

"This suite is amazing," Nikki said.

"I'm glad you like it."

Suddenly, he found himself looking at the room through her eyes. He wasn't the neatest traveler. His laptop was plugged in on the desk by the window with papers scattered nearby. His suitcase was open on a luggage stand revealing his tumbled clothing.

For a man who traveled constantly, he'd never had any interest in being anal about organization. He was more likely to toss things in and hope for the best. His system hadn't failed him yet.

Now that he finally had Nikki within ten feet of his bed, his brain seized up and threatened to shut down. He was hard all over. And breathless. A thirty-seven-year-old man who could barely speak.

"Um," he said, as he undid his tie and tossed it aside with his jacket. "Would you like something to drink?"

Nikki set the desserts on a table and removed her coat. "I'd rather not. That's what got us into trouble in Atlantic City. If we're doing this, I want to be all in, not woozy."

"Fair enough." So much for smoothing anyone's nerves with alcohol. "There's an extra robe in the bathroom. If you'd like to get comfortable."

She kicked off her sexy high heels and padded across the room to where he stood. "I kind of thought you'd be the one getting me out of my clothes."

Holy hell. "Nikki…" He nearly swallowed his tongue when she placed her small hand, palm flat on his chest, right over his heart. Her fingers burned his skin through the expensive fabric of his dress shirt.

She went up on her tiptoes and kissed him. "I have a babysitter on the clock. And I'm *interested.*" She hesitated. "Have I shocked you?"

"Lord no." He lifted her off her feet and walked toward the bed, her legs dangling. When he set her down, the smile she gave him fried a few more synapses. "I didn't think this would happen tonight," he said. "Or ever. Forgive me if I'm off my game."

She ran her hands through his hair while he reached

behind her to unbutton her skirt and lower the zipper. What he saw then paralyzed him even more. Nikki stepped out of the skirt casually, as if undressing for an audience was no big deal.

The lacy white garter belt, thong panties and silky stockings she wore were pure fantasy. He touched her warm thigh. “Damn, Nik. If I’d known you were hiding this, we’d have skipped dinner altogether.”

Her small smile was smug. The little tease was enjoying his discomfiture. “I ordered all of it online after you left my house Wednesday. I’m glad you approve.”

He removed her sweater next, lifting it over her head, trying not to mess up her hair. The bra he found matched the rest of her undies. Except that it had a panel of fine mesh on the top edge that revealed her raspberry nipples.

With his heart slugging in his chest, he scooped her up in his arms, folded back the covers one-handed and laid her gently on the bed. “Don’t move,” he croaked.

He began to strip with a marked lack of coordination, tossing pieces of clothing wildly until he was down to his black knit boxers.

Nikki no longer smiled. Her gaze fixed raptly on his erection, outlined in stretchy cloth. “You are a beautiful man, Jake Lowell,” she said softly. “I thought I might have embroidered the memory of you naked, but it seems not.”

He dispensed with his underwear and joined her on the bed.

When he touched her, he understood that time really could stand still. The room was hushed. Traffic noise from the street below barely penetrated his consciousness.

He ran his fingers through Nikki’s golden-red tresses,

spreading her hair on the pillows. She was a sensual woman. A siren. A goddess.

He refused to dwell on his grief for the years he had missed.

Timing. It all came down to timing.

"Jake?" She said his name softly, with concern. As if she could sense his turmoil. "Are you okay?"

He nodded slowly, running one hand from her shoulder to her belly to her silken-clad legs. "Oh, yeah," he said. "I'm good." He removed the panties but left everything else in place. When he played with her nipples through the bra, she moaned and arched off the bed. Her cheeks flushed. Her eyelids fluttered shut.

For one breathless moment, she was there in front of him. Ripe for the taking.

That one night in Atlantic City was a blur to him now. This felt like another first. A second chance. Was karma offering him closure, or an opportunity for redemption?

Slow burn. Yes. That's what it was. The need to take her rose through him like a forceful, uncontrollable wave.

"Nikki..." He whispered her name, not even sure what he wanted to tell her. If he hadn't run away all those years ago, *this woman* might have been his.

Emotion burned his throat, scored him with pain, but not as much as the regret crushing his chest.

He wouldn't let the negative emotions ruin this. Not now. Not tonight.

Carefully, he touched her center and found her wet and slick with heat.

Belatedly, he remembered the condoms in his shaving kit. He rested his forehead on her belly, breathing hard, shaking like he had a fever. "I'll be right back."

When he returned seconds later, Nikki turned her head

and smiled at him. The look in her eyes nearly brought him to his knees.

He joined her again, but when she tried to curl her fingers around his shaft, he grabbed her wrist and held her at bay. "Later," he said gruffly. "I don't think I can wait."

He took care of protection and moved over her, spreading her thighs and fitting the head of his sex at her entrance. They both gasped when he went deep. So much for wooing her with his technique.

Nothing about this was smooth or practiced. Just two people yearning, straining against each other. Her skin was soft and warm. When he lifted one stocking-clad ankle onto his shoulder, the sight of her shot another bolt of heat through his gut.

"I adore these stockings, Nikki. You look like a pinup girl from a wartime calendar."

Her smile was sleepy and happy. "Glad you approve." She raised her hips, urging him on.

Fear like he had never known intruded—a fear he didn't want to admit. This was a mistake. Like that night in Atlantic City, he was rocked with wild emotions. He didn't know how to control the feelings. This was more than sexual desperation. So much more…

What did it mean?

Now he and Nikki were forever connected because of Emma. He couldn't pretend he was a ship passing Nikki's in the night.

He had left her twice before.

In the midst of unprecedented passion, the knee-jerk instinct to run was strong. But even scarier was the yearning, the need to stay.

She cupped his face in her hands, testing the late-day stubble on his chin. Her eyes searched his. "It's okay, Jake. Don't worry about it. This is just you and me scratching an itch. No declarations. No promises. Give me what I want."

"Gladly." He closed his eyes and pumped his hips, breathing raggedly, blind with need and confusion. Nikki's body welcomed him, drew him in, squeezed him. If he had been the kind of man to believe in love, this might have changed him.

But he wasn't and he didn't, so he concentrated on taking Nikki with him to the top and then holding her as they tumbled over the edge.

When it was over, they were both breathing heavily, the sounds audible in the silent room. He felt dizzy and warm and limp with satisfaction.

As he rolled onto his back, Nikki curled her body into his, her head resting on his shoulder. "Wow. You're good at this."

"I'm glad you think so." He mumbled the words, his eyes closed. He was so tired suddenly that he teetered on the brink of unconsciousness.

After a few moments, Nikki stirred. "I have to go, Jake. It's a long way back. Please don't get up. You're in a warm bed. I'll grab a cab or a ride share."

He tried to process her words. And then it hit him. Nikki wasn't free to spend the night. He knew that, of course, but the knowledge had been pushed to the back of his brain. "I'll take you," he said.

"No, really." She climbed out of bed and scooped up her underwear and clothes, then went toward the bathroom, still wearing the garter belt and stockings. God help him. "Stay where you are," she said. "I'll text you when I get home."

He stumbled after her, pulling up short in the doorway to the small en suite. The long mirror over the sink reflected a woman who looked like a weary angel…if angels had red hair and white skin and a stubborn tilt to their chins.

"Don't be ridiculous," he said. "I'm getting dressed."

His clothing was scattered all over the floor and the furniture. He grabbed everything except his sport coat. When he was ready, he avoided looking at the bed. Would he be able to sleep there tonight?

Nikki wasn't like the other women he had bedded. She never had been.

What was he supposed to do with that knowledge?

They made their way down to the car in silence. The snow had picked up, but it wasn't sticking to the roads.

Nikki tried once again to convince him to let her leave without him. He shut her up by leaning her against the car and kissing her hard. Then he tucked her into the passenger seat and closed the door. Once the engine fired, he turned up the heat.

"You okay, Nik?"

She nodded. "I'm good."

When she reached out and put a hand on this thigh, he felt like he had won the lottery. "What's your schedule like this week?" he asked.

"On Wednesday, I only work half a day. I could fix dinner and you could have some time with Emma."

"Any chance I might spend the night?" His hands gripped the steering wheel.

The long silence made his stomach curl. He heard his passenger sigh. She sounded conflicted. "I'll have to think about it, Jake."

"Is there a downside?" He asked the question lightly, as if he was merely curious instead of stung by her palpable reluctance.

"I want you, but I don't want to get involved. My life and yours are both complicated. You've left me twice now. And both times nearly killed me. So I like to think I'm smarter than I used to be."

"You don't think much of my character, do you?"

"It's not your character. It's *my* self-control."

The rest of the trip passed in silence. Jake chewed on her words, unable to put a positive spin on them. She cared about him, but she didn't want to get hurt when he inevitably left again.

She wasn't wrong. He wasn't cut out for Falling Brook. Hell, he wasn't cut out for anywhere permanent. That was why he wandered. But could he change? Did he want to?

"Will you still come to Joshua's wedding with me?" he asked.

"Of course. I said I would. Besides, it will be fun. Your brother is a super guy. I'm so glad he and Sophie found each other."

The snow was coming in heavier bands. Jake focused his attention on the road, glad of the excuse to drop the conversation. Talking about his brother's happy nuptials made his own life seem empty and meaningless.

When they finally pulled up in front of Nikki's modest house, she leaned over and kissed his check—a brief peck, nothing to get hot and bothered about.

"I enjoyed tonight, Jake. Thanks for dinner…and everything."

"I'll walk you to the door," he said.

"No. Keep the car warm. I'll talk to you soon."

And then she was gone, though her scent lingered.

Jake waited for the front door to open and close. Then he put the car in gear and headed back to Falling Brook. The long drive gave him plenty of time to think. Too much time. Why were people so complicated?

As soon as Josh's wedding was over, there would be

no reason to stay. Except for the trial, of course. But even those legal proceedings didn't demand Jake's presence. He didn't care what happened to his father.

Not at all…

But he couldn't lie to himself. He was falling for Nikki all over again. Which scared the hell out of him…

Nikki spoke briefly with Nella, and then urged her to go home before the roads got any worse. She handed the girl an envelope with cash in it. "Thank you so much for staying late. I really appreciate it."

"No problem, Ms. Reardon. She was a lot of fun, and she went to sleep as soon as I put her to bed. Call me again anytime."

When the babysitter left, Nikki closed the front door and leaned her back against it. She had shed her coat when she walked in, but now her cashmere sweater and wool skirt felt too hot. Nella must have run up the thermostat.

It was fine, really. Emma sometimes tossed off her covers during the night. Nikki wanted her baby girl to be warm.

In the bathroom, she tried to avoid looking at herself in the mirror. She felt as if she was wearing a neon sign—*I had sex tonight...with Jake Lowell.*

Who really cared? If Nikki kept her head in the game and didn't lose sight of the fact that Jake would leave New Jersey sooner than later, she couldn't get hurt. Right?

After a long hot shower, she put on her oldest, comfiest pair of flannel pajamas and climbed into bed. When she closed her eyes, Jake was there in the bed with her. He had touched her hungrily but with such tender care. As if she was breakable.

She wasn't. Not anymore. Life had knocked her down more than once, but she had picked herself up and kept going.

Though it was late, and her daughter would be up early, Nikki couldn't sleep. She replayed the night with Jake over and over, stirring restlessly in her lonely bed.

No other guy she knew was as smart or as funny…or as dangerously masculine and attractive.

The sex tonight had been revelatory. Nikki responded to Jake like no other partner she had ever known. Not that there was even a handful to compare.

He drew something from her. Some deep expression of her femininity. With Jake, she felt sexual, sensual, elementally human in the best possible way.

For the first time, she let herself wonder if there was a way forward that included the two of them as a couple. They shared a child. It wasn't so far-fetched an idea. They certainly had sexual chemistry. And a deep history. Similar backgrounds. Shared values.

What if she allowed herself to open up to him? To drop her resentment and anger and disappointment? What if she took Jake into her bed and into her life with a blank slate? Was there any possibility she might really be able to love him again? Did there exist a part of her that never *stopped* loving him?

If she lowered her defenses and let her emotions run wild, would Jake be able to reciprocate? It was scary to think of saying "I love you" and then being rejected.

When he had suggested that she and Emma visit Switzerland, the invitation had been couched in very temporary terms. To say Jake was skittish about commitment was like saying a zebra had stripes.

Nikki wanted more from a man. She deserved more.

A life partner. Someone who would encourage her to grow and flourish, and who would love and support her.

Being honest with herself about the current situation was getting harder and harder. She wanted to dream.

By the time Wednesday rolled around, she had second-guessed herself a million times. She picked up Emma after Mom's Day Out, stopped by the store and then rushed home to throw together a homemade lasagna. Soon, the kitchen was all warm and cozy and filled with the wonderful smells of tomato sauce and cheese and garlic.

Jake had sent a text, offering to pay for a babysitter so they could go out to dinner again, but Nikki had declined politely. Perhaps it was unfair, but she felt the need to test Jake's reactions in a boring family setting. He couldn't always splash his money around and expect to make problems go away.

Nikki liked being pampered as much as the next woman, but this relationship with Jake had three sides, not two. Tonight's focus would be Emma. After Emma went to bed, all bets were off. Nikki hadn't planned that far ahead. Some things were best left to chance.

Jake hadn't asked again about staying over, and she hadn't brought it up.

Unfortunately, the weather had taken a raw turn. The flurries they'd had for a few days were predicted to become accumulating snow sometime during the night. She wondered if Jake would cancel, and then felt sheepish when she realized how very much she dreaded that phone call.

She could tell herself all she wanted that she was keeping an emotional distance, but the truth was far different. Jake was deeply involved in her life already. She had allowed it, encouraged it and enjoyed it.

The real question was…did she want him to *stay* involved?

When the doorbell rang at five thirty on the dot, she dried her damp palms on her pants and took a deep breath. Emma was playing in her room, but she would soon be asking for dinner.

Nikki had decided to dress casually. Her stretchy black leggings and gold ballet flats were comfortable and cute. The off-the-shoulder sweater was turquoise. She looked like what she was—a middle-class suburban mom home for the evening.

The bell rang a second time. Evidently, she had dithered too long.

Scuttling through the house, she swept her fingers through her clean hair and checked her reflection in the hall mirror. Not bad. Her eyes were perhaps too bright, her smile too big. She inhaled sharply and let the air escape slowly. *Calm, Nikki. Calm.*

It took her two tries to grab the doorknob. At last, she flung open the door, letting in a rush of cold air and revealing the identity of her visitor, not that she'd had any doubt.

"Jake. Hi. Come on in."

In a quick glance, she saw everything about him. Leather jacket unzipped over a tailored blue cotton shirt. Jeans that were just the right amount of worn. Jeans that hugged his legs and man parts in a very distracting fashion. And my gosh, were those…?

She blurted it out. "Are you wearing *cowboy boots*? Mr. Sophisticated World Traveler, Jake Lowell?"

"Let me in, Nik. It's freezing."

"Sorry." She stepped back quickly.

He brushed past her, bringing in the scents of the outdoors. "These are for you."

The large bouquet of deep yellow roses definitely didn't come from a run-of-the-mill supermarket. The blossoms were huge and fragrant. She took them automatically. "You didn't have to bring me flowers."

He shot her a glance that included irritation and banked lust. "I know that. Put them in water, Nik." He glanced down the hall. "I brought Emma something, too."

"Honestly, Jake. Gifts aren't necessary. She'd just a little kid."

Without warning, he kissed her, his lips lingering, pressing, summoning memories of the night in his hotel room. "She's more than just a little kid. She's my daughter."

Ten

Jake noted the stricken look on Nikki's face, but he couldn't quite pinpoint the cause. Was he being too abrupt about claiming his parental rights? Did his words sound like a threat? He hadn't meant them that way.

Giving Nikki a chance to regain her composure, he shrugged out of his jacket and rolled up his sleeves. The little house was cheery and warm. "Dinner smells amazing."

At last, Nikki's posture thawed. "I hope you like lasagna."

He followed her into the kitchen and watched as she rummaged under the sink for a vase. Her position gave him a tantalizing view of her perfect, heart-shaped ass.

Just as his libido began to carry him down a dangerous path, little Emma appeared in the doorway. "Is it time, Mommy? I'm hungry." She turned to Jake. "Hi! Are you eating with us?"

Jake nodded. "Sure am. And *I'm* hungry, too. Maybe we should get out of the way for a bit and let Mommy get everything on the table." He shot Nikki an inquiring look. "Unless you need help."

Her cheeks were pink. "I'm good. Give me five minutes."

In the living room, he handed Emma the gift that was wrapped in shiny red paper.

She cocked her head in a movement eerily reminiscent of her mother. "It's too early for Christmas."

"This isn't a Christmas present. It's just something your mom told me you liked." He had wrestled with his conscience and finally decided he wasn't above buying a child's affection if it landed him a few extra points in a sticky situation.

Emma's excited screech brought her mother running. Nikki stopped in the doorway, her expression frazzled. "What's wrong?"

Emma beamed and held up the toy, not realizing she had scared her mother. "Look what Mr. Man got me!"

Nikki mouthed at Jake, *Mr. Man?*

He shrugged. "I thought you told her to call me that."

"No."

Emma demanded her mother's attention. "Look, Mommy. It's the special one."

What Jake had procured at an appalling price was the princess from the latest animated movie. She was the deluxe edition with eyes that opened and closed and a fancy dress with two additional outfits. The doll had been advertised heavily on television and was out of stock in stores across the area despite the fact that Black Friday hadn't even happened yet.

Nikki squatted to give the princess her required admiration. "She's beautiful, Emma. Did you thank Mr. Jake?"

Without warning, Emma whirled and wrapped her arms around Jake's knees. "Thank you, thank you, thank you."

He touched her head, felt the long, soft golden hair. "You're very welcome." Emotions buzzed inside his chest. Alien emotions that weren't particularly welcome. He had decided he wanted to know his daughter. But that had been a cerebral decision. He hadn't anticipated actually *feeling* things.

Nikki rescued him. "Dinner's ready," she said calmly, rising to her feet. It almost seemed as if she could detect his internal agitation.

The meal could have been awkward. Emma's nonstop chatter made it less so. The roses were displayed in an inexpensive glass container. They matched the yellow stripe in Nikki's woven place mats.

Emma turned up her nose when her mom put a small serving of salad on her plate. It must have been a battle the two females had fought before, because the younger one sighed and gave in to the older.

The three of them ate in harmony, though Jake was unable to keep from imagining Nikki naked and at his mercy. Such inappropriate mental pictures probably reflected poorly on his qualifications to be a dad, but he couldn't help it. Three entire days and most of a fourth had passed since he had seen his lover.

Though Jake had kept busy, the mental movie reel made him itchy and restless and disrupted his sleep. He'd brought an overnight case this trip and left it in the trunk of the car. He couldn't read Nikki on this particular subject, but he wanted to be prepared.

Emma liked her mother's lasagna and cleaned her plate.

Jake ate three helpings himself and groaned when he

finally pushed back from the table. "I had no idea you could cook like that."

"Thank you." Nikki served her daughter a very small dollop of warm apple pie with ice cream.

When she offered some to Jake, he shook his head ruefully. "I overdid it with dinner. I'll have to wait for some of this to shake down."

"Of course."

Emma asked to be excused and was given permission. Just like that, the atmosphere in the kitchen went from homey to horny. At least on his part.

Nikki's face wasn't giving away anything.

Jake finished his glass of wine and poured himself another. "I'm glad she liked the doll."

Nikki stiffened visibly. "Presents aren't a substitute for quality time."

He stared at her. "I only found out I was a father a short time ago. You could cut me some slack, Nik. Are you trying to pick a fight with me?"

All that wild red hair was caught back in a ponytail at her nape, but it didn't take much effort to remember it fanned out across his sheets.

Her jaw jutted. "I want to make Christmas special for her. You just undercut me."

He frowned. "Were you planning to give her that doll?"

"No. You know I can't afford it. But now, whatever Santa brings will look paltry in comparison."

"I doubt she knows the word *paltry*, and you're her mom. She's going to love whatever you and the jolly old man put under the tree."

Nikki's ire deflated visibly. "Whatever." She chewed her lip. "You could make it up to me."

He grinned. "I like the sound of that."

"Get your mind out of the gutter, Lowell. I'm talking about actual useful *work*."

He glanced around him at the dishes. "You want me to clean up the kitchen? Sure. I'd be happy to—"

"No. Not that. I need help with the Christmas tree."

"What Christmas tree?"

She looked at him and rolled her eyes. "The one in the closet. I like to put up the tree the day after Thanksgiving. But since I've asked off for the wedding this coming Saturday, the diner has me down to work Friday *and* Saturday of Thanksgiving weekend. With you here tonight, we could put up the tree together in no time, and Emma could hang a few ornaments before she goes to bed."

"If you want, I could buy you a tree, fully decorated, and have it delivered tomorrow." Which would free up time for the two grown-ups to fool around later.

Nikki touched his arm briefly, making his skin hum. "Trimming the tree is part of the magic of Christmas," she said. "I appreciate the thought, but I love decorating. It makes me feel good."

"I get it. But why artificial?"

"For one, Emma has allergies. Besides, a live tree can't go up this early. They dry out. Surely, you've done this before."

"As a kid," he said, feeling defensive and trying not to show it.

Nikki stared at him, her beautiful eyes wide. "Are you telling me you haven't put up a Christmas tree in fifteen years?"

"Why does that shock you, Nikki? I live alone. I'm always on the road. It's a lot of hassle for one person."

"But what about the holidays? What about Christmas Day? How did you celebrate?"

Her inquisition brought back memories that weren't always exactly pleasant. "Well, for starters, sometimes I'm in a country that doesn't observe the Christmas holiday."

"Okay. I get that. But other years?"

"Occasionally a friend will invite me over. Or if I'm traveling, I'll find a church and go to a service. It's not a bad thing to skip the commercialism and the sappy sentiment. I haven't missed much."

Her eyes darkened with some emotion he couldn't name. "Oh, but you have, Jake. You just don't realize it."

"Where's this damn tree?" he growled. "Let's get it over with."

Nikki pointed him toward the closet, though she seemed troubled. Jake carried the long, rectangular box into the living room and opened it. Fortunately, the tree was one of those prelit deals. All he had to do was lock together the three sections and make sure the stand was attached tightly.

At Nikki's direction, he positioned it in front of the window. Though he wouldn't dare say so out loud, the poor fake evergreen was not the snappiest tree in the forest. Honestly, it looked a bit dilapidated. Even sad…

"I know it's not great," Nikki said, studying the tree with her nose wrinkled. "I got it on clearance the year I was pregnant with Emma. But the decorations cover up its imperfections. Emma," she called. "We're ready to put ornaments on the tree."

Emma came running, holding her doll from Jake. "Can I do the first one?"

"Sure, baby."

Jake had planned to sit back and watch while the womenfolk did their thing. He was sadly mistaken about his role. First Emma, and then Nikki, chided him.

Soon, he was selecting ornaments from a jumbled plastic container and placing them on the tree. When the ornament box was finally empty—hallelujah—the adults added shiny silver tinsel, starting at the top and winding it around the tree. Nikki got down on her stomach and spread out a red velvet tree skirt, twitching and pulling until it was straight enough to meet her exacting standards.

Jake would have offered to help, but he was afraid he would be tempted to do more than twitch if he was down on the floor with Nikki. She looked like a holiday treat in her fluffy turquoise sweater. It was the color of the Aegean Sea. Maybe he could convince her to take a trip with him to Greece. Sunshine. Warmth. Blue skies.

He cleared his throat and tried to think about icebergs and cold showers. "Are we done?" he asked.

Nikki stood, stretched her back and nodded. A piece of her hair had tangled with one of the lower branches. Jake smoothed the strand and rubbed his thumb over her cheek. "The tree looks great, Nik."

It was true. Somehow, the collage of ornaments had transformed a shabby artificial tree into something beautiful.

Emma stared at it, her doll in her arms. "Turn the lights off, Mommy."

In the dark, the tree was even better. Jake pressed a surreptitious kiss beneath Nikki's ear and nipped her earlobe with his teeth. "I keep picturing you naked," he confessed, his words too quiet for the child to hear. He slid a hand under the back of Nikki's sweater and caressed the length of her spine.

Nikki shivered, but didn't move away. Instead, she leaned into him, letting him support her weight. Her hair tickled his nose.

Finally, she turned in his loose embrace, touched his lips with her fingers and spoke as he had, in a low voice.

"It's snowing really hard now. You shouldn't drive back to Falling Brook. Why don't you spend the night?"

A rush of heat settled in his groin. His mouth dried. "On the sofa?"

He saw the multicolored lights from the Christmas tree reflected in her laughing eyes. "In my bed."

"What about Emma?" His voice sounded funny, perhaps because he was struggling to breathe.

Nikki gave his chin a quick kiss, then eyed her daughter. "We'll set an alarm," she muttered. "You can move to the sofa at five. It will be fine."

Nikki bathed her daughter, washed her hair and dressed her in warm pajamas. The temperature was dropping and would soon leave a crust of ice on the new-fallen snow. As Nikki tucked Emma into bed, her daughter cuddled the new doll sleepily. "Why isn't Mr. Man reading me a story tonight?"

"It's late, baby. Decorating the tree took all our time."

Emma yawned and snuggled deeper in her covers. "I like the tree. It's bootiful."

Nikki grinned. "Yes, it is. But remember, it's still a long time until Christmas. We put up the tree a little early this year. You and I will enjoy it every day and every night, and I'll let you know when it's time to look for Santa."

"I can wait, Mommy. I'm good at waiting."

"Can I ask you a question, love?" She smoothed her daughter's still-damp hair. "Why do you call Jake 'Mr. Man'?"

Emma yawned again, her eyelids drooping. "He's a boy and we're girls. I like Mr. Man."

Nikki managed not to laugh. "Fair enough."

When she turned off the light and tiptoed out, she was

pretty sure her daughter was already asleep. Nikki found Jake in the kitchen wiping the last of the countertops. The dishwasher was humming, and the kitchen was spotless.

"Jake," she said, feeling guilty. "You're our guest. I would have done all this."

His grin curled her toes. "First of all," he said, "I needed to earn my keep. And second of all…" He crossed the room and scooped her up on her toes for a fast, breath-stealing kiss. "I wanted you to be free for whatever comes next."

"And what would that be?"

"Lady's choice."

She nuzzled her cheek against his broad, hard chest, listening to the steady *ka-thump* of his heart. "What if we start by drinking cheap wine in the dark and enjoying the Christmas tree?"

"Cheap wine?"

"You tell me." She threw open the cabinet where she kept a single bottle of red and then opened the fridge and pulled out two bottles of chardonnay. "Your pick."

He winced. "I could have brought some."

"I suppose a man who visits fancy vineyards in France and Italy is above five-dollar vino?"

Jake's expression was droll. "If you paid five dollars for these, you were robbed."

His disgust made her giggle, though she was breathless with wanting him. "How about coffee? I have some beans in the freezer. And a grinder. Though it's probably dusty," she admitted.

He cupped her face in his big hands and kissed her eyelids one at a time, his expression searing and intense. "How about a glass of water, and then we go make out on your couch?"

"I'm fine without the water," she gasped. They were

pressed together so closely she could feel the hard length of him against her abdomen. "And we *could* go straight to the bedroom."

Jake was suddenly the one with patience. "Tree first, woman. We worked hard on that masterpiece."

He took her by the hand and drew her down the hall to the living room. Nikki had opened the drapes before she put Emma to bed. Now, streetlights illuminated the heavily falling snow. The tree cast a warm glow over the room.

"You couldn't have driven home, anyway," Nikki muttered. "Look at it out there. Did you bring an overnight bag? You should grab your stuff from the car before it gets any worse."

Jake sat down and pulled her onto his lap. "You agreed to make out with me. Don't change the subject. And yes. I packed a few things. Just in case."

Nikki shivered. How many times over the years had the two of them fooled around like this? When she was in high school and Jake was in college, she had lived for the weekends when he came home to Falling Brook. He'd told his mother he needed to wash clothes. He'd told Nikki he needed *her*.

Now, Jake's hands were everywhere…caressing, arousing. When he stroked the center seam of her leggings, the one that lined up with her aching sex, she arched into him and whimpered. "Yes, Jake. Yes."

They kissed ravenously, straining to get closer and closer still. His lips bruised hers. His hands tangled in her hair. "I want you, Nik. I haven't been able to think about anything else but making love to you since I brought you home Saturday night. Please tell me I'm not the only one with this obsession."

"You're not," she panted, her tongue soothing the

small hickey she had left on his neck. "Where are the condoms? Don't say they're in the car."

He shoved her aside and jumped to his feet, reaching for his billfold. "Two," he croaked. "Right here."

"Good." She stood also, then stripped her sweater over her head. The house was warm, but her nipples furled tightly when Jake reached for her, his gaze hot.

"Let me help you with that bra," he said. Seconds later, the bra was in the air and Jake was sitting on the sofa again with her on his lap so he could play with her breasts. He plumped them between his hands and buried his face between them, inhaling her scent. "You still wear the same perfume," he said softly.

"Yes."

"I caught a whiff in a department store one time and got a hard-on. I love the way it smells on your warm skin. I could eat you up, Nik." Then he caught one nipple between his teeth and tugged. That simple contact sparked fireworks all over her body.

When she cried out, he glanced up at her, his cheeks flushed. "Too much?"

She smoothed his hair with a shaky hand. "No, Jake. Never too much."

He rewarded that confession by giving the neglected nipple equal time. In moments, Nikki's knees were weak and the thrum of arousal low in her belly was impossible to ignore. "Take off my pants," she begged, standing up clumsily.

The stretchy fabric cooperated easily when Jake slid his hands inside and dragged her pants down her legs. He took her ballet flats, too, leaving her in nothing but a pair of lacy black undies.

"God, you're beautiful," he breathed, his expression reverent.

"You have too many clothes on."

She started unbuttoning his shirt, but his patience ran out. "I'll do it."

Suddenly, she realized the drapes were still open. "Oh, my gosh." The living room was dark, but still. Scuttling backward into the shadows, she hissed at Jake. "My bedroom. Now."

They tiptoed down the hallway, past Emma's closed door, and made it unscathed into the master bedroom. *Master* was a misnomer. The bedroom was scarcely larger than Emma's, but it did have a bathroom, so the lady of the house didn't have to use the one in the hall.

Jake exhaled. "Does this door lock?"

The room was dark. "Yes. Hang on." She found the bedside table and turned on the lamp. When she saw Jake's face, her heart stopped. He looked like a pirate intent on capturing a prize.

Rapidly, he removed the rest of his clothes. He made her feel young again, and reckless.

She turned back the quilt and the sheet and climbed onto the bed.

Jake joined her quickly. "This feels good," he said as they rolled together, their limbs tangling.

"The mattress isn't great," she mumbled, wrapping her hand around the most interesting part of him.

He shuddered. "I don't give a damn about the mattress. I'd take you outside in the snow if that was the only way to have you. You excite me, Nik. I guess that's obvious. I'd like to see you sunbathing nude on a private terrace in Greece. Just the two of us. Drinking ouzo and eating cheese. How does that sound?"

Since he was touching every erogenous zone on her body and a few that were surprisingly mundane most of the time, she was in a cooperative mood. "Sounds wonderful. Would you buy me a gold anklet and let me ride a donkey down to the sea?"

He choked out a laugh. "I'd buy you a whole damn town. And every man who walked by our dinner table at night would see you in candlelight and be jealous that they weren't me." He moved away long enough to don protection, then came back to her.

Reclining on his hip, he entered her with two fingers, feeling the slick warmth of her body. Gently, he stroked the spot that centered her pleasure. "I want to take you hard and fast, but I also want it slow and easy."

Nikki skated her palm over his sculpted, warm shoulder, loving the feel of him, the intimacy. "Why choose?" she asked quietly. "We can have it all."

He rose over her and thrust hard, making both of them gasp. She wrapped her legs around his waist. The movement forced him deeper. He thrust again, and she climaxed, the world going hazy as she concentrated on wringing every bit of pleasure from her release. It had come too fast. She wanted more. But already Jake was finding his own nirvana, taking her body and making it his own.

At last, breathing hard, he rolled away, linking her hand with his. "That was amazing, Nik." The words were slurred. His breathing deepened as he fell asleep.

She reached for the lamp and turned it off. Then with one hand, she set an alarm on her phone. In the dark, tears stung her eyes. Christmas was the season of miracles, but something told her Jake Lowell wouldn't stick around long enough for Santa to show up.

Nikki squeezed his hand, holding on as if she could keep him forever. "I love you, Jake," she whispered.

Eleven

When Jake opened his eyes, he was disoriented by the dark. This wasn't his hotel room. And then he was fully awake.

Shifting carefully to the side of the bed, he stood and stumbled to the bathroom. When he returned, his eyes had adjusted fractionally to the black of night. Nikki must have installed room-darkening shades on her windows.

A glance at his watch told him it was only two. In the silence, he could hear the almost imperceptible sound of Nikki's breathing. He climbed back under the covers and turned into her warmth. The curves and valleys of her body had him hard again.

But he was cold inside, and there was a block of ice where his heart should have been. Nikki had thought he was asleep when she said those four incredible words. *I love you, Jake.*

Had she really meant it? How could she? After everything that had happened…

As he tried to steady his panicked breathing, a memory popped into his head. He'd been twelve, maybe thirteen, camping with a friend and his family at Yellowstone. A park ranger gave a talk about the west's low humidity and had warned that if the remnants of a campfire were not separated and scattered well enough, an ember, a slow burn, might remain for hours, days. And then spring back to life when the wind conditions were right.

Now here Jake was. Did he still love Nikki? Or did he even care enough to try? And with a kid in the mix, what was the fallout if he wanted to be the man Nikki deserved, but failed?

His erection mocked his indecision. *Take her*, the devil on his shoulder urged. *Protect her*, said his better self.

In the end, he knew the answer. Moving her gently in the bed, he shook her awake. "I need you, Nik. Again? Please?"

She nodded sleepily, murmuring her pleasure when he kissed her long and deep, teased her lips, thrust his tongue inside to stroke her tongue. The fire burned hot again.

Reaching for the nightstand on his side of the bed, he found the remaining condom and managed to rip it open. When he was ready, he faced her on his side. Carefully, he lifted her leg over his hip, pulled her close and joined their bodies.

It was perhaps the most intimate thing they had done. Their breath mingled. They met as equals. Neither in charge. Both of them taking pleasure and giving it in return.

Nikki curled her arm around his neck and kissed him. "I'm glad you stayed tonight," she whispered.

Her kiss took him higher. He felt invincible. "Me, too, Nik," he groaned. Fire swept down his spine, flashed in his pelvis. His fingers dug into the soft curve of her ass. He wanted to say something, to tell her how he felt, but the storm swept him under. He came so hard he might have lost his wits for a moment.

He rolled to his back at the end. Her cheek was smashed against his chest. Stroking her glorious hair, he tried to steady his breathing. His brain spun out of control, and he tasted fear. How could he hurt the woman who had been his whole world?

"Jake?" she said, petting his chest like he was a big jungle cat.

"Hmm?"

"I'm wide-awake now. Tell me about the wedding. I know you said it's at two o'clock, but is it going to be a huge affair? Where are they getting married?"

He tried to focus. "You remember the Bismarck Hotel downtown?"

"Yes."

"They've remodeled the top floor into a large entertainment space. Josh and Sophie had the choice of including only family and close friends or planning for a crowd of a thousand or more. You know how it is in Falling Brook. Once you start inviting people, it's hard to draw the line. Plus, with all the Black Crescent mess in the news again this year, my brother and his fiancée thought it would be in poor taste to spread a bunch of money around. Last I heard, the guest list hits around fifty. Small and intimate."

"What about a rehearsal dinner?"

"Nope. Not even that."

"Good for them."

The conversation was a pleasant diversion, but Jake

had arrived at the moment of truth. Things were getting far too cozy. He released her and scooted up against the headboard, forcing himself not to touch her.

Nikki reached for the lamp and flipped the switch. He hated that. He didn't want her to see what was coming.

If he had any guts at all, he wouldn't let her have hope. He raked his hand through his hair, feeling the cold sweat on his forehead. "I don't think I'm going to stay for my father's trial, Nikki."

She sat up, too, pulling the sheet to her chest, covering her breasts. Her hair was a tumbled, fiery cloud around her face. Her eyes were huge. "I don't understand. Why not? You need closure, Jake. If you don't face Vernon, you'll never get over what he did. He'll always be the bogeyman."

Perhaps there was truth in what she said, but he didn't want to hear it. He didn't want to admit it. "He's nothing to me. I don't care what happens to him. He destroyed us, Nikki. I can't forgive him for that."

Every bit of color leached from her face. He thought for a moment she might be sick. "That's not true," she said. The words were sharp.

He stared at her. "Of course it is."

The heartbreak dawning in her eyes was familiar. He'd seen it fifteen years ago. He might have seen it five years ago in Atlantic City if he'd left when she was awake. She lifted her chin, visibly angry. "*You* destroyed us, Jake. Not your dad. He disappeared, but you could have come back anytime, and you didn't."

The attack came out of nowhere.

He gaped at her. Nikki was always on his side. Always. "I *had* to leave. He'd made my life impossible. Everywhere I went, reporters followed me. One of them shimmied up a ladder and tried to climb into my bedroom. It was hell, Nikki. And all of it, his fault."

"I know it was hell. I was there, remember?"

"Well, at least your dad died. He paid for his sins. You didn't have people thinking that you and your mother were hiding a fortune somewhere."

"That's a terrible thing to say." Her pallor increased. "I loved my dad, even though I hated what he did. I also hate how your dad and mine tore lives and families apart. But time moved on, Jake. I'm not stuck in the past. I've had to build a new life from the ground up. I have a child who loves me and a mother who depends on me for emotional support. I'm not that frightened high-school girl anymore."

"The implication being that I'm a coward?" His temper simmered.

She hesitated. "Not a coward. No. Not that. But you're emotionally stunted. You've had every resource in the world at your fingertips, and yet you couldn't bring yourself to grow up and come back and do your part. We all needed you, Jake. Oliver. Your mother. Joshua. Me."

Her words chipped away at him, exposing his weaknesses. It wasn't that he'd been too lazy or immature to share the burden—he'd been afraid. Afraid that he would come home and make things worse. "I offered Josh my help more than once. But he assumed I was a screwup, so he wasn't interested."

"That was in the past. My God, Jake. He offered you the helm of the company recently. How much more does he have to do to prove he believes in you?"

"I've lived on the road too long to change my ways. People aren't always who you want them to be, Nikki. You expect too much."

Her eyes were wet. Her jaw wobbled. "Do I? Maybe

so." One tear broke loose and ran down her cheek. "I think you should go sleep on the sofa now."

There it was. The death blow.

He had brought it on himself. Provoked this confrontation. The ice in his chest melted, leaving a gaping hole. It hurt. Dear God, it hurt. But he didn't know how to fix it.

Nikki stared at him, anguish on her face. "What about Emma?"

"I'll still see Emma. She has nothing to do with my father."

Now Nikki's smile was bitter. "I think you're wrong, Jake. How you relate to your daughter has everything to do with this chip on your shoulder. You've carried it far too long. It's crippled you."

He took the hit stoically, but he fought back, lashing out. "What did you say your college degree was in? Surely, not psychology." He heard the sarcasm and condescension in his words, but he couldn't seem to stop this train wreck of a conversation. "I'm a grown-ass man, Nikki. I think I can handle my own life."

She huddled against the headboard, her knuckles white where she gripped the sheet. "Maybe you can. But I have to ask, what about the wedding? I don't want to be rude to Joshua and Sophie."

"You'll come to the wedding with me. My family is expecting it. I've told them about Emma, so they'll want to see you."

"Won't that be fun," she said bitterly. "I'll find my own way there, Jake. I wouldn't want to inconvenience you."

"Don't be absurd. I'll pick you up at noon."

"And what happens to you and me after the wedding?"

He saw it then. Despite everything he had said and done, in Nikki's despairing gaze he saw one last remnant of hope amid her pain. "I don't think there is a 'you and me,'" he said, the words brusque and flat. "Lots of people share custody of children. I know who I am. And who I'm not." He slid out of bed and found his knit boxers. Grabbing up his shirt and pants, he started getting dressed.

Nikki wrapped the sheet around her body, toga-style, and went to her closet. "I'll get you some sheets for the sofa," she said.

Suddenly, he couldn't stand to be near her for another second. It was tearing him apart. "No," he said curtly. "I'm leaving."

She whirled around, frowning. "Don't be stupid, Jake. The snow is deep. And it's still coming down. You'll wreck your car."

He shrugged, staring at the woman who had shown him a glimpse of what his life *could* be like. "Don't worry, Nik. I always land on my feet."

As he grabbed his cowboy boots and the rest of his things and walked to the living room, he waited for her to follow him. Instead, the house was still and quiet. It would be a few more hours until dawn arrived. No need to worry about Emma getting the wrong idea. By the time she woke up, Jake would be back in Falling Brook at his impersonal hotel.

The Christmas tree mocked him with a cheerful glow. It was still lit, because Jake and Nikki had been too desperate for each other to pay attention. When he was completely dressed, he listened one more time to see if Nikki was going to waylay him. To lecture him about road safety. To tell him what a stubborn, closed-off bastard he was.

But nothing happened.

The front door had one of those twist locks that didn't require a key to be secured from the inside. When he was bundled up, he opened the door, stepped out into the hushed silence and waded through the snow.

He was alone in a deserted landscape.

Nikki cried for an hour, cried until her nose was stuffed up and her chest hurt. For long minutes, she had expected a knock on the front door. She had strained to hear it. Because it would be Jake admitting that the weather was too bad to leave.

Apparently, risking life and limb was preferable to staying with her.

How could he make love to her so beautifully and feel nothing?

If Jake had shown any glimmer of interest in a permanent relationship, Nikki would have fought for their future. She would have traveled anywhere with him. Emma hadn't started school yet. And Roberta might soon be going back to the friends she had known for decades.

But Jake had run from Nikki yet again, because of shadows from his past. She was long beyond what had happened fifteen years ago. She wasn't reliving old hurts, not anymore. She deserved a man who would love her, body and soul. Maybe he was out there somewhere.

In the meantime, she had to let Jake go. The hurt was like severing a limb, but it would only hurt worse if she refused to face the truth. Jake Lowell didn't love her. He couldn't. He was too empty inside.

The trouble with heartbreak and emotional meltdowns was that the world kept on turning. Emma bounced into Nikki's bedroom at seven, her impish personality bolstered by a good night's sleep.

Nikki managed not to groan. "Hi, baby."

"Where's Mr. Man?"

"Why would you ask that, hon?"

"It was snowing last night. You told me we couldn't drive in snow. Remember?"

"Ah. Well, that was us. Mr. Jake is a very good driver. So he went home after you were in bed."

"When is he coming back?"

"I don't know." Nikki, in desperation, changed the subject. "Let's get you some breakfast, so you'll be ready to play when Grandma gets here."

In typical Jersey fashion, the weather pattern had shifted again. It was too early in the season for sustained cold temps. The snow was already melting, and the sun was out. The streets were a slushy mess. But not particularly dangerous.

Nikki's shift at the diner started at ten today. Though she was glad it wasn't any earlier, she still didn't know how she was going to make it through eight hours of on-your-feet work. Lots of caffeine maybe. And a stone-cold commitment not to think about stupid, emotionally stunted rich men.

Roberta Reardon didn't spare Nikki's feelings when she arrived. "You look terrible. Are you getting the flu?"

"No, Mom. I'm fine. I just didn't sleep well."

"I see you have your tree up. How did you manage that since I last saw you?"

Emma answered, innocently. "Mr. Man helped."

Roberta's eyebrows went up. "Mr. Man?"

"Jake. He had dinner with us." Nikki glanced at her daughter. "Go take off your pajamas and get dressed, please."

When Emma headed for her bedroom, Roberta pressed for more. "And?"

"And nothing. He's getting to know Emma. He wants to be part of her life."

Her mother's smile was gentle. "You don't seem happy about that."

"It will be difficult," Nikki admitted, her throat tight.

"Because you're in love with him?"

"Mom!" Aghast, Nikki turned to look down the hall, making sure Emma hadn't picked up on the adult conversation. "She'll hear you."

"So it's true?"

"No, Mother," Nikki lied. "Jake and I are friends who share a child. That's all we'll ever be, and I'm okay with that."

She waited for the lightning to strike or for a huge sinkhole to open up and swallow her for telling such a whopper.

Roberta seemed disappointed. "Okay then. I believe you."

"I have to finish getting ready."

Nikki fled the room, telling herself she absolutely would *not* break down and cry. She was a grown woman. Not some fragile schoolgirl fixated on romantic fantasies that had no base in reality.

She made it to work with ten minutes to spare, so she grabbed a cup of coffee and took it to the storeroom. This place, this small restaurant, had become a familiar home. She liked her coworkers, and she liked her customers. The days had a comfortable routine.

Everybody needed to eat. And, surprisingly, a lot of people needed someone to talk to when their lives were empty. Nikki could do worse than stay here at the cozy retro diner indefinitely.

But the truth was, the salary for assistant manager wasn't all that great. When Emma was older and her needs were more expensive, Nikki would need a different job. Perhaps one that made use of her degree in communications.

She had thought about working for an ad agency. Maybe doing PR for a local business. She was a decent writer, and she didn't mind speaking in public.

Her moment of quiet time ended abruptly when one of the line cooks swung open the door and grabbed a can of baked beans. He glanced at the clock with a grin. "You hiding out in here, Nikki? Rough morning?"

Her face must have looked worse than she thought. She managed a smile. "Not enough sleep. You know. Kids..."

"Don't I ever."

The door closed, and she took a deep breath. Nothing had to be decided today. She would stay the course until after Christmas. January was a good month for resolutions and starting over. Maybe Falling Brook was the answer. Maybe Joshua really would offer Nikki and her mother a lifeline. Who knew what the future held?

The only certainty was that *Nikki's* future didn't include Jake Lowell.

Twelve

After Jake left Nikki's house in the predawn hours, he made a concerted effort to spend time with his family. If he was leaving after the wedding, he needed to fulfill his responsibilities as a son and a brother.

Oddly, the movie with Oliver, the rushed lunch with Joshua at Black Crescent and the afternoon tea at his mother's Friday afternoon were cathartic. He'd had in mind offering his support to *them*, but he ended up being the one who felt comforted.

His mother, especially, surprised him. They bypassed the pleasantries quickly and waded into deep water. "How are you doing, Mom? Really, I mean. I know you went to see Dad."

Eve Lowell looked much as she always had. Younger than her years. Dignified. Stylish. She was older now, of course. But she still had the posture of a beauty queen.

She wrinkled her nose at his question. "It was all small

talk. But enough to show me that it's time to move on. I'm not the same person I was. It took me a long time to find my strength, but I did. I still have my rough days, but I'm in a good place now, just like Oliver. When Oliver told me about his visit and how he came to the same conclusions, I was glad he went. It was healthy and positive for both of us."

"Do you still love Dad?" Jake hadn't known he was going to ask that question. When his mother was silent, he wished he hadn't. Finally, she shook her head slowly. "It depends on what you mean by love. Your father was declared legally dead. I'm no longer bound to him by law. But I said vows a million years ago. Vows I meant at the time. I certainly didn't know my husband was going to become a felon."

"So, is that a yes or a no?"

She looked at him wistfully. "We can't always choose whom we love, and we can't always stop loving them simply because they don't deserve our love. I know your father sent you away, Jake."

"He didn't send me away." Anger snapped in each word. "He left. He left you. He left me. He left all of us. And I couldn't handle the gutter press. They hounded our family and made us miserable. Because of *him*." Jake shook with sudden fury—fury he hadn't realized he'd pushed down, and had pushed down forever, it seemed.

"My poor boy. He left you homeless, didn't he?"

Jake felt raw suddenly. And he hated that vulnerability. "I owe you an apology, Mother," he said formally. "I never should have left you to face everything on your own. I'm sorry I didn't stay. I'm sorry I didn't come back."

"I had Joshua," she said, waving a hand. "We got by."

Though her words weren't meant to wound, Jake felt

them cut deep. He loved his brother dearly, but always being cast as the screwup was not a role Jake relished.

"Is there anything you need?" he asked. "I've done well financially."

"Jake, dear boy." She patted his hand. "Over the years you've sent me jewelry and artwork for my birthdays and Christmas. I never felt forgotten. I knew why you couldn't come home. But I hoped that one day the hurt would fade." She paused, her expression turning crafty, mischievous even. "Now tell me about Nikki and this baby of yours. Joshua has filled me in on the basics."

Jake hunched his shoulders. "Emma is four. She's mine. I'm making arrangements with Nikki, so I can fly in for the occasional visit. And, of course, we can video chat."

His mother's face fell. "I don't get to see my granddaughter?"

"I suppose that's up to you and Nikki."

"It strikes me that I haven't heard you talk about Nikki and *you*."

"There's nothing there, Mom."

"You made a baby together."

"That was five years ago. We bumped into each other one evening in Atlantic City and…well, you know."

Eve's smile was sweet. "I may be getting older, son, but I do understand sexual chemistry."

"We've been apart fifteen years. Whatever we had is gone."

"I find that hard to believe."

"Why?" He frowned at her.

"Because you've never found another woman to settle down with and make a home. That strikes me as odd. You have a huge heart, Jake. A generous spirit. And though you'd chew glass before you'd admit it, you're a sensitive and loving and wonderful man."

"I thought you were disappointed in me," he said gruffly, caught off guard by her praise. "I failed you."

"Nonsense," she said stoutly. "You followed your own path. Don't hide in the shadows forever, dear boy. You may not get too many chances for happiness. Seize this one before it's too late."

In that moment, he knew he was tired of running, tired of being so slow to change and grow. Despite all evidence to the contrary, he felt a fillip of hope that something new might be close at hand. He was ready to reach for happiness. But he still wasn't sure he could handle it or how to get there.

Maybe it was too late…

Though Jake appreciated his mother's support, his intentions were all over the map. Maybe Falling Brook wasn't as bad as he remembered. After all, the town had been nothing more than an excuse, a convenient bogeyman.

He'd had no contact at all with Nikki. He couldn't bring himself to text her. What would he say? Her words still rang in his ears. *You destroyed us, Jake. Not your dad.*

Apparently, Nikki Reardon was not as forgiving as Eve Lowell. Mothers always made excuses for their misbehaving sons. Lovers simply walked away.

Though, in all fairness, Jake had been the one to leave. He'd given up the wild, glorious uncertainty of Nikki's bed for the cold comfort of his iron-clad, selfish rules.

Never stop moving. Never put down roots. Never look back.

On the morning of the wedding, he ran out of options. He sent a brief text: I'm picking you up at noon.

It took ten minutes for Nikki's reply: I'll be ready.

He sighed. Thanksgiving was five days away. Maybe he should get out of New Jersey. The sooner, the better. Nothing was the way he thought it would be. Too many messy emotions. Too many people. Too many regrets.

He pulled up in front of Nikki's now-familiar house at twelve sharp. Before he could exit the car, she started down the walk, her long legs shown to advantage in silver heels. He met her halfway. "Hello."

She eyed him coolly. "Hello."

Though she carried a winter coat over her arm, the silvery-pink scarf around her shoulders protected her from the light breeze.

She looked stunning. Her golden-red hair was caught up on top of her head in a fancy knot of loose curls. The lustrous strand of pearls around her neck complemented the fabric of her dress. He wondered if Roberta had managed to hang on to one piece of valuable jewelry for her daughter, or if the pearls were costume.

The dress's strapless bodice and fitted waist fluffed out in what Emma would probably call a princess skirt. It ended midcalf. Jake opened the passenger door for Nikki and helped her in, carefully tucking in her skirt so the door wouldn't catch it.

When he ran around and slid behind the wheel, Nikki's familiar scent enveloped him. Her perfume wasn't heavy. Perhaps she had barely spritzed her throat. But he was intensely aware of it. And of her.

He started the engine. "You look beautiful, Nik. That dress was made for you."

She stared out the windshield. "Thank you."

"Are we going to act normal today?"

"I don't know. You tell me."

"C'mon, Nikki. Can't we call a truce?"

Now her head snapped around in his direction. Her eyes shot fire. He'd always thought that was just an expression, but Nikki nailed it. "You mean a truce during the wedding or until you leave town?" she asked.

He counted to ten. "For my brother's wedding. It's an important day."

"I know what weddings are, Jake. I had one, remember?"

The reminder hit him hard. He'd tried to forget that. "I know," he said, reeling from the pain of imagining it. Suddenly, he wanted details. "Was it a big wedding?"

"Mom and I were broke. Timothy and I went to the courthouse."

"I'm sorry it didn't work out." He said the words quietly, but he meant them. "You deserve to be happy."

"Thank you." She crossed her arms. The curves of her breasts peeked over the silky fabric that covered her chest. She looked lush, untouched, intensely feminine.

She belonged to him. The certainty came out of nowhere. Implacable. Undeniable. What was he going to do about it?

They arrived in Falling Brook and parked in a garage near the hotel. The half-a-block walk wasn't bad. Nikki put on her coat. Jake helped. The bare nape of her neck gave him ideas, but he reined in his impulses. It would be hours until he could get her alone.

Weddings happened every day, all the time. Half of them ended. He hoped his brother and Sophie would not be one of the failures, but who knew? Jake wasn't a sentimental man, or at least he hadn't been. But today, the woman beside him and his brother's big day were making Jake *feel* things.

At the Bismarck, they left Nikki's outerwear at the coat check in the main lobby. In the elevator, riding up to the twentieth floor, he studied her. She wasn't looking at him, so it was easy to sneak a peek.

She was so beautiful, it made his chest hurt. As a seventeen-year-old teenager, she had been cute and pretty and full of life. Now, she carried the maturity of a woman—a woman who had faced many of life's challenges and persevered.

Her magnolia skin, so often associated with redheads, was still the same. Soft, unblemished. Begging to be touched. Lust stirred uneasily in his gut. Today was about his brother, his twin. But despite the occasion, or perhaps because of it, Jake was drawn to his wedding date, his Nikki. He had missed her fiercely the last two days. The strength of that feeling convinced him he needed to move forward carefully.

He cleared his throat, feeling claustrophobic in the small space. "Joshua and Sophie asked their guests, in lieu of gifts, to make a donation to Haley Shaw's charity. I wrote a check. But I also sent Sophie a large potted orchid this morning from you and me with best wishes for a wonderful wedding day."

Nikki's head came up, and she actually smiled. "That was a lovely gesture. Thanks for including me."

The elevator dinged, and they exited. The entire top floor of the Bismarck had been completely transformed. Plate-glass windows in every direction showcased the view. One section of the giant room was set up with rows of white chairs and a center aisle marked with a satin runner. At the front, seasonal live flowers covered a trellised arch. Along the center aisle, candles burned inside crystal globes atop brass stands.

"This is beautiful," Nikki said, scanning the room with interest.

"C'mon. Let's get a seat." The front row on the right-hand side was reserved for Jake's mother, for Oliver and his fiancée, Samantha, and for Jake and Nikki. Jake watched as Nikki greeted each member of his family. Then they sat down.

Eve shot her son a knowing glance, but he ignored it.

The area set aside for the ceremony filled up quickly. The guest list might have ended up closer to sixty than fifty, but the crowd was still small enough to be described as intimate. A buzz filled the space as anticipation mounted.

Suddenly, Jake needed air. He had been blind for far too long. He was beginning to know what he wanted, but he had to make plans. Now he was trapped by the time. Three minutes before the hour.

From a side alcove, Joshua appeared, beaming. The minister accompanied him. The two men took their positions. A stringed quartet had been playing for the last twenty minutes. Now they paused and began the first notes of "Pachelbel's Canon."

Nikki touched his forearm. He jumped at the unexpected contact. His skin felt too tight for his body, and his chest was constricted.

She looked at him with concern. "Are you okay?" she whispered.

Nikki knew without any doubt that Jake was definitely *not* okay. He ignored her question. They stood with the other guests as the bride began to walk down the modest aisle. The expression on Sophie's face when she looked at Josh made Nikki's eyes damp with emotion.

Weddings always got to her, but this one more than most. Joshua had borne the weight of his father's sins and had worked for years to restore the community's trust in Black Crescent. He deserved to be the man of the hour.

His bride was stunning in an off-the-shoulder white satin gown with dozens of cloth-covered buttons down the back. Her hair was twined with tiny white flowers. She had opted for no veil.

Sophie and Joshua held hands and faced the minister. Their voices as they spoke their vows were clear and strong. They had chosen a traditional wedding liturgy with phrases like "love, honor and cherish" and "'til death do us part."

At last, the minister placed his palm over the couple's hands for a blessing. Then he said words that rang out over the small assembly: "I now pronounce you husband and wife. You may kiss the bride."

Everyone cheered and clapped. Josh bent Sophie over his arm and kissed her enthusiastically, not seeming to mind that they had an audience.

Nikki, without thinking, twined her fingers with Jake's, fighting a flood of feelings that threatened to overwhelm her. When he shot her a surprised sideways glance, she realized what she had done and dropped his hand immediately. But it was too late. She had inadvertently let him know how much she cared about him. Her face heated with humiliation.

The bride and groom exited. Everyone stood up and moved toward the reception area, talking and laughing.

Nikki spoke in Jake's direction without actually looking him in the eye. "Excuse me," she said stiffly. "I'd like to speak to Haley Shaw." She fled, managing not to run.

Fortunately, Haley was nearby. She had been sitting with Chase Hargrove. But Chase had moved away to chat with someone else.

"Hi, Haley," Nikki said. "You look beautiful."

Haley beamed. "Thanks. So do you."

"I didn't get a chance to say everything I wanted to the day I showed up at Black Crescent to talk to your boss."

Haley seemed surprised. "Oh?"

"I never thanked you for all those years you've stood by Black Crescent. Your loyalty to Vernon and my dad. And the way you stayed to help Joshua after everything fell apart."

Haley grimaced. "Well, I felt guilty, to be honest."

Nikki gaped at her. "Why?"

"Because I saw both of them that morning—Vernon and your dad. And I knew something was going down. But I never said anything to anybody. And then it was too late."

"Oh, gosh no, Haley. What could you have done? None of us had a clue what they were planning."

"Maybe. But you should know—I stayed with Black Crescent because I loved working there, and Joshua is a great boss."

Nikki shook her head slowly. "Life is strange. I've felt guilty all these years, too. I was still living at home back then. I overheard pieces of several odd phone calls. Conversations that made me uncomfortable. But I never said anything, either. I blamed myself afterward. Jake blamed me, too."

"Well, he must have gotten over it. The way he looks at you gives me the shivers. The man is in love with you in a bad way."

"Oh, no," Nikki said quickly. "You're mistaken. We're old friends, that's all. He asked me to be his plus-one because he's been gone forever and doesn't really know any women in Falling Brook."

Haley wrinkled her nose, unconvinced. "I think you're kidding yourself. Chase and I had our ups and downs and misunderstandings before we got engaged. Relationships are difficult. We had to learn to trust each other."

"I didn't know you were engaged."

Haley held out her hand, showing off her ring. "Yep. No wedding date yet. I'm waiting to see if Josh is going to be able to find a new CEO before making plans."

"I thought he had been interviewing candidates."

"He has. For months. But it has to be the right fit. Look at the Lowell men over there. It's probably what they're talking about right now."

The groom had separated from his bride for the moment. Sophie was surrounded by a crowd of family and friends. Joshua stood in a tight circle with Oliver and Jake. The three men were gorgeous. With both twins in dress clothes, Jake looked far more like his identical brother than usual.

"You're probably right," Nikki said. "I think I'll go get some food. I skimped on lunch. And I see that your handsome fiancé is headed this way."

Joshua, Jake and Oliver were deep in conversation when Nikki slipped past them. She picked up enough words here and there to know Haley was right. They were talking about the CEO search. Maybe the Lowells should sell Black Crescent. She wondered if any of the three had floated that idea.

Feeling somewhat out of place, Nikki picked up a plate and began filling it with appetizers. The cake would be cut later. She found a corner and sipped her champagne. The day, unlike the expensive alcohol, had gone flat. She shouldn't have come. Things with Jake were rocky at best.

She was looking down at her glass when a deep voice startled her. "There you are."

"Jake," she said.

"So you do remember my name. That's a start."

His attempt at humor failed.

"Don't feel like you have to entertain me," she said. "I know you have lots of catching up to do with old friends." Even after fifteen years, she and Jake knew many of the guests personally.

"How about a dance?" he said, taking her empty plate and glass and setting them on a nearby tray.

"I don't think so."

"We agreed to a truce, remember?"

His gentle smile and half-hearted grin made her stomach curl with anxiety and heartbreak. "Sure."

He tucked her tiny beaded clutch in his jacket pocket, then took her by the hand and led her out onto the dance floor. Other couples had the same idea. Jake put an arm around her waist and pulled her close. The string quartet had yielded to a bluesy band that began playing romantic standards.

When the musicians launched into "I Only Have Eyes for You," Nikki stumbled and gasped. "I don't want to dance," she said, trying to pull away.

Jake held her tightly, looking almost as miserable as she felt. "Dance, Nik. For old times' sake."

He might as well have stabbed her through the heart. She wanted to run away. This was agonizing. She loved him, but he didn't feel the same.

No matter the pain, she wouldn't cause a scene at Josh and Sophie's wedding.

She kept her gaze focused on the third button of Jake's pristine white dress shirt, trying not to cry. His body was big and hard and warm, and he smelled amazing. His hand clasping hers was strong and tanned. He had mentioned Greece. Probably because he had a favorite villa there that he rented whenever the mood took him.

What kind of women did Jake *entertain* when he went

to the Mediterranean? The odd thing was that Nikki didn't really care about all those faceless females. She loved him as he was—imperfect, fierce, generous, sweet with Emma…and the perfect lover in Nikki's bed.

Once, he had been her whole world. Having him back in Jersey now, even fleetingly, had shown her why her marriage hadn't worked out. It had also underlined the truth that some feelings never die. She loved Jake Lowell, and she probably always would.

The dance finally ended. Jake and Nikki stood at the edge of the floor, not speaking, and watched as the bride and groom enjoyed their first dance. After that, the tempo picked up. Alcohol flowed freely, and the crowd became more raucous.

"I have to go to the restroom," Nikki said. She pulled her clutch from Jake's pocket and slipped away before he could say anything. In the ladies' lounge she found a seat and repaired her lipstick. One glance in the mirror told her she was hiding her feelings fairly well. Only her eyes gave her away. She pinched her cheeks and put a wet paper towel on the back of her neck.

She wanted badly to go home. But it was a very long way. If she hired a car, it would cost a fortune.

When she returned to the reception, Jake was nowhere in sight. Some kind of buzz circled the room. Clumps of guests stood here and there, looking either startled or worried or both.

Nikki found Haley, who looked shell-shocked. "What happened?" Nikki asked. "I can't find Jake. What's going on?"

Haley lowered her voice. "Somebody just brought word that Vernon has escaped from custody."

"Oh, no. Poor Joshua. Poor Sophie. What a dreadful thing to happen today of all days."

Suddenly, Joshua strode across the room in their direction. His face was stormy. When he stood right in front of the two women, he sighed. “Jake is gone, Nikki.”

She gaped at him. “What do you mean *gone*? I don’t understand.”

“He and Oliver left to go find our dad.”

Nikki shook her head slowly. “No. That doesn’t even make sense.”

Josh rubbed his forehead and pinched the bridge of his nose. “I know that. Neither of them was particularly rational when we got the news.”

“Vernon could be anywhere,” Haley said.

Nikki felt sick. “I’m so sorry, Josh. Is Sophie upset?”

At last, he smiled. “My new bride is a saint. We’re going to contact the travel agency and delay our honeymoon for a few days. Once again, Vernon has screwed me over. I don’t know how this keeps happening.”

Nikki touched his arm. “Is there anything I can do?”

“Maybe keep my twin from losing his mind.”

She winced. “I don’t have any control over your brother. Sorry. He told me he was leaving Falling Brook as soon as the wedding was over. He was pretty insistent about it. I tried to talk to him, but we had a big fight.”

Haley frowned. “But you came to the wedding together.”

“We had a temporary truce,” Nikki said. “I guess it’s over.”

Joshua glanced over his shoulder, clearly looking for his bride. “I’ve got to get back to the lovely Mrs. Lowell. Jake sent you a text, Nikki. Check your phone. I’ll see you ladies later. God help us if they don’t find Vernon. I don’t know if this town can handle that kind of news.”

Thirteen

Nikki kicked off her high heels and stared at the message on her phone for the hundredth time:

I called a limo to take you back to your place. The driver will be in the lobby to greet you at five. Sorry I had to leave…

She didn't know whether to laugh or cry. Here she was, sitting in a fancy, over-the-top hired car heading home from the ball without the handsome prince. It was a miracle her dress hadn't turned into rags and the car into a pumpkin. In the whole history of bad wedding dates, today had to rank right up there in the top five.

This was the end. Jake was who he was. She was never going to change him. Perhaps she should be glad Jake even remembered he *had* a date. *Damn* Vernon Lowell to hell and back. How could he do this to his sons, his ex-wife, the citizens of Falling Brook? Nikki's heart ached for the man she loved. But at the same time, she was angry and hurt. How could Jake treat her this way? Whatever she thought she had with him was over.

In fifteen years, Jake hadn't managed to deal with his father's betrayal. This stunt would rip open the wound for sure. She wanted to talk to Jake, but she was afraid that if she called, he wouldn't answer. And that would hurt even more.

It was better not to know. It was better to call time of death on this relationship.

She huddled into her coat and listened to her stomach growl. The original plan with Jake had been to go out to dinner after the wedding. As it was, Nikki was destined to eat peanut butter and jelly with Emma.

Finally, the ride ended.

Roberta lifted an eyebrow when her daughter walked into the house. "Was that a *limo*, Nicole Marie Reardon?"

"Yes, Mom." Nikki squatted and hugged her daughter. "Hi, baby. I missed you. But I brought you some bubbles from the wedding reception. And some M&M's." The candy was imprinted with the bride's name and the groom's. Yellow for Sophie. Navy for Josh.

"How was it?" Roberta asked.

"The ceremony was lovely," Nikki said.

"I hear the reception took an exciting turn."

Nikki shot her mom a startled glance. "You know?"

Roberta nodded. "It's all over the internet."

"Oh, lordy. Did you find out any details?"

"No. The story I read said they think he must have paid off one of the guards. The feds are investigating."

"Great. Just great."

"How did Jake react?"

"Not well, Mom. He and Oliver went haring off to try to find Vernon."

"Oh. I'm sorry."

"Yeah, me, too. That was the final straw for me. I can't wait forever for Jake to get his life together. I can handle the future on my own. I don't need a man who spooks like a skittish horse. I wanted him to share my world, but that's not going to happen."

Emma looked up, clearly not interested in the conversation. "I'm hungry. Can we eat now? And is Mr. Man coming over?"

Sunday evening, Nikki sat on the end of her bed and checked her texts…again. Nothing but yawning silence from Jake. Why was she surprised? Though she had hoped against hope that he might lean on her in the midst of his crisis, Jake was on his own…again.

If they'd had any chance at being a couple, it was gone. His silence said louder than words that he didn't need her.

It hurt, far worse than she could have imagined.

In the hours since law-enforcement officials had apprehended Vernon at the Canadian border—midday today—the judge had issued a statement. On Tuesday morning at 10:00 a.m., anyone who had been wronged by Vernon Lowell and his partner, Nikki's father, would be given the opportunity to address the defendant directly. To state their grievances. To bear witness to the misery and pain Vernon and Everett had caused.

The only caveat was that in order for anyone to speak, he or she must first notify the judge via email and receive a confirmation.

Nikki was torn. She called her mother and posed the question. Roberta refused flat out. "I have no interest in going," she said firmly. "Anyone in that room will probably still assume I knew what my husband was doing. They'll hate me for what happened. My being there will solve nothing."

"Are you sure, Mom? Don't you even want to ask Vernon the questions you can't ask Dad? Aren't you curious?"

There was a brief silence, and then Nikki heard her mother sigh. "I can't change the past, Nikki. Go if you want to. I know you're worried about Jake."

"I'm not positive he'll be there. He was pretty insistent about leaving right after the wedding."

"Things have changed in the last two days. It's hard for me to believe he would simply walk away. I'll keep Emma. If it will make you feel better, go. Go see Vernon. Go speak to him. Ask what you want to ask."

"Maybe I will."

"When you sign up with the judge, you can always drop out if you change your mind."

"True."

"Do you *want* to speak to Vernon?"

"Maybe. Mostly, I just want to be in the room and see what happens."

"Then do it. There's not a downside. Judges are leaning more and more toward giving victims the right to face their abusers. Vernon hurt a lot of people and abused their trust. That pain runs deep. You've seen it in dear Jake. Go, Nikki. Be there to support the Lowell boys if nothing else. It will make you feel better, and maybe you'll get a few of the answers you've wanted for fifteen years."

Nikki slipped into the courtroom at twenty minutes before the hour. It had taken longer than she anticipated to get through security. The chamber was crowded, but she found a seat in the back corner. Many of the faces she recognized. Some she didn't.

The Lowell men were sitting in the front row with their mother, Eve. Sophie was there, too. And Samantha. Just looking at the back of Jake's head made Nikki tense and weepy. What was he thinking? How was he holding up?

The bailiff instructed everyone to stand. The judge entered. Then came Vernon Lowell in handcuffs, his gaze downcast. He was wearing a standard-issue orange jumpsuit. His scruffy beard and longish hair were a mix of gray and white. With his stooped shoulders and weary air, it was almost impossible to reconcile this version of the man with his past self.

At one time, Vernon had been one of the richest men in the tristate area. The boutique hedge fund he created from scratch had been wildly successful. It was rumored years ago that there was a waiting list of would-be clients hoping for a chance to "get in."

Nikki didn't know if that was true or not, but it made sense. The very elite reputation of Black Crescent had made it all the more attractive to the high-profile citizens of Falling Brook. Those lucky enough to have their millions in Vernon's care had seen those millions multiply.

But then everything went south. The fiscal dreams rotted on the vine.

Vernon and Everett absconded with money that wasn't theirs.

The judge banged a gavel and made opening remarks, explaining why he had allowed this somewhat unprecedented hearing. Still, Vernon stared at the floor.

Nikki's stomach tightened as the first name on the list was read aloud. The judge instructed Vernon to lift his head and face his accusers. Nikki wondered if there was any particular order. The first person to stand and walk toward the front of the room was Zane Patterson. There was a small podium for the Falling Brook visitors. Zane's words were calm but held an underlying bitterness as he laid out for Vernon a litany of what had happened when the Pattersons lost everything.

Each person on the judge's list was allotted ten minutes. Some took the entire time. Some ended abruptly. Though the wounds were fifteen years old, the stories sounded fresh. Raw.

It was painful to hear. Jessie Acosta was on the list. Like Zane, her father had been a client of Black Crescent.

Nikki was shocked when Chase Hargrove stood. As far as she knew, his family hadn't entrusted their money to Black Crescent. But, apparently, Vernon had involved Chase's father with some scheme that ended with Chase's dad going to prison for fraud.

One after another, the people spoke. Many of them had been in their teens and twenties when the tragedy happened. Their lives had been shaped, broken, damaged by Vernon's actions.

Nikki held her breath, feeling waves of guilt for something that hadn't been her fault at all. But her father had been deeply involved.

Evidently, the judge was saving Vernon's immediate family for last.

Suddenly, the name read aloud was *Nicole Reardon.* She flinched. Why had she signed up? Why hadn't she had them strike her name when she first arrived?

"Ms. Reardon?" The judge repeated her name.

Nikki stood slowly, her heart thumping wildly in her chest. Dozens of people stared at her. Not Jake. He still faced straight ahead. Nikki swallowed, her mouth dry. "You can skip me, sir."

The judge frowned. “This is your moment, Ms. Reardon. I assume it’s been a long fifteen years. I’m giving you a chance to speak your piece.”

There was no backing out now. Nikki walked on shaky legs to the front of the courtroom. Not once did she cast her gaze sideways to see Jake. She stood at the podium and faced Vernon.

Until this very instant, she hadn’t known what she was going to say to him. But the words came tumbling out as if she had rehearsed them for five thousand empty days. Not a single other person had asked Vernon a question. They had vented, accused, mourned. Now it was Nikki’s turn.

“Mr. Lowell…” She paused, feeling overwhelmed. Hopefully, she wasn’t going to keel over. “Mr. Lowell. You and my father were best friends, colleagues, business partners. Clearly, you both were involved with the destruction of Black Crescent. But tell me this. You got away scot-free. My father crashed his car fleeing the police. Why wasn’t he with you?”

For a moment, emotion broke the stoic expression on Vernon’s face.

The judge addressed him. “Please answer Ms. Reardon’s question. She deserves to know the truth.”

When Vernon spoke, his voice was almost defiant. “Everett wanted to say goodbye to you and your mother. I told him he was a fool. Partway back to the house, the chase started. He had to turn around. He never made it.”

“Oh. Thank you.” Why was she thanking Vernon Lowell? How stupid. She turned to go back to her seat. As she moved, Jake looked at her across the small distance that separated them. He didn’t smile. He was visibly ashen.

Nikki kept on walking, comforted in the smallest possible way that her father had wanted to say goodbye.

Next up was Eve Lowell, Vernon's wife. When the judge read her name, she shook her head. Like Nikki, she must have changed her mind. The judge didn't press her. He went on. *Oliver Lowell.*

Oliver stood and shrugged. "I learned in recovery not to blame other people for my addiction," he said. "You're a wretched bastard of a father, and I'll spend the rest of my life trying not to be like you. End of story."

Joshua Lowell. Joshua went to the podium and spoke quietly about his regrets. Mostly, he mentioned his mother and his two brothers. He sat down.

Then came the name Nikki had dreaded hearing. *Jacob Lowell.* Surely, Jake was the last one. It was almost noon.

Jake walked to the podium, his shoulders stiff, his eyes blazing with strong emotion. When he reached the designated spot, he stood there for a moment. The courtroom was completely silent. Hushed. Waiting.

Outside, the noise of New York City was audible, but muted by the thick walls and closed windows.

Even Vernon seemed affected by the somber atmosphere.

Jake shoved his hands in his pockets as if he didn't know what to do with them. "I'm not going to address you as *Father* or *Dad*," he said. "You gave up that right long ago. But I will say that I have hated you for far too long. I've let your shadow hang over my life, blighting it. Constraining it. I told myself I traveled the world because I loved the freedom and the adventure. The truth is that I've been afraid to come home. What you did nearly destroyed me. Not because I was destitute or on the run from the law. But because you convinced me that my

DNA carried some sort of poison. If you could do what you did, maybe I was doomed to be as black-hearted a person as you."

Jake paused, maybe to catch his breath, and then continued. "I'm not a perfect human being. I have my faults, plenty of them. But from this day forward, I will no longer let your treachery determine the course of my life. I don't hate you. I don't love you. You are nothing to me at all…"

The gathered crowd exhaled almost in unison as Jake returned to his seat.

Moments later, the judge tapped the piece of paper in front of him, shook his head slowly and gave the bailiff a nod.

"All rise," the uniformed officer instructed the gathering.

Another set of officers stepped forward, helped Vernon to his feet and led him away.

When the judge and the prisoner were out of sight, the bailiff said, "You're dismissed."

Nikki was sitting in the back corner. No one needed to climb over her. She wasn't in anyone's way. She remained as the room emptied. At last, Oliver and Samantha walked out. Then Joshua and Sophie and Eve.

Jake never stood up. She watched from the back corner of the room as he leaned forward, elbows on his knees, and stared at the ground. His posture suggested that he was unapproachable.

Suddenly, Nikki couldn't bear the thought that he might speak to her or think she had been waiting for him.

She jumped to her feet and slid around the back of the last bench, escaping into the crowded hallway. When she saw the nearest stairwell, she made a beeline for it, not willing to wait for an elevator.

Six flights of steps. The courtroom had been higher up in the building than she had realized. At last, she popped out onto the street. The crisp, cool air felt good on her hot cheeks. She felt weird. Sad. Depleted. It had been an emotional morning.

But maybe there was closure now. Maybe everyone could move on.

She set off down the street, feeling tiny icy pellets of snow land on her face. Nothing that would amount to much. At least the weather felt Christmassy. Every shop she passed was fully decorated. Though Thanksgiving was still two days away, hardly anyone waited for that marker to get ready for the December season.

Behind her, someone called her name. "Nikki. Nikki. Stop. Wait up."

When she turned, she saw that it was Jake. She shivered, a combination of the cold and the way she always reacted in his presence. He'd had plenty of opportunity to speak to her in the courthouse. Why had he followed her now?

She stepped into the sheltered doorway of a large building and waited. This was not a confrontation she relished. Prior to this morning, the last she had seen of Jake was when she went to the ladies' room at the wedding reception three days ago.

He caught up to her, panting. "Where's your car?" His hair was tousled, and his cheeks were ruddy with the cold. He looked like a male model in a winter catalog. Sophisticated. Gorgeous. Out of reach.

"In the garage on the next block."

"We'll take mine," he said, sounding as arrogant as a man who thought he had all the answers. "I'll get one of Joshua's guys to drive yours home."

"No, thank you," she said politely.

She left the alcove and continued her journey.

Jake took her arm. “Don’t be ridiculous, Nik. We need to talk. We’ll ride together. My car is more comfortable.”

Anger swept over her, dissolving any squeamishness she had felt at facing him. “Don’t you *dare* call me ridiculous,” she said curtly, conscious of the many passersby. “I’m not the one who took a woman to his brother’s wedding and then slipped out like a thief in the night.”

His jaw tightened. “Maybe a poor choice of words.”

“Sorry,” she muttered.

“You knew where I was.”

“I knew that you and Oliver lost your minds. You hadn’t seen your father in fifteen years, and yet somehow you thought the two of you could track down Vernon better than the FBI? Sorry, Jake. That doesn’t cut it.”

“I made a mistake,” he said. “I was running on shock and adrenaline.”

“The mistake was mine,” Nikki replied, her throat clogged with tears.

“Let me explain,” he said urgently.

Nikki refused to be a pushover. “I know you’re Emma’s father. I won’t play the villain. But when you decide on a visitation schedule that fits your life, I’ll make plans for you to spend time with her in the company of either my mother or yours. I don’t want to see you again.”

His face was frozen in tight planes. His eyes burned. “Give me a chance, Nik. I have things I need to say.”

She shored up her resistance. “I’m cold, and I’m hungry. Goodbye, Jake.” She started walking again, blind to her surroundings. All she could think about was getting away. It hurt too much to be with him.

He followed her, took her arm in a gentle hold and spun her around, his eyes filled with anguish. “Don’t go.” He kissed her then, a kiss that held more desperation than passion. At first, his lips were cold against hers, but then the slow burn kindled again, and they were clinging to each other like survivors of a shipwreck.

In a way, the comparison was apt. Fifteen years ago, their love had crashed on the rocks of tragedy, and they had been one step from drowning ever since.

Jake's kiss was achingly sweet one second and roughly possessive the next. Nikki went on her tiptoes, striving to get closer. She was courting more heartbreak. She knew that. But how could she be strong when everything inside her was melting with yearning for him?

At last, he stepped back, but he kept her hands in his. "One hour," he said hoarsely. "That's all I'm asking. One hour."

"And you'll feed me?"

Not even a glimmer of humor lightened his face. "Yes."

They ended up at the same scruffy neighborhood grill where the two of them and Joshua had eaten after their abortive attempt to visit Vernon in jail. Jake asked for a booth in the back. As they took off their heavy coats, he tried to sit with Nikki like last time, but she waved him to the other side of the table. She needed a buffer zone.

Jake didn't ask her opinion about the meal. He motioned for a waitress. When the woman arrived, he ordered two burgers, medium, with no onions and extra pickles, plus a couple of Cokes. How many times as teenagers had they ordered that exact meal and then laughed that they were so perfectly matched?

While they waited for the food, awkwardness loomed between them, filling the space, making conversation almost impossible. Finally, Nikki broke the silence. "Have you learned anything at all about the stolen money?"

Jake scowled at his drink, poking his straw through

it. "Mom spoke briefly to the lawyer this morning. According to him, Vernon claims there never was a theft. He told counsel that he and Everett were *hoodwinked* by an unscrupulous deal. They saw a chance to quadruple Black Crescent's coffers and took it. But the investment went belly up, and they were too ashamed to admit the truth, so they fled."

"Do you believe that?"

"I don't know. Maybe. I've read reports from the officers who apprehended my father. He wasn't living in luxury."

"I suppose that makes more sense than the two men suddenly deciding to embark on a life of crime. Doesn't that make you feel better?"

"No. Because they should have stayed and faced the music."

The server arrived with the burgers. Nikki dug into hers, ravenous despite the circumstances. Some women didn't eat when they were stressed. Nikki wasn't one of those. She had gained twenty pounds after her father's death and Jake's departure. Gradually, she had come out of her funk and started taking care of herself again, but it had been a struggle.

She and Jake barely spoke while they ate. The waitress brought drink refills and the check. Eventually, plates were clean, and the awkward silence returned.

Nikki looked at her watch. "It's been an hour," she said bluntly. "I have to go."

Jake frowned. "We haven't even talked."

She glanced around at the bustling eatery. "This place isn't exactly private, and it's too cold outside for a long walk. Let's call it quits, Jake. Please. You. Me. It's a no-go. There's nothing left." Her chest ached.

He was everything she wanted, but there might as well

have been an ocean between them. Soon, there would be…when Jake returned to Europe.

The line of his jaw was grim. He flagged down their server one last time. Jake handed the woman the check and three one-hundred-dollar bills. "We'd like to keep the table for a bit. No interruptions, please."

The woman stared, dazed, at the cash in her hand. "You mean no change?"

"No change. No drink refills. No nothing. Is that okay with you?"

She nodded vigorously, wonder dawning in her eyes. "Yes, sir. Cone of silence. I've got it." Tentatively, she touched the sleeve of his jacket. "Thank you, mister. This will make Christmas pretty special at my house."

When the woman disappeared, Jake shrugged out of his suit jacket and rolled up his sleeves. It was warm in the small restaurant. They were tucked in a far back corner. No one had any reason to pass by their table. Because the lunch rush had now waned, the booth next to them was empty.

The situation wasn't ideal, but under the circumstances, it would have to do. Nikki fanned herself with a napkin, wishing she had chosen something other than wool when she got dressed that morning. She had worn the red sweater and black skirt again with more sensible shoes.

Jake must have read her unease. "I could grab us a hotel room for an hour. If privacy would make you more comfortable."

She gaped at him. "You'd spend two hundred and fifty dollars for one hour in a hotel?"

He shrugged. "More like five hundred probably. It's the holidays. But, yes. If you were there, I would."

Nikki knew what would happen if she found herself

in a hotel room with Jake. The chemistry she had tried so hard to deny would spark and flame. That fantasy wasn't conducive to holding her ground. "No hotel," she whispered. "Just say what you want to say."

Jake stared at her. His eyes were more gold than green at the moment, and his gaze was hot and beautiful and determined. "I'm in love with you, Nikki."

Fourteen

Jake saw his companion flinch and knew he had his work cut out for him. Nikki's body language was guarded in the extreme. Her chin was up, and her eyes were dark with anxiety. He saw her throat work.

"No, you're not," she said quietly. "You've been under a tremendous amount of pressure, and you're trying to make a grand gesture. It's not necessary to placate me in order to see your daughter."

His temper flared. "That's not a very complimentary assessment of my character. I know my past behavior hasn't been exemplary, Nik, but I've changed. Or I'm trying to," he added, in the spirit of honesty. "I love you."

Tears spilled from her beautiful Irish-hued eyes, rolling down her cheeks unchecked. She swiped at the dampness with the back of her hand and reached for her purse and coat. "I can't do this."

"Don't leave me, Nik," he begged, his heart like shards

of glass in his chest. "Don't be afraid of this, of us. We lost it all once before, but our time has come. You have to believe me. Things are different now."

She didn't slide out of the booth, but she was close to bolting.

"What makes you think so, Jake? I don't see it."

He swallowed hard. "I spoke to Josh this morning. Before we went to court. I told him I had changed my mind about Black Crescent. That I was prepared to take over as CEO." Even now, his stomach churned about his decision, but he wouldn't let Nikki misinterpret his nerves. "Josh was thrilled and supportive," he said.

Nikki seemed less so. She gnawed her bottom lip. Her restless fingers shredded a paper napkin. "You'll be bored with it in a month. And you'll disappear again."

It was his turn to flinch. "Wow," he said, stunned at how much she could hurt him. "You're not making this easy."

Now she was angry. "There's *nothing* easy about us, Jake."

"I heard you say 'I love you,'" he muttered. "That night I made love to you at your house. You thought I was asleep."

She closed her eyes and shook her head slowly. When she looked at him again, he finally saw how much his abandonment had cost her. "It was the sex talking."

"Don't be flip. Not now. I heard you say it, and I was too chickenshit scared to say it back. But I'm saying it now. *I love you.* I'm not leaving. I'm not running away. If it takes me ten months or ten years to convince you, I'll do it. I. Love. You."

"Stop," she begged, her gaze agonized.

He clenched his hand on the table as he resisted the urge to pound something. "When we ran into each other in Atlantic City five years ago, it was like being struck by lightning. You were everything I had left behind, everything I had lost. That night we spent together was incredible. But you weren't a teenager anymore. You'd lived your life far more bravely than I had. I was knocked on my ass and swamped with so many feelings I couldn't handle it. I'm sorry I left you, Nikki. I've regretted it every day since."

Nikki put her face in her hands, her shoulders bowed. He couldn't tell for sure, but he thought she was crying again. When she finally looked up at him, her mascara was smudged, and her eyes were still wet. "How can I believe you, Jake? I want to, but I'm afraid. Afraid you'll smash my heart again. I don't know how many more times it can recover."

Slowly, he reached for his wallet. "Maybe this will convince you," he said quietly. He opened the leather billfold and extracted a piece of paper that was ragged at the creases. It was yellow stationery with a row of pink daisies at the top. He handed it to Nikki. "Do you remember?"

She stared at the note, her eyes wide. Though the letter was upside down from Jake's perspective, he didn't need to read it. He had memorized the contents years ago. Nikki had slipped the plea to him at her father's funeral.

In the days before smartphones and texting, she had written, "Take me with you to Europe…"

Her hands shook as she traced the girlish handwriting with a fingertip. "I can't believe you kept this."

He sat back and sighed. "I tried to throw it away a hundred times. The guilt crushed me when I looked at it. Over and over."

"You shouldn't have felt guilty. It was outrageous of me to ask."

"Was it, Nikki?" He cocked his head and soaked in her grace and her courage, painfully aware of how his life might have turned out differently. "I kept this, too." He handed her a graduation picture, wallet-size. It was Nikki, smiling at the camera, her hair vibrant, her eyes filled with joy.

"Oh, Jake." She teared up again.

He inhaled sharply and dropped the last of his protective cloak of secrets. "I love you, Nikki Reardon. I suspected it in Atlantic City. I think I knew it deep down the moment I came back to Falling Brook and saw you face-to-face. And heard I had a daughter. But I couldn't accept the truth."

"But you—"

He waved a hand, cutting her off. "I'm not finished. I've loved you in one way or another my whole life, Nik. Everywhere I traveled, I wanted to share new adventures with you. Sunsets and storms. People and places. You were always in the back of my mind, those big emerald eyes telling me how much you cared. I was wrong, Nicole Marie Reardon. I was a coward. I let inertia keep me on a path that led nowhere." He reached across the table, across the miles and years of loneliness. "I love you. I adore you, in fact. I want to spend the rest of my life with you and Emma."

And finally, at long last, the sun came out.

She smiled at him through her tears. Her fingers gripped his. "Yes," she said, the word barely audible. "I love you, too, Jake. So much it hurts."

They sat there for seconds. Minutes. Their gazes locked. Their hearts healing.

Finally, Nikki glanced around the restaurant, seeming dazed, noting the people going about their business.

She took a sip of her watered-down drink. "If you're still serious about that hotel thing, I'll take you up on it."

And just like that, his body went hard all over. Except for his heart. That organ was embarrassingly soft and filled with love for this incredible woman.

"Let's go," he said gruffly.

Outside the restaurant, he hailed a cab, not wanting to waste the time it would take to retrieve his car. Pulling Nikki against him in the back seat, he trembled when she laid her head on his shoulder.

He directed the driver to one of the city's premier luxury hotels.

Nikki balked briefly when she saw the iconic facade. "We don't have any luggage," she whispered.

"They won't bat an eye."

It was true. The front desk ran Jake's credit card and confirmed his request for a suite. The man handed over two keys.

Jake dragged Nikki with him to the small gift shop. Her face turned bright red while he bought protection.

Then they were on the elevator, streaking toward the top floor. When they were in the room, Nikki exclaimed over the view of Central Park. The light snow had dusted the tops of the trees.

Jake took her hand and went down on one knee. "Nikki, will you marry me? We'll shop for a ring together."

She tugged on his arm. "Yes, yes, yes," she cried. Her eyes glowed with happiness.

He stood and scooped her up. "Is it too soon to try out the bed?"

"Honestly," she said, with a mischievous grin, "I thought you were moving kind of slow for a well-traveled bachelor bad boy."

He carried her into the bedroom. Though the ache in his body urged him to do everything in hyper speed, Jake knew this occasion was too important to rush. He set Nikki on her feet and started undressing her, pausing to caress her smooth skin, soft curves, lush hills and valleys.

Her body was a wonder to him. Feminine. Unbelievably arousing.

While Nikki settled herself in the sumptuous covers, he stripped in record time and joined her. "I'm sorry," he groaned, burying his head between her breasts, feeling the ragged thump of her heart. "I'm sorry we've wasted so much time."

She stroked his hair, shivering when he tasted her nipples. "We've learned a lot, Jake. We've grown up. We've faced battles and won. Life won't ever tear us apart again, because we won't allow it. Make love to me, my dearest heart. Now. Like it's our first time. Like we have forever ahead of us."

"We do, Nikki. We do." He gave her his pledge and entered her slowly, stunned by the pleasure as her body welcomed his. The fit was snug, the stimulation almost unbearable. She deserved romance, but the lust he had bottled up for days and hours roared to life.

They moved together wildly, straining for dominance. It was heat and blessing, madness and perfect bliss. He took them to the peak and then slowed, tormenting them both. Trying to make it last.

Nikki arched and cried out beneath him, her fingernails scoring his shoulders. "Don't stop," she begged. "Don't stop."

He was beyond reason then, blinded by the need to find release, wrapped in the realization that their love had risen from the ashes against all odds.

The end was hot and hard and fast, draining, as close to perfection as mere mortals could get.

He held her after that, his breathing rough and jerky. Though it had been far too long since he had done so, he thanked the deity for not giving up on him.

Nikki's body was a warm, sweet gift in his embrace. "You're everything to me, Nik," he muttered hoarsely. "Now and always. I love you."

She smiled softly and reached for his hand, curling her fingers with his. "Emma and I will go wherever you go, Jake. You don't have to run Black Crescent if you don't want to…"

Shaking his head slowly, he exhaled. "I'm back where I belong. Here with you. And with my family and Falling Brook. I'm not leaving again."

A tiny hesitation betrayed her last reservation. "You're sure?"

He nuzzled her hair, letting sleep take him. "You can count on it, my love. You can count on it…"

* * * * *

THE WIFE HE COULDN'T FORGET

YVONNE LINDSAY

This story is dedicated to my fabulous readers,
whose continued support I cherish.

One

She hated hospitals.

Olivia swallowed hard against the acrid taste that settled on her tongue and the fearful memories that whispered through her mind as she entered the main doors and reluctantly scoured the directory for the department she needed.

Needed, ha, now there was a term. The last thing she needed was to reconnect with her estranged husband, even if he'd apparently been asking for her. Xander had made his choices when he left her two years ago, and she'd managed just fine, thank you, since then. Fine. Yeah, a great acronym for freaked out, insecure, neurotic and emotional. That probably summed it up nicely. She didn't really need to even be here, and yet she was.

The elevator pinged, and its doors slid open in front of her. She fought the urge to turn tail and run. Instead, she deliberately placed one foot in front of the other, entering the car and pressing the button for the floor she needed.

Damn, there was that word again. *Need.* Four measly

letters with a wealth of meaning. It was right up there with *want.* On its own insignificant, but when placed in the context of a relationship where two people were heading in distinctly different directions it had all the power in the world to hurt. She'd overcome that hurt. The pain of abandonment. The losses that had almost overwhelmed her completely. At least she'd thought she had, right up until the phone call that had jarred her from sleep this morning.

Olivia gripped the strap of her handbag just that little bit tighter. She didn't have to see Xander if she didn't want to—even if he had apparently woken from a six-week coma last night demanding to see her. Demanding, yes, that would be Xander. Nothing as subtle as a politely worded request. She sighed and stepped forward as the doors opened at her floor, then halted at the reception area.

"Can I help you?" the harried nurse behind the counter asked her, juggling an armful of files.

"Dr. Thomas, is he available? He's expecting me."

"Oh, you're Mrs. Jackson? Sure, follow me."

The nurse showed her into a blandly decorated private waiting room, then left, saying the doctor would be with her shortly.

Unable to sit, Olivia paced. Three steps forward. Three steps back. And again. They really ought to make these rooms bigger, she thought in frustration. The click of the door opening behind her made her spin around. This was the doctor, she assumed, although he looked far too young to be a neurological specialist.

"Mrs. Jackson, thank you for coming."

She nodded and took his proffered hand, noting the contrast between them—his clean, warm and dry, hers paint stained and so cold she'd begun to wonder if she'd lost all circulation since she'd received the news about Xander.

"You said Xander had been in an accident?"

"Yes, he lost control of his car on a wet road. Hit a power pole. His physical injuries have healed as well as could have been expected. Now he's out of the coma, he's been moved from the high-dependency unit and onto a general ward."

"And his accident? I was told it happened six weeks ago? That's a long time to be in a coma, isn't it?"

"Yes, it is. He'd been showing signs of awareness these past few days, and his nerve responses were promising. Then last night he woke fully, asking for you. It caught the staff by surprise. Only his mother was listed as next of kin."

Olivia sank into a chair. Xander? Asking for *her*? On the day he'd left her he'd said they had nothing to say to each other anymore. Were they talking about the same man?

"I…I don't understand," she finally managed.

"His other injuries aside, Mr. Jackson is suffering from post-traumatic amnesia. It's not unusual after a brain injury—in fact, studies show that less than 3 percent of patients experience no memory loss."

"And he's not in that 3 percent."

The doctor shook his head. "Post-traumatic amnesia is a phase people go through following a significant brain injury, when they are confused, disoriented and have trouble with their memory, especially short-term memory loss. Although, Mr. Jackson's case is a little more unusual with some long-term memory loss evident. I take it you were unaware of his accident?"

"I rarely see anyone who is in regular contact with him and I was never particularly close with his mother. I'm not surprised no one told me. I haven't seen Xander since he walked out on our marriage two years ago. We're just waiting for a court date to complete our divorce."

Olivia shuddered. Even now she couldn't keep the bitterness from her voice.

"Ah, I see. That makes things problematic then."

"Problematic?"

"For his release."

"I don't understand." Olivia furrowed her brow as she tried to make sense of the doctor's words.

"He lives alone, does he not?"

"As far as I know."

"He believes he's coming home to you."

Shock held her rigid in her chair. "H-he does?"

"He believes you are still together. It's why he's asking for you. His first words when he woke up were, "Tell my wife I'm okay."

Dr. Thomas began to explain the nature of Xander's injuries, but his words about loss of physical form due to the length of his coma and difficulties with short-term memory on top of the longer-term memory loss barely filtered through. All she could think of was that after all this time, her estranged husband wanted her.

"Excuse me," she interrupted the doctor. "But just how much *does* Xander remember?"

"As far as we can tell, his most recent clear memory is from about six years ago."

"But that was just after we married," she blurted.

That meant he remembered nothing of them finishing renovations on their late 1800s home overlooking Cheltenham Beach, nothing of the birth of their son five years ago.

Nothing of Parker's death just after he turned three.

She struggled to form the words she needed to ask her next question.

"Can he…does he…will he remember?"

The doctor shrugged. "It's possible. It's also possible he may never remember those lost years or that he may only regain parts of them."

She sat silently for a moment, letting the doctor's words sink in; then she drew in a deep breath. She had to do this. "Can I see him now?"

"Certainly. Come with me."

He led Olivia to a large room on the ward. There were four beds, but only one, near the window, was occupied. She steeled herself to move forward. To look at the man she'd once pledged her life to. The man she'd loved more than life itself and who she'd believed loved her equally in return. Her heart caught as she gazed on his all-too-familiar face, and she felt that same tug anew when she saw the similarities to Parker. They'd been like peas in a pod. She rubbed absently at the ache in the center of her chest, as if the motion could relieve the gaping hole there.

"He's sleeping naturally, but he'll probably wake soon," the doctor said at her side after a cursory glance at Xander's notes. "You can sit with him."

"Th-thank you," she replied automatically, lowering herself onto the seat at his bedside, her back to the window and the sunshine that sparkled on the harbor in the distance.

Olivia let her eyes drift over the still figure lying under the light covers. She started at his feet, skimming over the length of his legs and his hips before drifting over his torso and to his face. He'd lost weight and muscle mass—his usually powerful frame now leaner, softer. A light beard covered his normally clean-shaven jaw, and his hair was in dire need of a cut.

She couldn't help it. She ached for him. He would hate being this vulnerable and exposed. Xander was a man used to action, to decisiveness. To acting rather than being acted on. Lying helpless in a hospital bed like this would normally drive him nuts. Olivia started in shock as Xander's eyes opened and irises of piercing gray met hers. Recognition dawned in Xander's gaze, and her heart wrenched as he smiled at her, his eyes shining in genuine delight. She felt the connection between them as if it were a tangible thing—as if it had never been stretched to the breaking point by circumstances beyond both of their control. Her lips automatically curved in response.

How long had it been since she'd seen his smile? Far, far too long. And she'd missed it. She'd missed him. For two awful, lonely years Olivia had tried to fool herself that you could fall out of love with someone just as easily as you had fallen in love with him, if you tried hard enough. But she'd been lying to herself. You couldn't flip a switch on love, and you couldn't simply shove your head in a hole in the ground and pretend someone hadn't been the biggest part of your life from the day you'd met him.

She loved him still.

"Livvy?" Xander's voice cracked a little, as if it was rusty and disused.

"It's me," she replied shakily. "I'm here."

Tears burned in her eyes. Her throat choked up, and she reached out to take his hand. The tears spilled down her cheeks as she felt his fingers close tight around hers. He sighed, and his eyes slid closed again. A few seconds passed before he croaked one word.

"Good."

She fought back the sob that billowed from deep inside. On the other side of the bed Dr. Thomas cleared his throat.

"Xander?"

"Don't worry—he's sleeping again. One of the nurses will be by soon to do observations. He'll probably wake again then. Now, if you'll excuse me…?"

"Oh, yes, sure. Thank you."

She barely noticed the doctor leave, or one of the other patients shuffling into the room with his walker and a physical therapist hovering beside him. No, her concentration was fixed solely on the man in the bed in front of her and on the steady, even breaths that raised his chest and lowered it again.

Her thoughts scattered to and fro, finally settling on the realization that Xander could have died in the accident that had stolen his memory and she might never have known about it. That she might never have had another opportunity to beg him for one more chance. It opened a whole new cavern of hurt inside her until she slammed it closed. He hadn't died, she reminded herself. He'd lived. And he'd forgotten that he'd ever ended things between them.

Xander's fingers were still locked around hers. As if she was his anchor. As if he truly wanted her to be there with him. She leaned forward and gently lifted his hand up against her cheek. He was warm, alive. Hers? She hoped so. In fact she wanted him as deeply and as strongly right now as she had ever wanted him. A tiny kernel of hope germinated deep inside Olivia's mind. Could his loss of memory allow them that second chance he'd so adamantly refused?

Right here, right now, she knew that she'd do anything to have him back.

Anything.

Including pretending the problems in their past had never happened? she asked herself. The resounding answer should have shocked her, but it didn't.

Yes. She'd do even that.

Two

Olivia let herself in the house and closed the door, leaning back against it with a sigh as she tried to release the tension that now gripped her body. It didn't make a difference. Her shoulders were still tight and felt as if they were sitting up around her ears, and the nagging headache that had begun on the drive home from the hospital grew even more persistent.

What on earth had she done?

Was it lying to allow Xander to continue to believe they were still happily married? How could it be a lie when it was what he believed and when it was what she'd never stopped wanting?

You couldn't turn back the clock. You couldn't undo what was done five minutes ago any more than you could undo what happened in the past two years. But you could make a fresh start, and that's what they were going to do, she argued with herself.

It might not be completely ethical to take advantage of his amnesia this way, and she knew that she was running a risk—a huge risk—by doing so. At any moment his memory could return and, with it, Xander's refusal to talk through their problems or lean on her for help of any kind. Yet if there was a chance, any chance that they could be happy again, she had to take it.

She pushed off the door and walked down the hall toward the large entertainer's kitchen they'd had so much fun renovating after they'd moved into the two-story late nineteenth-century home a week after their marriage. She automatically went through the motions, putting the kettle on and boiling water for a pot of chamomile tea. Hopefully that would soothe the headache.

But what would soothe the niggling guilt that plucked at her heart over her decision?

Was she just doing this to resolve her own regrets? Wrapped in her grief over Parker's death and filled with recriminations and remorse, hadn't she found it easier to let Xander go rather than fight for their marriage—hell, fight for *him*? She'd accused him of locking her out of his feelings, but hadn't she done exactly the same thing? And when he'd left, hadn't she let him go? Then, when she'd opened her eyes to what she was letting slip from her life, it was too late. He hadn't wanted to even discuss reconciliation or counseling. It was as if he'd wiped his slate clean—and wiped his life with her right along with it.

It had hurt then and it hurt now, but time and distance had given her some perspective. Had opened her eyes to her own contribution to the demise of their marriage. Mistakes she wouldn't make again.

The kettle began to whistle, momentarily distracting her from her thoughts. Olivia poured the boiling water into the teapot and took her favorite china cup and saucer from the glass-fronted cupboard where she displayed her antique china collection. After putting the tea things on a tray, she carried everything outside. She set the tray down on a table on her paved patio and sank into one of the wood-and-canvas deck chairs. The fabric creaked a little as she shifted into a more comfortable position.

Bathed in the evening summer sun, Olivia closed her eyes and took a moment to relax and listen and let the sounds of her surroundings soak in. Behind the background hum of traffic she could hear the noises of children playing in their backyards. The sound, always bittersweet, was a strong reminder that even after tragedy, other people's lives still carried on. She opened her eyes, surprised to feel the sting of tears once more, and shifted her focus to pouring her tea into her cup. The delicate aroma of the chamomile wafted up toward her. There was something incredibly calming about the ritual of making tea. It was one of the habits she'd developed to ground herself when she'd felt as though she was losing everything—including her mind.

She lifted her cup, taking a long sip of the hot brew and savoring the flavor on her tongue as she thought again about her decision back at the hospital. The risk she was taking loomed large in her mind. So many things could go wrong. But it was still early days. Xander had a long road to recovery ahead, and it would be many days yet, if not weeks, before he was released from hospital. He had yet to walk unaided, and a physical therapy program would need to be undertaken before he could come home again.

Home.

A shiver ran through her. It wasn't the home he'd lived in for the past two years, but it was the home they'd bought together and spent the first year of their marriage enthusiastically renovating. Thank goodness she'd chosen to live with her memories here rather than sell the property and move on. In fact, the decision to stay had very definitely formed a part of her recovery from her grief at Parker's death followed so swiftly by Xander's desertion of her, as well.

She'd found acceptance, of a sort, in her heart and in her mind that her marriage was over, but her love for Xander remained unresolved. A spark of excitement lit within her. This would be their new beginning. After his release from hospital, they'd cocoon themselves back into their life together, the way they had when they'd first married. And if he regained his memory, it would be with new happier memories to overlay the bitterness that had transpired between them before their separation.

Of course, if he regained his memory before coming home with her, it was likely they'd never get the chance to rebuild their marriage on stronger ground. She had to take the risk. She just had to. And she'd cope with Xander's real world later. The world in which he worked and socialized was not hers anymore. Keeping his distance from his friends and colleagues would be easy enough, initially—after all, it's not as if his bedside cabinet had been inundated with cards or flowers. Just a card signed by his team at the investment bank where he worked. Until he was strong enough to return to his office anyway. By then… Well, she'd cross that bridge when they got there.

Xander's doctors had categorically stated he was in no condition to return to work for at least another four weeks, possibly even longer depending on how his therapy progressed. It should be easy enough to fend Xander's colleagues off at the border, so to speak, Olivia thought as she sipped her tea and gazed out at the harbor in the distance. After all, with Xander in the high-dependency unit at the hospital, and with family-only visitation—which she understood equated to the occasional rare visit from his mother who lived several hours north of the city—it wasn't as if they'd be up-to-date beyond the minimal status provided by the hospital. She'd call one of his partners in the next few days and continue to discourage visitors at the same time.

She felt a pang of guilt. His friends had a right to know how he was, and no doubt they'd want to visit him. But a careless word could raise more questions than she was comfortable answering. She daren't take the risk.

It was at least two years late, but Xander's amnesia was offering her another chance, and she was going to fight for him now. She just had to hope that she could successfully rebuild the love they'd shared. The fact that he woke today, obviously still in love with her, was heartening. Hopefully, they would have the rest of their lives to get it right this time.

Xander looked at the door to the hospital room for what felt like the hundredth time that morning. Olivia should be here by now. After a heated debate with Dr. Thomas about whether or not he'd go to a rehab center—a debate Xander had won with his emphatic refusal to go—the doctor had finally relented and said he could go home tomorrow, or maybe even later today. He'd used the mobile phone Olivia had left with him—his had apparently been pulverized in the accident and his laptop, as well, had been smashed beyond repair—to call the house and get her to bring him some clothes. He'd missed her, and she wasn't answering her mobile phone, either.

He'd go home in his pajamas if he had to. He couldn't wait to get out of here and back to their house. He liked to kid himself he could even see its green corrugated iron roof from the hospital window. It gave him a connection to Olivia in the times she wasn't here.

It had been three weeks, but, God, he still remembered that first sight of her when he'd fully woken. The worry on her exquisitely beautiful face, the urge to tell her that everything would be all right. Sleep had claimed him before he could do anything more than smile at her. This damn head injury had a lot to answer for, he cursed inwardly. Not only had it stolen the past six years from his memory but it had left him as weak as a kitten. Not even capable of forming proper sentences on occasion. Each of the therapists he'd seen had told him he was doing great, that his recovery was progressing well, but it wasn't enough. It would never be enough until he could remember again and be the man he was before his crash.

He couldn't wait to be home. Maybe being around his own familiar things in his own environment would hasten the healing process. He looked out the window and cracked a wry smile at his reflection in the glass. At least one thing hadn't changed. His levels of impatience were right up there where he always remembered them being.

Xander caught a sense of someone in the doorway to his shared room. He turned and felt the smile on his face widen as he saw Olivia standing there. Warmth spread through his body. A sense of rightness that was missing when she wasn't with him.

"You're looking happy," Olivia remarked as she came over and kissed him on the cheek.

Her touch was as light as a butterfly. Even so, it awakened a hunger for more from her. He might not be at his physical peak, but the demands of his body still simmered beneath the surface. They'd always had a very intense and physically satisfying relationship, one he couldn't wait to resume. He laughed inwardly at himself. There was that impatience again. One thing at a time, he told himself.

He swung his legs over the edge of the bed. "I might be able to come home today. I tried to call you—"

"Today? Really?"

Was he imagining things or did the smile on her face look a little forced? Xander rejected the thought immediately. Of course she was as genuinely excited as he was. Why wouldn't she be?

"Dr. Thomas just wants to run some final tests this morning. Provided he's happy I should be able to leave here later this afternoon."

"Well, that's great news," Olivia said. "I'll shoot back home and get some things for you."

Xander reached out and caught her hand in his. "In such a hurry to leave me? You just got here. Don't go yet."

Her fingers curled around his, and he turned her hand over before lifting it to place a kiss on her knuckles. He felt the light tremor go through her as his lips lingered on her skin and her fingers tightened, saw the way her pupils dilated and her cheeks flushed ever so slightly.

"I miss you when you're not here," he said simply, then examined the hand he held more closely. Her nails were short and practical, and even though she'd scrubbed at them, he could still see traces of paint embedded in her skin. It made him smile. "I see you're still painting. Good to know some things haven't changed."

She bit her lower lip and turned her head, but not before he saw the emotion reflected in her eyes.

"Livvy?"

"Hmm?"

"Are you okay?"

"Sure, I'm fine. I'm just worried I'm going to have to cart you home in those," she said lightly as she tugged her hand free and pointed at his striped pajamas with a disparaging look on her face. "And yes, I'm still painting. It's in my blood. Always has been, always will be."

He laughed, like she wanted him to, at the line he'd heard her say so many times. He saw the strain around her eyes lift a little.

"Fine, you better go then, but come straight back, okay?"

"Of course. I'll be as quick as I can," she said, bending down to kiss him on the forehead.

Xander leaned back against his pillows and watched her departing back. He couldn't quite put his finger on it, but something wasn't right. They'd talked about him going home for days. Now that the time was finally here, was she afraid? He mulled the idea over in his head. It was possible. He'd been through a lot, and maybe she was worried about how he would cope on his reentry into the real world. She was such a worrier, always had been. He guessed that came with the territory of being the eldest out of four kids growing up on a farm without their mother. His Livvy was used to micromanaging everything around her so that nothing would go wrong.

When he'd married her, he'd silently promised himself that he would never be a burden to her—that he would never make himself one more responsibility she had to shoulder. Even now, he was determined to make certain that his recovery didn't weigh her down. He'd do whatever it took to ensure that the rest of his recuperation went smoothly so that the worry would disappear from her eyes once and for all.

"Nothing will go wrong," he said aloud, earning a look from the guy in the bed opposite his.

Olivia hastened to the car parking building and got into her car. Her hand shook slightly as she pressed the ignition, and she took a moment before putting on her seat belt and putting the car in gear.

He was coming home. It was what she wanted, so why on earth had she run like a startled rabbit the minute he'd told her? She knew why. It meant she would have to stop putting her head in the sand about the life he'd created when he'd left her. It meant taking the set of keys that she'd been given, among the personal effects the hospital had held since his accident—ruined blood-stained clothing included—and going to his apartment to get his things.

She knew she should have done it before now. Should have gathered together what he would expect to find at their home. His wardrobe, his toiletries. Those were pretty much all he'd taken with him when he'd left. There was nothing for it but to steel herself to invade the new home he'd created. At least she knew where he lived. That was about the only thing the legal separation documents had been any good for, she thought grimly as she drove the short distance from Auckland City Hospital to the apartment block in Parnell where Xander had taken a lease.

She parked in one of the two spaces allocated to his apartment and rode the elevator to the top floor. Letting herself in through the door at the end of the corridor, she steeled herself for what she would find on the other side. As she stepped through the entrance hall she found herself strangely disappointed.

It was as if she'd stepped into a decorator's catalogue shoot. Everything perfectly matched and aligned—and totally lacking any character. It certainly didn't look as though anyone actually lived here. There was none of his personality or his love of old things, no warmth or welcome. She walked through the living room and toward a hallway she hoped would lead to his bedroom. It did, and she was surprised to discover the bedroom was in the same pristine, sterile condition. Not so much as a stray sock poking out from the simple valance that skirted the king-size bed. It wasn't like the Xander she'd known at all—a man who was meticulous in all things except what she teasingly referred to as his *floor-drobe.* Maybe he had a cleaning service come through. Or maybe, the thought chilled her, he really had changed this much.

Anyway, she was wasting time. She needed to get his things and take them back to her house on the other side of the harbor bridge and then get back to the hospital again before he began to think she wasn't coming to take him home after all.

In the spare room closet Olivia found a large suitcase, and she quickly grabbed underwear, socks and clothing from the walk-in wardrobe in Xander's bedroom. From the bathroom she grabbed shower gel, cologne and his shaving kit. She wondered briefly if he remembered how to use it. It had been a while since he'd shaved properly. Only last week she'd teased him about the furry growth that ringed his jaw. Privately, she found she quite liked it. It made him seem a bit softer, more approachable than the cold stranger who'd stalked so emphatically out of her life.

She shook her head as if she could rid herself of the memory just as easily and wheeled the case to the front door. Should she check the refrigerator? She cringed a little at the idea of finding nine-week-old leavings rotting inside, but she figured she would have to do it sometime. She poked around in the drawers until she found a plastic garbage bag and then, holding her breath, opened the shiny stainless-steel door of the fridge.

Empty. *How odd*, she thought as she let the door close again. Not even a half bottle of wine stood in the door. If she hadn't taken Xander's things from his bedroom and en suite herself, she would hardly have believed he even lived here. She pulled open a pantry door and was relieved to see neatly labeled containers and a box of his favorite cereal stacked on the shelves. Okay, so maybe whoever had made the apartment look so spick-and-span had cleaned out the fridge, as well. She made a mental note to try and find out from somewhere, perhaps among his personal papers, if he had a cleaning service. If so, she'd need to put their visits on hold indefinitely.

She looked around the open-plan living room and dining area to see where he might keep his personal files and records. There was nothing to suggest a desk or office space in here. Maybe there was another bedroom? Olivia went back down the hall that led to Xander's bedroom, and spied another door. She opened it, stepped inside and immediately came to a halt.

Her heart thumped erratically in her chest as her eyes fixed on the photo on the desk in what was obviously Xander's home office. She recognized the frame as one she'd bought for him for his first Father's Day and in it was the last photo they'd taken of Parker before he died.

Three

Her hand went to her throat as if she could somehow hold back the sob that rose from the deepest recesses of her grief. She hadn't even realized Xander had taken the picture with him when he'd left. He must have hidden it away when, after the funeral, she'd packed up Parker's room and shoved all the boxes in the attic, along with his albums and the framed photos they'd had scattered around the house.

It had hurt too much to see the constant reminders of his all-too-short life.

If only…

Those two words had driven her almost insane. If only Xander hadn't left the gate open, or hadn't thrown the ball quite so vigorously for Bozo, their dog. If only Bozo hadn't run out into the street in pursuit of the ball and—even now, she gasped against the pain from the memory—if only Parker hadn't run out into the street after him. If only she hadn't told Parker to run outside and play with Daddy in the first place, instead of staying safely in the studio with her that day.

Racked with her own guilt and her anger at the world in general and Xander in particular, she'd done the only thing she could to alleviate the searing pain. She'd packed up Parker's short life and hidden it, telling herself she'd look at his things again when she was able. Every piece of clothing, every toy, every photo—hidden away.

All except this one. She reached out a finger and traced the cheeks of her little boy, locked behind the glass. A child forever—never to grow up and go to school, play a sport or meet girls. Never to stretch his wings, push his boundaries or be grounded for some misdemeanor or another.

Her hand dropped back to her side. She stood like that for several minutes before shaking herself loose from the memories and trying to remember why she'd come in here in the first place. Yes, the cleaning service, that was it. Olivia rifled through Xander's filing system—as linear and exact as she remembered—and found the number she was looking for. A quick phone call to suspend services until further notice was all that was required, and then she was on her way.

Before she left the room, though, she lifted the photo from Xander's desk and shoved it in a drawer. It hurt to shut her baby away like that, but if she had to come back here again, she couldn't bear to see the stark reminder of all they'd lost.

Thankfully traffic through the city to the harbor bridge approach was lighter than usual and she made the trip home in good time. She dragged the suitcase up the flight of stairs and into the guest bedroom, and quickly unpacked and hung up Xander's shirts and trousers and a few suits, still in their drycleaner bags, in the closet and shoved his underwear, socks and T-shirts into the small chest of drawers. She put his toiletries in the bathroom across the hall. It wouldn't be a lie to tell him she'd moved his things in there so he could recuperate in his own space. She just wouldn't mention that she'd moved them from across town rather than from down the hall.

Before leaving the house again, she folded a set of clothes and a belt into a small overnight bag for him and then flew out the door. She was jittery with emotional exhaustion and lack of food by the time she got back to the hospital. Xander was standing at the window when, slightly out of breath, she finally arrived.

"I was beginning to think you'd changed your mind about taking me home," he said lightly when she approached him.

Even though his words were teasing, she could hear the underlying censure beneath them. And she understood it; really she did. Under normal circumstances she would have been back here much earlier. But their circumstances were far from normal, even though he didn't know that yet.

"Traffic was a bitch," she said as breezily as she could. "So, are we good to go? I have some clothes for you here, although I'm thinking you'll find everything on the big side for you now. We might need to get you a whole new wardrobe."

Her attempt at deflection seemed to work. "And I know how much you love shopping," he said with a laugh.

She felt her heart skip a beat. He'd always teased her about her shopping style. While she liked getting new things, she hated crowded stores. She had the tendency to decide what she wanted before she left the house and, with no dillydallying, get in, get the product and get right back out again as quickly as possible. No window-shopping or store browsing for her. Unless it was an art supply store, that was.

Olivia told herself it was ridiculous to be surprised that he'd remember that. After all, he hadn't lost all his memory, just the past six years. She forced a laugh and handed him the bag of his things.

"Here you go. Will you need a hand to get dressed?"

He'd had issues with balance and coordination since awakening from his coma. Physical therapy was helping him regain his equilibrium and motor skills, but he still had some way to go.

"I think I can manage," he said with the quiet dignity she had always loved so much about him.

"Just call me if you need me."

Xander looked her straight in the eye and gave her a half smile. "Sure."

She smiled back, feeling a pang deep inside. She knew he wouldn't call her. He was nothing if not independent—and stubborn. Yes, there'd been a time, early in their marriage, when they'd each been the center of the other's world. But that had all changed.

He was so lucky he didn't remember, she thought fiercely. Lucky that he was still locked in the best of their marriage and couldn't remember the worst of them both.

Xander took the bag through to the shared bathroom and closed the door behind him. A tremor ran through his body as he allowed the relief he'd felt when he'd seen Olivia return run through him. Ever since she'd left earlier today he'd been tense and uncomfortable, so much so the nurse preparing his discharge papers had remarked on the spike in his blood pressure.

He couldn't understand it. Olivia was his wife. So why had he suddenly developed this deeply unsettled sensation that things weren't what they should be between them? He shoved off his pajamas and stepped into the shower stall, hissing a little as the water warmed up to a decent temperature. He couldn't wait to be out of here. Even with Olivia's daily visits to break the monotony of sleep, eat, therapy, eat, sleep, over and over again, he wanted to be *home*.

Xander roughly toweled himself off, swearing under his breath as he lost his balance and had to put a hand on the wall to steady himself. His body's slow response to recovery was another thing driving him crazy. It was as if the messages just weren't getting through from his brain to his muscles.

He looked down at his body. Muscles? Well, he remembered having muscles. Now his build was definitely leaner, another thing he needed to work on. He pulled on his clothing and cinched his belt in tight. Olivia had been right. His clothes looked as if they belonged to another man entirely. He couldn't remember buying them, so they had to be something from his lost years, as he now called them.

A light tap at the door caught his attention.

"Xander? Are you okay in there?" Olivia asked from outside.

"Sure, I'll be right out."

He looked at his reflection in the small mirror and rubbed his hand around his jaw, ruffling the beard that had grown during his stay here. He looked like a stranger to himself. Maybe that was part of Olivia's reticence. The beard would have to go when he got home. Xander gathered his things off the floor and shoved them in the bag Olivia had brought and opened the bathroom door.

"I'm ready," he said.

"Let's go then," she answered with that beautiful smile of hers that always did crazy things to his equilibrium.

Had he ever told her how much he loved her smile, or how much he loved to hear her laugh? He couldn't quite remember. Another thing he would have to address in due course.

They stopped at the nurses' station to say goodbye

and collect his discharge papers, and then they began the walk down the corridor toward the elevator. It irked him that Olivia had to slow her steps to match his. It bothered him even more that by the time they reached her car he was exhausted. He dropped into the passenger seat with an audible sigh of relief.

"I'm sorry—I should have gotten you to wait at the front entrance and driven round to get you," Olivia apologized as she got in beside him.

"It's okay. I've had plenty of time to rest. Now it's time to really get better."

"You say that like you haven't been working hard already." She sighed and rested one hand on his thigh. The warmth of her skin penetrated the fabric of his trousers, and he felt her hand as if it were an imprint on him. "Xander, you've come a long way in a very short time. You've had to relearn some things that you took for granted before. Cut yourself some slack, huh? It's going to take time."

He grunted in response. Time. Seemed he had all too much of it. He put his head back against the headrest as Olivia drove them home, taking solace in the things he recognized and ignoring his surprise at the things that had changed from what he remembered. Auckland was a busy, ever-changing, ever-growing city, but it still disturbed him to see the occasional gaping hole where, in his mind at least, a building used to stand.

"Did the school mind about you taking time off to spend with me?" he asked.

"I don't work at the school anymore," Olivia replied. "I stopped before—"

"Before what?" he prompted.

"Before they drove me completely mad," she said with a laugh that came out a bit forced. "Seriously, I quit there just over five years ago, but I've been doing really well with my paintings since. You'd be proud. I've had several shows, and I'm actually doing quite well out of it."

"But it was never about the money, right?" he said, parroting something Olivia had frequently said to him whenever he'd teased her about not producing a more commercial style of work.

"Of course not," she answered, and this time her smile was genuine.

By the time they arrived at the house he felt about a hundred years old, not that he'd admit it to Olivia, who, to his chagrin, had to help him from the car and up the front stairs to the house.

As she inserted a key into the lock and swung the door open he couldn't help but twist his lips into a rueful smile.

"Seems like not that long ago I was carrying you across that threshold. Now you're more likely to have to carry me."

He regretted his attempt at humor the moment he saw the concern and fear on her face.

"Are you okay?" she said, slipping an arm around his back and tucking herself under his arm so she supported his weight. "You should rest downstairs for a while before tackling the stairs to the bedroom. Or maybe I should just get a bed set up down here for you until you're stronger."

"No," he said with grim determination as they entered the hall. "I'm sleeping upstairs tonight. I'll manage okay."

She guided him into the sitting room and onto one of the sofas.

"Cup of coffee?"

"Yeah, thanks."

While she was gone he looked around, taking in the changes from what he remembered. French doors opened out onto a wooden veranda—they were new, he noted. There'd been a sash window there before and—he looked down at the highly polished floorboards—there'd been some ancient and hideous floral carpet tacked onto the floor. Seems they'd done quite a bit of work around the place.

Xander levered himself to his feet and walked around the room, trailing his hand over the furniture and the top of the ornate mantel over the fireplace, which was flanked by wingback chairs. Had they sat here on a winter's evening, enjoying the warmth of the fire? He shook his head in frustration. He didn't know. He sat in one of the chairs to see if it triggered anything, but his mind remained an impenetrable blank.

"Here you are," Olivia said brightly as she came back into the room. "Oh, you've found your chair. Would you like the papers?"

"No, thanks. Just the coffee."

"Still struggling with concentration?"

He nodded and accepted the mug she handed him. His fingers curled around the handle with familiarity and he stared for a while at the mug. This, he knew. He'd bought it at the Pearl Harbor memorial when they went to Hawaii for their honeymoon. He took a sip and leaned back in the chair.

"That's good—so much better than the stuff they serve in the hospital." He sighed happily and looked around the room again. "I guess we did it all, huh? Our plans for the house?"

Olivia nodded. "It wasn't easy, but we completed it in just over a year. We…um…we got impatient to finish and hired contractors to handle a lot of it. I wish you could remember haggling for those French doors. It was a sight worth seeing."

He must have pulled a face because she was on her knees at his side in a minute. She reached up to cup his cheek with one hand and turned his face to hers.

"Xander, don't worry. It'll come back in its own good

time. And if it doesn't, then we'll fill that clever mind of yours with new memories, okay?"

Was it his imagination or did she sound more emphatic about the new memories than him remembering his old ones? No, he was just being oversensitive. And overtired, he thought as he felt another wave of exhaustion sweep through him. It was one thing to feel relatively strong while in the hospital, when there were so many people in worse condition he could compare himself with. Quite another to feel the same in your home environment, where you were used to being strong and capable.

He turned his face into her palm and kissed her hand. "Thanks," he said simply.

She pulled away, a worried frown creasing her brow. "We'll get through this, Xander."

"I know we will."

She got up and smoothed her hands down her jeans. "I'll go and start dinner for us, okay? We should probably eat early tonight."

He must have fallen asleep when she left the room because before he knew it he was awoken with another of those featherlight kisses on his forehead.

"I made spaghetti Bolognese, your favorite."

She helped him stand and they walked arm in arm into the dining room. It looked vastly different from the drop-cloth-covered space he remembered. He looked up at the antique painted glass and polished brass library lamp that was suspended from the ceiling.

"I see you got your way on the prisms," he commented as he took his seat.

"Not without a battle. I had to concede to the ugliest partner desk in all history for the study upstairs to get this," she said with a laugh.

He smiled in response. There it was. The laugh he felt had been missing from his life for so long. Odd, when it had only been nine weeks since his accident. It felt so much longer.

After dinner Xander propped himself against the kitchen counter while Olivia cleaned up. He tried to help, but after a plate slipped from his fingers and shattered on the tile floor, he retreated in exasperation to the sidelines to watch.

"Stop pushing yourself," Olivia admonished as she swept up the last of the splinters of china on the floor with a dustpan and brush.

"I can't help it. I want to be my old self again."

She straightened up from depositing the mess in the kitchen trash bin. "You are your old self—don't worry so much."

"With Swiss cheese for brains," he grumbled.

"Like I said before, we can plug those holes with new memories, Xander. We don't have to live in the past."

Her words had a poignant ring to them, and he felt as if she wanted to say more. Instead, she continued tidying up. When she was done, she looked at him with a weary smile. Instantly he felt guilty. She'd been doing a lot of driving back and forth from here to the hospital and helping when she could with his physical therapy. And he knew that when she was painting, she'd often work late into the night without eating or taking a break. Why hadn't he noticed the bluish bruises of exhaustion under her eyes? Silently he cursed his weakness and his part in putting those marks there.

"I don't know about you, but I'm ready for an early night," Olivia said with a barely stifled yawn.

"I thought you'd never ask," he teased.

Together, they ascended to the next floor, too slowly for Xander's liking but an unfortunate necessity as his tiredness played havoc with his coordination.

"Did we change bedrooms?" he asked as Olivia led him to the guest room at the top of the stairs.

"No," she answered, a little breathlessly. "I thought you'd be more comfortable in here. I've become a restless sleeper, and I don't want to disturb you."

"Livvy, I've been sleeping too long without you already. I'm home now. We're sleeping in the same bed."

Four

Sleep in the same bed?

Olivia froze in the doorway of the guest bedroom and watched as Xander made his way carefully down the hall to the master suite. She followed, then halted again as she watched Xander strip off his clothes and tumble, naked, into the side of the bed that had always been his. He was asleep in seconds. She watched him for a full five minutes, unsure of what to do. In the end, she grabbed her nightgown from under her pillow and slipped into the en suite bathroom to get ready for bed. By the time she'd washed her face and brushed her teeth her heart was pounding a million miles a minute.

He'd done so many things automatically in the few short hours since they'd returned to the house. It had been reassuring and frightening at the same time. It showed the damage from his injury hadn't destroyed everything in his mind, but it certainly raised questions, for her at least, about how long she'd have before he might remember everything.

Olivia gingerly slid under the bedsheets, trying not to disturb Xander, and rolled onto her side—taking care to stay well clear of him—so she could watch him sleep. She listened to one long deep breath after another, finding it hard to believe he was actually here. His breathing pattern changed, and he suddenly rolled over to face her.

"What are you doing all the way over there on the edge? I've missed you next to me long enough already." His voice was thick with sleep; he reached an arm around her to pull her toward him and snuggled her into his bare chest. "You *can* touch me. I'm not made of spun glass, you know."

And with that, he was asleep again.

Olivia could barely draw a breath. Every cell in her body urged her to allow her body to sink into his, to let herself soak up his warmth, his comfort. He felt so familiar and yet different at the same time. But the steady heartbeat beneath her ear was the same. And, right now, that heart beat for her. How could she not simply relish the moment, take pleasure in it, accept it for what it was worth?

Gold. Spun gold. Jewels beyond compare.

How many achingly lonely nights had she lain here in this very bed since he left her? Made futile wish after wish that they could lie here together, just like this, again? Far, far too many. And now, here he was. All her dreams come true, on the surface at least.

They said you couldn't turn back time, but isn't that effectively what his accident had done?

She sighed and relaxed a little. The moment she did so her mind began to work overtime. If his memory came back, would he forgive her this deception? Could he? She'd basically kidnapped him from the life he'd been leading before the accident. Brought him here to resume a life he'd chosen to leave behind.

She'd never been a deceitful person, and now it felt as if a giant weight hovered above her, held back by nothing more than a slowly fraying thread. One wrong step and she would be crushed; she knew it. Doing this, bringing him home, acting as if nothing bad had ever happened to them? It was all a lie. She felt it was worth telling—would he feel the same way? Only time would tell.

Olivia drew in a deep breath through her nose, her senses responding to the familiar scent of the man she'd already lost once in her life. She wasn't prepared to lose him again. She had to fight with all her might this time. Somehow she had to make this work.

She shifted a little and felt Xander's arm close more tightly around her, as if now he had her in his arms he wouldn't let her go, either. It gave her hope. Tentative, fragile hope, but hope nonetheless. If, in his subconscious mind, he could hold her like this, then maybe, just maybe, he could love her again, too.

Olivia woke to an empty bed in the morning and the sight of Xander standing naked in front of their wardrobe with the doors spread wide-open.

"Xander?" she asked sleepily. "You okay?"

"Where are my clothes?" he asked, still searching through the rails and the built-in drawers.

"I put them in the spare room when I thought you'd be convalescing there."

He made a sound of disgust. "Convalescing is for invalids. I'm not an invalid."

Olivia sat up and dropped her legs over the edge of the bed. "I know you're not," she said patiently. "But you aren't at full strength, either. What is it that you want? I'll see if I can find it for you."

At least she hoped she'd be able to find it for him. She hadn't brought everything of his from the apartment.

What if he had something he particularly wanted to wear and she'd left it behind? Now he was home it would be a lot harder to go back to his apartment and get more of his things. She castigated herself for not thinking about that sooner.

"I want my old uni sweatshirt and a pair of Levi's," Xander said, turning around.

Olivia's eyes raked his body. He'd lost definition, but he was still an incredibly fine figure of a man. There was a scar on his abdomen, pink and thin, where his spleen had been removed after the crash. The sight of it made something tug hard deep inside her. He could so easily have died in that accident and she wouldn't have this chance with him. It was frightening. She already knew how fragile life could be. How quickly it could be stolen from you.

Her gaze lingered on his chest where she'd pillowed her head for most the night. Beneath her stare she saw his nipples tighten and felt a corresponding response in her own. She sighed softly. It had been so very long since they'd been intimate and yet her body still responded to him as if they'd never been apart. And his, too, by the looks of things.

"Why don't you grab your shower and I'll go get your clothes," she suggested, pushing herself up to stand and heading for the spare room.

The sheer need that pulled at her right now was more than she could take. She had to put some distance between them before she did something crazy—like drag him back to bed and slake two years of hunger. As if he read her mind, he spoke.

"Why don't you grab it with me?" Xander said with a smile that make her muscles tighten.

"I'm not sure you've been cleared for that just yet," she said as lightly as she could.

Before he could respond, she headed into the hallway and hesitated, waiting until she heard the en suite door close and the shower start. Then she went to the narrow spiral wooden staircase that led to the attic. Her foot faltered on the first step, and she had to mentally gird herself to keep putting one foot on each step after another.

Somewhere along the line, the attic had become the repository for the things she didn't want to face. But right now she had no choice. She closed her eyes before pushing open the narrow door that led into the storage area lit only by two small diamond-shaped multipaned windows set in at each end. Another deep breath and she stepped inside.

Keeping her line of sight directly where she had stored the large plastic box of clothing that Xander had left behind, she traversed the bare wooden floor and quickly unsnapped the lid, digging through the items until she found the jeans and sweatshirt he'd been talking about.

She dragged the fabric to her nose and inhaled deeply, worried there might be a mustiness about them that would give away where they'd been stored, but it seemed the lavender she'd layered in with his clothing had done its job. There was just a faint drift of the scent of the dried flowers clinging to the clothing. With a satisfied nod, Olivia jammed the lid back on the storage box and fled down the stairs. She'd have to come back later and get the rest of Xander's clothes. She certainly couldn't just take a box down to their bedroom right now because she didn't want to invent explanations for why his things were stored away, either.

In her bedroom—*their* bedroom, she corrected herself—Olivia laid the jeans and sweatshirt on the bed and was getting her own clothing together when Xander came out of the en suite wrapped in a towel, a bloom of steam following him.

"I see we got the hot water problems fixed," he said, coming toward her.

"Yeah, we ended up installing a small hot water heater just for our bathroom." Olivia nodded. "Did you leave any for me?"

"I invited you to share," Xander said with a wink.

She huffed a small laugh, but even so her heart twinged just a little. He sounded so like his old self. The self he'd been before they realized they were expecting a baby and would be dropping to one income for a while. While they'd never been exactly poor, and her income as a high school art teacher had mostly been used to provide the extras they needed for the renovations, it had still been a daunting prospect. Of course, since then, Xander's star had risen to dizzying heights with the investment banking firm he now was a partner in. And with that meteoric rise, his income had hit stratospheric levels, too.

"Hey," Xander said as he walked over to the bed and picked up his clothes. "You expecting me to go commando?"

"Oh, heavens, I didn't think. Hang on a sec."

Olivia shot into the guest bedroom and grabbed a pair of the designer boxer briefs she'd brought back from his apartment. She tossed them at him as she came back in the door.

"There you are. I'll grab my shower quickly. Then I'll get some breakfast together for us, okay?"

Xander caught the briefs she'd thrown at him and nodded. "Yeah, sounds good."

The bathroom door closed behind her, and he sat down on the edge of the bed, suddenly feeling weak again. Damn, but this was getting old, he thought in exasperation as he pulled on his boxers and stood up to slide on his jeans. They dropped an indecent distance on his hips.

He stepped over to the chest of drawers and opened the one where he kept his belts. He was surprised to find the drawer filled with Olivia's lingerie instead. Maybe he'd misjudged, he thought, opening another drawer and then another—discovering that the entire bureau was filled with her things. That wasn't right, was it? It was as if he didn't share a room with her anymore. She said she'd moved his clothes to the guest room, but it seemed odd that she'd have moved everything. And shouldn't there be empty spaces left behind where his things had been?

Xander spied the pair of trousers he'd worn yesterday, lying on the floor. He picked them up and tugged the belt free from its loops. As he fed the belt through his Levi's he wondered what else he'd forgotten. What else was so completely out of sync in this world he'd woken up to? Even Olivia was different from how he remembered her. There was a wariness there he'd never known her to have before. As if she now guarded her words, not to mention herself, very carefully.

Olivia came through from the bathroom, and his nostrils flared as he picked up the gentle waft of scent that came through with her. A tingling began deep in his gut. She always had that effect on him. Had right from the first moment he'd laid eyes on her. So how was it that he could remember that day as if it was yesterday, yet his brain had switched off an entire chunk of their life together?

They went downstairs—Olivia tucked under his shoulder with her arm around his back, he with one hand on the rail and taking one step at a time. His balance and coordination were still not quite there, and he fought to suppress his irritation at being so ridiculously helpless and having to depend on his wife to do such a simple thing. He normally flew down these stairs, didn't he?

"What would you like for breakfast?" Olivia asked when they reached the kitchen.

"Anything but hospital food," he replied with a smile. "How about your homemade muesli?"

She looked startled at his request. "I haven't made that in years, but I have store-bought."

He shook his head. "No, it's okay. I'll just have some toast. I can get that myself."

Olivia gently pushed him onto a stool by the counter. "Oh no you won't. Your first morning home, I'm making you a nice breakfast. How about scrambled eggs and smoked salmon?"

His mouth watered. "That sounds much better. Thanks."

He watched her as she moved around the kitchen, envying how she knew where everything was. None of it was familiar to him. The kitchen was different to the poorly fitted cupboards and temperamental old stove that had been here when they'd bought the property in a deceased estate auction. The place had been like a time capsule. The same family had owned it since it had been built. The last of the family line, an elderly spinster, had lived only on the ground floor in her later years, and nothing had been done to modernize the property since the early 1960s.

The aroma of coffee began to fill the room. Feeling uncharacteristically useless, Xander rose to get a couple of mugs from the glass-fronted cupboard. At least he could see where they were kept, he thought grimly. Automatically he put a heaping spoon of sugar in each mug.

"Oh, no sugar for me," Olivia said, whipping one of the mugs away and pouring the sugar back in the bowl before putting the mug back down again.

"Since when?"

"A couple of years ago, at least."

Just how many of the nuances of their day-to-day life did he need to relearn, he thought as he picked up the mugs and moved toward the coffee machine. She must have seen the look that crossed his face at the news.

"It's okay, Xander. Whether I take sugar or not isn't the end of the world."

"It might not be, but what about important stuff? The things we've done together, the plans we've made in the past few years? What if I never remember? Hell, I don't even remember the accident that caused me to lose my memory, let alone what car I was driving."

His voice had risen to a shout, and Olivia's face, always a window to her emotions, crumpled into a worried frown—her eyes reflecting her distress.

"Xander, none of those things are important. What's important is that you're alive and that you're *here. With me.*"

She closed the distance between them and slid her arms around his waist, laying her head on his shoulder and squeezing him tight as if she would never let him go. He closed his eyes and took in a deep breath, trying hard to put a lid on the anger that had boiled up within him at something so simple, so stupid, as misremembering whether or not his wife took sugar in her coffee.

"I'm sorry," he said, pressing a kiss on the top of her head. "I just feel so bloody lost right now."

"But you're not lost," Olivia affirmed with another squeeze of her arms. "You're here with me. Right where you belong."

The words made sense, but Xander struggled with accepting them. Right now he didn't feel as if he belonged here at all. And the idea was beginning to scare him.

Five

Olivia could feel him mentally withdrawing from her and it made her want to hold on to him all the harder. The medical team had warned her that Xander would experience mood swings. It was all part and parcel of what he'd been through and what his brain was doing to heal itself. She gave him one more squeeze and then let him go.

"Shall we eat breakfast out on the patio?" she asked as brightly as she could. "Why don't you pour our coffees, and then maybe you could set the table out there for me while I finish making breakfast."

Without waiting for a response, she busied herself getting place mats and cutlery and putting them on a large wooden tray with raised edges so that if he faltered nothing would slide off. She couldn't mollycoddle him all the time, but no one said she couldn't try to make things easier for him, either. She went ahead and opened the doors that led onto the patio, ensuring that the way was clear for him with nothing to trip over.

"There, I'll be out in a minute or two," she said after

he'd filled both mugs with coffee. He seemed to hesitate. "Something the matter, Xander?"

"I didn't notice yesterday if you still take milk or not."

His voice was flat, with an air of defeat she'd never heard from him before. Not even after Parker died.

"I do, thanks."

She turned around to the stove and poured the beaten eggs into the pan rather than let him see the pity that she knew would be on her face. As she stirred the egg in the pan, she listened, feeling her entire body relax when he picked up the tray and slowly began to move out of the kitchen. When the eggs were almost done, she sprinkled in some chopped chives from her herb garden and stirred the egg mixture one last time before loading the steaming mix onto warmed plates. She garnished the egg with some dots of sour cream, another sprinkle of chives and some cracked pepper, then added the smoked salmon shavings on the side. Satisfied the meal looked suitably appealing, she carried the plates out to the patio.

Xander was standing on the edge of the pavers, staring at the cherry blossom tree he'd planted when they moved in.

"It's grown, hasn't it?" Olivia remarked as she put the plates down on the table. "The tree. Do you remember the day we planted it?"

"Yeah, I do. It was a good day," he said simply.

His words didn't do justice to the fun they'd had completing the raised brick bed and then filling it with barrow loads of the soil and compost that had been delivered. After they'd planted the tree, they'd celebrated with a bottle of imported champagne and a picnic on the grass. Then, later, made love long into the night.

"Come and have breakfast before it gets cold," Olivia said, her voice suddenly thick with emotion.

They'd made so many plans for the garden that day,

some of which they'd undertaken before their marriage fell apart. She hadn't had the time or the energy to tackle the jobs they'd left undone on her own. In fact, she'd even debated keeping the house at all. Together with the separate one-bedroom cottage on the other side of the patio, where she had her studio, the property was far too big for one person alone.

But now he was home again, the place already felt better. As if a missing link had been slotted back in where it belonged. She pasted a smile on her face and took a sip of her coffee.

Xander desultorily applied himself to his plate of eggs.

"Is it not to your liking?" Olivia asked.

"It's good," he replied, taking another bite. "I don't feel hungry anymore, that's all."

"Are you hurting? They said you'd have headaches. Do you want me to get your painkillers?"

"Livvy, please! Stop fussing," he snapped before throwing down his fork and pushing up from his seat.

Olivia watched as he walked past the garden and out onto the lawn. His body was rigid, and he stood with his hands on his hips, feet braced slightly apart, as if he was challenging some invisible force in front of him.

She stared down at her plate and pushed her breakfast around with her fork, her own appetite also dwindling as the enormity of what she'd done began to hit home. He wasn't a man to be pushed or manipulated; she'd learned that years ago. She'd made decisions before that had angered him. Like the day she brought Bozo home from the pound without discussing it with him first. And the day she stopped taking her birth control.

A shadow hovered over her, blocking the light. Xander's hand, warm and strong and achingly familiar, settled on her shoulder.

"I'm sorry. I shouldn't have reacted like that."

She placed a hand on top of his. "It's okay. I guess I am fussing. I'll try to keep a lid on it. It's just that I love you so much, Xander. Hearing about your accident terrified me. Thinking that I could have lost you…" Her voice choked up again.

"Oh, Livvy. What are we going to do?" he said wearily, wiping a stray tear from her cheek with his thumb.

She shook her head slightly. "I don't know. Just take one day at a time, I guess."

"Yeah." He nodded. "I guess that's all we can do."

He sat back down at the table and finished his breakfast. Afterward, he looked weary, as if every muscle in his body was dragging. Olivia gestured to the hammock she'd only recently strung up beneath the covered rafters.

"You want to test-drive the hammock for me while I tidy up?"

"Still fussing, Livvy," he said, but it came with a smile. "But yeah, that sounds like a good idea."

She gave him a small smile in return and gathered up their things to load the tray he'd brought out earlier.

"Do you want another coffee?" she asked.

"Maybe later, okay?"

She nodded and went back inside. After she'd stacked the dishwasher she intended to tackle the hand washing, but all of a sudden she was overwhelmed with the enormity of the road ahead. She closed her eyes and gripped the front of the countertop until her fingers ached and turned white. For a moment there, outside, when he was staring at the garden, she'd been afraid he'd remember that fateful day when he'd been playing with Bozo and Parker in the yard. She still remembered his shout at Parker to stop. There'd been something in his voice that had made her drop her paintbrush, leaving it to splatter on the floor as she'd turned and run outside in time to hear the sickening screech of tires.

A shudder ran through her body, and she pushed the memory aside. She'd dealt with all of that. Dealt with it and put it away in a filing cabinet in her mind and locked the drawers as effectively as she'd taped the boxes of Parker's things closed before hiding them in the darkest recess of the attic.

Olivia opened her eyes and applied herself to scrubbing her cast-iron pan clean and wiping the stove top and the benches down until they gleamed. She cast a glance outside to where Xander lay in the hammock, asleep. Maybe now would be a good time to bring his clothes down from the attic and filter them in among the items she'd brought from his apartment. *And* put the whole lot back in their bedroom where he believed they belonged.

And they did belong there, she affirmed silently. Just as he belonged here, with her.

Mindful that she might not have much time, Olivia moved quickly. This time she managed to avoid looking at the boxes of Parker's things altogether, right up until she turned around with the storage box and headed back to the door. She had to pass the shadowy nook where she'd put her child's entire history. If only it could be as easy to put away the pain that crept out whenever she least expected it and attacked her heart and soul with rabid teeth.

The all-too-familiar burn of tears stung at the back of her eyes, and Olivia forced herself to keep moving toward the stairs. She wouldn't cry. *Not now. Not now. Not now,* she repeated down each step on the spiral staircase. In her bedroom—*their* bedroom, she corrected herself again—she shoved her things to her side of the wardrobe and, after grabbing a few extra hangers, she shook out and hung up the clothes that had been packed in the box. Then she went to the spare room and transferred all the things she'd put in there to the bedroom, clearing the bureau drawers that she'd taken over and putting his clothing away.

It didn't look as though he had much. Certainly not as much as she'd left behind at the apartment. Would he notice? Probably. She *was* talking about Xander, after all. A man who was precise and who took planning to exceptional levels. Detail was his middle name. It was part of why he was so good at what he did and why he'd rocketed through the company ranks. She doubted she'd be able to sneak another visit to his apartment now he was home, not for a while anyway. And if she did that, it would only cause more problems when he discovered she'd added more clothing to his existing wardrobe. No, she'd just have to stick with what she'd already done.

And hope like crazy that it would be enough.

Xander woke abruptly. At first confused as to his surroundings, he let his body relax when he realized he was home, lying in the hammock in the garden. He let his gaze drift around him, taking in the familiar and cataloguing the changes that they'd obviously made over time. They'd done a good job, he had to admit—if only he could remember actually doing any of it, then maybe he'd feel less like a stranger in his own home and more as if he belonged here.

Carefully, he levered himself to a sitting position and lowered his legs to the ground. He wondered where Olivia had got to. He couldn't see her through the kitchen window. He got up and shuffled a few steps forward. Then, as if his brain had taken a little longer to wake up and join the rest of him, he moved with more confidence.

"Livvy?" he called as he went back inside the house.

The creak of floorboards sounded overhead, followed by her rapid footsteps on the stairs.

"Xander? Are you okay?" she called before she reached the hallway where he stood.

He watched as she did a quick inventory of him and suppressed the surge of irritation that she'd immediately jump to the conclusion there was something wrong. It wasn't fair of him to be annoyed with her, he told himself. This was all as new and as intimidating for her as it was for him.

"I'm fine," he said calmly. "Just wondering what you were up to."

"I put your things back in our bedroom," she said breathlessly. "It took me a little longer than I expected. Sorry."

"Don't apologize. You don't have to be at my beck and call."

Some of his irritation leaked out into the tone of his voice, and he wished the words back almost immediately as he saw their impact on her face and in her expressive eyes.

"I might want to be at your beck and call, Xander. Have you considered that? It…it's been a while since I've had you here."

He felt like a fool. Once again he'd hurt her and all because she cared. He reached out and grabbed her hand before tugging her toward him. He felt the resistance in her body and looped his arms around her, pulling her even closer.

"I guess when we promised the 'in sickness and in health' thing we didn't think it would ever really apply to us," he said, pressing a kiss to the top of her head.

He felt her body stiffen, then begin to relax until she was resting against him, her head tucked into his shoulder and her breath a soft caress on his throat. His arms tightened, trying to say with a physical touch what he couldn't seem to say with words. After a few minutes, Olivia pulled away.

"What did you want to do today? Go for a drive maybe?" she asked. "We may as well make the most of it today because your physical therapist will begin home visits tomorrow."

She smoothed her hands down her jeans, making him wonder what she was nervous about. The action had always been her "tell" when something made her uncomfortable. Had it been their embrace? Surely not. They'd always been a physically demonstrative couple. In private anyway. Memories of just how demonstrative they'd been filled his mind and teased his libido into life. Good to know not everything was faulty, he thought cynically.

But even though that part of his body appeared to be in working order, it was as though there was some kind of a barrier between him and Olivia right now.

"Xander?" she prompted, and he realized he must have looked as if he'd zoned out for a while—and probably had.

"You know, I'd like to stay home today. I tire all too damn easily for my liking. How about you show me what you've been working on in your studio lately?"

Her face brightened. "Sure. Come with me."

She slid an arm around his waist—apparently more comfortable with aiding him than accepting physical comfort from him, he noted—and they walked outside and across to the small cottage on the property.

The cottage was one of the reasons they'd bought the property in the first place. He knew that it was Olivia's dream to give up teaching and paint full-time, and if he had it in his power to help her achieve that dream, well he'd been prepared to do whatever he could to see her do it.

Stepping over the threshold and into what was originally an open-plan living/dining area but was now the main part of Olivia's studio almost made him feel as if he were trespassing. This was very much her space, and she'd made it so right from the start.

He could understand it in some ways. In her childhood, she'd never had a space to call her own. Instead she'd been too busy caring for her siblings, supporting her father where she could, right up until she'd graduated high school and come to Auckland for her degree. Even then she'd lived in a shared-flat situation with ten students in a dilapidated old house.

"You've made some changes," he commented as they stepped inside.

"Not recent—" she started, then sighed. "Oh, I'm sorry. That was insensitive of me."

"Not insensitive," he said, looking around at the canvases she had stacked on the walls. "Don't worry about it."

He walked over to the paintings and gestured toward them. "Can I look?"

"Of course you can. I'm doing this harbor series for a gallery showing a bit closer to Christmas."

"Your style has changed," he commented. "Matured, I think."

"I'll take that as a compliment," Olivia said from behind him as he lifted one canvas and held it at arm's length.

"It's meant as one. You've always been talented, Livvy, but these…they're something else. It's like you've transformed from a very hungry caterpillar into a butterfly."

"That's a beautiful thing to say, thank you."

"I mean it. No wonder you gave up teaching."

She ducked her head, her hair—loose today—fell forward, obscuring the blush he caught a hint of as it bloomed across her cheeks.

* * *

Olivia kept her face hidden so he wouldn't see her sudden change of expression. She'd given up teaching six weeks before Parker was born. It had nothing to do with her art. Keeping up this facade was as difficult as it was emotionally draining.

"Do you miss it? The teaching?" Xander asked, oblivious to the turmoil that occupied her mind. He gave a snort of irritation. "I feel like I should know all this. I'm sorry if we're going over old ground."

She lifted her head and looked him straight in the eye. "Don't apologize, Xander. You don't need to. You didn't ask for this to happen—neither of us did. We both have some adjusting to do."

Not least of which was his casual reference to Parker's favorite book. When Xander had likened her improvement in her painting to that of a very hungry caterpillar morphing into a butterfly, she'd wondered if he recognized the reference. Wondered if, deep down inside that clever mind of his, he still could recite, verbatim, the book he'd read to Parker every night.

Six

"Is this what you're working on right now?" Xander asked, coming to a halt in his traverse of her studio to stand in front of a large canvas she had on her easel.

It was a broad watercolor of Cheltenham Beach, only a block down the hill from their house. A place where she usually took daily walks to blow away the cobwebs of the past that continued to stubbornly cling to the recesses of her mind.

"It is. I'm nearly done," she replied, watching him as he stared at the picture.

Would he remember the times they'd taken Bozo for a run on the white sand, laughing as he'd chased seagulls—his short legs and long hairy body no match for the svelte grace of the birds? Or when they'd taken Parker to the beach for his first swim in the sea? Their son had been such a water baby. Crawling flat out on his pudgy hands and chubby little knees to get back to the water every chance he could. In the end they'd had to bundle him into his stroller and take him home, amid much protesting.

Her heart gave a sharp twist. This was going to shred her into tiny pieces—this wondering, the waiting, the fear that he'd remember and the hope that he might not. But was that entirely fair—to hope that he would never recall the past? He'd been a loving father and a good, if initially reluctant, dad. Was it fair that he shouldn't remember all that he'd been to Parker and the love that had been returned from child to father?

"I like it," Xander said, interrupting her thoughts. "Do you have to sell it? It would be perfect over the mantel in the sitting room, don't you think?"

She'd thought that very thing. And there it was. The synchronicity she and Xander had shared from the day they'd met. Just when had they lost it so completely? she wondered.

"I don't have to sell it," she said carefully. "But it's the focal point of the collection."

"Maybe I'll need to buy it myself," Xander said with a wink that reminded her all too much of the reasons she'd fallen in love with him in the first place.

She laughed. "I hope you have deep pockets. It'll command a good price."

"Maybe I have an 'in' with the artist," he said suggestively. "We might be able to come to reciprocal agreement."

Her body tightened on a wave of desire so sharp and bittersweet she almost cried out. It had been so long since they'd bantered like this. So long since it had led to its inevitable satisfying and deeply physical conclusion.

"We'll have to see about that," she said noncommittally and stepped away just when Xander would have reached for her. "I was thinking of baking cheese scones for lunch. You keen?"

"I shouldn't be hungry after that breakfast, but I am,"

Xander conceded but not before she saw the hint of regret in his eyes.

Had he wanted her in that moment when they were teasing? She'd certainly wanted him. She wished she had the courage to act on it. The doctors hadn't said outright that they shouldn't resume normal marital relations. Thing was, theirs was no longer a normal marriage. She'd be taking even greater advantage of him, wouldn't she, if she gave in to the fierce physical pull between them?

Of course she would, she told herself. No matter how much she might wish it to the contrary, it would be lying to him. *Like you are already?* that cynical voice in the back of her mind intruded. *How much worse would it be?*

She shook her head slightly, as if she could rid herself of the temptation that way.

"Come on," Olivia said firmly, slipping her arm around Xander's waist in a totally nonsexual way and turning him away from the painting. "You can do battle with the coffee machine for me while I whip up those scones. We can discuss the painting later."

Two weeks later saw them settled into a more comfortable routine. The physical therapist came to the house twice a week, putting Xander through his paces and working with him to improve his balance and coordination. In between his visits, Olivia helped him through his exercises. She realized, with regular home-cooked meals and the physical exercise, he was slowly returning to normal. Physically, at least.

Mentally, he was still adrift in the past and none too pleased about it. He'd taken to spending a bit of time in his office upstairs each day, familiarizing himself with his client backgrounds all over again. Olivia was thankful he was nowhere near ready to return to work yet, but eventually he would be. She wouldn't be able to cocoon him within their home forever.

It occurred to her that at some point in time, if his memory didn't show any signs of returning, she'd have to tell him they'd had a child. It was too risky not to. Someone at his office could just as easily raise the subject when he returned to work, and she needed to head that train wreck off at the pass if she could. But now wasn't the time. He had enough to cope with, relearning everything in their current world.

Olivia picked up her palette, squeezed some colors onto the board and selected a brush to work with. She tried to force her mind to the small canvas she'd started this morning when Xander had been with the therapist, but her mind continued to drift back to her husband. To the man she loved.

She'd never struggled to focus on her work before. On the contrary, in the two years since Xander had left her, it had been an escape she'd sought with grateful abandon. Even before their separation, she'd guarded her alone time with a single-minded purpose and actively discouraged him from sharing her creative space. But now the gift of his return to her life made her want to spend every moment she could with him.

She put down her brush and palette and took them over to the small kitchen to clean. It was useless to keep trying to work today when all she wanted was to be near him. After she'd tidied up she walked across her studio to the bedroom on the other side. It was a large room, longer than it was wide. Its southerly aspect didn't allow for the best of light, which had made it useless to her as a work space, but it would work well for Xander as an office. He could even access it through a separate door so as not to disturb her when she was working, if he wanted to. And if they relocated his things down here, she'd be able to be near him as she felt she needed to be.

She tried to kid herself that this new overwhelming need to keep an eye on him was nothing more than that of a concerned wife for her recuperating husband, but in all honesty the need was pure selfishness on her part. Sure, she would worry less about him possibly losing his balance on the stairs if he was here in the single-level dwelling with her while she worked. But worry wasn't the only thing that drove her to consider the change. No, it was much more than that. It had more to do with grabbing this second chance at happiness and holding it close. Nurturing it. Feeding it. And never letting him go again.

Fired up by her decision, she went into the main house and straight up the stairs to the room Xander had set up as his office when they'd moved in. The door was open. When she noticed Xander, she hesitated in the doorway, her hand ready to knock gently on the frame.

He was slumped in his chair, his elbows on his desk and his head resting in his hands.

"Xander?" Olivia flew to his side. "Are you okay?"

"Just another of these damn headaches," he said.

"I'll get your pills."

Less than a minute later she was back at his side with the bottle of heavy-duty painkillers the hospital had prescribed and a glass of water to knock them back with.

"Here," she said, spilling the tablets into the palm of his hand. "Take these and I'll help you to our room. You've been pushing yourself again, haven't you?"

He'd already had a therapy session that morning and, for the past two hours after lunch, had been up here in his office. It was more than his tired body and damaged brain could handle—that much was obvious to her if not to her stubborn husband.

"Maybe," Xander grunted.

His admission told her more than he probably wanted to admit, which, in itself, worried her even more. He grew paler as she helped him to his feet and for once he made no pretense about not needing her support as they slowly made their way across the hall to their bedroom.

Xander lay down on the bed with a groan, and Olivia hastened to draw the drapes and cast the room into soft half light. She brushed a light kiss on his forehead and turned to leave the room. But Xander had a different idea.

"Come lie with me, Livvy, please?"

It was the "please" that did it for her. Carefully, she eased her body on the bed next to him and curled to face him—one hand lifting to gently tousle his hair and massage his scalp. Beneath her fingertips she felt the scar tissue that had formed as he'd healed during his coma. It both shocked and frightened her, and she started to pull her hand away.

"Don't stop. That feels great," Xander protested.

It felt ridiculously good to her to be needed by him. Most of the time since he'd been home he'd fought for independence—begrudgingly accepting her help only when he had to or when she insisted. But here, now? Well, it made her decision to bring him home all the sweeter. To be able to fill a need for him, in the home they'd created together rather than know he was alone in that barren and soulless apartment he'd been living in, gave her a stronger sense of purpose than she'd felt in a long time.

The first thing Olivia became aware of when she woke was Xander's face immediately in front of hers. His eyes were open, and his face so serious, so still, that for a split second she was afraid he'd remembered. But then his eyes warmed and he gave her that special half smile of his.

"Livvy?" he asked, lifting a hand to push a hank of hair off her face.

"Mm-mmm?"

"I love you."

Her eyes widened and her heart went into overdrive. How long had it been since she'd heard those precious words from Xander's lips? Far too long.

She turned her head so she could place a kiss in his palm. "I love you, too."

She snuggled up closer to him, loving the fact she could.

"I mean it," he said. "I was thinking about the accident and wondering when the last time was that I told you how much you mean to me. It frightened me to think it might have been a very long time ago, and that I might have died without ever telling you again."

She was lost for words.

Xander continued. "And I wanted to thank you."

"Thank me? Why? I'm still your wife." She gasped in a sharp breath. Would he pick up on the slip she'd made, referring to herself as *still* being his wife?

"You've been so patient with me since I was released from the hospital. I appreciate it."

He leaned in a little closer until his lips touched hers in the sweetest of kisses. Olivia felt her body unfurl with response to his touch—her senses coming to aching life. She couldn't help it; she kissed him back. Their lips melded to each other as if they had never been apart at all, their tongues—at first tentative, then more hungrily—meeting, touching and tasting. Rediscovering the joy of each other.

Xander's hands skimmed her body, lingering on the curve of her waist, touching the swell of her breasts. Her skin grew tight, her nipples aching points of need pressing against the thin fabric of her bra. He palmed them, and fire licked along her veins. And with it an awareness that doing this with him was perpetuating another lie.

With a groan of regret, Olivia caught at his hands and gently eased them from her aching body. She wriggled away from him and swung herself into an upright position. Drawing in a deep breath, she cast a smile at him across her shoulder.

"If that's how you show your appreciation, remind me to do more for you," she said, injecting a note of flippancy into her voice that she was far from feeling.

"Come back," he urged.

She looked at him, took in the languorous look in his eyes, the fire behind them that burned just for her. Even in their darkest days, they'd still had this physical connection between them. A spark that wouldn't be doused. A need that only each other could fulfill.

"I wish I could, but I've got work to do," she said, getting to her feet and straightening her clothing. "You stay in bed though. You're still a bit too pale for my liking. How's the head?"

"It's fine," Xander replied, also getting up.

As Olivia went to leave the room, he stepped in front of her. "Livvy, stop. You won't break me if we make love."

"I know, and I…I want to—don't get me wrong. I just think it's too soon for you, and on top of your headache, as well—" She broke off as the phone rang.

Grateful beyond belief for the interruption, she dived for the phone next to the bed.

"It's the gallery," she whispered to Xander, covering the mouthpiece once she identified who it was. "I'll be a while."

He gave her a piercing look, one that reminded her all too much of the determined man he'd been, and then turned and left the room. Olivia sagged back onto the edge of the bed, her pulse still beating erratically, her mind only half engaged with the gallery owner's conversation. She must have said all the right things in all the right places because the twenty-minute call seemed to satisfy the gallery owner's queries.

After replacing the phone on the bedside table, Olivia reached out and smoothed the covers of the bed. The indentations of where they'd been lying together were easily erased. If only it was as easy to erase the demand that beat like an insistent drum through her body. Sure, she could have given in to him, but the sense of right and wrong that had made her pull away still reared up in the back of her mind.

It would be unfair to make love with him when he didn't know about their past—about the problems that had driven them apart two years ago. She'd been a fool to think she could live in a make-believe world where the past never happened and everything was still perfect between them. She did love him, deeply, and that was more than half the problem. If she didn't, she would have been able to take advantage of his overture to make love, would have been able to lose herself in his skillful touch and the delirium of his possession without guilt holding her back.

She'd been nuts to think she could just bring him home from hospital and keep him at arm's length and not have to face a situation like this. He'd always had a high sex drive, and hers had mirrored his. It had been a long time since they'd found their special brand of perfection together.

Not for the first time, she felt strong misgivings about what she'd undertaken. She'd wanted to give their marriage a second chance. But once he knew what she'd done, how she'd used him and taken advantage of his injuries, where would that leave her?

Where would that leave either of them?

Seven

As she exited the bedroom she heard Xander back in his office. She crossed the hall and leaned against the doorjamb.

"You're supposed to be taking it easy," she said.

He swiveled around in his chair to face her. "I need to do something. Aside from the memory loss, I've started feeling better. I'm bored. With you working on your paintings, I was thinking about calling the office and seeing if I could go in for a few hours a week. Ease in gently, y'know?"

A fist of ice formed around Olivia's heart. If he did that, it wouldn't be long before he'd learn about her deception. And what chance would she have with him after that?

"You haven't been cleared by the doctor yet. Why don't you give it another week or two? See what he says when you go for your checkup?

"Look, I know I need to be working, but there's no reason why you can't be familiarizing yourself with the markets and what's been happening while I'm painting. Why don't we relocate your office to the bedroom off the studio? That way you can work and I won't have to worry about you. We can keep the single bed that's in there so that if you get another headache, or simply need to rest, you can just lie down."

"And you can keep hovering over me like a mother hen?" he asked with a raised brow.

She pulled a face. "If you want to call it that. I prefer to think of it as caring. Besides, at least that way you won't be bored and we can keep an eye on each other."

He inclined his head. "Okay, when you put it that way. You always lose track of time when you're painting, anyway. I'll be able to make sure *you* keep to *your* breaks."

"So, is it a deal?"

He stood up and brushed her lips with his. "It's a deal."

"Let's go and work out where we'll put everything," she said, turning to leave the room.

He followed close behind, and she hesitated to allow him to catch up so she could walk down the stairs with him. Yes, he was getting stronger every day, but she still worried.

"Y'know, I'm kind of surprised you're willing to give up your space to me," Xander commented as they hit the ground floor and started toward the doors that led out to the cottage.

"Why's that?" Olivia asked, although she had an idea she knew where this was heading.

"You've always protected your work space. I don't remember you ever suggesting we share it before."

She shrugged. "A lot can change in a few years. Would you rather not move your office down here? We don't have to."

"No, I'd prefer it. We can always use an extra bedroom upstairs for when we have those kids we've obviously kept putting off having."

Olivia stumbled as weakness flooded her body at his words. They hadn't put off having kids. Would things have been better if they had? Would they have been spared all that suffering if she'd stuck with the five-year plan Xander had painstakingly created for them? He hadn't thought they were ready to be parents—but she'd wanted a baby so badly. She could never regret the time they'd had with Parker, but if they'd waited…if she'd been a few years older, a few years wiser when she became a mother, would she have made better decisions? Would it have changed anything if Xander had been given more time to adjust and prepare himself to become a father?

She'd taken the decision out of their hands when she'd gone off her birth control pills without telling him. He'd been angry at first, when she'd told him she was pregnant, but he'd eventually warmed to the idea. Although she'd always suspected that in many ways he held a bit of himself back. As if he was afraid to love Parker too much.

She'd even accused him of loving their son less, in those immediate dark days after Parker had died.

"Hey, you okay?" Xander said, putting a hand to her elbow. "I thought I was supposed to be the clumsy one."

"I'm okay," she insisted, focusing on her every step even as her mind whirled in circles.

"About those kids?" Xander started. "I think we should do something about that as soon as we can. Life's too short and too precious to waste. If my car wreck has taught me nothing else, it has taught me that. I'd like us to start trying."

Outside the cottage Olivia hesitated. "Are you sure about that, Xander? You've only just begun your recovery. Do you really think having children right away is a good idea?"

She didn't even know if she wanted another baby, ever. Was her heart strong enough to take that risk? Loving Xander was one thing, and she'd lost him figuratively the day he'd left their home and she'd almost lost him literally in the wreck that had stolen his memories.

"Aren't you the one who usually accuses me of putting things off too long? Why the change of heart? Talk to me, Livvy."

"Xander, can't we just wait until you're better? You've never wanted to rush into this before."

"But what if I never get *better*? What if my memory doesn't return and those years stay locked away forever?"

There was a part of her that wanted that to happen. But Olivia knew that wouldn't be fair to him or to her. If they were to truly make this marriage work, there couldn't be any secrets between them. Even so, she couldn't bring herself to raise the subject of their separation or the tragedy that had triggered it with him just yet. Not when she was still unsure how he would react.

She'd learned as a child that it was best not to face the pain of loss—it was far better to tuck it away where it couldn't be felt. Her father had taught her that. After her mother had died, her dad had told Olivia that looking after "the wee ones," as he'd called her siblings, was up to her now. And then he'd thrown himself into his farm work with a single-mindedness that didn't allow for grieving.

Whenever Olivia had felt the overwhelming loss of her mother, she'd just buttoned it down and turned to the work she had at hand—whether it was her schoolwork or helping her siblings with theirs. And there were always chores to do around the farm and the house. Following her father's staunch example, she'd never allowed herself time to think about her loss or the pain she felt. And that's exactly how she'd coped after Parker's death.

"Livvy?" Xander prompted.

"We'll cross that bridge when we get there," she said stoically. "Right now the things that matter are getting you strong again and being happy together. And if having you here, sharing my space, means I can stop you from reaching the breaking point like you did earlier today, then that's all to the good."

"And vice versa," he reiterated, lifting a finger to trace the circles she knew were under her eyes. "You work too hard yourself."

She cracked a wry smile. "Pot, meet kettle."

Xander laughed, and Olivia felt some of the weight that had settled in her heart ease a little. They'd discuss the issue of children later. Much later. Which reminded her, she needed to go back on the Pill.

Inside the cottage they debated the best way to set up the bedroom to serve Xander's needs. She'd have to contact a contractor to run the separate phone line Xander had to his office upstairs, to the cottage, as well. The Wi-Fi proved patchy, so that was another thing to be looked into. Privately she was relieved that his access to the internet would be a little restricted here initially. What if he took it into his head to do a search on himself or her? There was bound to be some archived newspaper article that would spring up with the details of the speeding driver who had killed their son and their pet with one careless act. Again Olivia accepted that she'd have to tell him about that dreadful day at some stage, but as long as she could put it off, she would.

"How are we going to get my desk in here?" Xander asked as they surveyed the space. "I'd like it under the window, but I doubt we'll be able to manhandle it between the two of us."

"Wouldn't you rather get a new desk?" Olivia asked hopefully.

She hated the behemoth he'd insisted on installing upstairs in the early days of their marriage. It had been their only bone of contention back then.

"Don't think I don't remember how much you dislike my desk. But I love it, and if I'm moving in here, it's moving with me," Xander said with mock severity.

Olivia sighed theatrically. "Well, if you insist. Mrs. Ackerman next door has a couple of university students boarding with her. They might like to earn a few extra dollars manhandling it down the stairs and into here. With any luck, they might even drop it."

She added the last with a giggle that saw Xander reach for her and wrap her tightly in his arms. "I've missed that sound," he said before tickling her. "But I'm afraid I'm going to have to punish you for that comment."

By the time she'd managed to extricate herself from his hold she was weak with laughter and it felt good. She could almost believe that everything was going to be okay after all.

The next morning, Xander moped around the house at a complete loss for what to do with himself that he knew was at odds with his old self. Olivia had gone out to do some shopping while he was busy with the physical therapist. She'd been gone several hours now. Since he was alone in the house, he decided to use the time for some exploring. He went through each room, starting downstairs, poking through the kitchen cupboards and then examining every item in the living room, dining room and formal lounge. Some things spoke to him; others held their silence. No matter what, he felt as if something vital was missing, and he hated it. He wanted his life back. Hell, he wanted himself back.

On a more positive note, the weakness that had plagued him since awakening from the coma was receding, and his physical therapist was extremely pleased with his progress to date. Olivia had suggested turning the tool room, which only had access from outside on the ground floor, into a home gym. With his physical therapist's suggestions it had been outfitted so that he could keep up his program every single day without fail.

Pushing himself felt good but wasn't without its own problems. It often left him shaking and struggling to stay upright under the weight of yet another of those wretched headaches.

He picked up a silver-framed photo that had been taken of him and Olivia on their wedding day, and he felt a strong tug of desire as he studied her face and the creamy curve of her shoulders, exposed by the strapless figure-hugging beaded gown she'd worn. At least that continued to remain the same, he thought as he replaced the picture on its shelf. The bond between them was as strong as ever. She'd been of immeasurable support to him, even if she was still shy about making love. Those barriers would come down eventually. Their relationship had always been too well-founded and their attraction too strong to allow something like his brain injury to keep them apart for very long.

The sound of footsteps coming up the front path caught his attention. A visitor? They'd had no one since he'd come home from hospital. He'd had little to no contact with anyone else, even his mother, who lived in the far north. He'd called her once, to tell her he'd been released from hospital, but their conversation had been as short as it always was. He was fine, she was fine—end of conversation. The prospect of a fresh face was instantly appealing, and he was at the front door and ready to open it before the doorbell could even be rung. He felt his face drop as he recognized the uniform of the courier standing with his finger poised to press the bell.

"Package for Mrs. Olivia Jackson. Could you sign for me, please?"

The courier handed his electronic device and stylus over to Xander for his signature, then passed Xander the large flat envelope he'd had tucked under his arm. With a cheery "Thanks" and a wave, he was gone.

Xander slowly closed the front door and turned the envelope over in his hands. "Oxford Clement & Gurney" was printed on the envelope. Family law specialists. A frown furrowed his brow as he stared at the black print on the white background. He repeated the name of the firm out loud, knowing that there was something about it that was familiar. But no matter how hard he reached for the key in his mind to open that particular door, it remained firmly closed and out of reach.

Family law specialists—what on earth would Olivia be needing them for? The envelope was poorly sealed, just a slip of tape holding it down in the center of the flap. One small tug would be all it took to open it and check the contents inside. Maybe he'd find something that would fill in some of the gaps in his Swiss cheese for brains. But what if he didn't like what he discovered? And how would he explain to Olivia that he'd been prying in her personal mail? There was no question it was addressed to her and not to him.

Maybe something had been going wrong in their marriage before his accident. Maybe things weren't as he remembered and that was why Olivia remained cagey about the past six years. He hadn't pressed her too hard for any of it, and he now wondered if that wasn't in self-preservation. Were there things he really didn't want to know? Things he was actively suppressing?

The doctors said there was no permanent damage to his brain from the accident and only time would tell if the amnesia would be permanent or not. It was vague and frustrating as hell to know that he had no timeline to full recovery. But perhaps he didn't want to remember. If things hadn't been good between him and Olivia, to the extent that she'd been talking to lawyers, then could he have chosen to forget?

Even as he chewed the thoughts over and over in his mind, he couldn't believe that could be true. Or was it simply that he didn't *want* to believe? Without his memory, without her, what did he have left?

"Argh!" he exclaimed and tossed the envelope onto the hall table in disgust. "It's in there somewhere—I know it is," he raged.

He went through to the kitchen, poured himself a glass of cold water and downed it quickly. His hand shook as he put the glass back down on the counter and grimaced against the all-too-familiar shooting pain in his temple that was the precursor to another headache. He reached for the painkillers Olivia kept on the counter for convenience's sake and quickly threw a couple of them down with another drink of water, then went and lay down on one of the large couches in the sitting room. He'd learned the hard way that the only thing that would rid him of the headache was painkillers and sleep. With any luck, when he awoke, Olivia would be back home with some answers for him about the envelope that had arrived.

Eight

Olivia came in through the back door and was surprised to find the house silent. Had Xander gone out for a walk by himself? Fear clutched at her throat. They'd discussed this and agreed that he wouldn't go out on his own just yet. Even his physical therapist had agreed it probably wasn't a great idea until he was a bit stronger, at least not without a stick and Xander had flat-out refused to use one of those.

"Livvy? I'm in the sitting room," he called out. Olivia felt her entire body sag in relief.

"Coming," she answered, putting down the few extra grocery items she'd bought to cook a special dinner with before going to find him.

He was reclining on the largest of the couches in the sitting room, late-afternoon sunlight spilling over him and, no doubt, responsible for the flush on his cheeks. Even so, she automatically put a hand to his forehead to check for fever. Xander's hand closed around hers.

"Still expecting the worst, Livvy? I'm just a little

warm from the sun. That's all." He sat up and tugged her into his lap. Catching her chin between his fingers, he turned her face for a kiss. "Now, that's the proper way to say hello to your husband," he chided gently.

Her lips pulled into a smile and she kissed him again. "If you say so, husband. So, have you been behaving while I've been gone? No wild parties? No undesirable behavior?"

"All of the above," he answered with a cheeky grin. "I wish."

His expression changed under her watchful gaze. "What is it? Did something happen? Did you hurt yourself?"

He rolled his eyes at her. "No, I did not. But there was a delivery for you. An envelope from some law firm in town."

Olivia stiffened and got up from his lap, her movements jerky and tight. "An envelope?"

She turned away from him and closed her eyes. Hoping against hope that the thing hadn't triggered any memories for him.

"I left it on the hall table." He rubbed at his eyes. "Man, I feel so groggy after these naps. They're going to have to stop."

"Did you have a headache?"

"Yeah."

"Then you know the naps are the only thing to really get rid of them. Maybe it's the painkillers that leave you feeling dopey. We can talk to the doctor about it if you like, maybe ask about lowering the dosage?"

"Good idea."

He got up from the couch and walked through to the kitchen. She heard him pour water into a glass. While he was there, she quickly went into the hall and retrieved the envelope.

"I'm just going upstairs to have a quick shower and get changed," she called out. "I'll be back down in a few minutes."

Without waiting for a response she flew up the stairs and into the bedroom. She grabbed some jeans and a long-sleeved T-shirt and carried them and the envelope into the bathroom, where she closed and locked the door. She turned on the shower, then sat down on the closed toilet seat and tugged open the envelope, allowing the contents to slide into her lap. Her heart hammered an erratic beat as a quick scan of the letter from her lawyer confirmed that the two-year separation that was required under New Zealand law before a couple's marriage could be dissolved had passed. Also enclosed was a joint application for a dissolution order for her signature. It had already been signed in advance by Xander.

Olivia looked at the date he'd signed the paper. It was the same date he'd crashed his car. That meant the document had been lying around somewhere, waiting to be actioned. A shiver ran down her spine. What would have happened if it had been sent to her more promptly? If she'd received it before Xander had woken from his coma and asked for her? She'd probably have signed it and returned it to her lawyer and it would have been duly processed through the court.

She reread the cover letter more carefully. In it, her lawyer apologized for the delay in getting the documentation to her. Apparently a changeover in staff had meant it was overlooked. Just like that, her life could have been so drastically different. She and Xander could already be divorced, rather than still very much married.

Bile rose in her throat, and she swallowed hard against the bitterness. She had to put a stop to the divorce proceedings somehow, but how? She couldn't instruct Xander's lawyers for him. How on earth was she going to get around this? Not signing the papers was a start. She shoved them roughly back into the envelope and folded it in half as if making it smaller would diminish the importance of its contents, too.

She'd have to hide it somewhere where Xander would never think to look. She opened the drawer on the bathroom vanity where she kept her sanitary items and slid it into the bottom. There they'd be safe and he certainly wouldn't accidentally come across them.

She quickly shed her clothing and dipped under the spray of the shower before snapping the faucet off and drying and dressing to go downstairs.

"Good shower?" Xander asked as she came into the kitchen. "I started scrubbing the potatoes, by the way. Earning my keep."

"Thanks," she answered as breezily as she could manage given how she'd rushed through everything. "Good to see you have your uses."

And so it began anew, the teasing. The easy banter that had been one of the threads that had bound them together through the days before they'd become parents. Before everything had become so serious. Before they'd been driven apart.

A light spring rain meant they couldn't eat outside tonight, so Olivia laid the table in the dining room, setting it with their best cutlery and the crystal candleholders they'd received as a wedding gift from her father. Her fingers lingered on them, remembering how they'd originally been a gift to her parents for their wedding and, in particular, remembering the words her father had shared with her when he given them.

"I know your mum would have wanted you to have these, and I hope you and Xander can be as happy together as your mother and I were. We didn't have as long as we should have had, and I regret not telling her every single day that I loved her, but you can't turn back time. Don't leave love unsaid between you and Xander, Olivia. Tell him, every single day."

Recalling his words brought tears to her eyes as she leaned forward and lit the candles. She'd gotten out of the habit of telling Xander she'd loved him, long before Parker had died. She'd been so absorbed in her work at the high school and their renovations on the house. Then her pregnancy and subsequently their new baby. Loving Xander had never stopped, but telling him had.

"I'm sorry, Dad," she whispered as she blew out the match she'd been using. "I let us all down, but I'm not going to do that again. This time I *will* make it work. I promise."

And, later that night, when they went to bed, she curled up against Xander's back and whispered to him in the darkness.

"I love you."

His response was blurred with weariness as he mumbled the same words in return, but it was enough—for now.

The rain had cleared by morning. After breakfast, Olivia suggested they go for a walk on the beach. With Xander's balance and strength improving daily and his coordination almost back to normal, she was sure they'd be able to tackle the softer sand areas. If it proved too much, at least they were only a block away from home. Worst-case scenario, she'd leave him on a bench seat, get the car and pick him up. Not that he'd admit defeat or even let her consider doing something like that, she thought to herself as she finished stacking the dishwasher.

"Ready?" she asked as she straightened from her task.

Olivia looked at Xander, who was leaning up against the counter, watching her.

"Never more so," he said. "It'll be good to get out. Home is great, but I think I'm beginning to suffer a bit of cabin fever."

She'd expected as much, and dreaded it. Living as they had, cocooned together on their property, had been remarkably simple. Her brief weekly updates to Xander's boss, and her reiteration that he wasn't up to visitors or calls just yet, had meant his colleagues hadn't called to talk to him. And with Xander not being cleared to drive yet, his independence had been severely curtailed. Making it all the easier to keep up the pretense that their marriage was in healthy working order.

But was it a pretense? It didn't feel like it. Not when they spent their nights wrapped in each other's arms, their days either in the cottage together or with her painting while he did his physical therapy. She knew this was an idyll that couldn't last forever. Real life would have to intrude eventually, even more quickly if, or when, he began to recall the years he'd lost. She'd have to talk to him soon. She'd have to find a way to present the truth without all the ugliness or the pain or the accusations.

The downhill walk to the beach was a gentle one, the last few hundred meters on level ground. Getting back up the hill toward the house might be another story, but she decided to tackle that when it was time. A bit of an example of how she lived everything in her life right now, she realized.

A brisk breeze blew along the beach, so there weren't too many people about. Just a few hardy souls like themselves, wrapped in light jackets and enjoying the fresh air.

"I forgot how good it feels to be out on the beach,"

Xander commented as they strolled slowly along, arm in arm. "Although I miss running along here like I used to."

His eyes were wistful as he watched a guy power along the beach with long graceful strides, his leashed dog running right alongside him, tongue lolling in its mouth.

"You'll get that back, I'm sure," Olivia said with a squeeze of his arm.

"We should get a dog," Xander said, his eyes on the retreating figure of the runner. "In fact, didn't we have a dog?"

Olivia felt a chill go through her that had nothing to do with the wind that tugged like a mischievous child at her hair. And here it was, the moment she'd been dreading. Having to tell him the truth, or at least a part of the truth about a returning memory from the time he'd lost.

She took a deep breath before answering. "Yes, we did have a dog."

"Bozo?"

"You weren't too impressed with the name, but that's what he came home from the pound with."

A smile spread across Xander's handsome face, and his gray eyes glinted with satisfaction. "I remember him. But what happened? He was young, wasn't he?"

Yes, he was young. Only a year older than their son had been when they'd both been hit by the speeding driver.

"Yeah, he was just a puppy when I brought him home. He was only four when he died."

She held her breath, fearfully wondering if he would press her for more details and praying that he wouldn't at the same time. Her prayers were answered.

"We should get another dog. It'll be good for me, get me out of the house to exercise regularly—and you, too," he said with a wink as he hugged her in close to his body. "I know you—when you're working on your paintings nothing else exists, right? You neglect yourself when you're working."

Olivia swallowed against the lump in her throat. She'd been working the day Parker had died. She'd sent him out of the studio because he was playing havoc with her concentration. If she'd only allowed him to play around her, he would still be alive today.

She'd found it hard to get beyond that guilt. In fact, she doubted she ever would completely. Logically she knew it was a combination of events that led to tragedy that day, and that no single action was at fault, but it didn't stop her wondering how things could have been different.

"Speaking of neglecting yourself. How are you doing? Not too tired? Maybe we should head back," she said, turning the subject back to Xander. It was far easier than allowing the focus to be on her.

When Xander agreed to turn back she was surprised. It wasn't like him to concede anything—and it worried her. Back at the house she went to make them coffee while he rested in the hammock on the patio. When she came out again, he was asleep. He'd pushed himself too hard on the sand, she thought as she settled down at the table and watched him. He was still a little pale, but his cheekbones were less prominent than they'd been when he'd come home from the hospital, his shoulders a little heavier.

Slowly, he was gaining weight and condition again, but he still had a long way to go. The body's ability to heal never failed to amaze her. It was his mind that remained an unknown. The sense that she was living on borrowed time bore down on her. She just knew she'd have to find a way to tell him the truth soon.

It was the small hours of the next morning when Olivia woke in her bed with a sense that something was very wrong. She reached out for Xander and only felt the space where he should have been sleeping. In the gloom, she could see their bedroom door was open. She quickly got up from the bed and flew to the door. She could hear Xander, his voice indistinct as he muttered something over and over again.

Where was he? She followed the sound, feeling her heart pound in her chest as she realized he was in the bedroom that had been Parker's. What had driven him there? At the doorway she hesitated, wondering what she should do. Turn on the light? Wake Xander? But if she did that, it might leave him asking questions she had no wish to answer right now.

Cautiously she stepped into the room.

"Xander?" she said softly and placed a hand on his arm.

He muttered something under his breath, and she strained to hear it—her blood running cold in her veins as she made out the words.

"Something's not right. Something's missing."

His head swiveled from side to side. Even though his eyes were open, she knew he was still asleep.

"Everything's all right, Xander. Come back to bed," she urged gently and took his hand to lead him back to their room.

At first he resisted, repeating the words again, but then she felt his body ease and he followed her back down the hall and into their bed. She lay on the mattress, tension holding her body in its grip as Xander slid deeply back into a restful sleep. She didn't know how long it was before she managed to drift off herself. All she did know was that the writing was on the wall.

While his conscious memory was fractured and had wiped the slate clean of all memories of their son, his subconscious was another matter entirely. Deep down he knew something was out of sync with their life, which begged the question: How much longer did she have before he realized exactly what it was?

Nine

Xander watched through the studio's French doors as Olivia worked, lost in concentration and in the composition of another piece for her exhibition. He loved observing her when she was unaware of his scrutiny. It gave him a chance to see her as she really was and not the face she projected to him each morning and through each day.

Something was obviously worrying her—deeply, he suspected—but she was a master at hiding how she felt about things. When they'd first met, he'd actually admired that about her, had recognized her resilience and strength and found them incredibly appealing. Olivia never showed weakness or dependency, but he'd learned that in itself wasn't necessarily a good thing. He knew she had to feel weakness at times—she just refused to show it. Refused to let him help. Marriage was about sharing those loads. Meeting problems head-on, together.

So what was playing on her mind now and how on earth would he get her to share it with him? Was it something to do with the envelope that had been delivered from those lawyers a couple of weeks ago? The envelope that had magically disappeared and that she hadn't discussed at all? He'd searched the name of the firm online and discovered that they were specialists in divorce and relationship property laws. The knowledge had left him with more questions than answers.

Was there something wrong in their marriage that she couldn't bring herself to discuss? Was this existence they now shared just some facade for a crueler reality? Somehow he had to find out. From the moment he'd seen her at his bedside at the hospital, he'd been assailed with a complex mix of disconnection and rightness. Logically he knew a lot of it could be put down to the head injury he'd sustained and the amnesia, but a little voice kept telling him that there was more he should know. Something vitally important.

But if it was so important, why then was Olivia holding back? He could sense it in her. The words that she bit off on occasion, the sudden sad expression in her eyes when she thought he wasn't looking. Even the furrows in her brow, such as she had right now, implied she was worried about something.

He would give her another few days and then he'd push her to find out what it was. Maybe the missing information was the key to his memory; maybe it wasn't. One thing he knew for certain, he'd be stuck in this limbo forever if he didn't get to the bottom of it.

He moved toward the studio doors. Olivia must have seen him because she turned to face him, her features composed in a welcoming smile that didn't quite reach those beautiful blue eyes of hers. She had some paint in her hair, another proof of her distraction. Sure, she was never immaculately tidy and controlled when she worked, but today she looked pressured, distracted even. Until she put on her face for him, that was.

"It's getting late," Xander said as Olivia put down her brush. "You should call it a day."

"I'm inclined to agree with you," she admitted, stretching out her shoulders and shaking out her hands. "Nothing's going right today."

"Clean up and come inside the house. I have a surprise for you."

"A surprise?"

Her eyes sparkled with interest, and he smiled in response.

"Don't get your hopes up too high. It's nothing spectacular. I'll see you back at the house. Five minutes, no more," he cautioned.

"I'll be there," she promised.

True to her word, on his allotted deadline he heard the back door open and then her footsteps coming toward the kitchen.

"Something smells amazing," she said, coming into the room. "Did you cook for me?"

"I did," he said, bending down to lift the dish he'd made from the oven.

"Oh my, did you make your moussaka?" she asked, coming closer and inhaling deeply. "I haven't had that since—"

And there it was again. That sudden halt in her train of thought. The words she left unspoken. He wondered what she'd have continued to say if she'd left herself unchecked.

"Since?" he prompted.

"Since you made it last, which was a while ago," she replied smoothly. "I'm looking forward to it. Shall I set the table?"

"All done."

"Wow, you're organized tonight."

"You were busy, and I didn't have anything else urgently claiming my attention," he joked. "Come on—we're eating in the dining room."

Carrying the dish, he led the way to the room he'd prepared with fresh-cut spring flowers and their best crockery and cutlery. A bottle of sparkling wine chilled in an ice bucket and tall crystal flutes reflected the glint of the light from above.

"Are we celebrating?" she asked.

"I've been home a month, I thought it appropriate."

"I feel like I should change," Olivia said, plucking at her paint-spattered shirt and jeans. "You've gone to so much bother."

"It wasn't a bother and—" he let his gaze sweep her body "—you look perfect to me."

A flush rose on her throat and her cheeks. "Thank you," she said quietly.

Xander put the dish on the table and took a step toward her. He raised one hand, cupped her jaw and tilted her face to meet his. "I mean it. You're perfect for me."

Then he kissed her. It started out gentle but swiftly deepened into something much more intense. His arms closed around her, and her body molded to his, igniting a sense of rightness that swept over him like a drenching wave. Needs that had been suppressed for weeks unfurled, sending hunger hurtling through his veins that had nothing to do with the meal waiting on the table for them and everything to do with this woman here in his arms.

Xander wanted nothing more than to push all the accoutrements from the table and lay Olivia on its surface. To feast on her and slake the appetite that demanded satiation. But he wanted their first time back together since his accident to be special, and he'd been planning this all day long. He was nothing if not a planner, and he knew that the long-term satisfaction gained would be all the sweeter for not rushing a single moment.

Slowly, gently, he eased back on the passion—loosening his hold on her and taking her lips now in tiny sipping kisses. After a few seconds he rested his forehead on hers. His breath was as unsteady as his hands, and desire for her still clamored from deep within his body.

"Now we've had our appetizer, perhaps we should move to the main course," he suggested, aiming for a light note that—judging by the languorous look in Olivia's eyes—he may have missed entirely.

"If you still cook as good as you kiss, dinner is going to be wonderful," Olivia said dreamily.

"Still?"

There was that hint of something he was missing again. They'd always taken turns cooking and often cooked together. But something in the way she said it made it sound as though she hadn't eaten his cooking in a long time.

"Oh, you know," she said with a flutter of her hand and stepped away from him, her gaze averted. "You've forgotten a lot of things—what if cooking is one of them?"

As an attempt at humor it fell decidedly flat, but Xander chose not to pursue it right now. Instead he tucked it away in the back of his mind, along with the other inconsistencies, to be examined another time. Tonight was meant to be a celebration, and he wasn't going to spoil that for any reason.

"I'm pretty sure you're safe from food poisoning," he said with a smile and held out her chair.

Once she was seated, he opened the sparkling wine and poured them each a glass. After taking his seat, he raised his crystal flute and held it toward Olivia.

"To new beginnings," he said.

She lifted her glass and quietly repeated the toast before clinking her flute against his. He watched her over the rim of his glass as they drank, taking in the shape of her brows, the feminine slant of her eyes and the neat straight line of her nose. Her features were exquisite, dainty, until you reached the ripe fullness of her mouth, which hinted strongly at her own appetites. Her lips glistened with a little moisture from her wine, and he ached to lean forward and taste them again. He reminded himself anew that the best things in life were to be savored, not rushed.

The meal proved he'd forgotten none of his prowess in the kitchen. After dinner they took the rest of the bottle of wine into the sitting room and watched a movie together, sipping slowly of the wine and of each other's lips. When Xander suggested they go upstairs, she didn't hesitate. As he rose from the sofa, where she'd been curled up against him, and held out his hand, she took it and allowed him to pull her upright.

He led her upstairs and into their bedroom. Filtered light from the street lamp outside drifted through the windows, limning the large iron bed frame and the furniture around the room and creating a surreal atmosphere. In some ways this *did* feel surreal. Knowing that they were going to make love again. To be what they'd promised one another they'd always be when they made their wedding vows.

Olivia's fingers went to the buttons on his shirt, and she made quick work of them before pushing the fabric aside and pressing her palms against his chest. Her palms felt cool to the touch; beneath them his skin burned in response, as his entire body now burned for more of her touch. Or, more simply, more of her.

A shudder went through him as her hands skimmed down over his ribs, across his belly and then lower, to the buckle of his belt. He shifted, taking her hands in his and lifting them to his mouth to kiss her fingertips.

"You first," he said, his voice rough with the strain of

forcing himself to take it slow. "I want to see you again. All of you."

Her delicious lips curved into a smile, and she inclined her head ever so slightly. It was enough to make his already aching flesh throb with need. She slowly unfastened each button of her shirt. When the last one was undone, she shrugged her shoulders back and allowed the garment to slide from her body. His eyes feasted on the sight of her. Her breasts were full and lush, pressing against the lace cups that bound them, swelling and falling with each breath she took. Olivia reached behind her, and he swallowed hard as, with the hooks undone, she slid down first one strap, then the other, before pulling the bra away.

He'd told himself he could wait, but he'd lied. He had to touch her again. Had to familiarize himself with the curves and hollows of her body. A body that had been imprinted on his mind and his soul over and over but that now seemed strangely different. He reached out to touch her—to cup her breasts in his hands and test the weight of them, to brush his thumb across the eager points of her nipples. And then, finally, to bend his head and take one of those taut tips with his mouth. She moaned as he swirled his tongue around her. First one side and then the other. Her fingers tangled in his hair and held him to her as if the very beat of her heart depended on it.

He made short work of the fastenings on her jeans and slid the zipper down before shoving the aged denim off her hips and down her legs. Xander slid one arm around her waist while the other dipped low, over her hips and to the waistband of her panties. Everything about Olivia felt familiar and yet different at the same time. There was a softness about her that he didn't remember. Her hips, once angular, were now more gently rounded, and her breasts seemed fuller and more sensitive than he remembered, too.

It was crazy, he thought. He knew her like he knew the back of his hand. She was still the same Olivia he'd fallen in love with and married and made a home with. She was the same Olivia who'd rushed to his bedside when he'd woken from his coma and the same woman who'd brought him home and cared for him this past month. And yet she was slightly altered, as well.

His fingers hooked under the elastic of her panties and tangled in the neat thatch of hair at the apex of her thighs. His long fingers stroked her, delving deeper with each touch until he groaned into the curve of her neck at the heat and moisture at his fingertips.

"You're so wet," he said against her skin, letting his teeth graze the tender skin of her throat.

"For you, Xander. Always for you," she murmured.

He felt a ripple run through her as he stroked a little deeper, the base of his palm pressing against her clitoris while he slid one finger inside her. The heat of her body threatened to consume him, to render him senseless with reciprocal need. He gently withdrew from her body and lifted her into his arms, ignoring her protest as he walked the few short steps to the bed and laid her down on the covers.

"You shouldn't have done that—you might have hurt yourself," she admonished in a husky voice that tried but failed to sound scolding.

"What? And miss doing this?" He wedged one knee between her legs and eased them apart, settling himself between them with the familiarity of the years of their love. He pressed his jean-clad groin against her and was rewarded with a moan from his wife.

"We're still wearing too many clothes," she pointed

out, her fingers drifting across his shoulders before tugging playfully at his hair.

"I'm getting to that," he answered, shifting lower on the bed and pressing a line of wet kisses down her torso as he did so. "One." Kiss. "Thing." Kiss. "At." Kiss. "A." Kiss. "Time."

With the last kiss he tugged her panties to one side and traced his tongue from her belly button to her center and slid his hands beneath her buttocks to tilt her toward him. As his mouth closed over her, his tongue flicking her sensitive bud, he heard her sigh. There was a wealth of longing in her voice when she spoke.

"I've missed this. I've missed you, so much."

And then she was incapable of speech or coherent thought, he judged from the sounds coming from her mouth. All she was capable of was feeling the pleasure he gave her. And he made sure, with every lick and nibble and touch, that it was worth every second.

She was still trembling with the force of her orgasm when he slid her panties off completely and shucked his clothes. He quickly reached into the bedside table drawer, grabbed a condom and sheathed himself. Settling back between Olivia's legs and into her welcoming embrace felt more like coming home than anything he'd felt before. The rhythm of their lovemaking had often been frenetic in the past, but, tonight at least, he wanted to take it slow. To truly live and love in each special moment. He positioned the blunt throbbing head of his penis at her entrance and slowly pressed forward, taking her gasp in his mouth in a kiss as he slid in all the way. Her inner muscles tightened around him, and he allowed himself to simply *feel*. Feel without pain. Feel without emptiness. Feel without frustration or loss.

Loss?

She squeezed again, and he stopped thinking and gave

himself over to the moment, to the beauty of making love with the woman he loved more than life itself. And moments after he'd slowly brought her to the brink of climax again, he pushed them over the edge and took them both on that wondrous journey together.

Later, as he drifted to sleep, his wife curled in his arms with her hair spread across his shoulder, he knew that everything had finally started to fall back into place in his world again. He might not remember everything, but he remembered this and he never wanted to let go of it—or of her.

Olivia woke before dawn with a sense that all was well with her world again. She'd slept better than she had in months, maybe even since before Parker had died. Xander slept deeply beside her, and she gazed at his profile in the slowly lightening room. She would never have believed it was possible to love a person as much as she loved him and she never wanted to lose him again.

That meant she had to talk to him. Had to tell him about Parker and his death; about their separation. But how on earth was she to start talking about something so horrible when they'd just reaffirmed everything about their love in the most perfect way possible? She didn't want the darkness of their loss and the cruel words they'd thrown at each other to taint the beautiful night they'd shared. Maybe they should take another day, or even a week.

It wasn't going to be easy telling him, whether he remembered eventually or not. But he deserved to know what had happened. Objectively and without emotion or harsh words clogging everything. It also meant facing up to the full truth about her contribution to the slow and steady breakdown of their marriage.

How did she explain why she'd taken decisions they

should have made together and made them herself? Decisions like getting Bozo—like stopping her birth control pills before they'd even really discussed when they'd have a family. They'd been in no way emotionally ready to be parents, but she'd forced the issue because she'd had an agenda and nothing and no one would sway her from it.

Looking back, she could understand why she'd behaved that way, but it didn't make it right. She'd had to become a mother at only twelve years old, caring for her three younger siblings—aged ten, eight and six—when their mother died. Waking them each morning, feeding them breakfast, packing their lunches and making sure they all got on the school bus on time. Then, at the end of each day, making sure everyone's homework was completed and a hearty meal was prepared and on the table when her father came in from the farm.

She'd hoped that taking care of everything would make him happy and proud of her. But it never seemed to work. She did everything she could to try and put some of the sparkle back in her father's dull blue eyes, but it seemed that no matter how hard she tried, no matter what she did, his grief over her mother's death locked his joy in life and his children in a frozen slab.

She became even more organized, more controlling of what happened around her, especially when it came to taking care of her family. And that didn't let up, not even when she went to university or began teaching. No, she continued to supervise and encourage her siblings' career aspirations, pushed them to apply for student loans and to enter university while working part-time jobs to help cover their living expenses just as she had. It was only after the youngest of them had graduated, and Olivia was teaching full-time at an Auckland high school, that she began to relax—and then she'd met Xander.

There'd been an aloofness, a self-sufficiency about

him that had appealed to her. While in some ways it had reminded her of her father and how he kept himself emotionally detached from his children, it also meant Xander wouldn't need her as much as her siblings had needed her. For the first time in years, she could focus on herself. She could be independent, to a point, and do what she'd always wanted to do. Paint and create her own family on her own terms. And she had done all that—but she'd forgotten the vital ingredient to a truly happy marriage. Making those big decisions as a couple, not as a pair of individuals.

She had a lot to make up to Xander for. Caring for him once he'd been released from the hospital had been a start. Repairing their marriage was next.

Xander's hand skimmed the curve of her buttocks even as he slept, and she smiled and closed her eyes again. She had plenty of time to work out when she would tell him everything. For now, she'd just revel in the moment.

Ten

When Olivia woke again, the sun was streaming into their bedroom windows. The space beside her in the bed was empty, and she could hear the shower running. A smile of deep satisfaction spread across her face as she stretched and relished the sensation of her naked skin against the sheets. Everything was going to be okay; she just knew it.

A perturbing memory flickered on the periphery of her mind. The condom Xander had used last night—she'd completely forgotten about them being in his bedside drawers. After Parker's birth, Xander had taken control of that side of things. They hadn't discussed it, but she suspected it was mostly because he didn't want to be hijacked into parenthood again. She'd had no objections. But how old would those condoms have been? And was the fact he'd reached for one so automatically an indicator that windows on the past were subconsciously opening for him again?

She leaned over the bed, slid open the drawer and

squinted a little as she tried to make out the date printed on the box. As she read the numbers her stomach somersaulted. Expired. Well and truly. She quickly put the box back in the drawer and closed it, her nerves jangling. Surely they'd still be safe, but just in case, she'd buy some more and replace the expired box.

Olivia grabbed her robe and shrugged it on. *A big breakfast*, she thought. Maybe pancakes made from scratch with maple syrup and bacon. She did a mental inventory of the contents of the refrigerator and her pantry as she made her way downstairs. After using the downstairs bathroom to quickly freshen up, she went into the kitchen and began whipping up the pancake batter.

She'd just put bacon on the grill when Xander came into the kitchen. She looked up and drank in the sight of him.

"Well, you look better than you have in a while," she said with a smile before crossing the kitchen to plant a kiss on his chin.

"I think we both know the reason for that," he said, playfully tugging on the sash of her robe and sliding his hands inside to cup her breasts.

Instantly her body caught flame. How had she survived without him all this time? she thought as he bent his head and kissed her thoroughly. Her body mourned the loss of his touch when he pulled away and straightened her robe.

"You hungry?" she asked. "I'm making pancakes."

"I'm always hungry around you," he said. "Are we eating in here or outside?"

"It's a beautiful day—why don't we eat on the patio?"

"I'll set the table."

While Olivia ladled batter into the heavy skillet she had on the stove top, Xander gathered up place mats, cutlery and condiments, and took them outside. She was humming with what she knew was a ridiculous smile on her face when the phone rang. After checking quickly on the bacon, she reached for the handset and answered the phone.

"Mrs. Jackson? It's Peter Clement here."

Olivia's joyful mood bubble burst instantly. Her lawyer. The one representing her in the divorce proceedings Xander had brought against her.

"Could you hold the line a moment?" she asked. Muting the phone, she popped her head out the back door. "Xander, could you keep an eye on the bacon for me and finish making the pancakes? I just have a call I need to take."

"Sure," he said, moving with his still-careful gait toward the house.

As soon as he was in the kitchen, Olivia went upstairs to their bedroom and sat on the bed.

"Sorry to keep you waiting."

"No problem," the lawyer said smoothly. "I've had a call from your husband's lawyers following up on the dissolution order I forwarded to you for your signature the other week. Did you receive it okay?"

"Y-yes, yes, I did. But there's been a change in circumstances."

"A change?" the lawyer pressed.

"Xander is back home with me. We…uh…I think it's safe to say we're no longer separated."

There was a long silence at the end of the phone before Olivia heard a faint sigh, followed by, "I see."

"Can we halt the divorce proceedings?"

"Is this something your husband is agreeable to?"

"Yes, of course." She crossed her fingers tight and prayed it wasn't a lie. It couldn't be. Not now. Not after last night.

"And has he instructed his lawyers in that regard?"

"Um, not yet. You see, he's been in an accident and unable to communicate with them—up until now, that is," she amended quickly. "But I'm sure he'll be in touch soon."

"This is quite irregular, Mrs. Jackson. Your husband has already signed the forms—"

A sound from behind her made her turn around quickly. Xander stood in the doorway. How long had he been there? How much had he heard? Too much, judging by the look on his face.

"Mr. Clement, I have to go. I'll call you later and confirm everything."

Before he could reply, she disconnected the call and dropped the phone onto the tangled sheets of the bed in which they'd made such sweet love last night. Her stomach lurched uncomfortably under Xander's gaze, and she reached out a hand toward him.

"Xander?"

"You mind telling me what that was about?" His voice was cold, distant and too much like that of the man who had left her two years ago.

"It…it's complicated."

She stood up, tugging the edges of her robe closer together—her hands fisting in the silky fabric.

"Then find simple words to explain. I'm sure I'll grasp them eventually even with my brain injury."

Sarcasm dripped from his every word, and she was suddenly reminded of the piercing intelligence he'd always exhibited, which she'd ridiculously assumed was impaired with his amnesia.

"Don't be like that," she implored. "Please."

"Then tell me, how should I be? Are you telling me I didn't overhear you instructing your lawyer to halt divorce proceedings? I'm assuming those would be *our* divorce proceedings?"

She quivered under the force of his slate-gray glare. "Y-yes," she admitted reluctantly.

"Divorce proceedings that obviously started before my accident."

She nodded, her throat squeezing closed on all the words she should have said long before now. She'd been an idiot. She'd had ample opportunity to be honest with him, and she'd held back the truth at every turn. Putting her own needs and desires, her own wish for a second chance, first before everything else. Including the man she loved. A sob rose from deep inside. Had she ruined everything?

Xander pushed a hand through his hair and strode across to the window, looking out at the Auckland harbor and the city's high-rises. That was his world—the one he had chosen. Not the enclosed space of this house they'd bought and renovated together, not the confines of the land surrounding it. This was supposed to be his sanctuary, not his prison, and she'd made it that by withholding their separation from him.

"How long had we been apart?" he demanded harshly, not even looking at her.

"Just over two years."

He abruptly turned around to face her, but she couldn't make out his features as he stood silhouetted against the window.

"And you brought me back here as if nothing had ever happened."

"Xander, I love you. I've always loved you. Of course I brought you home."

"But it's not my home anymore, is it?" he asked, his face tightening into a sharp mask of distrust. "That's why you didn't have all my clothes, why I didn't recognize everything...I can't believe you thought you could pull something like that off. What *were* you thinking?"

"I was thinking we deserved a second chance at making our marriage work," she said with a betraying wobble in her voice. "We still love one another, Xander. This past month has proven that to me as much as to you, hasn't it? Haven't we been great together? Wasn't last night—?"

"Don't," he said, slicing the air in front of him with the flat of his hand. "Don't bring last night into this. Do you have any idea how I feel right now?"

She shook her head again, unable to speak.

"I'm lost. I feel about as adrift as I did when I woke up at the hospital and found myself surrounded by people I didn't know and too weak to move myself without assistance. Except it's worse somehow because I should have been able to trust you."

Olivia moaned softly as the pain of his words struck home. He was right. She'd owed him the truth from the start.

"Why were we separated?" he asked, coming to stand in front of her.

Olivia's legs trembled, and she struggled to form the words in her mind into a sentence.

"We had begun to grow apart. I guess the gloss of our first year of marriage wore off pretty quickly. A lot of that is my fault. I made decisions about us that I should have included you in. Getting the dog was one of them."

She took in a deep breath, preparing to tell him about Parker, but an icy-cold fist clutched her heart and she couldn't push the words from inside her. Not yet, anyway. "We both got caught up in our separate lives and forgot how to be a couple. You spent a lot of time at work—initially, before you made partner, you put the time in so you could show them how good you were at your job. After that, you were proving you were worthy of the honor.

"I…I was unreasonable about it. I resented the additional hours you spent there, even though I knew you were doing it for us. We wanted to finish the house off quickly, and it was a juggle for us both. I was still teaching during the day and painting at night. When you were home, you expected me to be with you, but I had my own work to do, as well. We allowed ourselves to be at cross-purposes for too long, and we forgot how to be a couple."

What she said wasn't a lie, but it wasn't the whole truth, either. Their marriage hadn't been perfect before Parker had been born, but she'd ignored the cracks that had begun to show—plastering them up with her own optimism that as long as she stuck to her plan, everything would be okay.

But it wasn't okay. Not then and not now. Their marriage hadn't truly ended until they'd lost Parker—but the problems that had been in place all along were the reason why they hadn't been able to pull together after the death of their son. They'd gotten too used to going on their separate paths to find their way back to each other even in their time of greatest need.

"You don't exactly paint me in a very good light," Xander said. "I don't like the sound of who I was."

She stepped closer to him and laid one hand on his arm, taking heart when he didn't immediately shake her off. "Xander, it went both ways. I wasn't the easiest person to live with, either. We both had a lot of learning to do. We met, fell in love and got married so fast. Maybe we never really learned to be a couple like we should have. But I still love you. I've always loved you. Can you blame me for wanting to give us another chance?"

Xander looked at her and felt as if she'd become a stranger. She'd withheld something as important as their separation from him. A separation that had been on the brink of becoming permanent, according to the conversation he'd overheard.

And worse than the doubt and suspicion were the questions that now filled his mind. Why had he left her? Was there more to it than the growing apart? Was she keeping something else from him?

One thing she said, though, pushed past his anger and confusion to resonate inside him. She loved him; and he knew he loved her. Maybe that's why her betrayal in keeping the truth from him made him so angry. Was this the reason behind the disconnect he'd been feeling all this time?

Her fingers tightened on his arm. "Xander? Please, say something."

"I need to think."

He pulled away and left the room. Thundered down the stairs and out the front door. He vaguely heard Olivia's voice crying out behind him, but he daren't stop. He needed space and he needed time to himself. He powered down the hill, anger giving him a strength, coordination and speed he'd been lacking the past few weeks. His footsteps grew faster, until he broke into a jog. It wasn't long before a light sweat built up on his body and his lungs and muscles were screaming, reminding him that he was horribly out of condition and that if he kept this up, he'd likely be on bed rest again before he knew it.

He forced himself to slow down, to measure his pace. Automatically he went toward the beach. Seagulls wheeled and screamed on the air currents that swirled above the sandy shoreline, and he looked up, envying them the simplicity of their lives. But how had his own life grown so complicated? At what point had the marriage he'd entered into with Olivia become the broken thing she'd described to him just now?

He shook his head and began to walk along the beach, unheedful of the small waves that rushed up on the sand, drenching his sneaker-clad feet and the bottom of his jeans. The sand sucked at his feet, making walking difficult, but still he pushed on.

Why the hell couldn't he remember anything? The man she'd described, the driven creature who worked long hours and then expected her attention when he got home—that wasn't him. That wasn't who he remembered being, anyway. When and why had things changed so dramatically?

He remembered meeting Olivia at a fundraiser at an inner-city art gallery. He'd been drawn first to her beauty—her long red hair, porcelain-perfect skin and wide sparkling blue eyes had made his physical receptors stand up and take immediate notice. But it had been talking to her that had begun to win his guarded heart. He'd known he wanted her in his life right from that very first conversation, and it had been readily apparent that she felt the same way.

They'd spent that entire first weekend together. When they'd made love it hadn't felt too soon—it had felt perfect in every way. Six months later they were married and home owners and beginning to renovate the house he'd just fled from. Six years later they were separated and on the point of divorce. What on earth had happened in between?

He stopped walking and raised both hands to his head—squeezing hard on both sides as he tried to force his brain to remember. Nothing. Another wave came and sloshed over his feet, further drenching his jeans. He let his hands drop to his sides. He continued to the end of the beach and dropped down into a park bench on the edge of the strand.

Runners jogged by. Walkers walked. Dogs chased seagulls and sticks. Life went on. *His* life went on, even if he didn't remember it. There had to be something. Some way to trigger the things he'd lost, to remember the person he'd been. After ten minutes of staring at the sea a thought occurred to him. If he hadn't been living here in Devonport, with Olivia, where had he been living? Surely he had another home. A place filled with more recent memories that would trigger something in his uncooperative brain perhaps?

Olivia had to know where it was. The clothes she'd haphazardly shoved into their shared wardrobe had been a mixture of casual wear that he'd worn years ago and new items as foreign to him as pretty much everything else had become since coming home from the hospital. That meant she had to have picked up some things from where he lived. Which meant she could take him there.

He levered himself upright, his legs feeling decidedly overworked and unsteady as he turned and headed back on the paved path at the top of the strand and toward home. *Home?* No, he couldn't call it that. Not now. Maybe not ever again. Until he knew exactly why they were apart, exactly what his life had been like, he wondered if he'd ever belong anywhere ever again.

Eleven

Olivia clutched the now-cold mug of coffee she'd poured before sitting at the kitchen table. The breakfast she'd been cooking before the phone call from the lawyer had dried up in the warming oven. Xander had obviously finished cooking it, as she'd asked, and plated up their meals before coming to tell her it was ready. Before overhearing the conversation she'd have done anything to avoid sharing with him today. She'd finally had to throw the breakfast away, but she'd attempted to salvage the coffee. She'd even tried to drink it, but her stomach had protested—tying in knots as she wondered where Xander was.

She'd been frozen here since he'd left the house, alternately staring at the mug and then the clock on the wall as she worried herself sick about him. He'd been gone well over an hour. Unshed tears burned in her eyes. Where was he?

Maybe she should have run after him, wearing nothing but her robe, instead of remaining rooted to the bedroom floor until the front door had slammed closed. But she hadn't. Instead she'd showered quickly and dressed, then debated getting in the car and driving around looking for him. In the end she'd decided that would be a futile exercise. She simply had to wait for him to come back. *If* he came back.

A sound at the front door made her shoot up from her chair, unheeding as it tipped over behind her and bounced on the tiled floor.

"Xander? Are you okay? I've been worried sick—"

"I'm going upstairs to get changed. Then you're going to take me to where I've been living," he said bluntly.

"To where—?" Her throat closed up tight again.

He meant to his apartment. She couldn't refuse him as much as she wanted to.

"To my house, apartment. Whatever. Where I've been living. You know where it is, don't you?"

She looked up and met the accusation in his stormy eyes. She nodded slowly. "Yes, I've been there once, before you came home."

"Let's not call it home," he said bitterly. "It obviously hasn't been my home for a while."

She swallowed back the plea that she wished she had the courage to make to him. It could be his home again—it *had* been these past weeks. Why couldn't he just let them start afresh? She knew why. Xander was the kind of man who did nothing without weighing all the options, without being 100 percent certain of whatever he did. He didn't like surprises, and this morning had definitely been a very unwelcome one.

"Okay, let me know when you're ready."

"I'll be right down," he said and left the room.

Olivia took her mug to the sink and tipped out the congealed contents. Even thinking about the dash of milk she'd stirred into her coffee made her stomach lurch in protest.

The prospect of taking him back to his apartment terrified her. What if he remembered everything? The anger, the lies…the grief?

She had to face the truth. He may not want to even see her again after today. In fact, if he remembered the rest of his lost memories, he very likely would get on the phone to his lawyer and tell them to continue with the proceedings she'd requested a halt to. There was nothing she could do about it, and the helplessness that invaded every cell in her body was all-consuming.

Olivia found her handbag and car keys and went to the entrance hall to wait for him. The keys to his apartment were in the bottom of her bag, exactly where she'd left them the day she'd brought him home from the hospital. It felt like a lifetime ago.

Xander was dressed in a smart pair of dress trousers and a business shirt when he came back down. He'd obviously had a quick shower, and his hair was slicked back from his face. He'd trimmed his beard to a designer stubble. Now he looked far more like the corporate Xander who'd walked out on her two years ago.

"Ready?" she said, needing to fill the strained air between them with something, even something as inane as the one word she'd used.

Of course he was ready. He was here, wasn't he? Impatience rolled off him in waves.

"Let's go," he grunted and held the door open for her.

Even in his fury he couldn't stop being the gentleman he intrinsically had always been. His courtesy, however, brought her little comfort.

The drive toward the harbor bridge and into the city seemed to take forever in the frigid atmosphere in her car. Once they hit Quay Street, Xander shifted in his seat.

"Where are we going?"

She could tell it frustrated him to have to ask. "Parnell. You have a place on the top floor of one the high-rises."

He nodded and looked straight ahead, as if he couldn't wait to get there.

By the time Olivia pulled into the underground parking garage and directed Xander to the bank of elevators nearby, her nerves were as taut as violin strings. She felt as if the slightest thing would see her snap and fray apart. The trip up to Xander's floor was all too swift, and suddenly they were at the front door.

She dug in her bag and drew out the keys, holding them up between them.

"Do you want to do the honors?" she asked.

Xander took them from her and looked at the key ring. "I don't know which one it is," he said, a deep frown pulling between his brows.

She pointed to the one that would lead them inside and held her breath as he turned it in the lock and pushed the door open. Olivia followed him as he stepped inside. The air was a little stale, and there was a fine layer of dust everywhere after a month with no cleaning service. She almost ran into Xander's back when he stopped abruptly and stared around the open-plan living area off the entrance hall.

"Do you…is it… Is anything familiar to you?" she tentatively asked.

Xander simply shook his head.

He hated the place. Sure, it was functional—beautiful, even, in its starkness—and heavily masculine. But it didn't feel like home. The lack of a feminine touch, with not even so much as a vase on display in the built-in shelving along one wall, confirmed that he lived here alone. Of course, if he'd had a new partner, she'd have been the one at his bedside after he woke up, not Olivia.

He walked around the spacious living area and clamped down on the growl that rose in his throat. This place should at least feel familiar in some way. These were his things. His recent life. Yet he didn't sense even the remotest connection to anything, not like he did to some of the things back at the house across the harbor.

The anger that had buoyed him along since he'd overheard Olivia on the phone left him in a rush, only a deep sense of defeat remained in its wake. He looked around one more time. Still nothing. A hallway beckoned, but he found he lacked the energy to even want to push himself down that corridor and see what lay beyond it. A bedroom, no doubt. It would almost certainly feel as foreign to him as the rest of the apartment already did.

Weariness pulled at him with unrelenting strength. He didn't belong here, either.

"Take me back," he said roughly. "Please. I've had enough."

Olivia came to stand at his side. Everything about her seemed to be offering refuge, from the expression on her face to the arms she gingerly curved around his waist.

"Maybe losing your memory wasn't the worst thing, Xander. Have you stopped to consider that? We've been good together. Happy. It's proof we can do better together—*be* better together. Can't we just take that and build something great with it now all over again?"

He wanted to say yes, but some unnamable thing held him back. They started toward the door, then stopped abruptly at the sound of the doorbell, swiftly followed by the sound of a key being inserted and the door being opened.

Olivia's eyes opened in shock as a petite young woman let herself into Xander's apartment. She recognized her instantly. The woman had been an intern at Xander's office shortly after their marriage. Olivia knew she'd worked her way up since then. But what was Rachelle doing here, and why did she have a key to Xander's apartment? Her shock at seeing the woman was nothing to what came next.

"Rachelle, how are you?" Xander asked with a smile on his face that had been missing for the better part of today.

Olivia couldn't help it. She felt an immediate pang of jealousy. There'd always been something about Rachelle that had grated on her—a familiarity with Xander even when their marriage was at its best that had made Olivia feel as if she was operating off her back foot around her all the time.

Rachelle came forward and gave Xander a welcoming hug and kiss on the cheek. Olivia wondered if her eyes were turning an unbecoming shade of green as a wave of possessiveness swept through her. It was all she could manage to stand and smile politely, especially when what she wanted most was to drag the other woman off her husband and push her out the door. She took in a steadying breath. That wasn't her. She'd never been the jealous type, but Rachelle brought out the feral in her, always had.

"Xander! It's so good to see you," Rachelle gushed, still hugging him. "We were all so shocked at your accident. I'd have come to see you at the hospital, but they restricted visitors to immediate family only. But I called the hospital regularly and stayed up-to-date with your progress. Until recently, that is."

Rachelle finally looked at Olivia, who bit her tongue to keep from replying. The obvious reproach was there in the younger woman's words. Olivia lifted her chin, accepting the challenge.

"I've been in touch with Ken to let him know Xander was recuperating at home," she said firmly.

"Of course you have," Rachelle said with a slight curve of her lips. She turned her attention back to Xander. "I just thought I'd call in to see how Xander was and to see if there was anything he needed. This is his home, after all, isn't it? I didn't realize he was staying at your house." She turned to face Xander. "So, are you returning soon?"

Olivia held her breath. Was he?

Xander shook his head. "I don't know. I don't think so. Not yet, anyway."

Olivia fought to hold herself upright. No easy feat when she wanted to sag in relief.

"In fact," Olivia said with a forced smile, "we were just leaving."

"Oh," Rachelle said, disappointment clear in her face. "That's a shame. I've been looking forward to catching up."

Before Xander could respond, Olivia spoke again. "Perhaps another time."

She maintained eye contact with Rachelle, neither woman backing down from the silent challenge that hovered between them. Rachelle was the first to break.

"Of course," she muttered.

Xander excused himself to use the bathroom, leaving the two women alone in the foyer. Rachelle waited until they heard the bathroom door close before wheeling to face Olivia.

"He doesn't know, does he?"

"Know?" Olivia remained deliberately evasive.

"About you two. About your divorce. About Park—"

"He knows that we're separated and we're working through that. The doctors have said not to try and force anything."

"Olivia..."

"No." Olivia put up a hand as if she could physically stop the younger woman from doing anything she wanted to. "If his memory comes back, it will do so in its own good time."

"But what about when he comes back to work? Everyone there knows about his past. People will talk to him."

"But he's not fit to return to work yet anyway, so that's a bridge Xander and I will cross when we get to it."

Rachelle looked at her in disbelief. "I can't believe you're lying to him like this."

"I'm not lying," Olivia replied emphatically. *But I know I'm not exactly telling him the truth, either.* "Look I think it would be best if you leave. I'll take care of the plants before we go. You can leave your key with me."

Rachelle shook her head. "No. Xander gave me this key and if I give it back to anyone, it'll be to him."

Olivia didn't say anything, not wanting to push the issue and definitely not wanting to explore the idea of why Xander would give one of his colleagues a key to his apartment.

"You're going to have to tell him sometime," Rachelle continued. "If you don't, I will. He deserves to know. You can't just reclaim him like a lost puppy. He left you, Olivia. He had his reasons."

A sound down the hallway made both women turn and look. Xander—something was wrong, Olivia thought and quickly headed in his direction.

Xander stood at the basin in the bathroom, his hands gripping the white porcelain edge in a white-knuckled grip. A headache assailed him in ever-increasing waves. He had to lie down, to sleep, but he couldn't do that here. This place was all wrong. As angry as he was with Olivia, he needed her right now—needed to go back to their home. He must have called out, made some noise or something, because she was suddenly at his side, concern pulling her brows into a straight line and clouding her eyes.

"Another headache? Here," she said, rummaging through her handbag. "I brought some of your painkillers, just in case."

She pressed two tablets into his palm and quickly filled the water glass on the vanity with water and handed it to him.

He knocked the pills back with a grimace. "Take me back to the house, please."

"You don't want to take a rest here?"

He shook his head and immediately regretted it as spears of pain pushed behind his eyes. "Just get me out of here."

She slid a slender arm around his waist and tucked herself under his shoulder to support him. Slowly they made their way out of the room and down the hall. Rachelle still stood in the living room. He caught a glimpse of the shock on her face.

"I have to take him home," Olivia said with a proprietary note in her voice that even he, in his incapacitated state, didn't miss. "Please make sure you lock up behind you."

"Do you need me to help?" the other woman asked, stepping to his other side.

"We can manage," Olivia replied firmly and guided him to the door.

"Xander, I hope you're better soon. We miss you at the office…I miss you," Rachelle called out as they left the apartment.

The door swung closed behind them, and Xander winced again as it slammed. They made it down to the car and Olivia adjusted his seat back a little so he could recline and close his eyes. Throughout the drive back to

Devonport his mind continued to whirl around the stabs of pain that continued to probe his skull.

He'd thought the apartment would bring him answers. Instead it had only brought him more questions. Nothing had felt familiar or right or as if it truly belonged to him. Not the furnishings, not the clothes in the wardrobe he'd gotten a glimpse of before heading into the bathroom—not even the cups and saucers he'd seen in the kitchen cupboards when he'd looked there.

And then there was Rachelle. She'd been so familiar with him, as if they were far more intimately acquainted than mere work colleagues. Had he moved on from his relationship with Olivia so quickly? It seemed almost impossible to believe. Yes, Rachelle was attractive—if you liked petite brunettes with perfect proportions. But he had a hankering for slender redheads, one in particular—even if she had been holding out on him about them living apart.

But Rachelle. He'd recognized her. She was a part of his past, although he couldn't remember all of it. She was deeply familiar to him, more so than could be accounted for with his memories from six years prior. Did that explain why, when she'd come into the apartment, she'd gone straightaway to hug him and kiss him? The fact that her kiss had landed on his cheek had been a result of him moving slightly at the last minute; otherwise he knew she'd have planted one right on his lips. Judging by Olivia's reaction to the other woman, he doubted very much that she'd have been pleased about that happening.

Still, it made him wonder what his relationship with Rachelle was. She was more than just a work acquaintance. He knew that much from her behavior, not to mention the fact she had a key to his apartment.

Had he gone from one failed whirlwind relationship into another? It didn't seem right, not likely somehow.

If only he could remember!

Twelve

Olivia lifted Xander's feet up onto the sofa and drew the drapes in the sitting room to block out the afternoon sunlight. He hadn't even wanted to tackle the stairs when they'd arrived home. His headache must be bad, she thought, checking to see that his chest continued to rise and fall as he slipped deeper into sleep.

But she had him back here; that was the important thing. He could so easily have told her to leave him at the apartment. Maybe even leave him with Rachelle. The very thought painted a bitter taste on Olivia's tongue. She'd tried to like Rachelle on the occasions she'd met her at company functions, back before her marriage had ended. Had even attempted once or twice to be friendly. But the other woman had always carried herself with an air that implied she believed she was several notches above Olivia on the totem pole of life. How could she not be when Olivia had been, first, a schoolteacher, then, second, a stay-at-home mother while Rachelle was actively and successfully pursuing a high-flying career?

Rachelle had never made a secret of the fact she found Xander attractive, and Olivia had felt threatened by her confidence, not to mention the increasing number of hours in a week Rachelle spent with Olivia's husband. But Olivia had never once believed that Xander would embark on an affair. That simply had never been his style. But then, he'd changed so much after Parker's death. Maybe he *had* picked up with Rachelle after he'd moved out. Goodness only knew the woman hadn't been subtle about her attraction to him.

In the two years of their separation, Olivia had been working so hard just to keep herself from falling apart over the loss of both her son and her husband that she'd never stopped to consider that Xander might have gotten himself a girlfriend. Hadn't wanted to consider it, more like, she forced herself to admit. In fact, the idea hadn't even occurred to her when she'd brought him home from the hospital. Why should it, when the doctors had never mentioned Xander having any visitors other than his mother? Surely a girlfriend would have had some visiting rights?

She pushed the thought out of her head, preferring not to allow her mind to stray down that path. But she couldn't help it—she kept seeing Rachelle insert herself into Xander's arms and kiss him. And not only had Xander recognized Rachelle; he hadn't exactly pushed her away.

Olivia forced herself to do the math about just how far back in his memory Rachelle could be found. Rachelle had started at Xander's firm before Parker had been born. Did his memory loss stretch back that far or was he actually beginning to recall things and people from his missing years?

She checked on Xander one more time; then, satisfied he was deeply asleep, she went to the kitchen to make herself coffee. As she automatically started the machine and poured milk in a mug, her thoughts kept straying back to Rachelle and Xander—and how at home the woman had seemed in Xander's apartment. Just how large of a role did she play in Xander's life outside work, and how long had she been there? A year? Two years? Longer? Had she been hovering in the background even during Xander's marriage, just waiting to snatch him up as soon as he was free? And had Olivia herself furthered the woman's plans by not being the wife she should have been? Had her focus on her newborn son and then her developing little boy been so singular that it had driven her husband away from her and into the arms of another woman? It wouldn't be the first time in history that had happened.

But she hadn't been the only one wrapped up in Parker. While Xander hadn't initially been thrilled about the pregnancy, especially when he'd discovered it hadn't been a blessed accident but a decision she'd made without him, he'd been as besotted with their son on his birth as she'd been. Had they both gotten so caught up in being parents that they forgot to be partners? Was that something Rachelle had taught him how to be once more?

Fear and insecurity wended their way into Olivia's psyche like the persistent vines of a climbing weed. She couldn't lose him again—she simply couldn't. She hadn't fought when he'd left. And even though on the surface, at least, she'd looked as if she was coping, she'd still been too bruised, too grief-stricken, after Parker's death to have the energy. But she had energy now, and she knew she had to dig down deep and fight for her man. To consolidate her place in his life and in his heart so that they could work through everything together.

The second she'd seen him at the hospital, she'd known she'd do anything for him. She loved him as much now as she had when they'd first fallen headlong into love together.

Nothing, and no one, was going to get in the way of her repairing their broken marriage.

They deserved a new and better start together. She'd certainly learned from her past mistakes and accepted there had been many of them. She wasn't perfect by any standard, but, then again, neither was Xander. She loved him, imperfections and all. She'd grown as a person since he'd left. Deep in her heart Olivia knew that as long as Xander was willing, they could really make a go of things. They could build their marriage into the loving and lasting state of union she'd always wanted.

What if he wasn't willing? What if his recall, if it came, included every awful word she'd flung at him in grief and anger in the aftermath of Parker's death? What if he couldn't forgive her those things? She couldn't blame him if they were enough to make him leave. After all, they'd had that effect the first time around, hadn't they? She closed her eyes on the memory, and sucked in a deep breath. This time would be better. They had the cushion of time and distance now, and surely these past few weeks had shown him that they were far better together than apart?

So what could she do? There was only one thing that echoed in her mind. She had to give herself to him. Heart and soul, holding nothing back.

The afternoon passed in a blur. Xander locked himself in the office off her studio and told her quite emphatically he didn't want to be disturbed. She filled her afternoon packing her car with the paintings she needed to deliver to a gallery in the morning. With Christmas in only four weeks' time, she and her agent were hopeful for a high level of sales, especially now demand for her work was growing.

By the time she prepared their evening meal, Xander still hadn't come out of the office. Worried about him now, especially in light of the severity of the headache he'd suffered that morning, she risked knocking on the office door and popping her head in without waiting for him to respond.

"Xander? Are you hungry? Dinner's ready."

She'd gone to the bother of making one of his favorites—steak Diane with fresh spears of asparagus and baby potatoes. A pathetic peace offering given the day they'd had, but in lieu of being able to talk this out with him she'd felt she had to do something.

"I'm not hungry," he said without turning his head from the computer screen on his desk.

She ventured into the room, looking to see what held his attention so strongly. A ripple of unease went from head to toe as she recognized the staff profile page from Xander's firm. Up front and center was a photograph of Rachelle. Olivia's hands curled into impotent fists as she forced herself to breathe out the tension that gripped her. One by one, she uncurled her fingers.

"It's steak Diane. Would you like me to bring a tray out to you here?"

"Trying to butter me up?" he asked, finally turning to look up at her. A cynical smile twisted his lips.

"No. Well, not entirely. I'm not sure that any food could make up for the shock you had today. I'm sorry, Xander. I meant to tell you sooner. I just…couldn't."

Xander rubbed at his eyes wearily. "I guess it's not the kind of conversation you have on an everyday basis with a convalescent husband, is it?"

Olivia felt the tight set of her shoulders ease a fraction. It was an olive branch. One she'd grasp with both hands.

"Come, eat," she implored, gingerly putting a hand on his shoulder.

He lifted his hand and briefly laid it over hers. "I'll be through in a minute. Just let me shut everything down."

She wanted to stay and wait for him. To ask him if he'd discovered whatever it was he'd been looking for, but she knew she'd be pushing her luck. Slowly, she walked back to the kitchen and plated up their meal. All the while, the image of Rachelle's profile photo burned through her mind. Why was he looking at it? Was he remembering what they'd been to each other? Were his feelings for the other woman resurfacing? Thinking about losing Xander again just killed her inside.

The past weeks had taught her they belonged together, now more than ever. She loved him with every breath in her body, every movement, every thought. She just had to prove it.

Xander was surprised when Olivia went up to bed ahead of him. Then again, she hadn't slept half the afternoon away like he had. She'd been on tenterhooks all night, and he'd had the impression she'd been on the verge of saying or asking something several times, only to back down at the last minute.

Today had been a revelation for them both. He'd had the shock of learning about their separation, and Olivia had certainly looked stunned when Rachelle turned up at his apartment.

He thumbed the TV remote, coasting through the channels mindlessly as he turned over the things he'd discovered today. None of it made any sense to him, no matter how he approached it. He didn't feel as if he'd developed a romantic bond with Rachelle at all. Surely if they'd been a couple, he'd have experienced something when he'd seen her. He'd only felt mildly uncomfortable when she'd hugged and kissed him. Not like when he touched Olivia and certainly not at all like when they'd made love last night.

His fingers curled tight around the remote, making the plastic squeak. Even just thinking about his wife—and she was still his wife—was enough to awaken a hunger for her in him. How could things have gotten so bad between them that they'd separated? Why hadn't they been able to work things out?

With a harsh sigh, Xander switched off the TV and got up to turn off the light and head upstairs. He may as well lie awake in bed upstairs as sit here alone with the inanity of the TV clogging his brain.

He took the stairs confidently, but he hesitated when he reached the top. There was muted light coming from the bedroom, and a delicate scent wafted toward him. Vanilla maybe? His footfall was silent on the carpet runner that led down the hall toward their bedroom. He hesitated in the doorway, taking in the room and the setting Olivia had obviously gone to some lengths to create.

The drapes were drawn but billowed softly in the evening breeze. Dotted around the room—on top of the bureau, the bedside tables, the mantelpiece of the fireplace—were small groups of candles in glass jars. The scent in the room was stronger, and he felt his body respond to the seductive scene.

Olivia came through from the bathroom, wrapped only in a towel. His breath caught in his lungs as his eyes traveled hungrily over the smooth creamy set of her shoulders. His gaze lingered on the hollows of her collarbone before dropping lower to the shadowed valley of her breasts, exposed above the moss-green towel that was a perfect foil for her hair.

She'd clipped her hair up loosely, exposing the delicious curve of her neck, and silky strands tumbled to drift across her shoulders. He was struck with a sudden deep envy of those strands.

"Looks like you're trying to seduce me here," he said, his voice thick with desire.

"Is it working?" she said, her voice equally husky.

"I'm not sure. Maybe you need to keep going."

He watched as she slowly untucked the end of her towel. The material dropped away, revealing her beautiful body in one fell swoop. Xander's mouth dried. He swallowed, hard. Olivia reached a slender arm up and tugged a few pins loose, sending her hair cascading over her shoulders. Her nipples, normally a pale pink, had deepened in color and were tight buds on her full breasts—just begging for his touch, his lips, his tongue.

Xander's body felt taut and hot, his clothing restrictive as his erection hardened even more. She was so beautiful, and she was walking toward him. He forced himself to keep his hands by his sides as she stopped in front of him. Clearly she had an agenda—far be it from him to make any changes to whatever she had planned.

"How about now?" she asked.

She caressed one breast with her hand, stroking lightly across her nipple, and he watched, mesmerized, as her skin grew even tauter.

"Yeah," he answered, his voice gruff with the need that pulsed through him like a living thing. "It's working."

A tiny smile played around her lips. "Good," she whispered before going up on her toes and kissing his lips.

It was a tease, just the lightest of butterfly caresses, but it acted like a torch to volatile liquid. In that instant he was fully aflame—for her. She must have sensed it, because her fingers were at the buttons of his shirt, deftly plucking them open and pushing the garment off his shoulders to fall silently to the floor. Her hands spread like warm fans across his skin, rubbing and caressing him. He was hot for her, so very hot his blood all but boiled in his veins.

He reached up to touch her and pull her to him, but she grabbed his hands and held them at his sides.

"Let me," she whispered. "Let me love you."

She bent her head and kissed his chest, tracing tiny lines with her tongue and then kissing him again. And then her tongue was swirling in tight little circles around his nipple. He groaned out loud, couldn't help it, as a spear of need bolted through his entire body.

Olivia's hands were at his belt, undoing the buckle, and then at the button of his trousers, then—finally—at the zipper of his pants. She slid one hand inside the waistband of his briefs, her fingers like silk as they closed around his thickness. She stroked him slow and firm, and it was all he could do to remain a passive subject in this sensual onslaught on his body.

He felt her move before he fully understood her intentions, felt his trousers and his briefs disappear down the length of his legs, felt Olivia's hot breath against his thighs.

Felt her mouth close around his aching flesh.

"Livvy," he groaned, tangling his fingers in her hair as she used her tongue in wicked ways that fried his synapses.

And then he was beyond thought, locked only in sensation until even sensation became too much and he lost control, soaring on the wave of a climax that initially made his entire body rigid as pulse after pulse of pleasure rocketed through him then left him weak and shaking with its magnitude.

Xander pulled Olivia up and into his embrace, holding her close to him until his heart rate approximated that of a normal person's.

"Ready for round two?" Olivia asked softly.

"Round two?"

"Yeah. I have a lot of time and a lot of loving to make up."

"Don't we both," he agreed, pressing a kiss on to the top of her head.

He let her walk him backward toward the bed, where she pushed him onto the mattress and bent to remove his clothes from where they'd tangled at his feet. She rubbed her hands over his body, from the tips of his toes, up his legs and over his abdomen as she positioned herself on the bed over him.

"I've missed you, Xander," she said, her blue eyes staring straight into his—honestly burning there like an incandescent flame.

In the gilded light of the candles' glow she looked more beautiful than he'd ever seen her. Her hair was a tangle of gold-red waves that tumbled in glorious abandon over her shoulders to caress her skin. Her breasts were high and full, her nipples ripe for his touch—and touch them he did, taking them between thumb and forefinger and watching her face as he teased and tugged on them.

His body was quick to recover from his earlier climax, and he felt himself harden beneath the heat that poured from her. He slipped one hand between her legs, smiling as he discovered her readiness.

"Show me," he urged her. "Show me how much you missed me."

She reached for a condom she must have slipped under the pillow earlier and covered him, taking her time over it and turning the act into an art form of simultaneous seduction and torment. Then she positioned him at her entrance and slowly took him inside her body. Her thigh muscles trembled as she accepted him deep within.

"You feel so right inside me," she gasped with a strangled breath. "I never want to let you go."

Then she started to move, and all he could do was glory in the pleasure she gave him, holding on to her hips as she rocked and swayed and dragged them both toward a peak that arrived all too quickly and yet not fast enough at the same time. She melted onto his body, her curves fitting against him like a puzzle piece made only for him. He folded his arms around her and held her tight, lost in the perfection of the moment.

Much later, Olivia rose and disposed of the condom they'd used. He watched her through hooded lids as she extinguished one candle after another. The room softened into gray, then into darkness as she worked her way closer to the bed and climbed in next to him. He rolled her onto her side and curved his body around her back, marveling again at the perfection of how they fit together.

"Good night, Xander," she whispered in the darkness. "And…I'm sorry about today."

In response he squeezed her tight and pressed a kiss at her nape. He listened as she drifted into sleep.

As sorry as she truly seemed to be, he felt as though she still held something back. Something vital and just out of reach of his battered mind. Would he ever remember?

Thirteen

Olivia woke late the next morning feel both well used and well satisfied. She turned her head on the pillow and looked straight into Xander's clear gray eyes.

"I love you," she whispered. "So very much."

She pushed back his hair from his forehead and leaned over to kiss him before rolling over and getting out of bed. Xander caught her wrist, tugging her back down into his arms.

"Stay," he commanded, lifting her hair and nuzzling the back of her neck.

Goose bumps peppered her body. Oh, he knew all the right places, and he took his time exploring them over and over again. It was nearly eleven when they rose and Xander joined her in the shower.

"We should just spend the whole day naked," he said, slowly soaping up her body and sending her heart rate into overdrive all over again.

"I wish I could, but I have to take my work to the gallery. I'll be busy all afternoon and into the evening with the exhibition opening." She rinsed off, then pushed open the shower door. "I have to do this, Xander. It's my career now, my reputation as an artist."

"Then go do your thing. I'll find something to keep me occupied today."

"You could come, too," she offered, feeling a spark of hope light within her.

"Next time maybe, okay?"

Olivia bit back her disappointment. She knew it would probably be too much for Xander to be out most of the afternoon and evening, but she was reluctant to break the bubble of this new closeness they shared. She quickly dried herself then blow-dried her hair. Xander finished in the shower and then dried and dressed right next to her. Olivia tried to think back to the last time they'd been in the bathroom together like this. It was such a normal everyday part of life, and she'd missed it more than she realized as she teased him about hogging the mirror.

"You're taking your beard off?" she asked.

"Yeah," he said, lathering up with shaving foam. "I'm ready to be me again."

Olivia's brush tangled in her hair, making her wince. Ready to be him again? What exactly did he mean by that? She disentangled the bristles from her hair and put the brush and dryer on the bathroom vanity before sliding her arms around Xander's naked waist.

"I kind of like the person you are now," she said, pressing a kiss between his shoulders.

"You didn't like the old me?" he asked, halting midstroke with his razor, his eyes meeting hers in the mirror.

"I loved the old you, too, Xander. But we've both changed. I like the person I am now better, too. Maybe that was part of the problem before. I was always trying to be something or someone else. Maybe I need to take a leaf out of your book and just be me again."

She pulled away from him and finished her hair—the noise of the hair-dryer making further conversation difficult. The stress and worries of the day before still lingered too close to the surface for her. If she didn't have to be away from the house today, she most definitely wouldn't be. But she'd been telling the truth when she'd said that her career and her reputation rested on this show. The gallery was one of the most prestigious in Auckland, and she considered herself fortunate to receive an invitation to exhibit there. Of course the cut the gallery would get on any sale was substantial, she reflected, but the exposure her work would receive was worth more than money.

Later, after they'd had fluffy omelets with chopped fresh chives and bacon, hot coffee and toast, Xander helped her carry the last of her canvases out to her car.

"Thanks," Olivia said as she closed the back on her station wagon. "I'm not sure what time I'll be home, but I'll probably be late, after dinner anyway."

"I can look after myself."

"And you promise that if you get a headache, you'll take your pills and rest?"

"You don't need to babysit me, remember?"

"I know." She pressed her hand against his cheek. "But I worry about you."

"I'll take care, I promise," he said solemnly before turning his head to kiss the inside of her palm.

Across the street Olivia caught a glimpse of one of their neighbors putting Christmas lights up in the eaves of their house. It reminded her again that the holiday was less than four weeks away. It gave her an idea.

"Maybe when I get home—or if I'm too late, maybe tomorrow—we can put up the Christmas tree. I didn't bother when…" Her voice trailed off for a moment before she took a deep breath. She had to get over her reluctance to talk about the past. "When we were separated. It brought back too many memories of the fun we used to have. Anyway, I'll go up to the attic and get the stuff down for us when I get back, okay?"

"That sounds like a good idea," Xander agreed. "I'd like that. Now, you'd better get going. I thought you didn't want to be late?"

Olivia glanced at her wristwatch and exclaimed in shock. "Oh, is that the time already? You're such a distraction!"

He laughed and swooped in for another kiss, this time a lingering caress full of promise. "Hurry back—I'll be waiting."

Olivia drove away with a last glance in the rearview mirror. Xander stood in the driveway, hands resting on his hips, watching her go. He made it so hard to leave him behind, for more reasons than she cared to examine. The shadow of a passing cloud suddenly obscured the sun, darkening the road before her and making her push her sunglasses up onto her head. A shiver traveled down her spine. Olivia shook off the sensation, not wanting to examine the sudden sense of unease that gripped her.

It was just because she was leaving Xander for several hours on his own, she rationalized. Since he'd been home again, the longest she'd left him was a couple of hours while she ran errands or went shopping. It was natural to feel uneasy, but there was no cause for alarm. Nothing would go wrong.

Xander watched her car turn out the drive and the automatic gates swing shut behind it. The gate. There was something about the gate, some memory attached to it that was just out of reach. A sharp stab of pain made its presence felt behind his eye, and he closed his eyes and shook his head slightly to rid himself of the pain.

Take your pills. It was as if Olivia's voice were stuck in his head, he thought with a smile as he headed back into the house. Well, he'd promised her he'd look after himself. And, he had to admit, he had no desire for a repeat of the headache that had struck him yesterday. Inside, he found the painkillers and took the required dose, then retired to the hammock for a while until the nagging pain eased off. It didn't take long.

While he rested, he thought about what he should do to fill the hours until Olivia returned. The Christmas tree! Of course. He knew she'd mentioned putting it up together, but he also knew she'd love the surprise of seeing it decorated and lit in the large front bay window to welcome her home.

They'd always stored the tree in the attic, and, since she'd said she hadn't even put it up the past couple of years, he shouldn't have too much trouble finding it. Motivated by the idea of her pleasure in seeing the tree finished, he went inside and upstairs. The stairs to the attic were as narrow as he remembered them, and he fought back an odd sense of light-headedness as he placed his foot on the first tread.

At the top of the stairs, he pushed open the door into the attic, taking a bit of time to allow his eyes to adjust to the gloom. Light streamed in from the small diamond-paned windows at each end of the attic and dust motes danced on the beams. Xander sneezed and cursed under his breath.

Moving farther into the attic, he got his bearings and looked around at the boxes and shrouded pieces of furniture they'd stored there. He shifted a few cartons in an attempt to get to where he last remembered seeing the tree and decorations. If Olivia had told the truth, they'd be exactly where he himself had put them.

He straightened for a moment. *If* Olivia had told the

truth? Why would he think she'd lie about something like this? Why would she lie to him about anything? *Maybe because she lied to you about your separation*, a voice echoed in the back of his head. He pushed the thought down. She'd explained why she'd withheld that piece of information. Sure, he didn't agree with her choice, but if they were to move forward, he had to be willing to get past it. She'd accepted some of the blame for what had gone wrong between them. Considering what he knew of himself along with what she *had* told him, he could see how easily they could have drifted apart.

Born the youngest of two boys, he'd pretty much always been treated as an only child after his older brother died in a drowning accident when Xander was only about three years old. Looking back, he could see how his parents had each coped in their own ways. His mother by becoming a distant workaholic and his father, sadly, by retreating into himself and becoming unable to work at all.

Xander still remembered coming home from school and letting himself into their home, knowing his mother would still be at work and wondering if that particular day would be one where his father would be happy to come outside and kick a football with him or whether Xander would end up sitting on the floor outside his parents' bedroom, listening to his father sob quietly as he remained locked in grief for the son he'd never see grow up.

There was probably more of his mother's influence in him than his father's, Xander acknowledged. If nothing else, he'd always fought hard to live by his mother's example. Never letting life get him down, dealing with his grief privately and always striving hard for the future.

While he'd never seen his father as weak, because even as a child he'd understood what his father was going through had little to do with strength or weakness, he hadn't wanted to *feel* as overwhelmingly as his father had either. As a result, he'd always controlled his emotions strictly, keeping them on a tight rein. Xander hadn't dared to experience extreme highs or extreme lows in his personal life; he had, instead, poured himself into work and achievement. Now he wondered if that driven part of him had also been a part of what had put a wedge between him and Olivia? He couldn't remember, no matter how hard he tried.

What he did know was that he was prepared to give her the benefit of the doubt and to give their marriage another chance. Perhaps the accident and his amnesia were a good thing after all. He knew he could be stubborn and move on if he thought something wasn't working. Rather than work on their marriage, he would have rejected any overtures she'd made to work things out.

Even so, he couldn't deny the niggling feeling that there was more to their separation than the brief explanation she'd given him yesterday. And then there was the matter of Rachelle and the fact she had a key to his apartment. Something really didn't feel right about that, but he couldn't put his finger on it. He would, though. He felt so much better. Stronger both mentally and physically, except for these bloody headaches, he thought as he shifted a few more cartons, then squatted down to read the lettering on a box shoved to the back.

He recognized the writing—it was his own. The box was ignominiously labeled "Stuff." He tugged it toward him and opened the flaps. In it were framed certificates and some old photo albums. A surge of excitement filled him. Maybe the contents would cast some light over his lost years. He pulled out the first album and absently thumbed through it. It dated back to his years in university, before he'd met Olivia. No, there was nothing there that he didn't know well already.

He shoved the albums and certificates back in the box and pushed it back against the wall. With the digital age it was more than likely there were no physical albums of his more recent years. Maybe he needed to look harder at his computer files. See what was there that dated back from when he could last remember and up until now.

But before he could do that, he needed to find the Christmas decorations. Xander dug around a few more boxes but ended up with nothing more than a sneezing fit. He was just about to give up completely when he spotted two more boxes in a dark corner. Maybe this was what he'd been looking for.

He dragged the boxes under the remaining light. They weren't labeled like all the others were. Neither looked like the long narrow carton he knew had always stored the tree, but maybe one held the decorations. There was definitely something familiar about them.

A weird sensation swept through him, making him feel a little dizzy again as he rocked back on his heels. He shrugged it off, thinking that he probably just needed some fresh air. The tiny ventilation holes in the eaves near the windows weren't the most efficient. He'd been up there awhile already, and, with the sun beating down on the iron roof, it was getting pretty hot.

Xander tugged at the tape binding the first box with a grunt of determination. It came away with a satisfying sound. Once again that feeling of being off balance assailed him. Xander closed his eyes for a brief moment and waited for the sensation to pass. This one was worse than the last and left him sick to his stomach. He swallowed and forced his eyes open.

"Just this one," he said aloud as he lifted the flaps. "Then I'm heading back downstairs. What the—?"

His voice trailed off into silence as he pulled out the first of the items inside. A child's clothing, precisely folded in layers—a little boy's things, to be more precise. Xander put them to one side and reached in again. Toys this time. A teddy, a few die-cast trains and cars.

His stomach lurched, and Xander fought back the bile that crept up his throat. He *knew* these things. These pieces of another life, another time. The frustrating sense of limbo he'd been living in since waking up in the hospital began to peel away from him, layer after layer. The hairs on the back of his neck stood on full alert, and an icy shiver traced down his spine.

Without another thought he tore open the second box. Cold sweat drenched his body. More clothes, more toys and, near the bottom, photo albums. He lifted them from the box. Even in the muted light of the attic he could see the dates on the albums. He picked up the oldest of them and slowly opened the cover. There on the first page was a grainy sonogram picture. He traced the edges of the tiny blur on the picture with the tip of one finger as a powerful wave of déjà vu swept over him. And with it, a memory. A sense of excitement and fear and love, all in one massive bundle of emotion. And then loss. Aching, wrenching, tearing loss.

Xander turned the page of the album to a photo of Olivia, a younger and more carefree Olivia than the one he'd seen off today. There was a series of photos of her, first with a big smile and flat tummy, all the way through to a photo of her with her belly swollen with pregnancy and a finger pointing to a date circled on the calendar.

The next page saw him staring at himself, proudly holding a squalling newborn infant.

His son.

Fourteen

A sob tore from Xander's throat and his chest tightened, making every breath a struggle. *He remembered.* He remembered everything, all the way back to the day that Olivia told him she was pregnant—and the fight they'd had that night over her news.

He'd been furious with her for taking that step without his knowledge. It hadn't been an accident. It had been a calculated decision she'd made without him. He hadn't been ready. He could still recall the heady rush of their relationship, their haste to marry and build a life together. Hell, he'd barely come to terms with their closeness before she was telling him they had to make room for another person in their lives. A person who'd depend on them for everything.

Xander hadn't known if he had it in him to love even more than he already loved Olivia—at least not until he'd experienced the joy of Parker's birth. Tears ran unchecked down Xander's cheeks as he turned more pages, then reached for the next album and the next. Each one cataloguing their beautiful little boy's life, until there was no more. The last photos were of Parker's third birthday in the backyard. A pirate theme had been the order of the day, and even Xander had dressed in kind.

They'd been so happy. So complete. And then, with one stupid forgetful moment on his part, it had all ended.

The devastation of Parker's death, along with the certainty that he could have prevented it, had left Xander crushed by guilt. He wiped at his face, trying to stem the tears that wouldn't stop falling. This was what he'd forgotten. This was what he'd built walls around his heart and his mind for. To stem the searing, clawing pain that now threatened to tear him into tiny pieces.

Xander staggered to his feet, leaving the albums and the toys and clothes scattered around the cartons on the floor. He wobbled toward the doorway and stumbled down the stairs, as uncoordinated and clumsy as he'd been in those early days back in the hospital. At the bottom of the stairs he turned right and went straight to the bedroom next to his old home office.

Now he understood why his office had always been here. He'd hated every second he had to spend away from home when Parker had been alive. With this home office, he'd had the best of both worlds. Able to watch his son grow and learn every day, and meet the demands of his career and provide for his family at the same time.

His family. Their little unit of three. Xander could never have believed that the power of their triangle could ever have been torn apart. Hadn't understood that when you ripped away one edge of the triangle that the other two sides would collapse. Not together. No. But apart. In their grief, he and Olivia had inexorably turned away from each other.

He pushed open the bedroom door and looked around the bare walls and floor. The only thing that remained was a bureau that had stored Parker's clothes. Olivia had gotten rid of everything else. She'd wiped their son's existence from their home, in fact, from their very lives with clinical precision—just like his mother had when Xander's brother had died.

Xander dropped to his knees. Grief crashed over him with the power of a tidal wave. It felt as raw and as painfully fresh as if it had been only yesterday that he'd been forced to say goodbye to his son. The child of his body, of his heart. He roared in frustration and anger and sorrow, the sounds coming from deep inside him. Sounds he'd never allowed out, ever, but now it was as if he couldn't stop them.

He had no idea what the time was when he pulled himself back to his feet and made his way to his bedroom. No, not his bedroom anymore. Olivia's. He'd made his home elsewhere, and now he knew why. He went into the bathroom and showered again, all the while attempting to block out the memory of the last time, only hours ago, that he'd shared this same space with Olivia, and what they'd done.

The memory wouldn't be suppressed. His body, traitor that it was, stirred to life at the images running through his mind. He turned the mixer to cold, standing beneath the spray until the pain of the icy water was almost equal to the pain that pulsed in the region of his heart.

He leaned his forearms on the shower wall and let his head drop between his shoulders, allowing the water to pound on the back of his neck and down his back. Questions whirled in his mind. Why had she kept this from him? What had she been thinking? Why hadn't she told him everything when she'd had the chance to yesterday?

By the time he turned off the water and stepped out of the shower to dry himself he was no closer to finding any answers. She'd tricked him into coming here and she'd tricked him into staying—just as she'd tricked him into parenthood. Why?

Xander studied his reflection in the mirror, hardly recognizing the man whose tortured gray eyes stared back at him. He couldn't stay here. He couldn't listen to another lie from Olivia's lips. The betrayal of what she'd done was as excruciatingly painful now as the words she'd flung at him after Parker had died had been.

They'd still been in the emergency room. Pushed to one side while the doctors and nurses had worked frantically to save Parker's life. Until they accepted that nothing they did made any difference. Until the frenetic busyness fell silent and Olivia had turned to him and said it was all his fault. He hadn't wanted Parker and now her precious child was gone. Oh, she'd apologized afterward, but once spoken, the words couldn't be unsaid. Their hurt had spread in him like a voracious disease. Eating away at him until he had nothing left to give.

She'd blamed him for their son's death, but no more than he'd blamed himself. It had driven a wedge between them, creating a void that might possibly have been repaired had he needed her less and she'd needed him more. And he had needed her. The depth of his grief terrified him, made him afraid he would sink into the abyss of misery that had claimed his father. So he'd made a tactical withdrawal from his emotions, and, along with that decision, Xander had pulled away from his wife. And she'd done nothing to pull him back again—not until she'd shown up at his hospital room with a smile and a lie.

Xander picked his clothes up from the floor and bundled them up into a ball. They stank of his fear for what he'd discovered upstairs in the attic and of his grief and anger. He never wanted to see them again. He grabbed clean clothes from the bureau and the wardrobe, then yanked everything else he owned off its hanger and from its drawer and piled it all onto the bed.

Rummaging in the hall cupboard unearthed a suitcase that looked both new and familiar. He remembered buying it before a trip to Japan last year. Olivia must have brought his things from his apartment in it. He squeezed his clothing into the case and zipped it closed. Then he picked it and the bundle of clothes he'd discarded up and carried them downstairs. The case he left just inside the sitting room. The other things he shoved in the trash bin outside the back door.

He should just go, he thought. Leave now before she came back. But some perverse masochistic impulse urged him to stay. To face Olivia and to ask her what the hell she'd been thinking. Masochistic? No, it wasn't masochism to want answers. He deserved the truth from her, at last. No more subterfuge, no more lies or half truths. Everything.

Olivia was on a high when she pulled her car into the drive. The exhibition had been an enormous success. The gallery owner had been thrilled not only with the commissions they'd earned but also with the requests for more of her work in the future. There was international interest in her work, too. Sure, she knew better than to think her success from this point out was guaranteed, but tonight the world was her oyster. She couldn't wait to share the news with Xander.

She looked up at the house as she rolled to a stop outside the garage. It hadn't been dark long, but no lights were on inside. At least not at the front of the house. Maybe he was around the back or even in his office in the cottage.

Grabbing her bag and the bottle of champagne the gallery owner had given her before she'd left the exhibition, she got out of the car, quickly walked up the front path and let herself inside.

"Xander?" she called, clicking on the hall light.

A sound in the sitting room made her halt in her tracks and change direction.

"Xander? Are you okay?" she asked, turning on the overhead light in the room as she entered it. "I hope you're up to celebrating. The exhibition was fab—"

Her voice broke off as she took in the appearance of the man sitting in one of the armchairs, dressed in what she thought of as his "new life" clothes and with an expression on his face that sent a spear of alarm straight to her heart.

His voice was cold. "How long did you plan to keep the truth about Parker from me?"

She sank into a chair behind her, her legs suddenly unable to hold her upright a second longer. "I…I didn't plan to keep it from you. I just couldn't talk about it. I didn't know where to begin, what to say…I still don't."

He cocked one eyebrow. "Seriously? Even now you can lie to me, Olivia? Yesterday didn't give you ample opportunity to fill me in? Hell, any time in the last nearly *two months* wasn't enough time for you?"

He stood, and she fought to find the words she should have said anytime before now. "Xander, please. Don't go."

"A little too late to be saying that, don't you think?" he replied, his voice as sharp as one of the chef's knives in her kitchen.

"I tried, Xander. Honestly, I wanted to tell you."

"But you didn't. You packed our son's entire life into boxes and shoved them in a dark corner. You already wiped Parker's existence from our home and our lives once before—why wouldn't you continue to do that given the opportunity? I don't know you anymore, Olivia. Maybe I never did."

She pushed herself to her feet. Even though her legs trembled beneath her, she sifted through the shock that near paralyzed her to find something to say.

"Didn't you do exactly the same thing? Wipe Parker from our lives when you walked out that door, when you walked away from me?"

"I left you because I couldn't pretend that the past had never happened, like you did. It happened. I know it did, and I've regretted that day every conscious moment of my life since. You seemed to find it so easy to just pick up and carry on. As if Parker had never been born," he accused.

"I couldn't hold on to the past." Olivia clutched at her blouse as if doing so could ease the tightness deep in her chest. "It was killing me, Xander. But you couldn't see that. Holding on to Parker's memories, seeing the reminders of his life every single day? It was killing me inside, destroying me. I had to move forward or die. I had to put everything away, or I knew I'd end up being buried with him."

"Even at the price of our marriage? At the expense of *us*?" Xander shook his head. "And you say I did the same thing as you? I didn't. I couldn't. I loved our son with every breath in my body."

"So did I!" she shouted at him. "And I loved you. I still love you. That's why I did what I did. I brought you home, and I hoped against hope that you wouldn't remember because then we could forget the past and the hurt and the awful things we said to each other back then. We could be together, like we're meant to be. The way we have been. But you, you're running away again, just like you did last time. Why stand and face our problems when you can just walk away, right?"

The bitterness in her words stained the air between them.

"You have the gall to accuse me of running away? You

didn't want me anymore. You made that patently clear when Parker died. Sometimes I wonder if you ever loved me or if I just conveniently fit into the plan you had for your future. You certainly didn't need *me*. It makes me wonder why you even bothered to lie to me all this time."

Her throat choked up—just like it had the last time he left her. Her words, her fears, all knotted into a tangled ball that lodged somewhere between her heart and her voice and made her too afraid to tell him how she really felt.

Her words, when they came, were nothing but a stifled whisper. "I did it for us. For our marriage. It, no, *we* deserved a second chance, but you wouldn't listen when I said the past didn't matter. That it was our future that was important."

"*I* wouldn't listen? You shut me out, Olivia. You shut me out from the truth. From our son's memory, from our past. No!" He waved his hand in a short cutting motion in front of him. "You don't get to do this again. You don't get to make my decisions for me."

"What about our decisions, Xander? The decisions we should be making for *us*?" she pleaded.

"Us? There is no us."

Outside, she heard a car pull up and the driver toot the horn. Xander bent and reached down for the bag she hadn't seen standing there before. She recognized the suitcase immediately—after all, it hadn't been that long ago she'd packed it herself.

"Goodbye, Olivia. You'll be hearing from my lawyer—and this time the divorce is going through."

He started to walk toward the door, and she followed him, her movements jerky as if she were some marionette being played by a demented puppet master.

"Xander, please, don't go. Don't leave me," she implored. "We've been happy together. Things have been good again since you've been home, and this is *our home*."

He kept walking. Olivia put on a burst of speed, passing him and getting to the door before him. She pressed her back to the solid wooden surface, barring him from dragging it open and walking away from her.

"Think about how well we worked together with your rehab and how close we've become again. This is our chance to rebuild our lives. We made mistakes before—I know that. But we can work past them. Please don't throw away this chance for us to make it all right again. To rebuild our marriage."

He put his hands on her shoulders and physically steered her away from the door. She lacked the strength to fight him and just watched as he turned the brass knob and opened the door wide.

"You're good at this, you know," she murmured, using the only weapon she had left. "Walking away. You blame me for lying, for withholding the truth from you, but you're equally to blame for the way things fell apart. You always walk away instead of accepting or asking for help. You're prepared to share your body, but you've never shared your deepest feelings or your thoughts with me. Ever.

"Please, Xander. I can be there for you. We can work through this. Let me help you come to terms with your grief. You say I put Parker's life away into boxes, but you did exactly the same with your feelings. You stopped working at home and you spent every hour you could at work. We never talked. We never admitted how much we needed each other. Help me, Xander. Let me help you."

Xander shook his head again, his face a taut mask devoid of expression, his eyes cold. "You are the last person I will ever ask for help."

He stepped through the open door and out onto the

porch. Past his shoulder, out on the street, Olivia saw Rachelle get out of the car and look toward the house. Xander raised a hand to Rachelle in acknowledgment and kept walking.

Olivia stayed there, frozen in the entrance hall of her home, as she watched her husband walk away from her for the second time in their marriage. His parting words echoed in her mind. As the sound of Rachelle's car driving away faded into the distance, Olivia slowly shut the door and rested her forehead against its surface.

Every part of her body hurt from the inside out. She'd thought it was bad the last time he'd left her, but she'd still been so numb with losing Parker that she hadn't had the capacity to think or to feel too much. But now—given all that had developed between them since he'd been back, given how much she still loved him—she hurt in ways she'd never dreamed possible.

Where did this leave them, exactly? Wherever it was, she knew she didn't like it. Hated it, in fact. Hated that once again she'd allowed the best thing that had ever happened to her to walk out that door.

And still she loved him.

Fifteen

Xander sat in the car as Rachelle drove away from the house, his eyes fixed forward. *Look to the future*, he told himself, *away from the past*. Away from the hurt, the anger, the betrayal. Anger still simmered beneath the surface. At Olivia, at himself.

"Did you want to stop somewhere for a meal or a drink?" Rachelle said as they entered the harbor bridge approach.

"No," he said abruptly. "Thanks," he added. "Just to my place would be fine."

She nodded, but he sensed her disappointment. He remembered now that before his accident they'd become closer than two people who simply worked together. Friends still, not lovers. But they'd been heading in a more romantic direction. Although, when he'd been honest with himself, he'd found it impossible to engage his emotions to the extent he needed to in order to embark on an intimate relationship with someone. He knew she was a lot more invested in developing their relationship than he'd been. At least she'd never hidden that from him, not the way Olivia had hidden so much.

His stomach tightened on an unexpectedly sharp pain. Why did it hurt so much to be leaving her again? He'd already done it once before—and now that he remembered why, he understood and agreed with the choice he'd made two years ago. This time shouldn't have been any different, and yet it felt as if he was leaving a vital part of himself behind.

Being a Friday night, traffic was quite heavy. The journey gave him far too much time to think and reflect. He was relieved when Rachelle pulled into the underground car park and drew to a halt in one of the parking spaces allocated to his apartment.

She turned off the engine and twisted in her seat to face him. The smile on her face didn't quite match the uncertainty he saw in her eyes.

"Xander? Are you okay? Do you want me to come up with you?"

"Look, thanks for the ride, but I'd prefer to be on my own right now."

Her smile faded. "You're not angry with me, are you? I wanted to say something to you when I saw you and Olivia at the apartment, but she wouldn't let me."

Xander sighed. He just bet Olivia didn't let Rachelle say anything. "Of course I'm not angry with you," he said and leaned forward to kiss her on the cheek. "I'll see you on Monday, okay? At the office."

"You've been cleared to come back to work? That's fabulous. We've missed you so much. *I've* missed you."

"Cleared or not, I'm coming back. Even if it's only for a few hours a day. I need to get back to normal." *Whatever normal is now,* he added silently. "Again, thanks for the ride. I appreciate you coming to get me at such short notice."

"Anytime, you just call me. I'm here for you. I could even get you some groceries now, if you like, and bring them back. It's pretty empty up there right now."

He shook his head emphatically. "No, that's fine. I'll get some things delivered in."

"On the weekend?"

"I'll deal with it," he said firmly and opened his door to get out of the car. "See you Monday."

She took the hint and nodded, but her disappointment was clear in her eyes. "Monday it is. Good night, Xander. I'm glad you're back to your old self."

After she'd driven off, he took the elevator to his floor and let himself into his apartment. The soullessness of the space was just what he needed right now. He didn't want memories or feelings or anything. Except maybe a shot of whisky. He walked over to the cabinet where he kept his liquor and grabbed a bottle of Scotland's finest before going to the kitchen, where he splashed two fingers of amber liquid in a crystal tumbler.

He walked over to the windows that looked out over the harbor and toward Devonport—toward Olivia—and took a sip of the spirit. It burned as it went down, not the deep satisfying burn he'd anticipated but something far less pleasant. Xander looked down at the glass in his hand and wondered what the hell he was doing seeking solace in alcohol. He'd never done it before, and he certainly shouldn't be starting now.

He strode to the kitchen and tipped out the contents of the tumbler into the sink. He needed a distraction, but whisky wasn't it. He stared at the large flat-screen TV mounted on the far wall of his sitting room. No, not even watching a movie or channel surfing appealed. Instead, Xander walked down the hallway toward his bedroom, stopping at the door to his office.

His hand was on the handle before he realized what he

was doing. Work had always been a panacea for him—why should that be any different now? He should still have some client notes here he could go over. He rued the fact his laptop had been destroyed in the crash. Not even its leather case had protected its harddrive from the impact. If he'd had the laptop, at least he could have looked forward to losing himself for a few hours by updating himself on his files and who had handled what in his absence.

The minute Xander stepped in his office he knew Olivia had been in there. The picture of Parker that he'd taken with him the first time he'd left her wasn't on his desk where he knew he'd left it. A roll of rage swelled inside him. Wiping their son's memory from their house had been one thing, but tampering with his apartment, as well? That was going too far.

He searched the office for the picture, his movements becoming more frantic the longer it took him to find it. The relief that coursed through his body when he found the frame, face down in a drawer, was enough to make him drop heavily into his chair. He looked at the beloved face of his only child. Felt anew the loss and grief that he usually kept locked inside. Relived the guilt.

Carefully he put the picture back on his desk where it belonged and stared at it for several minutes. Losing Parker was a reminder that he couldn't stray from the path he'd set himself. He didn't want to love again the way he'd loved Olivia and their little boy because when it all fell apart it hurt far too much.

He understood why his father had collapsed within himself the way he had. His grief and guilt over Xander's brother's death had been too much for him to handle, especially with the way Xander's mother had locked herself in a non-emotional cocoon and forged her way through the rest of her life. He hadn't had the support he needed. After losing his son and his marriage, Xander hadn't had any support to lean on, either. But he was tougher, more determined not to become a victim of his own dreadful mistake, and if that meant separating himself from emotion—the way his mother had—then that's what he would do.

It had been the longest two weeks of her life and Olivia felt decidedly ragged around the edges when she forced herself to get out of bed and embark on her new daily routine. Who was she kidding, she wondered as she padded downstairs in her dressing gown, her hair askew and her face unwashed. This tired, halfhearted attempt to continue on as though everything was normal was a step back into the past, hardly anything new.

The house felt empty without Xander there, and her heart echoed with loss. She'd spent the past fourteen days listlessly wandering around, feeling unmotivated and empty. Even a call from the gallery owner to say they'd just sold the last piece and had requests lining up for more of her work couldn't lift her spirits.

She'd screwed up. Again. So what now? She aimlessly went through the motions of making coffee and pouring it into a mug. As she lifted the brew to her lips to take a sip, the aroma filled her nostrils and turned her stomach. She'd been off and on different things for days now, and coffee was just another to add to the list. With a sigh she tipped the contents down the drain and turned instead to put the kettle on. Maybe a cup of peppermint tea would revive her flagging appetite.

As she pulled a teabag from the box in the pantry she forced herself to acknowledge that it would take more than a cup of herbal tea to make things better. There was only one thing—one man—who could make a difference in her life. The only one who had ever mattered. Xander.

She'd just finished brewing the tea when the phone rang. She recognized the number on the caller display with a sinking sensation that pulled at her stomach. Her lawyer wasted no time on pleasantries.

"Mrs. Jackson, we've been instructed by your husband's lawyers to expedite matters relating to your dissolution of marriage. Do you need us to forward new forms to you, or do you still have the ones we originally sent?"

So, he hasn't wasted time, Olivia thought as she acknowledged the lawyer's request. "No, I still have the originals."

"All you need to do is sign them, put them in the enclosed envelope and post them today. Or I could arrange a courier to collect them from you if you'd prefer. It seems Mr. Jackson is in somewhat of a hurry."

Olivia closed her eyes against the burn of tears. Her voice shook as she spoke. "I see. I'll get the papers back to you. There's no need to organize a courier."

There was a brief silence on the other end before she heard her lawyer clear his throat. "Thank you," he said. "And, Mrs. Jackson? I'm so very sorry things didn't work out for you."

"I am, too, Mr. Clement."

She hung up without saying goodbye, and the phone fell from her hands to the floor. She wrapped her arms around her waist and bent over as uncontrollable sobs racked her body. It was over and it was all her fault. If only she'd been up front with Xander from the beginning, he might have been receptive to starting again. But now, with the stupid decisions she'd made, with her inability to face the pain of the past, she'd ensured they had no future together at all.

Eventually she dragged herself back up the stairs and into her en suite. She pulled open the drawer where she'd stowed the papers and reached inside, her hand hesitating as it hovered over the sanitary products stored there. Something wasn't right. She reached into the drawer and grabbed the little pocket-size diary she kept a record of her cycle in and counted back the days. She was two days late. Nothing really to worry about. Unless you factored in the minor detail that her periods always came every twenty-eight days without fail.

Her hand trembled as she shoved the diary back in the drawer and slammed it shut—leaving the folded envelope exactly where she'd put it, forgotten now in light of what she was dealing with. She'd been under a lot of stress, hadn't been eating or sleeping properly. No wonder she was out of kilter, she tried to tell herself. But all the while she knew her excuses were a waste of time. She knew the signs as well as she knew her face in the mirror each morning. The lack of appetite, the need to nap at odd times of the day, not to mention her reaction to the coffee she'd made this morning. And then there was the metallic tang that had been in her mouth the past couple of days. A tang she remembered vividly from when she'd become pregnant with Parker. She'd been ignoring each and every sign. Choosing oblivion over reality—which was what had led her to this situation in the first place.

Pregnant. With Xander's child. What the hell was she going to do now?

Three days later Olivia had her confirmation. The nurse at her doctor's surgery had been filled with quiet excitement on her behalf. An excitement that Olivia was hard-pressed to feel. She had to tell Xander straightaway. This wasn't something she could, or would, withhold from him.

The minute she got home she called his cell phone. It rang only a couple of times before switching to his answering service. Olivia disconnected the call. He must have diverted her call the moment he'd seen her number on the caller display. The knowledge that he wasn't even willing to speak to her on the phone was a blow she hadn't expected. Not prepared to give up at the first hurdle, she dialed again. This time it went immediately to the service and she left him a message.

"Xander, I need to see you. It's urgent. Meet me tomorrow, please." She named a café in Devonport, a short ferry ride for him across the harbor, and stated what time she'd be there.

Now all she could do was wait.

Sixteen

Xander arrived before the time Olivia had indicated, but she had still gotten there ahead of him. She saw him the minute he came through the door, and he watched as her cheeks suffused with color and her eyes grew bright.

"I got your message," he said unnecessarily as he sat down opposite her at the table. "What do you want?"

"I'm glad you came. I didn't want to tell you this in a message."

"For two months you've held things back from me and *now* you want to tell me something? What is it?" he asked, not making any effort to keep the irritation out of his voice.

He wasn't prepared for what came next.

"I'm pregnant."

He stared at her in shock. *Pregnant?* Silence grew between them. A waitress came over to take their order, and he waved her away. Finally he found his tongue.

"What do you mean, pregnant?"

"What it usually means." Olivia gave him a smile, no

more than a twist of her lips really and certainly not the fulsome smile he was used to seeing on her face. It made him look at her more sharply and note the dark bruises of sleeplessness beneath her eyes and the pale cast of her skin. Concern for her swelled inside him, but he ruthlessly quashed it. It shouldn't matter to him if she slept or ate or looked after herself. Unless what she'd just told him was true.

"We're having a baby," she affirmed.

Every cell in his body rejected the words. *A baby. No. Not again. Never again.* They'd used protection. Even in his amnesiac state he'd followed the protocol he'd instigated after Parker's birth.

"But how—?"

"The condoms we used were expired," she said by way of explanation, her eyes not leaving his face for a second.

"Did you know that before we used them?"

"No! Of course I didn't. I'd forgotten all about them, to be honest. You must have bought them well before..." Her voice trailed off.

Before Parker died. And, yes, their purchase had been made well before then. There had been little intimacy between him and Olivia during Parker's last year. Their son had been plagued with virtually every cold and flu known to man after he began preschool and was exposed to germs from the other children. Olivia had said his immune system would strengthen eventually. However, it had meant she'd spent more nights curled up in bed with Parker, trying to soothe him back to sleep, than she had with Xander. Their lovemaking had become sporadic at best as she'd poured all her care into nursing Parker to health.

Now she was pregnant again. An icy shaft of trepidation sliced through him. What on earth did she expect from him? Was she trying to manipulate him again? She said she hadn't known the condoms were expired, but could he believe her? Maybe she'd planned to become pregnant all along, making the decision without him just like she had the first time. Binding him to her through an innocent baby when everything else she'd tried had failed, perhaps?

"You're telling me you didn't do this deliberately?"

"Of course I am. I swear I'm telling you the truth," she said, her voice raising slightly and making heads turn toward them. She continued, "If you'll remember, you were the one to initiate things the first time we—"

"I remember," he said, cutting across the words she'd been about to say.

Words that all too easily painted vivid memories in his mind of every single exquisite moment they'd spent together. The sounds she'd made when they made love. The scent of her body. The feel of her as she climaxed around him and as he spent himself inside her. The intense sense of belonging as they came back down to earth and fell asleep in each other's arms. He didn't want to remember. He couldn't risk allowing himself to feel.

"Is this why you haven't signed the papers yet?" he demanded.

"No! To be honest with you, I forgot all about them."

"Honest? That's a novelty for you these days, isn't it?" At Olivia's shocked expression he huffed out a sigh. "I'm sorry—that was uncalled for."

His mind scattered in a hundred different directions, but everything that passed through his thoughts settled back on one thing. Olivia was pregnant, and, if she was to be believed, they were equally responsible for this situation. The knowledge was a bitter pill to swallow. Either way he looked at it, another child of his would be on this earth, which meant he had responsibilities to that child. Responsibilities he had promised himself he'd never bear again.

Xander abruptly pushed his chair back from the table and stood. "Thank you for the information," he said and turned to go.

He was forced to halt in his steps when he felt Olivia's hand catch him on the arm.

"Xander, stay—please. We have to talk about this." Her voice rose again, attracting the same attention as before.

"Don't make a scene, Olivia. You asked me to come here and I did. You've given me your news and now I'm going. In the meantime, perhaps you could complete your part of the dissolution document and return it to your lawyer as requested?"

He stared at her hand until she let go. The second she did so he started for the door. But the short walk to the ferry building or the ride across the harbor back to the office passed in a blur. All he could remember were Olivia's words. *I'm pregnant.* They echoed in his mind, over and over again.

He couldn't do this again—didn't want to ever face being a father again—but circumstance now forced it on him. There were choices to make. Tough ones. Xander reached for the phone and hit the speed dial for his lawyer's office.

Olivia was working in her studio when she heard a van pull up outside her house. She walked over to the driveway to see who it was and was surprised to see a courier there. She wasn't expecting anything. The courier handed her an envelope, got her to sign for it and went on his way. Olivia felt dread pull at her with ghostly fingers as she identified the source of the envelope. Xander's lawyer.

Slowly she walked to the patio at the back of the house

and sat down at the table. She stared at the envelope, wondering what lay inside. She couldn't bring herself to open the packet; she didn't want to see in black-and-white whatever demand or dictate Xander had dreamed up in response to the news he was going to be a father again. She was still having a hard enough time coming to terms with the way he'd behaved when she'd told him the news yesterday. She didn't know what she'd expected him to do or say, exactly, but it hadn't been to simply get up and walk away from her—again.

A blackbird flew down onto the lawn and cocked its head, staring at her with one eye before pecking at the ground, pulling out a worm and flying away. She felt very like that worm must feel right now, she realized. At the mercy of something bigger, stronger and darker than she was. Helpless. It wasn't a feeling she was comfortable with, and it reminded her of all the things in her life she'd never been able to control. Control had become everything to her. It kept her world turning on its axis when everything else fell apart.

She picked up the envelope and turned it over and over in her hands. Had she really thought for a minute that Xander would be pleased with the news that she was expecting another baby? Maybe, in a sudden rash of idealistic foolishness, she had. The news had obviously shocked him—it had shocked her, too. She hadn't anticipated his utter indifference. So where did that leave them?

The obvious answer lay right there, in her hands, but still she couldn't bring herself to tear the envelope open. Instead, she placed it squarely on the table and went inside and brewed a pot of chamomile tea—taking her time over each step. Only after she'd carried her tea tray back outside to the table, poured her first cup and taken a sip did she pick up the envelope again.

She placed one hand on her belly. “Okay, little one, let’s see what your daddy has to say.”

With a swift tear it was open, and she pulled the contents out. She scanned the letter quickly, then read it more slowly on a second pass-through. Olivia went numb from head to foot. Xander’s feelings couldn’t have been spelled out more clearly. While he was prepared to offer generous financial support toward the child, he wanted no contact with the baby or with her whatsoever. There was a contract enclosed, setting out his terms and the sums he was prepared to pay, but she didn’t even look at it.

Slow burning anger lit inside her. How dare he dismiss their baby like that? It was one thing to be angry with her—to not want anything to do with her—but to reject their child? It was so clinical and callous.

Olivia tossed the letter onto the table and propelled herself to her feet. She paced the patio a few times and came to a halt outside her studio. Through the open door she could see the canvas she was working on—a commission she’d earned as a result of her exhibition. Painting had always been her refuge in the past—through sorrow, through loss—but she knew that she needed to work this anger out of her system before she picked up a brush again.

With a growl of frustration she closed and locked the studio doors before she took the tea tray and Xander’s wretched communication inside. Then, after grabbing her keys and sliding her feet into an old pair of sneakers, she went out the front door and down to the beach. She powered along the sand, oblivious to the sparkle of light on the rise and fall of the sea and the growing heat of the sun as it approached its zenith in the sky.

By the time she’d made it to the end of the beach and turned back again, she had worked the worst of her anger and, yes, her indignation, off. Olivia sat down on a park bench in the shade and waited for her breathing and heart rate to return to normal.

What had driven Xander to such a decision? she asked herself as she tried to rationalize his stance. This cold distance he insisted on maintaining was not something she recognized from the man she loved. She knew he could be distant and independent. He could also be stubborn and insanely detailed at times. But he wasn't the kind of man who could reject a child. Even as angry as he was about her pregnancy with Parker, he'd loved their son with an intensity that had often taken her breath away. Surely he couldn't *not* love another child of his?

She watched a lone gull as it circled on the thermals in the air before changing its direction and swooping down to the water. Was it that he wanted to be free like that gull there? Answerable only to himself? Had her lies and losing Parker the way they had made him incapable of loving ever again?

The answer that repeated in her mind was an emphatic no. In the weeks before he'd regained his memory she knew to the depths of her soul that he'd loved her. But if he was capable of love, why then would he withhold it from this baby?

Fear.

The word—so small, so simple and yet so powerful—came to her with blinding insight. He was afraid to love again—certainly afraid to love their baby but maybe even afraid to love her, too. After all, wasn't love based on trust? And hadn't she destroyed his trust in her not once but several times over?

Had she given him her shoulder to lean on in the wretched dark days after Parker died? No, she'd been filled with recriminations and pain and projecting her own guilt onto him. Had she tried to stop him leaving that first time? No, she'd been too numbed by grief to do anything.

She knew a little of his family's circumstances, even though Xander had never discussed it much and Olivia had never been close with her mother-in-law. Knew how his father had so grieved the loss of his firstborn son that he'd completely withdrawn from the family he'd had left. Understood that Xander's mother had worked hard every day she could to support her surviving son and her husband. His mum may not have shown her love with hugs and kisses, but she'd done the best she could to ensure their family was secure.

Was it any wonder then that Xander hadn't known how to express his grief? Why had she never thought about that before? He'd grown up with two complete extremes of how to cope with loss. Had anyone ever asked him how *he'd* felt about losing his brother, let alone his son?

She knew she certainly hadn't.

Where to now? How was she going to break through the armor Xander now protected himself and his emotions within? She'd already lost his trust, so was it even possible for him to forgive her and allow her back into his heart?

There were no secrets left between them now. She could only try. They'd made a child together out of love; that had to count for something. She owed it to Xander, to their baby and to herself to fight for what was right—to fight for their love and the chance to start again.

It was late when Xander listened to the latest message from Olivia. He'd been putting it off most of the day. Once he was home, he knew he couldn't put it off any longer. She'd been blunt and to the point. She'd acknowledged receipt of the offer through his lawyer, but she wanted to discuss it with him face-to-face first. She said that if he agreed to meet with her again, she wouldn't delay any further. Everything he wanted signed would be signed and returned at that meeting.

He knew he should call her back. Instead he dropped his phone on the coffee table in front of him and stretched out on the wide sofa that faced the view over the harbor. Lights sparkled in the inky darkness, like the stars of a distant galaxy. *Distant*, now there was a word. It described exactly how he felt when it came to just about everything in his life. Distant was safe; distant didn't flay a man's heart into a thousand shreds, nor did it betray a man.

He'd thought that distance was what he needed, what he wanted, and he'd tried to throw himself back into his work to gain emotional distance the way he always had when faced with personal upheaval. But in unguarded moments thoughts of Olivia kept creeping in. Her image when she came to the hospital, and he saw the love and concern so stark and clear on her face. Her determination to see him through the physical therapy he needed to do each day to regain muscle tone and strength after his coma. The sweet, soft sigh she made as he entered her body, as if, in that moment, everything in their world was perfect. And it had been.

And then there were the memories that went further back, to when Parker was alive, to the cute little family they'd been and how happy they were together. A visceral pain scored deep inside and reminded him anew that he'd never see Parker grow up. Pain laced with guilt that he'd been the one to leave their front gate open and that he'd been the one to throw the ball Bozo had chased out onto the road. Only two small things, each taken on their own, but put together they'd led to a tragedy of inestimable proportions.

The bitter irony that his little family had faced the

same awful loss as his parents had hadn't escaped him. But he wasn't his father. He wouldn't give in and buckle under the grief he felt. Instead he'd locked his feelings down. He would not be weak or needy. He would not, above all things, need Olivia more than she needed him. When it had become clear to him that she didn't need him at all, that she'd moved past their tragedy without him, Xander had left.

He groaned out loud. This was doing his head in. He needed a distraction, but what? Or who? He picked up his phone again and scrolled through his contact list. He wasn't in the mood for testosterone-driven company. His finger hovered over Rachelle's number. She'd made it more than clear these past few weeks that she was interested in picking up where they'd left off before his accident. In fact, she'd also made it clear she was willing to jump a few steps on that particular ladder.

Was that what would finally dislodge Olivia's presence from his mind? He could only hope so.

Rachelle arrived within thirty minutes of his call, and she glided into his arms as if she belonged there.

"I'm so glad you called," she said with a sultry purr as she lifted her face to his.

He kissed her and tried to feel something, anything but indifference, and failed miserably. Maybe he was just out of practice, he thought. *But what about Olivia? You didn't need any practice there*, came the insidious voice in the back of his mind. He pushed the thought away and led Rachelle into his sitting room.

"Would you like a drink?" he offered.

"Sure, a pinot noir if you have it," she replied, settling herself on the couch and crossing her legs.

He couldn't help but notice the way her skirt rode up on her shapely thighs. She might be petite, but there was nothing about her that wasn't perfectly formed—and she knew how to dress to highlight those assets, he acknowledged wryly. Again he anticipated the surge of interest, of desire, that should be starting a slow pulse in his veins. Again, nothing.

Xander snagged a bottle of wine from the wine rack and went to the kitchen to pour them each a glass. He returned to where she sat and passed her the wine. They clinked glasses.

"To new beginnings," Rachelle said with a glow of hope in her dark brown eyes, flicking her glossy black hair back over her shoulder. "And happy endings," she finished with a smile.

Xander nodded his head and took a sip of wine. Even that didn't taste right. In fact, nothing about this evening felt right at all. Rachelle began to talk about work—she'd recently received a promotion and was excited about bringing new ideas to the table. Xander enjoyed her lively conversation and approved many of her ideas, but when she turned the conversation to more personal matters and placed one dainty hand on his thigh as she moved a little closer on the sofa, he knew he had to bring the evening to a premature end.

"Rachelle, look, I'm sorry, but—" he started.

Regret spread across her face, but she mustered up an attempt at a smile. She lifted her hand from his leg and placed her fingers across his lips. "It's okay," she said. "I can feel you're trying, but it's not working, is it? And, really, you shouldn't have to *try*. The problem is—you're still too married to Olivia. Maybe not on paper and maybe not in your mind, but—" she placed a hand on his chest "—you most definitely are still married to her here, in your heart."

She leaned forward, put her wineglass on the table and rose from the sofa. "Don't get up," she said as he started to rise, as well. "I can see myself out. Oh, and I guess I'd better leave this with you, too."

Rachelle pulled a key out of a side pocket of her handbag and put it on the table next to her glass.

After she'd gone, Xander stared at the key on the table. He'd given it to her about a week before his accident. They'd been scheduled to attend a client function together, and he'd offered his place for her to get ready since she lived fairly far away. As she'd finished work ahead of him, he'd given her the key so she could let herself in and they'd then traveled to the venue together. He hadn't asked for the key back that night, or the next day, either, thinking that they would be developing their relationship further. He couldn't have been more wrong about that—accident or no accident.

He played her parting words over in his head. Was he really still in love with his wife? He got up and took the wineglasses to the kitchen. After pouring their contents down the drain and leaving the glasses on the counter top, he headed to his bedroom.

The room felt empty. Hell, *he* felt empty. It was past time to be honest with himself. He missed Olivia. And, more, he missed their life together and the new closeness they'd developed during his recovery. But could he forgive her? Could he let himself care for her—and for the baby on the way—when he knew they had the potential to hurt him so deeply?

No easy answers came to him through yet another sleepless night. They didn't come through a particularly arduous time at work the next day. He was tired and more than a little bit cranky when he arrived back at the apartment at eight o'clock that evening. The last person he wanted, or expected, to see was Olivia standing at his door, waiting for him.

Seventeen

Olivia straightened the second she saw him come out of the elevator and walk toward his apartment. Her face was pale and drawn, and he fought to quell the expression of concern that sprang to his lips.

"Olivia," he said in acknowledgment.

"I…I couldn't wait for you to return my call. I needed to see you."

"You'd better come inside."

He opened the door wide and ushered her into the apartment. His nostrils flared at the trace of scent she left in her wake, and instantly his body began to react. Why couldn't it have been like this last night? he asked himself. Why was it only Olivia who drew this reaction from him?

"Take a seat—you look worn-out," he commented as he put his briefcase down and shrugged out of his jacket. "Have you eaten?"

"Yes, thank you. I had dinner before I drove over."

"Were you waiting long?"

"Awhile," she answered vaguely.

He stood and watched as she took a seat.

"Xander, is it really too late for us?" she suddenly blurted, her hands fluttering nervously in her lap. "Can you truly not find it in your heart to forgive me and allow us to start over?"

He pushed a hand through his hair and breathed out a sigh. He'd asked himself the same question over and over last night and still he had no answers. Sure, his heart told him to give in and find a way to make their way forward in their lives again, but his head and his experience emphatically told him to walk away while he still could.

The thing was, he still felt so much for her. Even now every nerve, every cell in his body was attuned to Olivia—to every nuance and expression on her face, to the gentle lines of her body, to the fact she was carrying his baby. Reality slammed into him with the subtlety of an ice bucket challenge. Except this was no challenge. This was his life. The thing was, did he want it? Could he risk everything again and start a new life with Olivia and a baby?

"Xander? Please, say something."

Olivia's voice held a wealth of pain and uncertainty. A part of him wanted to reassure her, to say they could work things out. But the other, darker, side remembered all too well the child he'd been, the one who'd come home from school to a house filled with sorrow and devoid of emotional warmth—remembered the void left by his brother that was too big for Xander to fill on his own. A void like that left by Parker's death. One too painful to imagine even attempting to fill again. Love hurt, no matter which way you looked at it, and he was done with hurting.

He sat down next to Olivia, his elbows resting on his thighs and his hands loosely clasped. His head dropped between his shoulders.

"I don't think so," he finally said.

"At least that's more promising than a flat-out no," Olivia commented, although her voice held no humor.

He turned his head to look at her. Her features were so familiar to him. This was the woman whose gentle touch and quiet encouragement had helped him to recuperate and grow strong again. The woman he'd fallen even more deeply in love with as they'd lived together and made love. If he only let himself, he would be completely vulnerable to her again and to their unborn child. But he couldn't let go. He had to make the break and make it clean and fast.

"You'd better go. We have nothing to talk about anymore, Olivia," he said wearily.

"Not until you've heard me out," she insisted. "I have a right to tell you how I feel. I love you, Xander. Not just a little bit, not even a lot. I love you with every single thing I am. Every breath I take, every choice I've made since I met you. It's all about you. I know that some of those choices were the wrong ones, and I'm deeply sorry for those, but I'm learning as I go here. We both were—*are*," she corrected herself emphatically.

"I never asked for anything from you," he replied and started to rise. She grabbed his arm and tugged him back down.

"I know you didn't. I know you probably don't even want to admit that you want me, us, in your life at all. It's why you're pushing me away now. Why we probably lived such a parallel life before." She drew in a deep breath, then let it all go on her next words. "I've talked to your mother. I know what it was like for you when you were little."

"You what? Why? You had no right to talk to her."

Anger boiled thick and fast deep inside. Anger at Olivia for contacting his mother over something that was between the two of them only, and anger at his mother for talking to Olivia when she never spoke to him about the past.

"I needed to know, Xander. I had to find out if we had a chance. When Parker died, I did what I do. What I've always done for the past twenty years of my life. I picked up the pieces and I carried on."

"You didn't just pick them up. You boxed them up and put them away for good. You treated Parker's memory as if it was something to be forgotten, something to be swept away as if it had never happened."

Her voice was quiet when she replied. "It was all I knew how to do. I couldn't talk about it, Xander. We didn't talk about emotions in our house, and I suspect your house was very similar. Your mum told me about your dad, about how unwell he was. His grief went far deeper than mourning, and eventually it broke him completely.

"I don't want that for you, Xander. I want you to be whole. I want us to be whole, together. We can't do this on our own, apart. But maybe we can pull the pieces back together if we work together. Please, Xander, tell me you'll try. Tell me we're worth it." She took his hand and pressed it on her still-flat belly and begged him, "Tell me all three of us are worth it."

He looked down at his hand, then up to her face, where her eyes shone with unshed tears. His own eyes burned in kind.

"I can't tell you what you need to hear."

He could see this wasn't the answer she'd hoped for, but she rallied enough for one more try. "Think about it a little longer, Xander. Please. For all our sakes. Neither of us is perfect, but together we can make a good attempt at it. I know I pushed you away. I was as guilty as anyone of not sharing how I felt.

"It's not that I didn't care—I cared too much. If I let any of it out, how would I function? How would I manage to keep putting one foot in front of the other day after day? I couldn't let that grief float to the surface and still care for you at the same time. If I let it out, it would consume me. The only way I knew how to get through was to work. To put away all the reminders. To lose myself in being busy. I never meant to push you away."

"You didn't just push me away, Livvy. You pushed away every last physical memory we had of Parker, too. I felt like once he was gone, he didn't matter to you anymore. You never talked about him. You barely even mentioned his name."

"I never meant for you to believe that I didn't think Parker's life mattered. He mattered. You matter. *We* matter, don't we?"

She got up and began to pace the floor.

"After Parker died and you left, I threw myself into my painting. The time I spent working was the only time I didn't feel the pain of losing you both. All I could do was work, day in, day out. I couldn't sleep, couldn't eat, but I could paint, so I did. I produced my most emotive work ever. I even scored an agent from the paintings I did at the time, and they became the platform for my current success. But you know what?" She stopped pacing and faced him, her face a mask of pain and remorse. "I can't take pride in that even now. I feel like I cashed in on Parker's death. I painted out my grief, my frustration, my anger—my guilt."

"Guilt? What do you mean?" Xander stood up, his body rigid with tension, his hands curled into tight fists of frustration. "It wasn't you that left the gate open, nor were you the one who threw the ball for Bozo toward the road. That was all my fault."

A single tear slipped down Olivia's cheek. He ached to wipe it away, but he daren't touch her.

"I know I said it was your fault, Xander. It was far easier for me to point the blame at you than to admit my own accountability for what happened. Parker had been happily playing in my studio that morning—don't you remember? But the sounds he was making with his train set got on my nerves, and I couldn't concentrate on my work.

"I told him to go outside. If I hadn't done that—" Her voice broke off on a gasp of pain, and she hugged her arms around herself tight.

When he said nothing more, she went over to the sofa and grabbed her handbag. "I'm sorry, Xander. More than you'll ever know. I'd hoped, that if we talked—properly this time—that maybe we could work things out. But I guess the river runs too deep between us now for that to happen."

Before he could stop her or form a coherent sentence, she was gone. Feeling more horribly alone than he'd ever felt in his life, Xander sank back down onto the sofa and stared out the window. The last rays of the evening sun caressed the peninsula across the harbor. The peninsula where his home lay and, if he was to be totally honest, where his heart lived, as well.

He replayed Olivia's words over and over, thinking hard about what she'd said and in particular about her admission of fault in what happened that awful day when their world stopped turning. Why had she never said anything about that before?

I did what I do. What I've always done for the past twenty years of my life. I picked up the pieces and I carried on.

Of course she did. It was the example her father had set her and it was what he'd clearly expected of her after her mother died. In so many ways it was a mirror to what Xander had gone through as a child. Keep putting each foot forward straight after the other—no time for regret, no time for emotion. Do what needs to be done at all times. And whatever you do, don't talk about it.

Could he have made more effort to salvage their marriage after Parker died? Of course he could have. But he'd been turned in too much on himself. Focused too hard on protecting that facade that he'd spent most of his lifetime building, as his mother had built hers. He'd never seen his mother show weakness, never seen her so much as shed a tear. When the going got tough, as it had so often as she struggled to keep everything together, she just worked harder. And wasn't that exactly what he'd done, too?

When Olivia had told him they were expecting a baby, he'd thrown himself into work. He'd distanced himself from her and from the impending birth by doing whatever he could to ensure their financial security. He'd earned a promotion along the way. Successes like that he could measure, he could take pride in. What the hell did he know about being a father? Heaven knew he hadn't had a good example of one to call upon. He hadn't had any time to research it, to even get his head into the idea—they'd had no discussion, nothing, before she'd sprung it on him. And then to his amazement, when Parker had been born, the bond and the love had been instant. Equally rewarding and terrifying in its own right.

Fatherhood had become an unexpected delight. He'd been amazed at how effortlessly Livvy had transitioned from high school teacher to homemaker and mother. She did everything with an air of efficiency and capability that was daunting. Did she never question her ability to be a good parent? Did she never question his? If she had, he'd never seen any sign of it.

Part of his original attraction to her had always been to her self-sufficiency, but that very thing was what had slowly driven a wedge between them. It shifted the balance. But what he realized now, weighing her words and the feelings she'd finally opened up to him about this evening, was that in trying not to become a victim of his past, in trying not to be like his father, he'd fallen in the trap of behaving like his mother.

Why hadn't he been able to see that he didn't need to be a part of a dysfunctional relationship? When had he lost sight of all that was good and right about life? He thought back to the joy and excitement of meeting Olivia, of falling in love with her. He'd met a lot of women over time—beautiful, strong and successful women—and none of them had touched his heart the way she did. Why should it be wrong to be vulnerable to the one person he wanted to be close to?

Had he, with his own determined aloofness, contributed to the demise of their marriage? Of course he had. He had to accept that he couldn't be all things to all people. Surely his own mother's example had shown him that. Then why had he followed her path in life instead of his own?

He'd been a fool. A complete and utter idiot. He'd pushed away the one person in the world who loved him unconditionally. A woman who was flawed in her own ways but who needed him as much as he needed her. Of course he wanted, no, *needed* to be close to her. And that was okay. It didn't weaken him; it didn't diminish him as a man. It made him stronger because he loved her.

He got up and walked over to the window, one hand resting on the glass as he looked toward the dark bump on the distant landscape—the hill on which their home stood. So she'd made some stupid choices—hadn't he made some equally dumb ones? More importantly, could he forgive her for manipulating him when he'd come out of hospital?

The last vestiges of anger that had filled and driven him these past weeks faded away. Of course he could. They both needed to work on this. And now there was another life to consider, as well. How on earth had he even imagined that he could cut that child from his life? Not be there to see him or her be born and grow and learn and develop. It hurt to even think about it, and instinctively he began to shut down that part of him that felt that pain. But then he stopped. Pain was okay. *Feeling* was okay.

He closed his eyes and turned away from the window. Was he man enough, strong enough, to do this? To take a leap of faith and let love rule him and his decisions rather than depending on distance and control? He had some big decisions to make, and he had to be certain he was making the right ones. More importantly, he had to be making them for the right reasons.

Eighteen

It was Christmas Eve. Just under a week since Olivia had last seen or heard from Xander. She'd decided to make some effort with the decorations that morning and had gone up to the attic to find them. But the decorations had been forgotten when she'd stumbled across Parker's things that Xander had left scattered on the attic floor. She'd tucked away the clothes and toys, then picked up the albums. She was about to put them back in the box and seal it up again, but she changed her mind and took them downstairs instead.

Putting them back on the bookcase in the living room felt right. So did putting the framed photos of Parker back where they belonged. She got the toys out of the attic and loaded them into a carton in the room that had been Parker's. The room that would now become this baby's. After she'd done all that, she realized that the house felt different. Lighter somehow. Right. All of these things had been missing and, with them, a giant piece of her heart and soul.

She would never stop missing her firstborn, but at least now she could remember him with less of the sorrow that she'd been trying to hide from these past two years. And she could begin to forgive herself for her choices that day, too.

It was time for a new beginning. If only that beginning could be with Xander by her side. She'd lost count of the times she'd checked the answering machine at the house or the display on her cell phone to see if he'd called. It was time to face the awful truth. There would be no future together.

The dissolution order and Xander's offer of financial maintenance for the baby sat on the kitchen table in front of her. She had a pen clutched in her hand.

"Just sign the damn things and get it over with," she said out loud. Her hand fluttered to her belly. "We'll manage, you and me."

Before she could put pen to paper, the front doorbell rang. With a sigh of exasperation, she dropped the pen to the table and got up to see who it was. She felt a physical shock of awareness when she saw Xander standing there with one arm leaning up on the doorjamb, wearing his old uni sweatshirt and a disreputable pair of Levi's. Her heart picked up double time as her eyes raked his face, taking in the gleam in his slate-gray eyes and the stubble growing back stubbornly on his chin.

"Are you here about the papers?" she said, rubbing her hands down the legs of her jeans.

"Not exactly," Xander replied. "I have something for you, for Christmas. For you and the baby, actually."

Olivia felt confused. "For…?"

"Come and see."

Xander spun on a sneaker-clad foot and went down the path to the front gate. Beyond him, Olivia could see a family-friendly SUV. Clearly he'd been cleared to drive again, but she knew he'd never be seen dead in something like this. She was the one who'd always had the practical station wagon while he'd had the sporty little two-door foreign import. Maybe he'd borrowed the vehicle from someone else? Maybe his present was bigger than would fit in his car?

"Are you coming?" he called from the gate.

"Sure," she said, slipping through the doorway and down the stairs to the path. "Is this yours?" she asked, gesturing to the SUV when she got nearer.

"Yeah, I decided it was time to leave the racing cars to the experts and grow up a little. Grow up a lot, actually."

The back of the SUV was open. Through the tinted glass on the side Olivia could see an animal crate. She came to a halt behind the car and gasped when she saw the beagle puppy inside. Xander opened the crate and lifted the puppy out, depositing it squirming in Olivia's arms.

"Merry Christmas, Livvy."

The puppy lifted her head and enthusiastically licked Olivia on the chin, making her laugh out loud.

"But why?"

"Every kid needs a dog, right?" He grabbed a bag filled with puppy toys and food, tugged the blanket from inside the crate, then went to the front of the car and grabbed a pet bed from off the seat. "You mind if I bring these inside for you?"

"Oh, sure," she said, completely flustered. "Come in—have a coffee. Does it have a name?"

"She, actually. And, no, she doesn't have a name yet. I thought you'd like to choose one."

As they walked into the house Olivia saw Xander notice the photos of Parker that had gone back up on the hallway wall.

"You've put them back?" he asked, pausing by one

of the three of them—their faces alight with happiness and fun.

She swallowed past the lump in her throat. "They belong there. I…I should never have hidden them away. It wasn't right or fair—to him or to us."

Xander said nothing, but she saw him nod slightly. Tension gripped her shoulders, and she wished she could ask him what he thought, hoping that he'd at least tell her she'd done the right thing, but he remained silent. In the kitchen he spied the papers Olivia had been agonizing over signing.

"You were going to sign them, today?" he asked.

"I still can't bring myself to do it," Olivia admitted with a rueful shake of her head. "But I guess, now you're here. You may as well take them with you."

His face looked grim. "We need to talk."

Olivia felt her stomach sink. The puppy squirmed and whined in her arms. "Shall we take her outside first?"

"It's as good a place to talk as any."

Xander deposited the puppy's things on the floor and then he followed Olivia out to the patio where the puppy gamboled about, oblivious to the tension that settled like a solid wall between the two adults, all her attention on sniffing the plants and trees before she squatted happily on the grass.

"She's gorgeous, Xander. But why did you buy her?" Olivia asked, barely able to take her eyes from the sweet animal and hardly daring to look at the man standing so close by her side.

"I never had any pets growing up. My mother said she always had enough on her plate, no matter how much I begged and pleaded and promised to look after one. I guess I forgot how much I'd always wanted one and reverted to acting like my mother when you brought Bozo home that day."

Olivia couldn't help herself; she rested one hand on his forearm and reached up to kiss Xander on the cheek. He turned his head at the last minute, his lips touching hers and sending a flame of need to lick along her veins. Startled, she pulled back.

"Thank you—I love her already. She's beautiful."

"No, *you're* the one who's beautiful. Inside and out. I just never really appreciated how beautiful before. Livvy, I've been doing a lot of thinking. I've come to understand that I only allowed myself to see the outside, the surface. I convinced myself that was enough, that we could make a life together based on the physical attraction and chemistry between us. As long as it was just the two of us, I didn't have to delve any deeper into how I felt. I knew I loved you—but I don't think I ever really understood how much, and I hadn't really counted on sharing you with anyone else, whether it be dog or child."

He lifted a hand, gently tucked back her hair and cupped her face.

"Livvy, I'm sorry. I was a fool. I don't think I ever really knew what love was, or what lengths it could lead a person to, until I met you. I didn't deserve you, or Parker, or any of what we shared. If I'd been a better husband, a better father, maybe none of what happened that day would have occurred."

Olivia bit back a sob. There was so much pain and regret in his words, and she knew that he had little to apologize for.

"Xander, no. You were a great dad, and Parker loved you so very much. Don't sell yourself short. You weren't the one to make important life decisions without including me. You weren't the one to cast blame without seeing where blame truly lay. Those faults were all mine."

Xander shook his head. "I was his father. I should

have been able to keep him safe. It was my duty to him and to you, and I failed."

Her heart wrenched when she saw the tears that shimmered in his eyes. "The only person to blame that day was the guy driving the car that hit Parker and Bozo. If he'd been paying attention instead of texting, if he'd been driving to the speed limit instead of racing along a suburban road—then he'd have seen them run into the street and been able to stop in time. But we can't keep plaguing ourselves with 'what if,' and we can't keep blaming ourselves or one another for what happened. It happened. We can't turn back time, as much as we wish we could.

"I would have done everything differently that day too, if I could have, but nothing I do now will change that. And it's the same for you. Surely you see that? Xander, you *have* to see that and accept it to move past it."

Xander swallowed and turned away to watch the dog as she continued to explore the garden. "It doesn't make it any easier, though, does it?"

"And it's no easier handling it alone, either."

"No, you're right there. I watched my mother handle everything on her own while I grew up. She became so adept at it, so automatic about it all, that she wouldn't even accept help from me once I was able to give it. She told you that my father suffered a complete breakdown after my brother died, didn't she?"

Olivia moved to stand beside Xander, slipping her hand inside his. "Yes, she did. Until then I never understood how tough it must have been for either you growing up or for your mother—or even your dad, for that matter."

"I didn't really know any different at home. Sure, I knew what other families had and I knew our household was odd by comparison and that I couldn't bring friends home, but it wasn't until Parker died that I fully understood what my father must have gone through. I didn't want to fall down into that dark hole. In fact, I did everything I could to prevent that from happening. I never let out any of it—not my fears, my sorrow." He shook his head. "I tried so hard not to be like him. He couldn't even function without my mother there he depended on her so much. She had to go to work each day because if she didn't, we'd have nothing to eat, no roof over our heads. But from the second she left the house each morning to go to work, he'd weep. I'd let myself out the door to go to school, with the sound of his sobbing echoing in my ears. Some days, he'd find the strength to pull himself together, but as I got older, more and more often when I got home, he would still be crying.

"You know, when he died, I felt relief rather than sadness or loss because for the first time in years I knew he finally had peace. He couldn't forgive himself for my brother's death, couldn't talk about it, nothing. Most days he could barely get out of bed. He needed my mother for everything. I couldn't let myself be like him—not even the slightest bit."

Olivia squeezed his hand, hard. "Your whole family should have had more help."

Xander nodded. "Mum is not the kind of person who accepts help. She soldiers on. Does what needs doing and keeps looking forward. She was strong and capable and solid as a rock through all of it, and I really thought that was something to aspire to. In fact, I saw a lot of that in you, too. I don't think I ever saw her shed a tear or admit she couldn't handle anything.

"After Parker died, you coped with everything that had to happen afterward with the funeral—even giving our victim impact statement at the sentencing for the driver who killed him. Your composure scared me. Made me look at myself and question why I couldn't do those things. Was I my father's son?"

Olivia hastened to reassure him. "No, you weren't. You were grieving, too. Everyone copes in their own way, Xander. You couldn't be anyone other than yourself or feel anything other than what you were feeling at the time. Me, I pushed all my feelings aside, the way I learned how to do when I was a kid. Life goes on and all that," she said bitterly. "It got to the point where everyone in my family turned to me when it came to making choices about their life, even my dad. It became second nature to me, and it made me who I am.

"I never thought twice about involving you in the big decisions I made because I was just so used to following my own plan. And when I met you and we fell in love and got married, I thought I'd be able to craft the plan for both of us—for our life together. It's no wonder we fell apart through the very happening that should have driven us closer together."

Xander sighed. "It wasn't all your fault. Through our marriage I let you take control of everything because it was so much easier that way. It left me free to do what I saw as my role, the role my father never had in my memory. I needed to compensate for all the things he didn't do, but it wasn't without its own cost, was it? Do you think we can make it work? Give ourselves another chance at this thing called love?" he asked, still staring out at the garden.

"Yes, I *know* we can. Not because I want to or because you want to, but because we owe it to ourselves, and to Parker's memory and to the life of this new child we created, to do so—to be happy." She reached up to stroke his face and smiled when he turned into the touch and planted a kiss on her fingers. "I've never stopped loving you, Xander. I never will. I just needed to learn that to make a marriage work it needed to be a joint proposition—from start to finish—and I'm totally not ready for us to be finished yet."

Xander nodded. "Nor am I. I guess neither of us had the ideal example growing up, did we? And yet, somehow we managed to find one another—love one another." He looped his arms around her waist and stared deep into her eyes. "Will you help me, Livvy? Will you help me to grieve for our son properly? Will you let me help you, too? Will you let me love you for the rest of your life and raise this new baby, and maybe even others, with you?"

"Oh, Xander, I would love nothing else. I love you so much. I don't want a life without you. I want to be there for you, always. I want us to be the family we both deserve."

"As do I with you. Together, I promise. We're going to do this together, and we'll get it right this time, in good times and in bad."

He bent his head to hers and sealed his vow with the tender caress of his lips against hers. His touch had never felt more right or more special. Olivia knew, as her heart rate increased and as warmth began to unfurl through her body, that her heart beat for this man with a passion and a love that was equally reciprocated and that, together, they could do anything.

Xander looked across the lawn at the puppy who was now sitting down, staring at them both. "So, what are you going to name her?"

Olivia looked up at her husband, the man of her heart and the key to her happiness. "I think the question should be, what are *we* going to call her, don't you?"

As Xander's laughter filled the air around them and he squeezed her tight, Olivia knew without a doubt that this time they'd make it. This time was forever.

* * * * *

MILLS & BOON
MEDICAL

Pulse-Racing Passion

Set your pulse racing with dedicated, delectable doctors in the high-pressure world of medicine, where emotions run high and passion, comfort and love are the best medicine.

Six Medical stories published every month, find them all at:

millsandboon.co.uk